ETHEREAL VOICES

by Shona Jabang

ETHEREAL VOICES

by Shona Jabang

ISBN 978-1-326-52081-6

Published by AudioArcadia.com 2016

Publisher's Note:
This book contains adult themes.

Shona Jabang is a Jamaican-American. She is a language arts teacher at an American high school in the UK as well as a part-time writing instructor with the University of Maryland University College (UMUC - Europe). She lives with her husband and two dogs in East Anglia, UK.

Shona originally grew up in the UK but lived in Jamaica, Canada, and the US before returning to the UK. She has a BA in English, an MS in Education, and an MA in Creative Writing (MCW).

She enjoys writing stories, poems, and plays which are based on her cultural background and the places in which she has stayed.

CONTENTS

Page

PROLOGUE

Outside, the wind blows sharply, whipping the
energy of the day into frenzy.
Outside, the elements dance madly, and all around
are disturbed spirits, hollow voices and
displaced souls.
Outside, there is no peace.
Outside, hunger distends hope and dreams
to become the source of famine.
Outside, is the emptiness of existence.
Inside, is the promise of wonder and the touch of
true spirit.
Inside, is the warmth of the soul and the diamond
polished and rare.
Inside, is sanctity, mantras, chants, songs in
cathedrals, communion with deities.
Inside, there is the fulfilment of identity.

SISTER, SISTER

My mother sat with her long, blue, faded gingham skirt draped between her legs and an old, battered, chipped enamel bowl full of fresh green peas on her lap. Her fingers moved quickly down the center of each pod casing - snapping, breaking it open, and scooping out the peas which fell like green pearls into the bowl. She flicked the broken pods into another enamel bowl placed on the step below her.

I followed her every movement - a nine year old child who still found her mother fascinating. My enamel bowl was seated on my lap like hers, but my fingers were slower and less precise. My mother hummed. I hummed along, familiar with the tune, as I was familiar with those early Sunday mornings.

In my memory Sundays were always days that were light and breezy, damp with morning dew, echoing with the morning salute of our family roosters, and filled with the familiarity of us being us. Sundays were quiet mornings; mornings when Rex and Papa slept late. We were up early to make breakfast and to begin preparations for our typical Sunday dinner. Later on, we would get ready for eleven a.m. service and return by one-thirty p.m. to begin the actual cooking. Some Sundays, my brother and Papa came with us to church; some Sundays, they did not. When they did not accompany us, the day seemed even more special than the rest. I truly felt I had my mother all to myself.

This Sunday, when I was nine years old, my mother whispered to me, as we were shelling peas on the verandah early one misty, July morning, 'Pearl, I carrying a new baby inside me.'

I stopped, holding the partially shelled pea pod, and for a few minutes I did not know what to say because the second her words hit the air I felt a surge of jealousy flash through my body. I smiled and looked happy because Mama was smiling happily.

She said, 'Pearl, you going to be a big sistah now. Is time to tek you head out of de clouds, an' t'ink 'bout all de good t'ings you mus' help to teach dis baby dat we goin' have.'

There were no old time stories filled with fantasy and storks dropping babies from the skies. My mother rubbed her belly and looked proud. She had put into words something I had being trying to ignore - the fact that her belly had been getting bigger and bigger with each passing week. I had not wanted to believe it could possibly be anything more than Mama eating too much rice and too many yams.

Before Isa, my parents only had the two of us. We were our parents' late life babies and not regarded as being as solid or as sturdy as the other children. People pitied Papa and Mama. The Good Lord above had taken many years before blessing them with any babies in the first place, and then, after long waits in-between, we finally came along. We were fragile. Mama hoped the baby would be a boy. She hoped he would be a strong, solid, sturdy, earthy boy. She ate all the right 'boy' foods, prayed all the right prayers, and hoped.

Mama and Papa began crowing about the new baby like it was the second coming of Jesus or something, and the whole village buzzed with excitement.

Well-meaning aunties and mamas-in-waiting were always coming by to chat with my Mama. The bigger she got, the more they hurried to give her a hand with housekeeping matters. They sent their boys up and their daughters by to help with the goats, the chickens, and the little plots of vegetables and roots that Ms. G (short for Agatha), my mother, had trouble bending low to tend to.

I did not understand all the fuss. The bigger Mama became, the tighter I hugged her giant, pumpkin belly and snuggled against her. She was real and solid; the baby was all woman-talk and nothing I could touch or see or feel - not yet, not ever as far I was concerned. The women of Worsop had babies all the time. I pretended to never feel *it* moving, even when Mama made a big announcement about it and grabbed my hand and placed it on her stomach. I acted like I felt nothing.

Late one evening, right after rainy season, Mama went into labor. In-between crying out in pain, my Mama begged Jesus for strength and in the same out-breath told me to fetch her this and fetch her that as six or seven aunties crowded the house.

They tried to make her comfortable while bolstering up my Papa (a man who could guide a cow or goat through the birthing process and face a barging bull, with no worries, but who could not bear to see his wife suffering).

When Papa suggested getting the donkey ready, Mama screamed at him, 'Is what me look like, eh, de Virgin Mary? You tryin' to kill me on a donkey cart all de way to Ulster Spring? Is mad you mad?'

Ulster Spring was at the end of a long, rough, rocky road which dipped up and down before reaching the hospital that teetered on a little hill fifteen miles away.

'Both mi and the baby be good an' dead before we even get up top dat hill,' she said.

In any case, the baby was at least a week - possibly more - late, by her guess. She told my father he had better go and see if Mass Creton's pickup truck was working because now Kubba had died and no one had taken her place as midwife, it meant that, unlike my brother and me who had been birthed by Kubba, this baby would have to be born in the hospital as something was not quite right. All the aunties in the house did not feel they could handle a 'somet'in' was not quite right' situation. The hospital was the best place for the whole dilemma. The aunties nodded and murmured amongst themselves.

While all the discussions were taking place, my mother steadily moaned, 'Lawd! Lawd! Lawd!' Her voice became higher and higher and more frightening to me.

Thinking she might die, I started to hate the baby and wished it out of her body. As far as I was concerned, this baby was an evil troll. Thus began my secret name for my new sibling. I remember standing in the doorway feeling a heavy boulder of fear settling in the bottom-most part of my belly.

Papa stood, like a little boy, looking at the aunties who, throughout all the activities, had remained calm as they handled the business of bearing children. The baby was not coming properly - an unexpected complication.

Papa, lost in a trance, had to be pushed out the door on his way down the hill on his fastest and least stubborn donkey. He was headed to Mass Creton's shop because he was the only one with something that had four working wheels and was drivable.

Long distance traveling always was a problem in Worsop. It may have been the sixties, but life in tropic, hilly-mountain villages was sixty years slow. Old, achy, arthritic mules, donkeys which stopped in the middle of the road and brayed as if you were whipping the life out of them, or good old feet, were how most people traveled around.

Mass Creton's truck had been known to have bad days and nights and didn't always make it to the end of a journey, but it was all we had.

I thought to myself, as the air tensed with worry and anxiety, that this was all this baby's fault - this unknown thing, this nobody, this Troll.

Isn't it strange how childish feelings of love and hate stay with us even when we become older, and we should not feel those same feelings the same way any more?

I look back now and realize what eventually happened to Isa and me was already written from that night, birthed in the chaos and excitement. But I felt no joy and excitement, only the petulance of a young heart which felt it was losing its place.

The night Mama went into labor was crystal, cool, and clear. The sky pulsed with stars hung so low you could almost reach up and pluck one. Mass Creton's pickup, a rusty antique, sputtered and rattled up to our house. We stood outside in the night air with Uncle, Aunty, most of their children, and two of the village aunties. Wrapped in blankets against the night chill, we watched as Papa eased Mama into the truck and then hopped in and slammed the truck door closed. Mass Creton kept the engine revving as if he was worried it might die if his foot left the gas pedal.

Mama said, 'Rex, Pearl, don't give no trouble, you hear *mi*!'

'Don't worry,' Aunty said, 'you come back with a healthy baby, you hear mi now!'

'Everybaady ready? Is forty-odd minutes of bumpy roads ahead, so hang tight!' Mass Creton yelled out the driver side window and, in answer, my mother screamed out so loudly and so painfully, Mass Creton didn't say another word.

With midnight on their heels, they rattled off into the depth of darkness with our dogs chasing after the truck, barking their own safe travels. Aunty and Uncle left one of the older boy cousins in charge of us. The aunties walked home to see about their own children. The kerosene lamps burned until two in the morning when they snuffed themselves out because they had drunk up all the oil.

We curled up in our beds wishing our Mama home. Cousin said Aunty or he would be back over in the morning to check on us and make sure we didn't burn up the kitchen trying to make ourselves something to eat. He advised that it was best to wait and eat at their house. He left, and the house felt larger than it really was, and its emptiness grew enormous in our minds. We had never been home without Mama.

It took five days for Mama and Papa to come back home. I remember I was excited and happy they were back until I realized nobody was really paying me much attention. Mama looked tired, her skin looked tired, and her eyes were deep and dark. She stayed in bed for a day or two nursing the baby.

Papa would bring the baby to me and say, 'Pearl, look at your new sistah! Look at har! You going have someone to play with and watch ovah, Pearl!'

I would quickly close my eyes and cover my ears and make promises to God as I wished her away back to the place where babies come from; back to her being a no one; back to her being a nobody. I wanted her to go back to where she was a being beyond knowing. But when I opened them, she was still there.

I took one look because one look was all I needed for me to realize *I* would never be fooled by those doll-like dimples. She looked like an angel, wrapped so warmly in her baby blanket. But I was *not* having it. Nothing about her made me want to even touch her. I was not impressed by her blacker than the middle-of-midnight curly hair or the pointiness of her little turned up nose. In that moment, I had made up my mind I would never love her.

One cold Trelawny night, I crept to the cot where she lay purring with butterfly breaths. I took another look. *I* was supposed to be the Princess Perfect. Tears traveled from my throat to my heart as I began to cry. I felt the stardust slip from my hair and softly, silently, sprinkle and sparkle in hers.

I always loved my Mama in a way that was almost too deep even for a daughter. I was hurt when Mama kept telling me she wanted another boy because girls were too much trouble. I never set out to be a problem. I did things as soon as they got into my head without thinking them through to the end.

My only brother, Rex, read all the time. I thought of him as a true prince because he was a phenomenon in school (a word I heard Head Teacher use to describe him). I was not, as I was told by Head Teacher, a phenomenon. I was hard headed.

Rex was fourteen, five years older than I was, when my Mama brought the baby home. I never minded *him* getting treated special because he was a special boy. He used mile-long words all the time and received A-plus on all his papers in school.

He spent many evenings and weekends at the home of our Head Teacher (the head of the two teachers in our little school) and her husband, where they provided him with extra lessons because they truly believed he would one day be incredible.

Head Teacher even spoke about the possibility of his becoming a politician and what an honor such ambition would bestow on our little hill village. He never had to do much at home because his nose was always nestled happily in some book or the other, and generally he was called gifted. He never said much, but we were close. He read poetry to me from a big book Head Teacher had given him, and he told me stories about princesses and dragons, flying beds, and magic carpets.

On his fourteenth birthday, Papa got him a flashlight so he could read even after the kerosene lamps had been blown out and the tar pitch, country night had completely invaded the little two-room dry wood house we lived in.

He could do maths in his head, tell you about the planets, the moon, and the stars, and he was always cutting up some insect or lizard to see how they worked on the inside. I was used to him being a bit more special than I was.

Yet, I had always felt I had my own unique spot. I was the baby. Everyone called me Mama's wash-belly, the last baby, but with Isa's coming she became the new wash-belly. Slowly, I came to feel like she washed all traces of me from my Mama's belly.

When my Mama was carrying Isa, I tried not to give her too much trouble, but God had given me this God-awful character of always talking back and getting things done according to my own impulses.

I had these wandering feet which took me to places I knew I had no business going. Without thinking, I would wander off down country roads, or brave a path through the bushes, or saunter down to Mass Creton to play the juke box, or listen to cricket on his transistor radio. Mass Creton always sent me home, eventually, but if Robby, his youngest son, was there alone, he would let me stay at least an hour or so.

I never thought too long about what I planned to do on any given school day. I started out with good intentions, but school made my head ache. Sometimes, I would leave the house on the way to school, complete with my slate, chalk, composition book, lead pencil, protractor, ruler, and all, but never actually made my way into the old, mud-brown, two-roomed school house which was disintegrating before your very eyes, with its broken window and its leaky roof.

I stashed my school supplies under bramble bushes and picked them back up on the way home. There were things to do down by the river. Things that fascinated me and didn't involve a bamboo cane smacking my palm because I could not spell "category" or when I committed other academic or social sins. There were fresh-water fish which swam in families to try and catch and then allow to escape, as well as new plants to discover, pretty colored river rocks to collect and hide in my secret places, and birdsongs to imitate.

My only girl cousin, on my father's side, Moira, (child cousin number four of the seventeen), drowned there one shimmering, close-to-the-sun, summer day, way before the baby was even thought of. I was five when she died.

Mama said, 'Jesus allows us to be bowed down low when we don't live right. Moira sneak off dat day she drowned. She should 'ave been in school an', if she had been, we would be tellin' you a different story, an' she might be de one doing de tellin'.'

She had been nine years, like me, when I started giving my Mama trouble. It was our bone of contention, Mama said, and my bottom would hurt for days after news raced to our house as to where I really was getting an education. It seemed as if everybody, even other children, watched out for us because they were so quick to tell on us.

In our village, many children never went to school, or they went on and off (more off than on, when the crops were ready).

If they were boys, they worked with their papas in yam, cassava, sweet potato, banana and plantain

16

fields; they made sure the cows were happy, or moved the goats from one place to the next.

If they were girls, especially girls with some years on them, they had brothers and sisters to keep a constant eye on, cassava to mash, peas to shell, chickens to feed, coops to clean, red tile floors to polish with coconut brushes, and washing loads to balance on their little heads and take to the river.

All of us, except for Rex (because he was too delicate), were the water-gatherers as there was no running water in our houses. We went to the Stand Pipe with huge empty buckets and returned with our heads swirling with grown up gossip which we gathered secretly by eavesdropping on grown folks' talk.

We knew we had no business repeating what we heard. We tossed gossip between us like a ball as we waited for our turn to fill our buckets. We returned sopping wet from water spilling over from those same buckets which, when full, we carried on our heads. It would take two trips when I got home from school to get our cooking water, and water to brush our teeth and drink for the next day.

Mama said that was hard enough work for her girl-child, and she was glad Worsop was so close to the clouds because the heavy rains didn't have far to fall. We collected drums of water for bathing and kept them carefully covered to keep the mosquito babies from swimming around in them.

We washed clothes in the little stream skipping across shiny, multi-colored pebbles and tiny rocks. It flowed merrily close to the farm fields. We were grateful we never had to go all the way to the river to do this.

All the families in the hilly village of Worsop were farmers, even Mass Creton. He farmed, but in his little shop he sold small bits of everything. He would put in special orders for supplies, if you asked him to, and he would let you barter or take a chicken or goat as payment, though he much preferred real shillings and pounds. He was one of the original one-stop shops - selling everything from sardines to Bayer's aspirin to chicken feed to paint to face powder and rose water. His farm stretched out languidly behind his shop and rolled for acres before dipping down the hillside.

Most farms were scattered and acres apart except for my paternal Uncle and Aunty's land. My Uncle, his wife, and their large brood of children lived across the road from us. Some farms tottered on the sides of the red-dirt hills; some dotted the road from Worsop leading to other villages and to Ulster Spring and then to Falmouth.

The land had been passed from one generation to the next; it had been bequeathed by sons and daughters to their sons and daughters down to our time. Seemed like our feet were planted firmly in this brick-red dirt which stained clothes and was the devil to remove, even with the most vigorous of washing.

The rains kept the dirt rich, and the farms fed and clothed their families. We were all poor, but we were well-fed. Papa took our crops to market by using a team of mules and donkeys heavy laden with hampers on either side of their fat bellies. He was gone for days at a time.

Mama always thought it was important for the both of us to go to school. When I got home, I took care of the major chores because Rex had to eat and work on his school work. I hated school. I went, when I went, because I had to. I never had to work half as hard as the other girls though. Mama wanted us to *live* and my 'play' relatives (relatives who were not really our relatives), our 'play' grannies and 'play' aunties from all over the village, understood her fears.

We seemed so fleeting because we had been sickly and thin for most of our young lives. People were pleased when we made it from one birthday to the next. The whole village felt they had a hand in our survival. When I became an adult, I learned my Mama had lost three babies before Rex and I came along, which was the reason everyone worried so much about us.

Mama took in sewing and sometimes people came from miles to give her clothes to sew for them because she was one of the best seamstresses in the area. Between sewing, cooking, and cleaning, she planted her own little crops, kept our free roaming chickens fed, collected eggs and determined which hen or rooster would wind up as supper.

When there were big jobs to be done on the farm, my cousins came to help. At the end of the harvest, there was a huge cook-out, a run-down, they called it, with big drums of food simmering and cooking on open fires; goats were roasted on long metal spikes turning slowly over firepits full of fragrant wood. People brought even more food to add to the festivities such as fried chicken, fried fish, yams, boiled bananas, fried and boiled plantains, cassava, breadfruit, and Manish water soup which was passed around by the gallon. There were Johnny cakes, callaloo, cucumber salad, potato salad, cabbage salad, corn sweet on the cob, sweet potato pone, rum punch, ginger beer, beer, and Guinness.

Everyone danced to the sound of banjos, harmonicas, and djembe drums until the sun began to wake from sleep and the moon closed her eyes and went to bed.

During this time, the time when Isa was not yet born, Papa was gone to market for many days during harvest. He said he would soon have one more mouth to feed, and he needed to be prepared. Mama was tired all the time from moving her big baby belly around.

Sometimes, I got away with going in the opposite direction of school. I learned to take advantage of this time when I was not completely watched. Sometimes no one remarked on my absence, and I got away scot-free, and sometimes some little bare-footed, bare-chested, dusty boy would find his way to my house to say I was where I was not supposed to be. I often wondered why no one worried that these tattle tales were not in school themselves.

The other children called me 'Duppy Baby, a Ghost Child', and laughed at me. If Papa was away, Mama waited until I made my way home, and then she would whoop me. When her belly got too big, she would say, 'Chile, what am I to do with you? You wait till Papa come. He will jus' have to sort you out.'

I was never too bothered by this. Often, it could take days to get to Brownstown to market. On the

20

way back, most of the hampers were empty except for the ones carrying things which were particularly needed from Brownstown such as cloth and supplies ordered by Mass Creton. The trip back was faster but, by the time he came home, the threat of punishment had usually mellowed down considerably.

'Little girl,' Papa said, in his stern voice, 'fine your Bible quick, you hear me! I see your soul needs to be reminded of where de good path is; you need redirection. You Mama tell mi you been running wild like de heathens of Africa. We cannot have dis behavior go on, you hear mi?'

I nodded in repentance wondering whether it would be the easier Psalms or Proverbs or the dreaded Leviticus or Deuteronomy that would whoop me into shape.

He would, tiredly, pick Bible verses at random for me to memorize and recite at a forgotten later date. I could feel Mama rolling her eyes at him in the background.

Later, I would hear them whispering in their bedroom when they thought I was asleep, but I did not think being a heathen was so bad. I said my prayers anyway and hoped God forgave me for whatever sin I committed on any particular day.

No matter how much I twanged her nerve strings, I knew my Mama loved me. Many nights before she left for Ulster Spring hospital to have Isa, she was braiding my hair, as she did every night.

The crickets sang outside the window and a moon so big lit up the sky. I was warm and cozy, my mother's hands weaving magic in my hair as I sat on the red-tiled floor. Her belly still allowed her to bend but only a little, little bit; my elbows rested unsteadily on her knees as her stomach bumped them off every now and again.

'You know you is my little, precious girl, a girl name Pearl, a special girl name Pearl,' she said, as she braided my hair. 'Pearl, what do you want to be when you get to be a big young lady?'

I said, 'A Mama, like you!'

'Oh, baby,' she replied, 'bein' a Mama is hard work! You know, mi would like you to be a nurse. Yes, mi can see dat for you. Yes, I can really see dat for you. But you have to get serious about life, Pearl. It seems all you want to do is play. Life is not always playtime, chile. Life is hard work and then maybe you get some time to play. Farm life is dyin', Pearl, an' you 'ave to look furthah out now past Worsop. You have to t'ink biggah dan runnin' to de rivah an' not goin' to school. You 'ave to t'ink big, Pearl. No time for little, bitty dreams.'

When she said it like that, I could see it for myself, although I did not know at the time what a nurse really did. I had never been to a hospital or to a doctor except for Shepherdess who knew all about healing herbs and tonics.

We were often reminded that although we had been sickly children, we had been healed by prayers. God took away our sickness. I had never seen a real doctor or nurse except in pictures at school when we did health studies.

'Does bein' a nurse mean goin' to more school?' I asked.

When she nodded, I lost interest immediately and didn't ask any more questions. I wanted to be a juke box operator, but I kept this dream to myself.

Many nights she sang to Rex and me as we lay in our beds. She sang old folksy, Jamaican, country songs. They were songs people often sang walking late at night along dirt roads lit by millions and millions of brilliant stars and usually a happy moon in its various shapes and sizes.

'Evenin' time, work is ovah now its evenin' time; we dey walk pon mountain, dey walk pon mountain, dey walk pon mountain side! Work is ovah now it's evenin' time; we dey walk pon mountain, dey walk pon mountain, pon mountainside.'

My Mama had a sweet, low voice, and her singing always made me feel safe and would put me to sleep even after one of my most troubled days. I especially loved it when she sang whilst she braided my hair.

'Is long time, gal, mi nevah see you! Come let mi hol' you han'! Is long time, gal, mi nevah see you! Come let mi hol' you han'! Peel neck John Crow, sit pon de tree top, pick off de blossom! Let mi hol' you han', gal! Let mi hol' you han'!'

My hair was really long, thick, and knotted easily. I was tender-headed, but my Mama had gentle hands and, as her quick fingers oiled and three-way twisted my hair, she would tell me stories about her Mama and her Mama before and about people in the village. Her stories were filled with spirits and 'duppies' and country magic. She had a song to match every story, she told me.

'It was undah de coconut tree, dahling, it was undah de coconut tree! You promise to marry to me, dahling, it was undah de coconut tree!'

23

She would call me her beautiful, brown-skinned, brown-eyed girl. Her made-up song for me went 'Brown girl, berry brown, loves to dance and spin around. Brown girl, eyes so bright, what will you do on this moonlit night?'

I had to come up with a response and sing it back to her. We would do this call and response until I ran out of things to do on a moonlit night, and I started making up things that were so silly we ended up laughing hard. Mama would hug me and call me ridiculous. I knew I was special to her.

The night Isa was born everything changed.

Isa had been home for a few days. The house saw people coming and going because everybody heard how pretty she was. On days when there were too many people in the house, I stayed outside and played in the bushes and in the trees. I was bored and lonely.

Rex was often at Head Teacher's house for his special lessons, and sometimes he stayed there overnight. When he wasn't home, I had no one to talk to. I threw big stones at mangoes which looked red and ripe and were within reach; I played with the lizards and put long, glassy, green grass blades into swarming black ant holes (resisting the urge to put the smaller lizards in as well); I idled away my time, but I didn't leave the front yard of the house.

My ears pricked up when laughter and conversation drifted outside; I was waiting to hear my name. Aunties and mamas-in-waiting, young and not so young, play grannies, papas and papas-in-waiting, manly and not so manly, play grandpas, and children, little ones and big ones, they all came to visit the new baby. The children tried to push me into play, but I was content with my own company. After a while they left me alone and created their own games without me.

People were coming in and out of the house with plates of this and bundles of that and leaving like they had seen a miracle. I got tired of them not seeing me until they saw Isa first; I got tired of them looking right through me as they patted me on the head and brushed by, talking baby talk as they went. I practised rolling my eyes like I had seen Mama do.

In our tiny house they still had to make paths through others to get to see the baby. Ms. G's miracle baby! Her big surprise! Her old age blessing! Her new wash-belly; her last child baby!

I sucked my teeth as I viciously used a jagged rock to slice the tail off a little green lizard. 'Don't worry,' I told it as it scurried off in disgust, 'you going grow anothah one.'

'She beautiful,' they said.

'What a pretty, pretty baby!' they said.

'Look pon dat 'ead of hair!' they said.

'Lawd! Har dimples can hol' water; dem so deep!' they cooed.

'Har de perfect color,' they said, 'not too, too light, but not dark at all.'

Rex had fallen in love with her the minute she arrived, and I felt completely betrayed. Papa and he would hold her like she was made of whipped egg whites, as if she was going to melt.

'Take care of lil sistah!' were Rex's last words on the nights when Head Teacher came to get him for his studies.

Isa was almost white when she first came home. She was a pale baby, covered with light yellow hair all over her body, especially her face. Mama, laid up in bed, watched her. She kept an animal-like sense of her every whereabouts and who was holding her.

Once or twice each day she remembered to ask where I was (I could hear her voice as I amused myself outside) and if I was all right. Usually a voice said I was fine, fine, fine, but I didn't think she was really that interested.

Feeling more and more like an afterthought, I often drifted out the door across the verandah and tried to distract and distance myself by turning in on my imagination.

In Pearl Land, I was the only Princess, and all this attention was for me, only for me being Pearl, Precious Pearl, Princess Pearl, and a Perfect Pearl. I waved to my subjects as I had seen Queen Elizabeth do on Mass Creton's black and white TV; my royal wave blessed everyone as they bowed before my beauty on bended knees.

In the evening I got tired, testy, bored, and hungry, but I stayed out in the front yard for as long as I could, or I went to sit on the veranda, rocking back and forth in Mama's chair. This became my routine until people began to leave. Their voices drifted back on the evening breeze as they embarked on their walks to their homes. They acted as if they had been to a really good party; I felt as if I hadn't been invited. My steps were always lead-like when I finally came in.

By late evening, everyone was gone. I always walked in with some sense of dread because I really did not want to have anything to do with this sister. I never asked for her. She came without my permission, and now nothing was ever to be the way it was before.

One night, after I felt Mama had had enough time to rest, I asked her to braid my hair.

She said, 'Oh baby, Mama is jus' too tired! Give me a few days, Princess. You Aunty say she will do it. She will do it when she cum check pon me an' baby.'

It was a numbing blow to me because our sacred bonding sessions took place when she braided my hair. No matter what bones of contention I managed to dig up throughout the day, she always braided my hair at night. Aunty would do it but only after she had made sure *the baby* was all right first. I knew then, with an all in all sureness, that I was now only the third best: Rex, first, Troll, second, and the true Princess, third. My dislike for this little bundle of bother was a solid mass permanently positioned in my heart. I went back outside and sat on the veranda, staring up at the big balloon moon. I would have to pray for forgiveness because I knew it was a sin not to love your own sister.

On a pristine night as moonbeams streamed through the windows, the baby was asleep in her cot, which was in the corner of Mama and Papa's bedroom. I did not look in her direction; I looked past her and walked through the back door to the kitchen which was separate from our main house. I gobbled down some food, drank some water, washed my hands, face, privates, and feet, in a basin; I patted myself dry and put on my bed clothes.

When I went back to kiss my Mama good night, she was breathing softly, her face pleasant and peaceful. Papa was sitting in a chair by the cot looking at his diamond, his new daughter. He kissed my cheek as he wished me good night and went right back to gazing at his gem. I blew out the lamp and crawled into my bed, hoping the cricket songs and the bull frogs would help to put me to sleep.

Later on, I would get up to go look at the baby in order to try to understand how she had so sweetly taken my place. Papa and Mama were fast asleep and didn't hear me tiptoe into their room. The bright moonlight lit up the baby's face. I felt my heart sink because she looked so beautiful, like a baby angel. In my dream journeys, her perfect little face kept appearing. I awoke the next day to find my pillow wet with my tears.

Each time Isa looked at me, it was as if she only then realized I existed. She always seemed so surprised to see me. I am not sure what I expected from her, but it was as if she had always been a being, and I was the one who was new.

Her self-confidence annoyed me. I hated the sound of her baby laugh, the way it made my parents, brother and whoever was around, laugh with her - but not me. Her apparent perfection irked me. My mother made me mind my manners, and I pretended to love her for my Mama's sake, but I never played with her unless asked.

When the photographer came to Worsop, they dressed us up in our best clothes. Isa wore a pretty, lacy pink frock, pink booties, and a pink bonnet. They placed her on my lap and posed us for photographs. Mama ooh-ed and ahh-ed, and Papa coughed many times because he was Papa and that was how he showed his pride.

Isa was small, smooth, sugary, and smelled like rash ointment, carbolic soap, and baby powder. The photographs of the three of us were displayed in special places. Everybody said what pretty girls we were and what a handsome boy Rex was. Mama said we were the greatest of all her joys in her entire, wonderful, world.

One day, when someone was admiring these photographs, I heard my Mama call Isa her 'Brand New Princess'. I felt my heart begin to freeze. In all the stories ever read or said, I remembered there being a one and only Precious Princess. I shook the last specks of shiny, stardust from my hair and watched them fall - disappear deeply and completely into the raw, red dirt.

Isa was a growing baby; she grew in little tiny spurts. There was a mad rush to get new cloth to make more baby clothes, even though she could still fit into all the other cutesy clothes cluttering baskets in the bedrooms. She was the best dressed baby in the whole of Worsop.

Her hair grew like Rapunzel's because she had growing hair like mine except hers was fine, silky and black, black, black. Her skin darkened to a milky coffee brown, two shades lighter than my own skin. Her eyes, when they finally settled on a color, were the color of light black mint tea - a liquid, green-black.

Rex liked to babysit her as soon as he got home from school. I preferred to imagine life without her, but I didn't go down to the river for many weeks because I was struggling to keep an attitude of goodness. I hoped my parents would notice, but they did not.

My old ways were never too far below a shallow surface and itchy feet were still my greatest sin. But I made the walk to school and tried to think about the square roots of numbers and when to use commas. My mind was a million miles in all directions and nothing sank in. The Head Teacher constantly compared me to Rex.

At home, I shadowed a baby sister. I was in a nowhere place. Women continued to come by our house to visit. We were on the way to Mass Creton's shop, and people had to pass our house when they were going to buy their necessities. Although an excuse to visit was never required in our home, they always said they had stopped by to see the baby who was now walking and learning her words.

She was a bright child and people remarked she was probably going to turn out like Rex. I received the passing nods, pats on the head, and the usual reminders. I needed to do better in school and stop running around like a wild child.

I was constantly told how lucky I was to have two siblings like Rex and Isa. No one expected much of me, and so I never knew how to expect better of myself. Most of the times, I felt as if I were as invisible as when she first got there. They never spoke to my eyes, even as they pleasantly patted my head. I said yes at all the right times, and they smiled distantly over the top of my head.

When Isa turned twelve months old, she was three times blessed. A man of holiness came to bless her. His wife, First Lady, came with him, dressed in her Baptist Sunday Church Holy and Sanctified dress and high heels which sank into the red dirt as she made her way down to the house.

She had sat sideways on a donkey, all the way from their house, and was shiny and moist with sweat by the time she arrived. We had already received blessing in morning church, but Pastor Robinson felt, based on our history of childhood illness, the house needed to be blessed as well. He wanted to do a special blessing for Isa in her own home as added protection.

Pastor Robinson was forever looking to put out the burning fires of hell and snuff out the smell of brimstone. He said God was coming back in five years' time on a Sunday in May. First Lady raised her eyes to the heaven and said 'Amen' and 'Yes, Lord.' Pastor Robinson laid hands on Isa as she lay in her bassinet in my parents' room. He put the Holy Spirit in her, and she was saved and sanctified.

Right after dusk, Shepherdess came with her flock of sisters. There were seven of them. They always did their holy work in a group of seven because seven was a blessed number, they said. The sisters danced, sang, and blew whistles to scare the devil as they banged away on tambourines.

The early night air was warm, and the moon was bright on Isa whose bassinet was in the middle of the front yard. The women danced around her. Shepherdess, with pencils tucked behind each one of her ears (she said God sent her messages to write down, but I never saw her with any paper), and all the moon-stained sisters, spun around in circles as their long, white dresses went up and down like washing in a strong wind. Their white turbans never budged from their heads, no matter how fast they spun around. They made me dizzy as I watched them from the veranda.

At midnight, the obeah man, Brata, came. He was an albino, and he had very, very strong magic. He was dressed in black with a tall black hat on top of his frantic, wiry, red hair, and a black coat with two V'd flaps in the back. They had moved Isa and her bassinet back into Mama's and Papa's bedroom.

Brata threw herbs and white powder over her and talked under his breath the whole time. The candle lights flickered as if they were little spirits. His voice rose like a warrior. 'Be gone evil spirits, duppies, and ole hags! Be gone, all you demons! Be gone all you shady shadows of envy, lies, deceit, and hatred!' he hollered, as I looked closely to see who he was talking to.

He sprinkled black powder over Isa. 'Be gone to de back of night! Go back to the deepest depths! Obey my voice, and stay far from dis chile!' He sprinkled more powder and, dipping his middle finger and his index finger into a bowl of chicken blood, he drew a star on Isa's forehead.

I watched from the doorway. I never liked Brata. I was scared of him because of what he knew. He communicated with the dead, and he only came out in the night time.

Isa was now three times blessed. My parents became more hopeful. Isa was going to live after all.

There had always been talk of moving to England. Everybody talked about England as the place to become rich, to find good work, to make real money, and to go to good schools. I never took much notice.

I had heard this talk all my life. I had heard it was a cold, wet, grey place with a lemony sun which came out once or twice a year. I saw pictures of it in books, and there were strange children with yellow, brown, and red hair, white, white skin, and pink lips. They wore nice clothes and went to proper schools. They looked clean with no red dirt on their knees or on their feet which were dressed in pretty shoes, not sandals falling apart around the edges. They wore no torn and repeatedly stitched clothes. They did not have nappy hair refusing to stay controlled by plaits, raggedy ribbons, or rubber bands.

I had never seen a white child. The closest to a white person in our village were the albinos and people who were very light-skinned black people. Our family was of the latter persuasion.

I could not imagine a place full of these kinds of people. I knew children who had a parent or two living in this place called England, but they were merely a few of them. I reasoned they, the black people who lived in England, must stay well-hidden so no one took pictures of them for our school books.

I also knew many people who had lived in our village but who now lived in England and sent money and clothes for their village relatives. The children they had left behind constantly talked about what they would do when they got sent for, to go and live in that cold, distant land.

It seemed to me everyone was rich in England because of the Queen. I still did not understand why anyone would want to live in a land with such a watery looking sun.

Back then, I did not know how poor we were and how much the farms were becoming too hard to keep up. I did not realise how many people were concerned about the future of life in the country.

I also did not understand how things were changing in the world and how life in Worsop did not offer much to us. I knew nowhere and nothing else. I thought we were doing completely fine. In my eyes, we needed nothing because we had each other, even with the unwelcomed addition of Isa.

I paid no attention to my parents' changing attitudes towards the farm. My father was my father, and if he chose not to go to the yam hills or to see about the bananas as often as he always had, that was of no concern to me. I was obsessed with trying to figure out what I could do to make Isa less special to everyone around me. Sometimes, my parents would stop talking when I came into the room. I would hear snatches of conversation which did not make sense. I was busy being a child with my own childish problems.

One Thursday, Papa went away without taking anything to sell. Mass Creton took him in his pick-up. He came home a few days later. I found out he had gone all the way to Kingston - to Town.

I was curious. In my life time, no member of my immediate family had ever had a reason to go to Town. I knew my parents talked about having gone there when they were younger, and I knew many others in our village who had gone there for one reason or the other.

Montego Bay was closer, and we had been there once so that Rex and I could see the ocean. The trip had been long and we had stayed with a relative of my mother's. The ocean had been the most beautiful thing I had ever seen, and they had to force us out of those warm, blue-green waters. I was six at the time, but we had never been back.

Next to Christiana, Montego Bay had been the only 'big' city I had ever seen. To me, Kingston was the Emerald City - a mythical place far removed from our country village, not only because of distance but mainly because of its bigger-than-life reputation. It was a place to make your fortune. It was also a place where danger lurked at every turn.

'Children, mi have a big announcement. Mi sell some land some time ago. Fifty acres to be exact. De time has come for us to make a big move out of Jamaica to a new land, a new home. People say England is goin' to close her doors soon; laws are changin', an' is not easy like it used to be in de fifties for Jamaican people to go an' fine a bettah life. If we wait too long, it may well be too late.'

Papa had sold fifty acres of land which had been passed down to us from our grandfathers; stretching back to at least three grandfathers before, all the way back to the days of slavery. It was idle land that we no longer farmed. In one hand he held a big, bulky, brown envelope.

'Papers to England,' he announced, 'finally come t'rough!' He held the envelope as if it were holy.

'Mi want you children to listen to mi good. Right now,' he paused, 'mi can only tek Mama, mi-self, an' one chile. We jus' don't have the means to tek all of us. When t'ings sekle down, we will sen' for you, Rex, an' you, Pearl.

'So,' he continued, 'when we get to London, we going to stay with you Mama's Cousin Kenneth and his wife, Puncie. He has a small, one room flat in a place called Hackney. Space will be tight. Is not much, but is all we can do for right now.'

Papa told us not to worry. In a short while we would all be together again.

'In de meantime,' he said, 'Aunty an' Uncle goin' to live in our house as dat will be more room for dere boys in dere house. When it is time fah you to leave, we plan to rent out de farm permanently. Dey goin' to tek care of de farm an' our overall interests. Now, mi speak to Head Teacher an' since Rex is recommended for Kingston College, he is goin' to live in Kingston wit Head Teacher's sister an' her 'usband. We know dey know people who know many, many important people in Kingston. His tuition is taken care of, an' Mama an' I have no worries dat he is goin' to be in good hands. He is goin' to a Christian home. Pearl, you will stay wit Uncle an' Aunty. We plan to sen' fah de both of you aftah graduation.' He stopped talking, finally.

I had long since closed my eyes and covered my ears when I heard they were leaving me behind. I stopped listening. I stopped breathing. I ran from the room to the baby's bassinet where she was fast asleep, breathing softly with butterfly breaths.

'No! No! No!' I screamed, as I ran.

Mama, Papa, and Rex ran in behind me. My tears poured like water from the clouds above Worsop when they were heavy with rain. All my Mama could do was hug me and whisper sweet things as she rubbed my aching head.

'Is all right, honey,' she kept saying, stroking my hair and hugging me as if she would never let me go. 'Everyt'in' is goin' to be alright, sweetness.'

I didn't hear the sugar in her words. I only knew one thing for sure - she was leaving me behind; she was going to be letting me go and taking Isa with her - Isa instead of me - not me with Isa. I refused to be sensible because after all Isa was a baby. There was a whirlpool rushing around in my head.

On the morning they left with her, I stood, silently, stiffly, a brewing storm, my arms folded, and my face solid with anger. They were on their way to Kingston where in a few days they would take a ship to England. I hurriedly turned away from the hurt look in my Mama's eyes when I refused to hug her and when I acted like I didn't see Isa's little arms reaching out to me.

'Pearl,' Mama said, 'come kiss mi an' Papa bye-bye, an' come kiss Isa. Don't fret. Time will go really fast, an' soon we all goin' to be back together as one family in de same place again!'

I did not say a word as I turned and started running down the road in the other direction. I wanted to run for a while. My legs had their own mind. I did not look back, even when they called to me to come back and say goodbye properly.

'Pearl! Pearl! Girl, come now. Stop dis nonsense! Pearl!' Their voices faded as I ran, and then I heard the coughing of the truck's motor. When I could hear them and the truck no longer, I knew they were gone. I did not stop running for a long time.

Eventually, I was aware I would have to face Aunty for my taking off like that.

In the beginning, Rex came home every other month but, in time, he stopped coming. I got long letters instead. Rex said we were all we had for now, even if he couldn't see me much. I wrote back in my chicken scratch handwriting which only he was able to understand.

'I miss you. How is you?' I wrote. 'I stay okay. Aunty and Uncle make sure I stay all write. Me miss you an Mama an Papa.' Whenever I tried to say I missed Isa, the words burned my throat and never made it to the tip of the pencil.

Two of my Aunty's and Uncle's oldest boys had started going back and forth to Kingston. The Stand Pipe gossip was that they were up to bad things in the city. Then one day they stopped coming home. I had known them all my life, and I began to feel this was now the way my life would always be. I would always lose people I felt deeply about. No one knew for sure what happened to them. For many long days and nights, Aunty cried for them

'Mi sons! Mi sons! Mi want mi children! Where are mi boys?' she wailed. She wore black, and refused to eat. She would only drink hot Cerasee Tea, as bitter as she could make it. We went out into the yard and pulled strands of the vine for her. It grew wild everywhere. We would pop the thick, orange pods (which were poisonous) and suck on the sweet, pulpy, red seeds which we spat out when they lost flavor.

Aunty sent letters to family in Kingston to see if they could help to find Lil Pa and Lee Van. All anyone was able to tell her was when they last saw the boys. After that, no one knew anything. Uncle and Aunty made one trip to Kingston - to Trench Town.

The police told them, 'Please, we 'ave no time to worry 'bout every country bwoy who come an' get caught up in Kingston life. Every day we find anothah body in some gully or on the side of some road. If you haven't heard from you boys in ovah two months, then we don't know what it is we supposed to tell you...'

It was Uncle who repeated to us what they had been told. Aunty stayed in her room for two days. Then one day she woke up and life went on. She had fourteen more mouths at home to fret over. Sweet black mint tea replaced her Cerasee Tea. She began to cook, clean, and take care of her chickens, vegetable gardens, and the womanly affairs of both her farms and ours. She resumed bossing everyone around. I realized I had had it good when she was in mourning and felt evil for thinking such thoughts.

Even before my cousins disappeared, I had always been afraid of Kingston. Aunty had taken me there to visit Rex in his first year living with Head Teacher's relatives. We had had to take public transportation through the heart of the city to get to the nicer area in which Rex now lived.

The city was fast. People moved like ants, scurrying everywhere. Mule and donkey drawn carts mingled with streams of cars, dusty trucks, leaning, multi-colored country buses, mini-vans, and taxis packed with people. It was loud, with the constant blaring of vehicle horns, the blasting of music from various types of speakers, and people laughing and cussing. It smelled of diesel fuel, asphalt, tar, garbage, and sweat - a city full of concrete buildings with people constantly hustling, selling and buying. Stray dogs and goats cruised the crowded streets.

I felt as if my lost cousins had been swallowed up by all the meanness that I had seen on so many people's faces when I passed through some rough areas on the country bus home. I wondered if they had ever regretted leaving the greenness of Worsop with its happy faces and polite, country ways. Aunty recovered from the loss, at least on the outside.

Uncle said, 'Mi always did know dis day was goin' to come.' He went on with his farming.

The months slipped into years. Changes started to happen in Worsop and in me. More of my cousins moved to other parts of the island, and soon there were only seven of them left. Of the seven, two talked all the time about leaving when the younger ones grew up a bit more. Aunty and Uncle started to sell parcels of their land but kept what they felt they could still manage and farm with the help of the remaining children.

Uncle said he had no intention of going to England, even if that was what Aunty was starting to talk about. Jamaica was his birthplace, and this was his land. He was not going to leave just because times were getting harder. He would die right where he had been born.

I grew taller and more hard-headed. Aunty spent a great deal of time asking the Lord to give her patience to deal with my foolishness.

'Pearl, you getting' to be a young lady now. You can't be runnin' here an' runnin' dere. People goin' to talk. Dey quick to say you doin' t'ings you might not be doin', but who knows? You act so flighty -

flighty all day long! Chile, you raisin' my blood pressure every day! What mi s'pposed to tell you parents? You an' you shenanigans! Not right fe a young lady, jus' not right!'

I refused to go to school. By the time I was thirteen, I was helping out in Mass Creton's shop most of the time. Eventually, everyone came to the agreement that at least when I was there, they knew where I was. My heart had birthed a tiny piece of ice which was steadily growing bigger the longer my parents were away. I felt abandoned.

Mama and Papa's letters had to make their way from the ships in Montego Bay, up the coast, and up the mountain to Worsop. They took a long time to arrive. But my parents always wrote to me, Rex, Aunty and Uncle.

Once a year they sent barrels of clothes and little toys and books for Rex, the younger cousins, and children they were especially close to, and me. They told Rex and me that soon they would have a real place for all of us.

They sent smiling pictures of themselves and of Isa. Isa and Papa standing in snow, playing in snow; Isa bundled up like a little mongoose, Isa in cute little summer dresses with the lemony sun smiling down on her with Mama standing closely behind, Isa with a teddy bear on what I knew was a swing even though ours hung from trees and was not as fancy as the one from which she smiled.

Aunty said, 'Lawd 'ave mercy! Little Isa is no longah a baby. She is a actual chile. Look how big she getting. Look at dose long braids! What a beautiful baby an' now a beautiful little sistah for you. Pearl, look at you sistah! Mi know you can't wait to see har again!'

I grudgingly looked at the pictures. 'Is jus' stupid pictures. All baby-pickney look de same!'

More often than not I would throw the pictures on a nearby table and, without another word, run off to Mass Creton's shop.

My Aunty, although she loved me, thought I was a 'facety' child because I could be very rude to her when Uncle was not around. She had made a promise to my parents: Uncle and she would never lay a hand on me. My parents had rarely ever hit us, or rather they had never raised a hand to Rex, whereas I had managed to suffer the consequences of their wrath on those rare occasions. They would never have wanted anyone else to touch us, but I knew that my mouthiness exasperated my Aunty. The way to correct children was with the belt or a switch from a plant or tree. Her boys had never reached an age where they could not be whipped. Still, my Uncle and Aunt respected my parents' wishes, and I managed to get away with behavior some elders in the village regarded as close to shocking.

'Mi goin' see if Uncle Creton need 'elp in de shop, Aunty!' I tossed the words over one shoulder before she could say or do anything to stop me.

I hated Isa so much more. I hoped one day to hear she had gotten lost in the winter whiteness in those photos or fallen off one of those little boats Papa liked to take her on in the summer time. After a while, I stopped praying for forgiveness. I figured God was tired of my foolishness, like Aunty and Uncle said they were.

Now I look back on those days, and I wonder if there was anything I could have done to stop the hatred building up in my heart. I wonder if I could have trusted my parents loved me as much as they did my baby sister. But I know now how much of a stubborn child I was and realize I had already made up my mind about the whole situation from the day they brought her home. My eyes were completely clouded by the jealousy and envy I felt for my sister.

Mass Creton's shop continued to sell a little bit of everything. On a Friday or Saturday evening, it was far less crowded than when my parents still lived in Worsop.

More young people, like my cousins, were leaving Worsop for places undrenched by mist and rain clouds; places with more than one juke box and one very old black and white TV which was unable to pick up the channels clearly - a clothes hangar being the new antennae. They left for places with electricity for everyone, proper toilets and indoor plumbing - not outhouses full of lizards, roaches and lingering odors left behind by decades of use, and places where hosepipes were not used for showers. Life in Worsop was slow and the conveniences of a modern world had not yet arrived - once they explored other towns, Worsop's backwardness became more glaring and less desirable.

The hilly village became top heavy with old people and young children who had been sent home from big cities in Jamaica and from abroad to be raised by relatives.

My parents sent enough money for Aunty and Uncle to buy one of the latest, most modern transistor radios. In the evenings, we would listen to *Semelina and Her Life in Town* which was a radio soap opera about a country girl who runs off to Kingston. ('Today Semelina finds herself in a heated argument with her gossipy neighbor, Dulce, who accuses her of stealing a valuable dress off the clothes line! Semelina's landlord gets involved and threatens Semelina with eviction if the dress does not make an appearance!')

We would listen to holy music and words from the radio Pastor at seven o'clock every evening.

'Brothahs and sistahs, de time is upon us; de Lord's time is at hand. We are merely days away from de end of dis wicked, wanton, worldly existence. Repent, Brothahs an' Sistahs, fall on your knees an' repent! Or burn in de damnation fires of hell!'

In cricket season, Uncle and his man-friends would gather at Mass Creton and drink rum and Guinness stout as they listened to the match. Sometimes, I went with my Uncle because, when I hung around my Aunty too much, I got on her nerves.

She had all boys (her only daughter being my cousin, Moira, who drowned in the river), and she seemed very partial to boys. She maintained that girls were nothing more than trouble.

She felt the need to constantly remind me to keep my legs closed and my heart pressed on Jesus, but I was too energetic for her to keep up with and too wily for her to keep an eye on all the time. She did not have to worry because I was not interested in boys.

Uncle took me along, and I would listen, cheer, and jump up with the men when their team did well. While the men spent the rest of the time slapping down dominoes and drinking rum, I would putter around with Mass Creton, checking on store supplies, or I would sit out in front of the store and play with his dogs.

No one seemed particularly concerned about my education. No one asked me when I was returning to school. My parents never mentioned it in any of their letters, and so the matter was dropped.

On hot Sundays, we sat fanning ourselves in our tiny Baptist church listening to Pastor Robinson and waiting for the end of the world on a day in May, but the dates kept changing so Aunty and Uncle said they were not going to pack anything until Pastor Robinson got the correct date from God or from the radio Pastor.

It took many years before I saw my parents and Isa again. By then the ice chip growing in my heart had become a boulder.

In 1967, I turned fifteen. I had, by this time, officially not gone to school in two years, but I could read and write enough to handle business in Mass Creton's shop. His son had moved to Kingston. Robby was in a ska reggae band and was hoping to go to England where Jamaican music was becoming popular, especially with white people.

A new singer was making musical waves. His name was Bob Marley. His ska band was putting Jamaica on the map.

Mass Creton sold off most of his farm and, in fact, no longer farmed. He, like my parents, rented out parcels of land to itinerant farmers, but he kept the shop going because it was the only one in the village.

Mass Creton's shop also operated as the post office. Mass Creton would go to Christiana on a weekly basis to get the local post. People would stop by his shop to see if they had any mail or sometimes, if he was going that way, he would personally take their mail to them. He was a good, solid man with a long-standing, deeply rooted level of respect in the village.

I was down to five cousins. The two who had planned to leave, did, but, unlike their lost older brothers, they ended up going to England and working on the railways in a place called Manchester. They made, it would seem, good money and always managed to send something home to Aunty and Uncle.

Aunty stopped talking about going to England when three of the sons, who still remained, fathered children. To her delight they were all boys. When they were with her, they were a handful especially when they were still young. As the months passed, they became harder to manage, and I would help out when they were around. I rather enjoyed running after them as they kept my mind occupied. I was good with the children and my interaction with them somewhat redeemed myself in the eyes of my Uncle and Aunty.

My Uncle and Aunty never moved into our farmhouse, as my Papa had said they would. Shortly after my parents left, they rented it out. The farms still managed okay; the remaining boys were content to stay put. I had no interest in the farm. I preferred to help out at Mass Creton's store or watch the young ones.

Rex had gone on to the University of West Indies, UWI, Mona Campus. He was nineteen years old now and wanted to be a doctor. His marks were so high that he had received a scholarship to UWI and was now living on campus.

On weekends he would stay with Head Teacher's sister and her family who had 'adopted' him as their own - with my parents' blessing. He hoped to transfer to a medical school in America. He was one of the few people I knew who talked about moving to America and not to England; that was his dream. He was tall, handsome, with soft curly hair, almond brown, slim, like Papa, and possessed a smile which made women, even old women, smile back.

I was not sure who I looked like. I had high cheekbones like Mama, but my big 'froggy' eyes (Rex said) came out of nowhere. I was tall, as well, and slim, too, but my body had curved into breasts and hips, and boys always paid me attention.

I visited Rex two or three times each year, although I still found Kingston too intimidating. The journey there took many hours and involved changing modes of transportation a variety of times, but I never really felt the need to stay long. Usually, I was allowed to stay for a day or two.

Kingston girls looked at me funny, and Rex's friends treated me like a little country idiot. The girls stared at my old Sunday-best clothes and long, coarse hair and giggled as they smoothed their hot combed or roller set 'do's and patted their tight jeans or tugged at their mini-skirts. They rarely said a word to me except the occasional, 'So, you is Rex sistah, eh? How old is you? You should live in Kingston, let we dress you up, girl!' Then they would turn away, giggling, before I answered.

The boys talked to me as if I were a five year old. Rex would tell them to leave me alone. Secretly, I had started to wonder if he wasn't a little embarrassed by me.

On one trip, he introduced me to his girlfriend. She was an Indian girl called Reena, with beautiful, straight, black hair which she often whipped up into sophisticated up-dos. She dressed like the girls I saw in magazines and came from a family who had a huge house close to the UWI campus.

During my one and only visit to her house, I was afraid to touch anything. She had visited many countries and studied at Cambridge University in England. Her voice was crisp and proper. I envied her her poise and confidence, and I knew she felt sorry for me. I could not partake in any of their discussions about the world and academics. I was always saying, doing, and wearing the wrong things, which was often confirmed by their raised eyebrows or little smiles.

I noticed how Rex was changing. He sounded more and more like a Kingston city boy - a city boy with education. His speech and his attitude were mature. I was still a country girl and very immature.

On one of these trips, Rex and I waited at the bus garage for the lopsided, rickety, blue, red, and green country bus which would be the first of quite a few buses to get me back home to Worsop. Around us, vendors hawked everything from snow cones to cut pieces of sugar cane to bags of seasoned shrimp.

Some sold roast corn and roast yams; others tried to get you to buy last minute items such as watches and baby toys.

It was hot and humid even though it was early morning, and the asphalt burned through the soles of my no longer white plimsolls. Raggedy boys ran in and out of the crowds of anxious travelers who were trying to find the right buses, and policemen walked up and down keeping the peace. Women clutched their purses tightly.

As usual, central Kingston grated on my nerves; there were too many people, too much noise, too many smells, and too much dirt. I longed for the peaceful quietness of home, and I was already thinking of a long dip in the river the following day. A man stepped on my foot and continued on without a word of apology. I rolled my eyes and brushed off my dirt covered plimsolls.

'Rude ass!' I muttered under my breath.

Rex laughed and asked me if my foot was okay. I nodded. 'Is downtown Kingston, Pearl, an' people always on the move. Nevah mind.'

'Yes, but dey could try to move wit some kind of politeness, don't you t'ink. Is a good thing up where you live is nicer.'

'Yeah, well, is a totally different part of Kingston. Down here you have to deal with a lot of ruffians; people forget their manners sometimes.' Out of the blue he asked, 'When Mama an' Papa send fah you, will you go?'

'Cha,' I said, 'mi no give dat much thought. Mi don't even t'ink mi is on dere mind at all. Anyways, all dat rain an' cold! Maybe is best if I fine a nice man an' stay right here in Jamaica.'

'I can't see why you would t'ink they not t'inkin' of us when every chance they get is a barrel or a lettah they send to you an' mi. Maybe is cause you just don't want to be near Isa,' he said, putting his hands in his pockets and whistling an out of tune tune while he looked up into the sky.

I punched him. 'Shut up! Who t'inkin' 'bout Isa? Don't be ridiculas. Me fine right 'ere. Jus' cause everyone runnin' to England, don't mean mi 'ave to run an' follow dem.'

'Pearl, why do you nevah want to write har or ask questions 'bout har? She is your sistah, you know. She still a little baby, an' you still har big sistah.'

I sucked my teeth and looked away.

'You know,' he said, 'I always thought you would grow out of it.'

'Grow out of what, Rex?' I continued to look away.

'This thing you have 'gainst Isa. Pearl, she is a little girl. Why you act like you don't like you own sistah?' He waited for an answer.

'Oh, look,' I said, ''ere come de bus!'

It was his turn to suck his teeth. I took my little travel bag from him, kissed his cheek, and gave him a quick hug before I hustled with the crowd of people on to the crowded bus. I was lucky. I pushed ahead with the shoving, despite all the cussing. As I made my way inside the bus, I found a comfortable place to stand. I saw him waving, even though he could not see where I was standing.

The bus eventually, after much commotion and settling of fares, chugged out of the garage. I put Isa out of my mind as I always did whenever she was

50

mentioned and resolved that this would be my last visit to Rex after the way his girlfriend acted. I had enough put-downs from my own relatives and other people in the village.

I knew full well that everybody was taking bets on how soon it would be before I turned up pregnant, but I felt I could take being looked down on from people I had grown up with rather than from strangers. We would write to each other like in the old days, I thought. After all, with his new friends, life, and girlfriend, I realized I was probably losing my brother as well.

Another year went by and then one more. It had been almost two years since my visit to Rex. I had grown comfortable and content. I felt I never had to really grow up. I still played around the village like a child at times although I maintained some sense of maturity when I was around adults.

I was turning seventeen, but Aunty would not give me her approval to have anything to do with boys. The ones left in Worsop were busy making eyes at me and trying to chat me up. I liked the attention but drew away from them if they even hinted at wanting to touch me in any way. Mass Creton put the fear of the Almighty into their young man-boy hearts, so my parents really had nothing to worry about. I was home at decent times. I had nowhere to go except the store. As my pool of friends slowly shrank, I kept to myself. What little trouble a young girl could get into in Worsop, I stayed out of.

One day, Mass Creton returned around midday with the mail from Christiana. I was busy taking inventory when he called my name.

'Pearl, lettah come fah you! Is from you Ma and Pa!' he said.

I hurried to the back room where he was sorting mail and putting the letters and parcels in alphabetical order.

'Pearl Waite, official mail!' he laughed. He handed me the familiar blue letter with the *Par Avion* label and flowers on the stamp. Mass Creton had become my best friend in the whole of Worsop. He understood me, and he talked to me like Papa used to. He was like Papa in so many ways. I knew some people whispered about me, this young girl, working in this shop, alone with this old man, but I trusted him with my life. He was always righteous in his actions towards me, and he ignored the talk as well.

His wife had died before I was even born, but Mass Creton never remarried. Many women tried to get him because of his good looks and nice ways. The fact he owned property as well as a shop was an added bonus.

He never had a girlfriend, and there were pictures of Matilda, his late wife, all around the shop and in his house. His house overlooked what used to be most of his farm. I thought it was funny how it faced backwards, but he said he liked the view when he sat on his veranda in the evenings, rocking in the old rocking chair that had belonged to his Matilda.

I walked outside to the back of the shop and ripped the letter open.

Dearest Pearl, we hope you are well and learning from working in the shop with Creton. We three are doing well. Papa have a new job in a factory and money is getting better. Your Mama is working too, making clothes in a factory. We moved to a little room in a place called Stratford, but this is for the moment. It is very hard to find places willing to let to us. Isa started going to a school nearby and she is happy. Aunty has sent us all the money the farm has made so far and from when we sell the other twenty-five acres and with our earnings we now have enough to put some money down on a little house in the Stratford area and we will still have a bit extra for furniture and to put away for rainy days. We went to see an estate agent yesterday and he took us to see a really nice place on a street called Chandos Road. Pearl, is a nice, nice house. Is called a terrace house. You and Isa will have your own room, and there is a room for Rex, if he decide to come. We should know for sure in a little while whether we get the place. There is a family living there now but they selling because they want to move to the country. Aunty has money put away for both of your fares and we been working on visas for you but that is no problem because Papa and I went and apply for British citizenship and we get approve, Pearl. So our children free to come here now once we file the proper papers. When you come you can go back to school, get an education, and be happy. We love you and miss you. We so sorry it take so long but we come here in our old age and it is always hard to start again in a new place when you are no longer a young person. We will send another letter or a telegram soon as we get the

*house. Love Mama and Papa, 6th June 1969. P.S.
As soon as we get your papers to come we will send
them.*

When I finished reading, I knew I had to make a decision. I stood there for some minutes with the letter in my hand until Mass Creton called out to ask if I was planning to come back inside any time before sunset.

Folding the letter, I tucked it into my brassiere and went back to finish the inventory and give Mass Creton a list of things we needed in order to restock. He looked into my eyes but did not ask why I looked so concerned. He knew I would tell him in my own time.

When I was free from working in the shop, I liked to wander through the country roads of Worsop. I would stop by our farm to talk to the coolie woman, Miss Inez, who rented out a patch of the land to plant neat, orderly rows of callaloo, yams, corn, and Scotch bonnet peppers. She always made me laugh and called me 'River Bird' because my long legs reminded her of the long-legged white river bird that delicately made its way along the shallows of Jamaican rivers. I told her I might be leaving.

'Lawd, chile! But mi goin' miss you! But is a good t'ing. Everybody want to go to Hengland!' She reached up and put her earthy, calloused palms on both my cheeks and kissed them. She was a sweet, hardworking woman who lived further on in the village with her heap of pretty, dark-eyed, dusky-skinned, half Indian children.

Her husband, a rough brute of a man who used to beat her on a regular basis, had left one day for a

54

visit to Kingston and never came back. My parents always included something for her in the barrels they sent over to us from the UK.

'Not so much mi, Mima,' I told her, calling her by the name the village children had always called her for as long as I could remember.

'T'ink only pon de good, Rivah Bird. It will work out fe you. One day you goin' to be jus' as posh like de Queen. T'ink what you will see an' what you will do an' who you will end up bein'. Mi will be right 'ere t'inkin' 'bout you!' She smiled. Her missing teeth (and there were many) never took anything away from the warmth of her smile. I kissed her cheeks, and she kissed mine. I walked on.

I walked where I used to love to run. I played with Shame-O'Lady plants, as I always had done, and laughed when they curled their leaves at my touch. I ate newly fallen mangoes lying scattered on the ground below free growing mango trees, and I lay on grassy beds, staring up at the blue, blue sky with its cotton-ball clouds.

On summer days, the heavens were so high, the clouds so milky white, and birds whistled and sang as they dipped and swooped alive with happiness.

I sat by the river and threw rocks, and decided to wade in up to my waist before totally immersing my body in the water's coolness. My hair became heavy and full of water, and I cried. Then I returned to the river banks and sat some more as the warm sun dried me.

I could almost hear the voices of my little friends now grown and mostly gone from the village. They had left Worsop for America, England, Kingston,

Spanish Town, Montego Bay, Cuba, Curaçao and Trinidad - wanting to be anywhere but here. I could plainly hear their laughter.

'When mi grow up...' had been our favorite game. 'When mi grow up, mi goin' to 'ave lots of money an' live in Hengland. Mi goin' to drive a big, big car an' eat plenty good food - mashed potatoes an' beef welly like mi Daddy say dem eat. Mi is goin' to eat mushy peas an' drink plenty ale an' Guinness. No yams fah mi, no suh! An' mi goin' put plenty shillings in de metah so mi nevah run out of 'eat like mi Daddy did las wintah!'

'When mi grow up, mi goin' to move to New York to be a doctah. Mi Mama send me plenty, plenty picture of New York. She work in a tall, tall buildin' wid elevatas. She say she work in janitorial services. Mi t'ink dat means she manage de 'hole buildin'! Mi goin' work in a buildin' even tallah dan de one she work in!'

'When mi grow up mi goin' to Kingston an' mi goin' become a politician an' run t'ings!'

We were all going to be movie stars, musicians, business owners, mayors of cities, and friends with the Queen.

It appeared that everyone abroad was doing well and making money. American dollars as well as pounds and shillings made their way slowly to Worsop to Mass Creton who was also emerging as a banker handling the foreign currency. In our minds, "foreign" was where the streets were paved in gold and silver, and where we imagined life was easy, fair, and prosperous.

Worsop was slowly dying. The stream on our land had dwindled to a mere trickle. Mass Creton stocked fewer items. The school was falling apart, the two churches in our village leaked heavily in the rain, and there was no money to fix anything. People were steadily leaving the village.

The ground was tougher, and life seemed rougher for many people who still had to struggle to live without the support of relatives in foreign places. Farms became overgrown as sons and daughters refused to help aging parents work the land before joining the caravan of fortune seekers. The talk was always of leaving.

I thought about my friends, my skipping school, and all my 'play' relatives. I felt the excitement of harvest celebrations, christenings, baptisms at the river, even funerals and nine-night wakes.

I saw in my mind's eye our village festivals when we danced in the streets, drums beating, Junkanoo dancers walking on mile long sticks, banjos and harmonicas twanging, and everyone eating plenty, plenty food.

I saw vivid images of Shepherdess and her flock dancing in their white dresses; the obeah man burning his incense and fire and chanting amongst the trees as we children sneaked and watched.

I thought about snuggling under warm sheets with little girl friends when the rainy, Worsop mountain mist descended on us; our Stand Pipe gossip, and the battle we never really won when we tried to wash the red dirt out of our clothes or from our feet. The feeling of loss was like a deep ache inside my very bones.

Everywhere I went in Worsop brought me to a place of memory. My memories of time with Mama,

Papa, Rex, and when the farm was still strong. I felt that if I left, I would be leaving my soul behind me.

I loved this little village with its country ways. I was not ashamed to be a country girl. That was who I was and wanted to remain. I dreamed about taking over our farm and surprising everyone by making it successful.

As I had grown older, I had slowly begun to develop an emerging interest in the land. My interest was in its early stages of infancy, but I was starting to ask questions and became more attentive when my Aunty and Uncle worked their land or talked about this business of farming.

When I was not at Mass Creton's store or watching children, I had started, much to everyone's shock, to follow Uncle and his sons to the field. My temper was being replaced by a sense of belonging.

Months later, I was in the field with Uncle, my hands deep in the red dirt as we harvested yams. A little boy came running to tell me Mass Creton had something important for me, and I should come right away.

It was a long walk to the shop, but Uncle said to ride one of the mules they had ridden out to the fields and have the boy ride it back to them after I had gotten to the store. The boy and I jumped on the smoke-grey mule's back. A light drizzle had been starting and stopping that afternoon, and I was a grateful I would have the chance to dry off when I arrived at Mass Creton's.

Mass Creton was standing outside the store smoking his tobacco pipe when I arrived. He greeted me with a big smile as he handed me the large envelope. I knew without opening it what it contained. There would be documents allowing me to travel.

'Pearl, open it quick. But mi a'ready know what this is. Chile, is the opportunity of a lifetime!' He had returned from Christiana after picking up the village mail. 'You goin' be wit your Ma and Pa an' little Isa. Cha, in England! You mus' mek sure you write mi all the time, alright? Mi want to know how you keepin'; what you doin'. Mi want to see how you turn out; but mi want to see it in your own words so you mus' write. You promise mi?'

It was as if I were leaving right then and there. My heart felt like lead. He looked deep into my eyes, binding me to the promise. He was getting old and arthritis knotted his fingers. He coughed a lot.

I marveled that no one had ever considered the fact I might not want to leave. It was just a given I would be grateful for this opportunity.

When my Uncle and Aunt found out I had gotten my travel documents, they beamed. I jokingly said they must be happy to finally see the back of me after all the trouble I had caused them. I was taken by complete surprise when my Aunty's face collapsed into sadness and a torrent of tears cascaded down her cheeks. I realized in that moment, despite my erratic behavior over the years, they loved me.

'Mi been watchin' you finally grow up,' she blubbered. 'Mi know dat dis is what de Lord wants fah you. You goin' in a new direction now. Remember we was good to you!'

My Uncle wiped a tear from his eye and put his rough hands on my shoulders. He looked deep into my eyes and said, 'Mek you parents proud, Pearl, an' mek us even prouder. You had it rough. We neva know from one day to the nex' how t'ings would turn out. T'ank God fah Creton watchin' ovah you. Is more 'im dan we keep you out of trouble, but t'ank God, you time fah you blessin' is 'ere. Mek us proud, chile, mek us proud.'

The following weeks were a flurry of Aunty sewing up new clothes for me and finding a small grip, a suitcase sufficient enough to hold my meager belongings. Uncle went all the way to Brownstown to find one. It was his gift to me.

The boys came up with something nice in my honor, and there was even a little party at church. I had attended these going away parties for other people. I never thought I would ever be one of them. I had never wanted to be one of them.

Despite all the jovialities, I knew I was hiding behind a fake smile. Still, no one asked me if I really wanted to leave. I did not want to disappoint them. This was supposed to be an honor and a blessing. Why did I feel so cursed?

As much as I longed for my parents, I had grown accustomed to their absence. I had Aunty, Uncle, the boys, Mass Creton, and everyone in the village. I had the green fields, the red dirt, the mist, the rain, the bright sunshine, the chilly nights, the peeny-wallie bugs blinking at nights, and a cacophony of millions of stars above at nights. I had good country food and fresh water.

What more did I need? Why did every one not see that these things were enough for me?

Rex came up from Kingston. He was leaving in a few weeks, on his way to America on a full university scholarship. He was making a goodbye trip. I was surprised he even bothered because he was such a town boy now with his straight legged pants, well-polished pointy shoes, and stylish shirt. His hair was slicked with pomade. His country accent was gone.

Rex looked like a more refined version of Papa. His voice, deep, his dimples, deep, and his whole attitude was that of a fully grown man. But when he laughed, it was as if we were back in the little bedroom we used to share, telling jokes, making up duppy stories, and hiding under the covers during thunder and lightning storms.

'Come, let's walk,' he said to me soon after his arrival.

'You sure you want to mess up you priss clothes an' shoes?' I teased him.

He took my hand, and we walked. People made a fuss over him as we meandered along.

'Ms. G's boy? Is dat you? Lawd 'ave mercy, but you de spittin' image of you Daddy. Lawd 'ave mercy!'

Rex responded politely to everyone we met along the way, but his words were often drowned out by their enthusiasm over seeing him again.

'Son, how propah you sound! All dat propah schoolin' teachin' you well! You sound jus' like you from foreign - like a membah of parliament! Me know you parents mus' be so proud of you. An' what is dis we hear? You goin' to 'Merica! Yes, son, you goin' be a big somebody soon! Don't forget dis little village up 'ere in dese Jamaican hills. Come back an' let we see how you turn out! An' Pearl? Sweet little Pearl! Off to Hengland! You Mama an'

Papa 'ave surely seen de full glory of de workin's of de Lawd. God is good!'

As soon as they could not hear him, Rex whispered in my ear, 'Not bad for two little duppy babies, eh, little sistah!' We cracked up laughing and then would meet up with another person singing our praises.

We made our way in early evening to my favorite place - the river. The mosquitoes were emerging, screeching and hungry, but even while slapping at our faces, arms, and legs, we talked long, we talked hard, and we both cried. We were losing each other to distance and losing our past to 'what used to be' and 'remember when'.

'Rex, everybody say mi should be so excited. Well, why mi feel like cryin' every second of every day?'

''cause this is all a new t'ing to you and mi,' Rex said.

'Not so much you, though. You been away all dis time. You lef' a long, long time ago,' I replied.

'Yes, but this nevah stopped being home,' he sighed. 'Change is hard, Pearl, it's hard for everybody. Goin' to America is goin' to be hard; leavin' everybody behind is goin' to be hard, but I am excited, too. I know it's the beginnin' for mi an' you!'

'Goin' to England feels like de end for mi.' My eyes filled with water. 'Dey nevah come back, you know.'

'What you mean?' he asked.

'Mama, Papa, Isa, all de othahs dat lef'. All 'cept the ones who jus' went to live in othah places in Jamaica. An' even dey stop comin' back aftah a while.' I took a long breath and continued in a melancholy voice, 'Dat means mi will nevah come back once mi leave.'

'Because they didn't, don't mean you won't come back. Life is different for every person. You don't know. If you want to come back one day then you goin' come back. It's all in the mind; it's all in how you plan you life. I know I will.'

'Will you, Rex?' I looked at him for a long minute. He sounded so proper, so educated. Before long, living in America would erase what was left of Worsop from him. I shook my head slowly from side to side as the first stars began to peep out of the greying fabric of the evening sky. Mosquitos, crazed with a thirst for our blood, sang as they continued their attack with full force. It was time to leave.

'No, Rex, mi don't t'ink you goin' come back.'

He looked at me and then looked out to the river. He looked up to the skies and then stood up. Turning in a full circle, taking his time, carefully, his eyes followed everything around him. He spread his arms out like they were wings. It was as if he were trying to wrap everything up in one big picture to keep with him for all those future days.

He made me feel sad all over again. And I began to cry. I felt he had come to say goodbye, not solely to me, but to all of Worsop. A single peeny-wallie firefly came close to his head, as if to kiss him, then flitted away.

The light of the day was dimming fast; the river waters were dark and still. A white owl, a Patoo, hooted in the woods then flew out of the trees and flapped its wings way over our heads as it made its way across the river. Right at that moment, as if by magic, a shooting star sped across the darkening sky. I felt it was a sign.

'Come, let us go. Aunty have a nice dinner waiting for us, and I have to get up early to make my way back to Kingston.'

He held out his hand and helped me up from the large boulder I had been sitting on. He kissed my tears. With his arm around my shoulder and my arm around his, we walked back along the trails we knew so well - even in the pitch of early night. We walked together singing silly songs like the ones we used to sing when we were so much younger.

MEMORY

Warmth, softness, my mother's arms
Gentle breath of my father, sanctity.
My brother sits rocking and whispering to himself,
My sister is impatient, staring out the window,
yearning, sighing,
The fireplace glows, warmth softness, light,
spreading throughout the room,
Living room windows, framed by heavy forest green
drapes drawn apart,
frosted on the outside, steamy on the inside,
Wink at grey, damp, London, twilight skies.
Stew peas and salt beef simmer in a pot
fills the house with sweetness.
A pretty, curved, glass of amber sits on the table
beside my father,
He takes a sip every now and again,
as black and white images flit across the TV box,
casting grainy flickers of electronic
Images, shades, and shadows flirting with light
from the old lamp in the corner.
My doll is missing one eye, she has no name, and
never wears any clothes, but she is always with me.
Her hair is singed on one side from when
She fell against the fireplace;
She is still my favorite.
Teacups lie scattered around the living room.
The naked bulb, hangs from the ceiling, no shade,
makes more shadows in the room.
I am safe.

MS. RAYMA

My mother used to say, 'Ms. Rayma was an ole woman when I was young and now that *I* am an ole woman she is still the same.'

She liked to tell me stories about the people she had known in her younger years growing up with her parents and her four brothers in the mist-drenched, mountain village of Worsop.

Ah, Ms. Rayma. When I think of all the people my mother grew up with, Ms. Rayma was perhaps the most peculiar of them all and the most fascinating.

After we moved back to Jamaica from England when I was nine, Mama would take me up to the country to see our relatives and to visit the little, three-room house with the outhouse and the outside kitchen area where my parents had birthed and raised thirteen children before I came along.

We would always visit Ms. Rayma whenever we went 'to country', as we used to call our visits. She lived in a one-room abode behind Mas Charlie's shop which was just off the main road that plodded up the hill to places populated by various members of our family, the Plummers, and others.

I remember the first time I actually met Ms. Rayma. It was 1970, and we were living in Kingston. I had only been on the island of Jamaica for a few weeks when my mother and one of my older brothers, who still lived in Jamaica, decided to make the five-hour trip.

Mama wanted to retrieve some items from the house which had been carefully preserved for us for some years by the family now renting it and our land. When we entered the village, my brother, Al, slowly maneuvered his brand new, cherry-red Cortina (his great pride and joy) up the gravelly, red-dusted, bending and curving country road. Even with much horn-blowing, he narrowly avoided randomly wandering goats, the occasional cow, wet, skipping children, men with machetes and rubber boots, and women with baskets full of the world on their heads.

An old man, so light-complexioned he was near white, came out of a small, dark, weather-wearied, corrugated-zinc roofed shop. My brother pulled to a halt. My mother rolled down the window and called out, 'Mas Charlie; Lord Jesus, Mas Charlie!'

He was delighted to see my mother after so many years. Rubbing his arthritic knuckles as he talked to her through the passenger window, his pleasure at seeing her was bright in his eyes and in his wide smile full of missing teeth.

A mist of rain swirled around him, but he didn't seem to mind the dampness that had seeped through his old, patched, khaki trousers, his blue plaid shirt, and the ancient, faded-brown fedora which perched lopsided on his mass of snow-white hair. He was short, thick, and had a bulbous, red nose, not to mention the biggest ears I had ever seen on an adult. He was somewhat odd - like a character in a story book.

'Come, come,' he said, as the three of us got out of the car. 'News come long time that you was on you way, Ms. G. So many people longin' to see you! My, my, is this the little baby you come back from Hengland to have nine years past! Lawd, but she little bit, but even so she not a baby no mo', fe sure. Some good Jamaica sunshine will mek har grow - though none here in Worsop at the moment.'

He laughed a deep belly laugh.

'Come, come, hurry out of dis drizzle. Ms. Rayma wasn't sure what time you was gettin' 'ere, but she been keepin' a pot of 'ot watah ready fe you to 'ave some tea. Lawd, 'is chilly dis afternoon - almos' December time - but den you 'member Worsop always cool to cold.'

He persistently rubbed his knuckles as we made our way through the dark interior of the sparse, kerosene-lit shop to what appeared to be his bedroom (it was quite dark, even though it was early afternoon), and then through a back door.

His accent was so thick I found myself struggling to understand each word, especially since my ears were used to a more East London vernacular. He spoke like he was singing. His voice rose and fell as if the words were notes in a song. I liked it. I liked him.

I wondered if Ms. Rayma was his wife. I knew from listening to snippets of my mother's conversations that people up in the country were 'Mas This' and 'Ms. That' instead of 'Mr.' and 'Mrs.' and 'Miss' and 'Ms.', just as they are in England. I was curious as to what she looked like. I imagined a similar version of Mas Charlie except in a female form. After all, I could not imagine anyone truly beautiful marrying someone like Mas Charlie. That never happened in any of the fairy tales I had ever read. Even frogs turned into handsome princes.

But when I asked, 'Is that your wife, Mr. Charlie?' he rumbled out another belly laugh and said, 'Good 'eavens, no, chile. Ms. Rayma is probably a good t'irty odd years or more oldah dan mi. Don't nobody on dis earth really know har true age, not even she. No, long, long time ago dis was har 'ouse, but she sold mi de front an' mi turn it into a shop. She kept the room in de very back of de house since she 'ad nowhere else to go.'

In the backyard we found a very tall, very thin, caramel-colored woman in an old yellow shift and an oversized black jacket that was obviously a man's. On her head was a huge, frayed straw hat dripping with the light rain. She wore a pair of black men's shoes, the leather of which was cracked with age and a lack of shoe polish, and which were a couple of sizes too big for her, even with her thick, black socks and droopy stockings.

She was tending to a large, black coal-pot in which red-hot coals burned. An oversized metal teapot - dented, old, and permanently scorched - rested on the coals. The whole thing was protected from the elements by a little zinc roof resting on cement blocks arranged around it to form a square. Four cement blocks had been placed on the zinc to keep it in place. Her back was turned to us as we emerged from the dimness of Mas Charlie's bedroom back into the grey afternoon. The light drizzle seemed determined not to end anytime soon.

Ms. Rayma turned around just as we came out, let out a squeal, and grabbed her head with both hands. She started to wail and moan which scared me at first until I realized she was happy to see us. 'T'ank you, Jesus! T'ank you, Jesus! Lawd 'ave mercy! Is you dat, Ms. G? Is truly you dat? Lawd, be praised!' she said, raising her hands in thanks to the grey, cloudy skies above. 'Come, come, come, come, mi cyaan 'ave you catch col' an' you jus' come.'

In one long step of her long legs she was in front of us, hugging my mother and kissing my brother and me. Our faces were scratched by the straw hat as she bent down to match our various heights. We were all a little damper by the time we entered her room.

Ms. Rayma's room, attached as it was to the back of the property, had its own door which she opened as she shuffled us in to sit on her queen-size bed and on the one chair which was placed beside the chipped mahogany dressing table.

There were no windows but, as rooms go, it was a fairly good size. It was cold in there, and after she placed her wet hat on a hook on the door, she dragged out musty blankets from a huge steamer trunk - in which I imagined she kept other belongings besides blankets - in the corner. We were too cold to refuse the blankets and soon got used to their mothball smell. A large kerosene lamp was burning and sat on the dressing table. A smaller one rested, unlit, on an upturned wooden crate in another corner of the room. Clothes hung from nails in the wood walls.

As we sat and the adults talked, I had the chance to have a good look at Ms. Rayma. She *was* old. She had many wrinkles and lines which mapped journeys across her face. Her long, bony neck was creased with rings of lines, and they reminded me of how the rings on their trunks told the age of coconut trees; her arms, hands, and fingers were thin, elongated; the skin was tight and brittle and ashy.

But her eyes were what surprised me. Even with age and in the dim light of the kerosene lamp, I could tell they had once been her best feature. They were a brilliant green although the whites had muddied just a bit. She had thin lips and high cheekbones. Her hair was tied up in a blue and green scarf, but the hair peeping out from the back and sides was straight and silvery white.

She had obviously once been beautiful. As I was thinking this, I noticed an old, black and white, silver framed picture of a young woman and a young man sitting on the dresser amidst other odds and ends such as a jar of Vaseline, a big bottle of Bays Water, and a bottle of Limacol. I could tell it was Ms. Rayma, and she had, indeed, been beautiful.

As my eyes adjusted to the dim light, I realized Ms. Rayma's wallpaper was, in fact, hundreds of old newspaper pages plastered to the thin wood walls. When I looked up, I saw that the ceiling was also plastered with old newspaper pages. I was instantly curious but struggled to be polite and remained sitting on the edge of the bed while they talked about my father's death.

'Ms. G, long time, so sad Bredda passed away. Mi would 'ave like to have seen 'im at least one las' time,' Ms. Rayma was saying in her husky, lilting accent, as a tear rolled slowly down her cheek. 'Good man, good man. Knew de word of de Lord backwards and forward an' did 'im bes' to live a good an' propah life. De 'hole of Worsop miss 'im like a dry rivahbed miss wata.'

Mas Charlie sat on the bed beside my brother and me while my mother sat in the rickety chair. Ms.

Rayma was sitting on another upturned wooden crate beside my mother who nodded in understanding as she reached out to pat Ms. Rayma's knee. Unable to sit still for too long and not wanting to start feeling sad about the father I had lost when I was four years old, I got up because I wanted to get a closer look at the walls.

'Chile, you need somet'in'?' Ms. Rayma asked.

Mama gave me a 'you better sit down and watch your manners' look, but I carried on, risking the future possibility of having my right ear tweaked as a reminder I had not been a good girl.

'Mrs. Rayma, may I please read your walls, please if it isn't a bother?' was the best way I knew how to ask.

Ms. Rayma threw her head back and laughed, 'Lawd, but you do talk like a propah little Henglish lady. Chile, dis room is full of 'istory. You' mothah can tell you. Dese paypahs go all de way back to even before she was born, back to 1900. But de light is bad in 'ere; you goin' hurt you eyes.'

She turned to my mother and said, 'If mi mine tell mi right, you was about dat age when you mother bring you 'ere to see mi. You 'ad a bad bellyache an' she 'ear mi 'ave a talent wid 'erbs an' country 'ealing. Back den dere was more of a 'ouse to dis room. You 'membah me 'usband? Good man, died too young. He use to tell mi people will t'ink me is a mad woman papahin' me walls wid newspaypah - mi start doin' it when mi was jus' twenty, maybe twenty-two or so, anyways a new wife mi was. We was married in June 1900 an' mi husband an' mi went to Kingston to celebrate. Nobady else was doin' t'ings like dat - no one was

72

doin' 'oneymoon an' t'ings like dat, dat is posh people livin', but mi 'usband, Josiah, said we should be diff'rent. So, mi bring back a newspaypah wid mi an' paste all de pages 'pon de walls of dis room - our bedroom - all dat left of the ole 'ouse we 'ad. Mi wanted to 'membah de time. After dat every time mi get a newspaypah mi paste de pages. Flour an' watah, mix up very light so it doan damage de paypah, but it last an' last.' She laughed as my mother and Mas Charlie listened intently, even though I knew they had heard all this before.

'It get so dat whenevah people go somewhere dey bring mi back newspaypahs. An' den when Josiah pass away in 1920, it become like a tradition an' sometimes me even get newspaypahs from people gon' a foreign. Newspaypahs mark when me children was born an' de years when dem die, all eight of dem - four as babies an' de four dat got grown. Newspaypah mark when Josiah went to meet his makah an' wait fe mi, even though it's been a long wait for de both of us. Newspaypah mark de years when mi whole family pass away, one by one, mi motha, mi fatha, all mi sista dem an' mi brothah dem, and leave mi one; newspaypah mark when mi friend dem gone an' when dere was war an' peace an' new invention, de good an' de bad dat 'as 'appened in dis world ovah eons. You not goin' find de names of mi children or mi family in those prints but fe mi when mi look pon the dates, when mi read de words it all come back to mi. Mi 'usband use dat firs' newspaypa over dere (she pointed to some mysterious point on the wall just above the intricately carved, mahogany bed head) to teach mi how to read an' since den de only t'ing mi read besides mi newspaypahs is de Bible. Chile! You can learn more from dese walls dan from any 'istory book.'

She got up and lit the small kerosene lamp that had a handle. Handing it to me, she told me to be careful holding it, although I was aware of the look of concern on my mother's face. But Mama didn't say anything as I took the lamp. Holding it as if it were the Holy Grail, I moved closer to one of the walls.

'So, tek you time, chile, an' look,' Ms. Rayma said, resuming her seat on the crate. ''ope de light is enough for now. An' when you next come back, look again 'cause it tek more dan jus' a little bit a time to see it all. So, you need to promise mi to come back. Al, you nevah been in dis room 'cause when you was a little bwoy you used to run from mi and call mi a witch!' She burst out laughing again, slapping her knee, two black front teeth merrily showing themselves.

My brother, Al, for all his twenty-six years, looked embarrassed.

And then my mother said, 'Mi would like to look again too; it's been a long time since mi read you walls, Ms. Rayma.'

The look of absolute pleasure which crossed Ms. Rayma's face took years off it. Before long, with Ms. Rayma holding the kerosene lamp, we were reading her walls and listening to her detailed reminiscences of people and times, forgetting about the tea until she suddenly remembered the boiling water on the coal pot.

She ran outside after handing the lamp to Mas Charlie, forgetting her hat, and the next thing we knew we were drinking sweetened black mint tea as we continued to read from the walls, the sound of rain drumming on the zinc roof of her room.

We stepped back into different times, places, and memories as my mother, Mas Charlie, Ms. Rayma and even Al lost themselves in memories, taking me with them to what was going on in Jamaica at the same time as major events were making headlines around the world.

We spent over three hours with Ms. Rayma before Mas Charlie reminded us there were other people who were waiting for us to show up. My Auntie, my father's older sister, had cooked a feast and readied a room for the three of us for the night, and longer, if we wished.

I met many other people on my first visit to Worsop, but Ms. Rayma remained my favorite. She was right: despite many visits with my mother, I never got through reading all the pages plastered to her walls. She died shortly after my mother and Mas Charlie died and just before I left the island, at seventeen, on my way to Canada to live with Al and his family.

I never forgot her nor the history lessons I learned in the dimness of her room with the smoky kerosene lamps, the rain often pattering down on the zinc roof, and a big, slightly-chipped porcelain mug of sweetened, black mint tea warming my hands.

GRAN

To her glory there is no measure;
She, from whose womb generations bloomed
gardens;
Ever-growing, ever-generating new generations.
She, Goddess.
She, woman strong, woman song.
She carries purpose on her lips;
Alpha and omega on her hips.
She is the tenacity of womanhood flowing
Back, back, back,
To her story entwined with history;
Back to sugar cane fields and hurricanes;
Walking steep country lanes
With heavy baskets straining necks,
Long trained for hard labor.
Scrubbing dirty clothes for rich folks.
She, back to whiplashes and girl children raped.
She, back to leaping over sides of ships; freedom on
her hips,
She, back to African Queen, walking splendid regal
with African King.
She, great love of Jesus and Muhammad.
She, Marabou spirit;
Mary Magdalene by the well and Isha's pride.
She, back to continents united;
to Gaia, Earth Mother.
She was Eve opening Adam's eyes.
She, back to God light and the creation of time.
She is Universe.
The sound the planets hum when they are at peace
She is cosmic cohesion and the Force of Gravity
She is simply, My Grandmother.

THE DEVIL AND LOLA

Lola had known the devil ever since she was a child, for the devil had taken shape and form and had morphed into the life-ravaged being of a trusted Uncle.

In the dead-time of late nights, when he should have been asleep, he had crept on cracked, calloused bare feet into the room she shared with her sister; he had lifted her from the warmth of rumpled bedsheets and taken her into the back room which he had claimed as his own and from which he had evicted her four older brothers. And there, with an unwashed hand muffling her cries, he had shown her all the sins she should never have known.

Lola was a child for only a short time in her life. She no longer feared the devil, and she no longer feared the dark. She was too bad for the devil now. He had taught her well. She swaggered as she walked, with her lips pursed in defiance, and her hips swaying in temptation. She sat, and she waited in the grim comfort of the dark.

When Lola was born in the nondescript Spanish Town street that ran behind the back of the market which was always littered with rotting produce and decaying animal flesh from said market, her father, Cyrus, balding, run-down, and painfully thin, took one drunken look at her and declared she was not his child. She did not 'favah' him in the least, and she did not 'favah' any of his other five 'pickney dem'. The only person she showed any resemblance to was Imelda and a dark-skinned local man called Isaiah.

'Is bun, you trying to give me? Is fool you t'ink me is? Me will show you who is fool?' he shouted at her. Even though Imelda was only a few hours past childbirth, Cyrus punched her in the face. She fell back against the pillow, and blood escaped from the busted lip now complementing her black eye and bruised cheek.

'Is your chile!' Imelda gurgled. 'Is fe you pickney! Mi swear, Cy! Mi would never go with any man but you! Mi swear pon mi dead Mama grave!'

'Lie! Is lie!' Cyrus thumped her in the head.

The afternoon was dank and humid. The room reeked of birth-blood and sweat, stale sheets, bay rum, and the liquor and nicotine oozing out of Cyrus's pores. Imelda had given birth at home because Cyrus said he had his suspicions. He thought the hospital would somehow cover up the evidence of his wife's indiscretion and wanted to see the baby first hand.

'Mi not feelin' dis chile. Mi not feelin' it at all,' he murmured for days before Lola was born. He drank more, and smoked more of the rancid tobacco he loved.

The other children stayed out of his way - even the last one, a girl who was born a year before Lola and who was the only one, he said, he could positively identify as his child. This baby, who was already walking and trying on the taste of words, seemed to understand there was rancor and discord in this household. She hid under chairs when Cyrus's rage inundated the house. The day of Lola's birth, she stayed with the older boys in the yard.

A next door neighbor, Miss Sugar, was Imelda's unofficial midwife. She stood by in a safe corner of the room, holding the newborn baby and watching as Cyrus beat his wife. Afterwards, she wiped

78

Imelda down with a rag soaked in a mop bucket full of icy water and tried to get her to hold the screaming little girl-child. Imelda pushed the baby away and turned her back to Miss Sugar.

Miss Sugar, who had six children of her own and was still breast feeding the last one, sighed. She took the baby next door where she remained for two weeks or so feeding on Miss Sugar's bountiful breasts until Miss Sugar's man made her give the baby back. No one had inquired after the baby's whereabouts.

Miss Sugar called her Lola and when no one suggested anything different, the name stuck. A christening never took place. Two years later, when Miss Sugar's house was badly damaged because of a grease fire in the kitchen, and the family was forced to move, Lola lost the only person in her life who had ever tried to protect her.

The sweet smell of rose water and Johnson's Baby Powder which always surrounded Miss Sugar and the gentle touch of her rough hands rapidly faded from Lola's memory and were replaced by the harshness of life in the Montrell household.

On the day of her birth, Cyrus, after beating his wife and threatening to throw the baby in the trash, left for the local bar and linked up with a plump, heavy bottomed, big breasted, wire-waisted, brown-skinned, wide-smiling girl of about the same age as his oldest son.

He never came back home. Throughout his drunken brawls and rants around town, he proclaimed that the reason for all his faults and failures sat firmly in the ample lap of his mocha-skinned, dimpled-cheeked, long-haired common-law wife, Imelda.

'Woman no good. Never was good. She lay down with all kind a dry-foot man as soon as mi back turn. Long time mi start wonder if all a dem pickney dem she breed really fe mi pickney.'

The plump, brown-skin girl and her parents, who lived out by the hospital way and with whom Cyrus now 'cotched', soon grew tired of him but were relieved of ever having to do anything about it when, a few months after they took him in, he drunkenly fell asleep under a blue and red country bus.

The next morning, the unknowing and later much traumatized bus driver drove over him. Cyrus never felt a thing. Imelda refused to bury him, and Cyrus was laid to rest in a pauper's grave somewhere on the outer edges of the town.

Imelda quite forgot Cyrus had always been a bit of an ass from times long before poor Lola came along. She quite forgot the child did indeed show a strong resemblance to Isaiah, a butcher in the market, and the truth was Lola had been conceived when Cyrus was away up country visiting his aged father who died soon after Lola was born.

Memories of the numerous beatings she received over the years had become blended and blurred, with a romanticized version of a Cyrus no one else had ever known.

She never bonded with the baby, and Lola almost died as an infant from her mother's various attempts at stretching out and watering down the baby formula.

From the time Lola was very young, her mother beat her for every minor infraction, and the beatings started long before Lola could walk. Cigarette scars and other mysterious markings with which she did not come into this world began to appear, scattered pox-like, all over her body.

Imelda hated Lola from her birth and blamed her for all her troubles with Cyrus. 'Bitch, a you make Cyrus leave an' gone. I regret de day you born. Mi wish mi could 'ave squeeze mi legs tight-tight, so you no get a chance to breathe God good air!' (A random blow would follow).

'Bitch, go empty de chimmy pot under mi bed. An' if you spill one drop, you goin lick it offa de floor - mark mi words!' (A random shove or push would add emphasis to what she said).

'Bitch, mi nuh know why you hangin' round dis kitchen. A who tell you sey mi feed stray dog?' (A well-directed, dirty dish cloth would strike the child directly in her face).

'Bitch, move out a de way! Move you nasty hind quarters and get off dat seat! You no see you sistah want to sit dere. See de stool in a de corner. You already know sey a your seat dat.' (A hit with a broom or pot or pan or anything else close to hand would cause Lola to run to the safety of the junky backyard, cutting her bare feet on broken glass and loose metal as she ran until she reached the broken-down fence).

'Bitch, a which queen you t'ink you is? A who tell you sey you can sit down when de yard no sweep, de floor no wipe, de toilet dirty, and de clothes still need wash.' (Lola soon became convinced that Lola was not her real name. She answered to 'Bitch' without a second thought).

Imelda's brother, Zeke, a tall, lanky, skeleton of a man with a melancholy disposition and a ready excuse for not ever having employment of any kind, came down from the country and lived with them. From the age of five, Lola was subsequently molested by him.

Imelda, in time, met up with a new man who preoccupied all her concerns, and within a short time she began to pay little attention to her children except for one, Arella, whom she regarded as her actual wash-belly, her real last child. Lola was neglected the most, and Zeke's behavior (yes, Imelda knew full well what happened when her eyes were shut and the covers were over her head) was never brought to question.

One by one, the older children dropped out of school in order to sell the local newspaper and Wrigley's chewing gum on the street corners or steal when the opportunity arose. Lola's Uncle continued to rape her and, after a while, the whole arrangement became the norm in Lola's household.

When Lola was fourteen, Zeke, still scrounging for a few dollars here and there, came up with the brilliant idea that Lola could make him easy money. He had two ideas, in fact. One was to train Lola in the ways of picking pockets, and the other was to sell her to other men. The more he thought about it, the more he realized he could actually combine the two 'businesses', and Lola could steal from the men with whom he arranged for her to sleep.

In his mind, Lola was nothing more than a mistake, and mistakes were born to be used. He mentioned none of this to Imelda in case she wanted to suddenly lay claim to her daughter or, more importantly, lay claim to whatever funds he could obtain by being Lola's pimp.

Imelda was working as a maid and cook for the Jewish people who owned the haberdashery on the high street. She solved Zeke's dilemma when she abruptly took all her belongings, left, and moved in with her boyfriend (not the butcher) out by Old Harbour Road.

The eldest boy, Cedric, and Lola stayed at the old place with Zeke, but rent was a constant stress. Imelda sent them nothing from her wages. The other children found homes among friends and some relatives because Imelda took only one child with her - the girl-child she considered her real wash-belly and last child, Arella.

Arella, sweet, delicate, café-au-lait, soft-as-cashmere little Arella, was smart and upright and progressing in leaps and bounds at the local secondary school, although only in her second year. She was Imelda's remaining hope for redemption as a mother. Imelda put her other children out of her mind. Just as a bird eventually refuses its nestlings if they are picked up by humans, Imelda turned her back on all her children, except for Arella.

'Huh,' Zeke said, 'is gone she gone fe true. Like mother, like daughter - the two of you are not'ing without a man. You good only fe one t'ing an' one t'ing alone. But you, Lola, how you feel when you look pon yourself and look pon your sistah? Dat is de kind of wife good man look for - even mi can see dat, and still and yet she is jus' a young girl but a young girl with prospects. Dat will nevah be you. Is

God sen' dat chile. You? You never know mother anyway. Is me you mus' look pon as your only family. Me is mother an' me is father to you. You hear wha' mi a sey. The only t'ing you have in this worl' is me alone. You hear me. You will always do what me tell you 'cause dere is no place for you to go, an' no one who will evah be on your side. You hear me.'

Lola, having never consciously felt her mother's loss, shrugged off Imelda's absence and digested Zeke's words. They say you cannot miss something you never had. Lola had never had her mother's love.

The closest thing she knew about love was the sweaty feel of Zeke's bony body grating on her soft skin; the spit in her ears when he held her head and whispered nasty things; the way he slapped her - just because he could - and scratched her back, to make her whimper. Sometimes, she would make overly exaggerated sounds of pain because she knew he liked that; it would make him finish faster, and she could go on with her time.

Her days were spent watching other children go to school and running errands for Zeke (liquor store, cigarettes, beef patties from the local shop, ice, a note slipped to a prospective client in the local rum and beer dive, and so on). She would get a dollar or so to get her something to eat as well. Other times, she stood at the entrance to the market and begged for money.

Nights were spent standing at the gate watching people, talking to one or two who did not think she was an untouchable. She would stand at the gate until Zeke decided it was time for her to come in, or

84

if it rained and she was forced to go indoors of her own free will. Sometimes, she would wait until she was practically soaked before walking, as if to the gallows, inside.

Zeke knew it was not hard to find men - especially men who had unsatisfactory wives/girlfriends. The word was soon out - skimming across agile fingers playing dominoes; wafting through local bars; mingling with casual street conversation; and careening through the narrow, cobbled, overcrowded streets. There was fresh meat in town - young, not entirely untouched, but young...and willing.

One day, shortly after her mother left, Lola came home from begging and a man - brown, big bellied, heavy jawed, dour, and knocking on fifty's door - sat in the living room drinking rum with Zeke.

The stench of man-sweat, cigarettes, and one hundred and eighty proof Appleton rum whirled on sordid waves of heat that were spun around by an ancient, dust encrusted fan which teetered in a corner.

The men looked up as she entered, carrying a bag of spiced shrimp and a Ting soft drink. It was her lunch. She glanced at them; they did not often have any company who just came to visit. Theirs was not a home that offered much that visitors would find enticing. The unknown man had prominent sweat marks under the armpits of his blue security uniform. A security hat was on a rickety table by the settee.

Zeke, dressed in a once-white-now-grey marina and khaki shorts, wore a New York Yankees' cap with the peak facing the back and a cigarette hanging from his lips. He was leaning casually on one side of the settee; his long, scarred-from-a-childhood-fire, legs stretched out in front of him.

The big man with the big belly was leaning on the other side, occasionally bending forward to flick the ashes from his cigarette into an empty tin can which sat on the battered little wood crate they used as a coffee table.

Zeke blew a heavy fume of tobacco smoke into the stale, rank air of the living room. Nobody did much cleaning any more, at least not enough to keep the roaches and the mice out or to make the house smell less like there was food hidden and rotting somewhere in its crevices.

'Afternoon,' she said, as she prepared to go to the back room which served as a dining room as well as the kitchen.

'Lola,' Zeke replied, 'dis is Mr. Clemonts. He come to see you.'

Lola stopped in surprise.

'Me? Fe what?' she asked.

Mr. Clemonts got up and so did Zeke.

Zeke said, 'The bedroom is right there, suh. We agreed thirty minutes, yeah?'

Mr. Clemonts nodded as his heavy-hooded eyes raked over Lola from her raggedy, plastic flip-flops to her face dark and shiny with the heat. His eyes X-rayed her thin, green, gingham dress. He made a sound deep in his gut. A lewd smile appeared on his fat jawed face and turned her stomach sour. She felt herself grow cold even though the living room was stuffy and hot.

86

'She a pretty, little, chocolate t'ing,' Mr. Clemonts drooled.

'Lola, go in with Mr. Clemonts. He 'ave somet'in' to show you.'

Lola looked from one to the other and then back again. She looked at Zeke, and her eyes begged him to tell her that this whole thing was not what she thought. In answer, Zeke grabbed her by the elbow and shoved her into a side room - one of the three tiny bedrooms that adjoined the living room, or front room, as they called it. Mr. Clemonts followed. Thus began the first of many of the worst thirty minutes of her life.

After Mr. Clemonts left, Zeke called her out to the living room where he sat, his long body curved into a sort of "S" on the battered blue settee. He threw five Jamaican dollars her way, told her to wash herself, and went out.

Lola sat on a chair in the living room for many minutes. Then she went to the back yard where a hose and zinc sheets served as a shower stall. The shower in the house had long since become useless.

She let the cool water wash over her body for as long she could but, no matter how long the water cascaded over her and no matter how hard she rubbed herself down with the red carbolic soap, she could not purge the stench of rum-flavored saliva laced with stale cigarettes or the stink of sweat infused with cheap men's cologne from her nostrils.

After three years, the men became the norm. The smells became the norm. Their rough hands and raspy breaths became the norm. Tall, bony men, like

Zeke, bruised her hips; the heavy ones, with their bellies and large hands, almost suffocated her.

They were always men years older than Lola. Men she knew had women waiting for them with cooked meals, warm beds, clean houses, and children - even girl children who were her own age.

Lola learned to leave her body and visit places where she was beautiful and loved and clean. While they grunted on top of her, she sailed on magnificent ships to exotic places on azure-blue seas, like the ones she had seen in Arella's school books when she was younger and Arella still lived at the house with their mother.

Zeke kept tabs on Lola's whereabouts. She was in demand. Three or four men came every day or every other day, and the rent became less of a concern. Lola was reminded that what he gave her was more than sufficient because he, yes he, was responsible for keeping the roof on top of their heads. After all, was he not the one who negotiated Lola's price? She should be grateful to him. She would never have been anything more anyway.

He laughed when she talked about doing anything to better herself. 'Uncle Zeke, you t'ink maybe mi could tek sewing lessons? A lady come by yesterday to talk with me 'bout maybe teaching me to sew. She sey she from the Salvation Army an' somebady tell her 'bout mi not havin' nobody an' sey maybe mi can use some training. Maybe mi can...'

He laughed so hard the tears ran down his face and pooled briefly in his hollow cheeks. It took him a few minutes to compose himself.

'You? A seamstress!' he spluttered. 'But is joke you a give me dis day, Lola.'

His face became as serious as sin. Looking her straight in her large brown eyes, he said, 'Let me remind you, Lola, dat you is a whore, an' dat is all you will evah be. Mek all de money you can now cause one day dat pum-pum goin' dry up, an' you will be not'ing more dan a ole whore. An' nobady want a ole whore.' He laughed. Then, because he suddenly felt pity for her, he raised her 'cut' to seven Jamaican dollars per 'client'.

Lola stopped talking about bettering herself. Per day, she could make over twenty Jamaican dollars for every three men. It was not bad money for a girl who was never going to make that kind of money any other way.

Under Zeke's tutelage, Lola learned to discreetly remove an extra ten or so when the men visited the makeshift bathroom outside to 'tidy' up. If they found it out later, they rarely made a fuss.

Most had wives and girlfriends who would not welcome gossip. Others would not want their illicit dalliances to become public knowledge. All wanted to come back for more of Lola. She was good - oh, so good. The men learned to be more guarded with their wallets.

Cedric left one day for Kingston and never came back. Lola's life became stagnant. At fifteen, Zeke took her to a woman who knew what herbs to give when women wanted to 'dash 'way' unwanted babies.

That one year, he took her there half a dozen times until her body stopped trying to reproduce, and her monthly cycles ceased of their own accord.

People talked behind their fingers whenever she was out. She stopped going out except for quick slips to the store or through the market to run Zeke's errands. Other women treated her as if she were mud around an outhouse, and men looked at her so hard it made her feel naked.

In the evenings, she would stand at the gate looking at the people passing by, but no one talked to her any more. They held their heads straight or made some remark seemingly directed at the setting sun, the sky above, one to another's face, or more directly to her face. The word 'whore' slipped out and floated with intentional imprudence towards her on many an evening breeze. She stopped standing at the gate.

At nights, she would sit in the uninviting back yard and gaze up at the multitudes entranced by the night's purity.

In the day time, she would often sit by the small window in the front room and drink or eat as she stared outside at the people passing the front gate. Since the house was so close to the market, the street was often busy, and watching people was a distraction from the dismal grey of her own existence.

She never knew for sure when it was she stopped feeling. She welcomed the complete numbness as it descended on her. Days turned into weeks, weeks stumbled into months, and months drifted by and became years. She had nowhere to go, and no one to go to. Lola decided it was better to stay with the devil she knew.

One Sunday evening, as she sat drinking tea by the window of the front room, she saw a pretty girl walking past and, as the girl walked, she stared at the house with an unsure expression. Lola recognized her sister, Arella.

Arella, dressed in a prim, pink dress with wide, white collars, turned back and stopped at the gate with a contemplative look on her face. Still looking unsure, she stared at the house. A little white purse hung from her shoulder, and a large Bible was in one hand. Lola glanced down at the light-blue shift she wore with its cornucopia of stains and hoped Arella was just, for some mysterious reason, passing by.

Arella raised her hand to smooth down her pristinely hot-combed, shiny, straight hair curling to her shoulders. She always had such pretty hair. She knocked at the gate. Lola, after some hesitation, came out. She was aware she looked unkempt. Her hair was sticking out in all directions as it valiantly attempted to escape the rubber band which tried to tame it into a rough ponytail. She had planned to take a hose shower after she finished her tea. She still smelled of the last man who had lain with her earlier in the morning.

Lola had not seen her older sister in some years. Arella was tall and slender, like she was, and she had deep dimples, like Lola, with the same wide eyes and straight nose. These were the prominent features of their mother, but this is where the resemblance ended. Arella had her father Cyrus's milk-coffee-brown skin color. Lola was much darker and, as she had grown older, her features had melded to resemble the face of a man who was still a butcher in the market.

The butcher heatedly swore up and down he had no connection with Lola, and he had no explanation for her 'favahing' him.

'Many unrelated people "favah" each other; is why all you questionin' my connection to dat gal? Mi never look pon no other woman 'cept mi wife, why would me? Is mad you t'ink me mad!' he declared, whenever the subject came up.

Arella appeared lamb-gentle and innocent; Lola looked thorn-scratched and worldly. Lola sashayed to the gate as Arella primly waited for her, casting an eye of disdain at the front yard with its strange flowers of junk, trash, and discarded items.

Zeke always told Lola that her hips, when she walked, sent signals to every man within viewing distance. She had learned to use her walk to her advantage, and it had become part of her nature. Arella raised an eyebrow as she watched her baby sister approach.

'Is what you want 'ere, Arella?' Lola asked with a dry voice. She felt no need for politeness. She merely hoped Arella had something to give her. Why else would she be at the house?

'Oh, Sistah Lola,' Arella's voice was so sweet. 'Mi come to ask you if you 'ave chosen Jesus? Have you given your heart to de Lord, my sistah? Mi hear dat you 'ave been dancing wit de devil. Is all ovah mi church. Of course, Pastor come an' spoke to me because everybody knows we are sistahs. He said it was mi duty to come to you an' see if mi can't help

92

you to find Jesus an' to admonish you, sistah, admonish you wit all of mi heart, dat de way of de harlot can only lead to death, damnation, an' burnin' in de fires of hell. You cannot dance wit de devil an' not get burned!'

'But see yah!' Lola said. 'You mean to tell mi, Mama sen' you wit you empty han' to come tell mi 'bout salvation? Where is any of you when mi belly is hungry? Mi nuh see hide nor hair of you for years an' not a word an' now 'ere you stan'. Eh, but what a libahty is dis. So, tell mi wha' you t'ink mi is?'

'A sinner and a whore, Lola. Everybody knows who you are, Lola. An' Mama did not send me. She would not be pleased to see me on dis street or at dis house. But once she knows it is where Jesus led me, she will understan'. Even though she don't come to church much, she knows de Lord is mi passion. One day, she too will see de light. No, my sistah, mi come to save you from bein' de whore of Spanish Town!'

She smiled like an angel. She seemed unaware she had not even taken the time to greet Lola properly before launching into the defects of Lola's soul.

Although Lola knew it, although she had heard the very same ugly word drop from other lips, even from the lips of the men she lay with, to hear it from Arella, in her sweet voice, was more than she could bear. She stifled her anger and said calmly, 'Sweet Arella, why you nuh come in an' tell mi more 'bout your Jesus.'

Arella, pleased she would be able to recount a story of success to Pastor, gingerly came through the gate and followed Lola into the house. Zeke was away. It had been a good day, and Lola had had six clients before it was two p.m. - especially in the morning while the churches around town were still in session. He had given her her share and then, as usual, went out. He would return later, and he had told her she was free for the night - his treat.

The house had no electricity as many years before the utility company had disconnected it. A kerosene lamp burned in one corner since the living room was always a little dark, no matter what time of the day it was.

The small window, with its years of accumulated dirt, was the only window which did not have a board covering it, due to missing glass panes. Lola had cleaned a good part of it so she could see the outside world. Arella wrinkled her nose in distaste as she sat on the edge of the worn settee. It was 1979, she thought - how could people still live like barbarians?

Lola excused herself and went to the kitchen. She returned with a much finger-printed glass, half full of water. Arella declined the offer as she wrinkled her nose. Lola drank the water herself.

Arella talked again about Lola's need for salvation. She talked, and she talked. Lola sat and then got up. She sat again. She got up again. She did this several times. She walked around the room as Arella talked, nodding and sighing as she warmed to her mission of saving Lola's soul and lightening her sister's blackened heart. Lola sighed along with her at appropriate times. Arella, thinking that Lola was really feeling the wonderful miracle of salvation, kept on talking.

It looked to her as if Lola's restlessness were a sign of her beginning to see the light. Lola's sins were probably causing her skin to itch and burn. Sin is like the acid in the bite of the most vicious red ants, and Arella felt pride in what was taking place. She thought perhaps this was her calling - the Lord's calling - to purge out the demons from sinners.

She thought maybe she would ask Pastor if he could teach her to lay hands on the unfortunates and infuse them with the power and glory that could only be found in the Word of the Lord, and which she was certain flowed through her.

An old lady in church had told her that one day all of Jamaica was going to know about her. One day, she would be holy news.

In Arella's mind's eye, she could clearly see people as they came in the hundreds to be healed in her very own church. Her voice became more passionate, louder, and high-pitched as she entreated her baby sister to change her sin-filled ways.

She thought about how people would look up to her as a true Christian for being able to save her lost sister. How her mother would be even prouder of her for taking the time to come to see her sister - a sister whom Imelda did not regard as her daughter.

Just like Jesus and the woman at the well, she would offer Lola redemption. After all, was not she, Arella, a shining example of virtue? She would be the example her sister needed to pull her back from the seven levels of hell that Pastor told the church was the destiny of all sinners.

Perhaps she could reunite Lola with their mother who might, with Arella's urging, forgive Lola for enticing men right from the time she was a little, little girl.

'Your sistah always had the disposition of a prostitute since de day she was born. Is why mi spirit could never tek to her even when she was a lickle pickney-child. She always disgrace me. Man always look pon her like dey can smell her. Since de day she was born, she been calling man.' Her mother had told her this with a face contorted in disgust, but there were no tears of sadness in her eyes.

Arella dearly loved her long suffering mother, but she was not a jealous girl. The church was teaching her the importance of family. Perhaps she was the one, the savior, the one who would lead them all to salvation if only they would let her. She would find her brothers next, she vowed to God, and save them as well.

'You must come to mi church with me, Lola. The congregation will tek you in as a prodigal daughtah who lost her way. You can only find forgiveness if you repent. Pastor sey ... Aiyaaaaaaaaaaaaa!'

Her scream was cut short. She realized in an instant that she had not noticed Lola walking behind her as she sat. The brick Lola brought down on her head knocked her out. With each subsequent blow, the life flowed out of her and blood soaked into her beautiful, pristinely hot-combed hair; the blood splattered the settee, the walls, and Lola. Lola found herself laughing as she pulled Arella's body into the back room where she slept.

She sighed when she re-entered the grimy, pungent, blood patterned living room. It was not

96

what she would have planned, she told herself. Arella, with all her propriety and righteousness, had brought out the devil with whom she danced every single day of her life - a devil who had long since taken up residence in her soul.

Lola had known the devil since she was a child. He had visited her in the form of a trusted Uncle late at nights when he should have been asleep in another room. Now she sat on a bloodied settee, in a dimly lit, stuffy, hot living room.

The brick had been replaced in Zeke's hiding place; a butcher's knife was under a tatty cushion on her lap.

Lola waited, patiently, for the sound of the front gate opening.

EMPTY NEST

The house on Elmer Street, stood silently.
We, dreamers, passed it every day,
Drawn to its solemnity; afraid of its darkened vigil.
It shrouded the fantasies of our imagination.
We, touched by imagined silence blaring from
empty rooms,
saw shadows in tattered, shivering, curtains;
Choreographed make-believed memories of lazy
days laced with euphoria,
celebrations, births and deaths, joys and heartbreaks,
shouted words, debutantes and rascals.
We made up stories as we passed inspired by past
auras shifting in the broken glass.
The house, sad, imbued with memories of
passionate love entwined, silly games, a cappella.
War and peace once bred by human togetherness.
Life, a game of hide and seek, shrill and full of
innocence.
We, loving the memory of its unknown, touched by
its loneliness,
Wanting to comfort the waiting, rusted tricycle in
the front yard.
The children, gone. The families, gone. A weathered
dog house.
Silent windows, though blinded by neglect,
Study each passer-by whose eyes are drawn to them.
Once we even thought we heard the voice of a child
silently shouting from the past, 'We were once
here…'

DEARLY DEPARTED

Cassandra stood by the grave as dirt hit the top of the coffin. She stood, dry-eyed, and declined offers of a ride back to the church reception hall where they were having a sort of mingle and reminisce get-together.

She felt no desire to hear her father's 'virtues' circulate amongst his relatives and friends or be overwhelmed with their attempts to console her by proclaiming him to be 'jolly good' and 'taken way too soon.'

'I'll be along later,' she said to inquiring eyes on their way to waiting cars. She was the last in her immediate family still alive - a dubious honor.

A misty rain added to the damp mustiness of the cemetery as gravediggers fulfilled their uninviting duty. Stoic and expressionless, they stifled their usual banter out of respect. As soon as she was sure everyone was gone, she put the umbrella down and let the cleansing, cold droplets of rain have their way.

'Papa, I can't say I'm sorry you're gone. You were a tyrant. It's over now.'

She looked up. An old man in a black suit stood a few headstones across from her; holding flowers, his head was down. He turned towards a section of the cemetery where many of her mother's relatives were buried.

There was something about him, something about the way he walked, that caught her attention and made her shiver. Cemeteries, funerals, and dreary British weather, she thought, a certified recipe for madness.

She turned, making her way through the slurping mud towards the road which led from the grave plots and to the cemetery gates.

She hoped she would be able to flag down one of East Ham's elusive taxis in order to attend, albeit unenthusiastically, the function being held at the church.

The day before the funeral, Cassandra visited her father's flat - a handkerchief pressed over her nostrils, nausea seeping up from her stomach and invading her oesophagus. She swallowed hard and repeatedly, unsure if she could survive the odor which suffocated the room.

Outside it poured like there was no tomorrow, and the skies hung low and thundered.

She walked around the dark, unkempt living room with its tatty, worn, mismatched furniture and wandered into the minuscule, cluttered kitchen with its dented pots, blackened pans, chipped crockery and scattered utensils.

A toaster with a suspiciously frayed cord rested on top of the world's oldest refrigerator. She shook her head. Her father had changed.

Next, she went into the only bedroom and was shocked. It was in perfect order; a white duvet covered the bed, complete with yellow, gingham pillows; the wardrobe was neat, if scanty, with items of clothing still hanging in anticipation; a pair of black loafers and a brown pair of ankle boots were lined up against a wall.

Above the scratched, mirror-less, wooden dresser hung an oil painting of her parents with their youthful smiles and sixties fashion; her mother wore a Jackie O suit with a pill box hat, her short hair

100

flipped at the ends; her father dressed in his usual black. The scenery was the standard photographic setting of the time - ocean, balcony, flower stand - painted in unnaturally vibrant color.

She remembered it hanging in the living room of the Stratford house. It brought back images of a father twirling her around - his grin wide and protective. She wondered if she imagined that father. Perhaps he was someone created by the positive energy of a four-year-old's innovative mind.

With more clarity, her most vivid memory was her father's slow and steady downward spiral into paranoia and bitterness which became unbearable when her mother passed. She picked up items from his dresser - a hairbrush, aftershave, *Old Spice*, of course, a few random envelopes - and she tried to put together scattered pieces of a jigsaw.

A year after her mother died, they took her into foster care. She was ten. Silence had fallen like heavy snow each day after her mother's death and slowly blanketed her life.

Her father would look through her when she tried to speak to him and then utter a dismissive word or two.

She learned to feed and care for herself and to hide under covers when lonely nights became too much.

A teacher noticed how thin and soundless she had become and called child welfare.

For twelve years after that, lost and abandoned, she received sporadic postcards filled with one or two grudging sentences from her father.

Her adoptive parents told her that her father had stopped working and lost the house. He moved from one council flat to another - a new address on each postcard. When he did something that warranted a complaint, the council moved him again. He said 'they' were against him but never said for sure who 'they' were.

He had lain dead in this flat on his sofa in front of his TV for two whole weeks before neighbors got someone on the other end of a phone line to take their complaints with more than a cynical retort. It was not a matter of concern but rather the fact that the smell superseded even the frequently appearing piles of rancid, raunchy garbage surrounding the junkie infested apartment building.

Two weeks after her father's autopsy (cause - Undetermined), death's perfume still ravished the flat. Cassie went to the mildewed bathroom and threw up in the sink.

She was almost at the road that led out of the cemetery when she noticed a black Peugeot sitting with its engine running and tinted windows up. Steam rose from the heat of its bonnet. She slowed her pace. The driver rolled the window down.

'Cassie!' he called. 'I wondered how you planned to get back! Thought I'd hang around. Girl, hurry and get in this car! You're soaked!'

'Aw,' she said to herself, 'Cousin Albert!'

They had greeted each other at the funeral although she could tell that he, like the others, was curious about her - a curiosity kept in check by the solemn occasion and a British code of politeness.

There had been a total of twelve other people at the funeral - six distant relatives and six friends, who had known her father for 'many, many, many years' and who eyed her slim figure with varying degrees of appreciation. Old men still longing for their past.

She smiled and said, 'That was awfully considerate of you…' She stopped. She was unsure of what to call him. Was he Cousin Albert, Uncle Albert, or just Albert? Jamaican custom dictated that you call older relatives and friends of the family 'Aunties' or 'Uncles'. She had not seen him since her mother's memorial and felt no connection. 'Uncle' implied history; he was just an outline of a memory.

'Call me Albert!' he replied, as if he could read her thoughts floating in a bubble above her head. He had the whitest teeth and a personality and build which filled the car. He was deep chocolate, like her father, with curly hair which hinted of their East Indian mix. Thick hands took up half the steering wheel.

'Shame about your dad,' he consoled her. 'George was all right. Ain't seen him in a long time. Back in the day, he was a character. I remember you when you were small. Quite the chatterbox! Like your Dad - always had something to say.'

'I'm sorry,' Cassie said, 'I only remember you from Mum's service. I can't remember you before then. You and Dad were close?'

'Close?' Albert's tone was warm and lively as he seemed to step back in time. 'We had each other's backs in those days, girl. Tore this London town up! Well, the east end of it at least. Fresh from the islands, you know; we came here on the same ship. Nineteen sixty! What a trip! George was like a horse waiting for them to open those gates so he could just take off running! I was the one who introduced him to your mother. Fine as wine, Miss Etta was! God rest her soul. Oh, excuse me, didn't mean to be crass.'

'No, it's okay,' she reassured him. 'I don't remember my parents talking much about the good old days. Bits and pieces, you know.' She was silent. The happy Dad was a ghost; the unhappy Dad was clearly etched in her memory.

'Nobody heard neither hide nor hair about you since your mother's passing. Seems like George was really broken up - changed his phone number, stopped coming by, moved. It was by chance that the police managed to find our cousin Sara's address and sent someone around to notify her. Rounded up who I could so he would have a half-decent little send off. Heard you were in America - seems they found some of George's mail.'

He rambled on. It took her a few moments to realize he had no idea what had transpired since her mother's death. She did not want to go into her adoption and moving to the States saga.

'Yes, I got a telegram from Sara a little under two weeks ago. Said there was going to be an inquest because of the circumstances and so any funeral arrangements would be delayed. I came as soon as I could. I'm staying in Central London. I haven't seen my father in a long time.'

'Oh, you don't say...' He waited for more, keeping his head turned towards the road while his eyes flicked to her for just a second.

She was silent.

He resumed talking. 'Well, it's a shame how someone can live close to you and still be so invisible. I swear, George's apartment building is not too far from me. Never knew. Never bumped into him on the street - oh wait, yes, I did - forgot about that day - he kept walking like he didn't hear me call out to him. I figured he didn't want to talk and went on my merry way. Glad Sara was able to sort things out for you. Hope the pennies we were able to throw into the pot helped.'

She was half listening as she gazed out at what was familiar and yet felt so distant. The rows of brick houses, cluttered streets, the dullness of the sky, the way the rain dribbled down the passenger window, the people hurrying with their umbrellas, the red double decker buses, the traffic - it felt as if she were watching a movie.

Then she went to live in East Anglia with the Crenshaws, a white family with two other adopted mixed race children. They eventually all moved to Maryland when Mr. Crenshaw acquired a civilian engineering position on Fort Belvoir, a military post in nearby Virginia.

That was seven years before her father's death. She had not seen him since the day the social workers came and packed up what there was of her things. She never saw the house on Colgrave Street again.

'My father had no insurance, nothing, but I had some money put aside for me. I used some of it,' she told Albert. The truth was that when she turned twenty-one, the trust fund her adoptive parents had set up for her became available. George's death was well-timed. At twenty-two, she had full access to the money, although she was none too happy about spending even one penny on her father.

They arrived at the church. Cassie braced herself for more questions and more sympathetic but inquiring eyes. She was glad Albert was there.

Someone is screaming. Someone moans, and the child tries to make them stop.

'Mummy, don't die, please, don't die, please, don't die.' The little voice spirals into a wail, and the walls of a concrete room echo with pain.

There is blood coming out of the side of pouty, full lips, lips turning blue, and one side of the thick, black hair is dark and wet with it.

The child tries to hold her, but her eyes roll back - the whites, ghoulish. The woman moans, and then she stops. Her head lolls to one side as thin little arms try to hold it up.

At the top of the stairs, a man stands, illuminated by light from the kitchen. The child cannot see his face. He makes no effort to come down and help her. Her screams continue. Cassie woke up, covered in sweat yet feeling disturbingly cold, to find the screams were coming from her.

The next day, Albert met Cassie to help her go through her father's things. The nasty smell was still pungent. It clung to the dingy walls of the flat, but Albert had the foresight to bring paper nose masks which helped a little but not much.

Once again, she struggled to keep her nausea in check. They opened every single functioning window in the flat and sprayed cans of air freshener which just made the already cloying odor worse.

She had made sure to eat nothing that morning and chewed on a wad of peppermint gum.

Albert was less sensitive. In a matter-of-fact-what-must-be-done manner, he proceeded to make suggestions about where they should start and what they should do first.

They taped boxes together in the hallway where the air was less heavy, except now they had to contend with the smell of stale urine and mold.

The hall carpet was filthy; the pattern and original color obliterated by years of neglect and the absence of regular hoovering. No one else was around, although music, burdened with a hefty baseline, blared from one flat, and the pungent smell of foreign cooking came from another.

A voice raised in anger screeched to a halt after something was thrown and hit a wall (Cassie hoped it was a wall) with a thud. They worked, silent and focused.

Albert remained in the hall and Cassie started taking boxes in. She was sorting through mountains of paper and clutter in the living room when she felt someone standing behind her. She turned. No one was there, but she could not help feeling that she was not alone in the darkly lit room.

The worn, greyish white, net curtains on the living room windows swirled as if they were performing a macabre ballet. A shudder threaded its way up her spine. She was grateful when Albert started tossing in taped up boxes, and even more relieved when he joined her.

'That should just about do it,' he murmured. 'Doesn't seem like he had much except junk, and the rest the council can clear out. You okay, you look a little pale. And you're shaking.'

'I'm good.' She gazed sadly around the melancholy flat. 'I just want to get this over with.'

'There, there.' Albert took her hand, patting it gently as if she were a little child. 'It'll be fine. We can take whatever you want to my place and sort through it. Tell me what you want to keep, and I'll ship what you can't cram into your suitcase.'

'Don't think I'll want much. I think we have way too many boxes as it is. Dad didn't exactly keep much of anything, from what I can see.'

'Much as I loved George, this place makes my skin crawl! So unlike George. Always was a neat freak; pressed and folded even his underpants - no joke - the brother was obsessive. When we were growing up, you could eat off those tiled floors in his house! You know, his Mum and Dad were rough on him, damn near came close to being abusive. Everybody used to call them Big Mama and Big Pap - only behind their backs, of course. No wonder he went a little wild when he came to England. Who would have guessed he would have ended up in this filthy, rat infested hole! Shame, shame, shame!' Albert shook his head in disbelief.

He held up various items for her review. She shook her head to indicate 'toss' and nodded to indicate 'keep'. Few items ended up in the 'keep' pile.

They rummaged through drawers and searched under furniture. Both were glad the building's caretakers had removed the sofa soon after the body was found, but the smell of death clung stubbornly to the walls and remaining furnishings.

108

Tucked away in one drawer, Albert found a framed picture of a woman - her mother. She looked to be in her twenties. Long, black hair hung loosely down past her shoulders; her blue eyes were alive and striking, and freckles were sprinkled across her nose. Her cheekbones were movie star caliber as she posed with her head turned to the side, wearing a demure Mona Lisa-type smile.

Albert looked sad. 'We all chased her, but she had eyes only for George. You have her eyes and her smile. Just as if she spit you out; you two look so much alike. Hope life cheers up for you.'

Cassie took the picture and looked deep into her mother's eyes as she ran her fingers through her own long, dark hair, and time rewound.

'Mummy, today I think we'll put your hair up. You look so pretty that way – same as Audrey Hepburn in *Breakfast at Tiffany's*. Remember how much you love Audrey Hepburn, Mummy? She's your favorite movie star, and that's our favorite movie. You always say you look like her except she needs more meat on her bones.'

She keeps talking. Her mother's eyes are on her, but her gaze is icy-blue, devoid of the present. Cassie reads to her silent mother, has lunch with her, feeds her, and then sits with her at the window in her private room.

Her mother stares out at the well-ordered garden. They watch birds flit from bush to bush, and the seasons change from summer rain or haze to falling leaves and then wintry frost and sleet. She chatters on about things she hopes will bring her mother back from that silent place only she alone can go.

'Time to leave, girl.' Her father arrives, rough-voiced, impatient, dressed in his black suit and black, suede fedora. He does not touch her mother or even look in her direction.

Her mother trembles, and her skin grows cold the moment he enters the room. For almost two years, this is Cassie's Saturday routine. It is the only day that her father brings her to see her mother for a few precious hours until her mother's heart dies late one Friday night. The following day would have been Cassie's ninth birthday.

Her mother's memorial service comes and goes - a blur of scanty relatives on her mother and father's side. No one bears the title of her mother's friend. After her mother's memorial, her grandparents pat her on the head. She never sees any of them again.

'Albert,' Cassie said, without lifting her eyes from her mother's, 'why did my father never reserve the grave for the two of them? He had Mum cremated. I don't even know what he did with her ashes. Dad's buried where her family bury their dead, and God knows where Mum is. Why?'

'Child, I wish I knew. I think at one time he said they were going to be buried in the same plot. Shocked all of us when he had her cremated. Right before your mother had the accident, your father was acting so damn strange. Hardly talking, drinking and, when he did talk, it was as if he thought the whole damn world was out to get him. I started backing off when he almost got us killed in a pub fight. Seems like he went from being mild-mannered and fun to being just plain mean. Something changed in that man. I used to tell him he might need to go and seek some kind of professional

110

help, but that advice almost earned me a fat lip because he said I was calling him crazy. So, I left it alone after that.'

Cassie held the photo for a long time before gently placing it on the 'keep' pile. This was beginning to sound more like the father she knew.

The last room to be sorted was the bedroom. There was little in there, and the room felt emotionless for all its neatness. It was all that remained of her father's grip on sanity. She well remembered his obsession with order.

The window could not be opened, no matter how hard they tried. The air had no movement, even with the bedroom door open, and the smell of her father's decaying body had permeated the cheap wooden furniture and bed linens. She felt herself shudder and, once again, her stomach turned. She kept the bile in its place by vigorously chewing on her peppermint gum.

Taking the oil painting off the wall, she placed it on the dresser before looking under the bed where she found an old shoe box. In it were a couple of ledgers, some old documents, a Bible, and a book that looked like a journal. Both the Bible and the book belonged to her mother. Her flowing handwriting penned her name in graceful letters on their front page.

The ledgers were of no use to her; the documents, the Bible, and the journal went into the one box she was taking back to the hotel. The oil painting went on the small pile of her father's personal effects that Albert would send to her in America. They were done.

She left the bedroom just the way it was - neat and orderly with the decorative pillows still in place. There was nothing for them to do except lock the front door and turn the keys in.

Albert went on to the car with a couple of boxes, Cassie stayed behind for just a second. She felt she should say goodbye. As she stood there trying to find the right words, a gust of cold air blew the curtains once more.

From the bedroom, she heard the sound of a heavy, sorrowful sigh. It was only the wind, she told herself, and then remembered that the windows were closed.

She hurried out as fast as she could. She balanced the box and her purse, while she locked the door with uncoordinated fingers.

Cassie declined Albert's offer of tea at his small terrace house which he said was close by. The journal was heavy on her mind. He looked disappointed. Before he could go full force into a diatribe about the loneliness of self-imposed bachelorhood and the scarcity of family companionship, she promised to visit at some point before she left the UK. Albert drove her to the nearest tube station.

That night, Cassie stayed in her hotel room. She ordered the salmon special with a bottle of Merlot.

After eating, she settled into the small armchair by her seventh floor window which overlooked the hotel parking lot. Up above and beyond the parking lot, the night skyline was filled with the flickering lights of the city. A glass of wine rested on the table beside her.

She flipped through the Bible which had various passages underlined - most of them were Psalms and Proverbs - her mother's favorite books. Words of comfort, she would call them. She read a few passages, but the solace they promised eluded her.

The Crenshaws never owned a Bible. She would often find Mrs. Crenshaw sitting Lotus style for hours until mindfulness reminded her she needed to put some food on the table for the kids before her husband came home. Cassie had a problem with God, regardless of who claimed to represent Him. He had let her down.

She put the Bible aside and picked up the journal. It had had a lock at one time - a fragile device that had been easily destroyed. Her mother's graceful cursive floated across the pages like musical notes. She traced the letters with her fingers - letting them rest on some, caress others, as a longing for her mother descended on her.

She took a long sip of wine and turned the hotel radio to a jazz channel. The journal was bound in rich, brown leather. She could feel something folded into the side pocket but decided to wait before pulling it out. Her mother wrote about the everyday events in a young mother's life, her loving husband, and the business of life in the city.

The entries were lighthearted but infrequent for the first few years of her marriage. They increased around the time Cassie turned five. They became dark and the words were burdened with some inner turmoil as her mother chronicled changes in her husband and in her life.

George changed from a loving, young groom to being suspicious and controlling. He questioned her about everything and insisted she spent her time at home. He dictated her every action, it would seem, even criticizing the way she wore her clothes and hair.

She wrote, *George told me tonight that I am a terrible mother. He threatened to send the baby to live with his parents to teach her discipline. I am hopeless at controlling a five year old child, at least in his eyes.*

He would call her numerous times throughout the day to check that she was home. She felt like a prisoner, hating her life and wanting a way out. He refused to talk to her and explain what she had done to make him treat her like his worst enemy.

A few pages had tear stains on them. Her mother's despair was poignant, and Cassie was moved by some of the entries she read.

After a few hours, she stopped reading. It was almost one a.m. The wine was all gone. Her head felt heavy. She put the journal down and crawled under the welcoming duvet of the hotel's bed. She pulled it over her head, as she used to do when she was a little girl, and cried herself into a restless sleep.

Early Tuesday morning it was pouring rain and dismal. The journal lay open to the last page Cassie had read when she awoke at five a.m. The entry she read had upset her. She had put the journal down to gather her thoughts.

Her mother had written: *George came home drunk, as he now does all the time. But tonight - this time it was different. Usually, he hurls insults my way, and after I give him his dinner, I can take*

Cassie and find comfort in my kitchen. It's always warm in there. It's the only place that feels safe now. But he didn't eat. He came in, threw his food in the rubbish, and accused me of trying to poison him so I could be with my lover. I asked him what he was talking about, and he said he was tired of my games, tired of my slutting around, tired of me acting like I was a good wife when I was really a whore, and worse, names I will not repeat. It was bad enough that he was attacking me, but then he started on Cassie. He said the 'little bastard' didn't even look like him. How can he say such a thing? I tried to keep her from him; she kept hugging my waist, and he came and pulled her away as if she was a dirty, little rag doll, and he told my child, MY CHILD, she was a child of sin and children born in sin pay for the sins of their parents. He yelled it in her face, and then he pushed her back to me, and walked out of the house. He just left! I can't take much more of this. Thank God she's sleeping now. Thank goodness, I feel I have a friend, but he's even scared to come by with George acting so erratic and suspicious. He's the only person I can talk to about all of this; the only person who knows what I'm going through. George can never find out he comes by. He already thinks the worst, but I need someone to talk to, and he's all I have.

Cassie tried to remember what happened, but it was an angry blur of raised voices. She had not understood why they were fighting. She never understood any of her parents' fights. They blossomed out of nowhere, took root, and withered away into those heavy silences which scared her.

She struggled to remember her mother having any friends, but it was so long ago. No matter how much she tried, no one came to mind. 'He' had appeared in other entries. Her mother never wrote his name. Cassie thought about asking Albert, but he had already told her he didn't see much of her mother once George changed.

'Got the feeling my "Welcome" mat had been removed,' he had told her.

She ordered coffee and toast from room service and ate without much appetite before settling once again into the armchair by the window. Outside, a hesitant sun played peek-a-boo with the clouds.

George came in and plopped a photo in front of me as I was sitting at the kitchen table. Threw it on the table and commanded me to look at it. It's an old photo, long before we became an item. God, we were only friends then, young, foolish. What does it matter? Why is he so upset about something that happened when we weren't even together? When I tried to explain, he wouldn't listen. Just said my lover gave it to him. He wouldn't explain. Have to go, time to get Cassie.

Cassie sighed again. She remembered there was something stuffed into the side pockets of the journal. Slowly, she pulled out a yellowed sheet of paper. Something was written on it.

George, do you really know your wife? Looking out for your best interests, see enclosed. Concerned.

The last entry in her mother's journal read: *Leaving tomorrow as soon as George goes to work, packed my bags, got Cassie's things ready. Mum says she planned for me to stay with Aunt Bess on the farm. George has never wanted to go. Be good*

116

to get away from London, to get out to the country.
Fresh air, a fresh start. Starting to feel more alive
now. Cassie's going to love the ducks. They were my
favorite when I was a child. Just one last thing to
do. I thought he was someone I could trust. I know
who's been filling George's head with all this
nonsense. If he wants to take someone else's word
over me, his own wife, then so be it. I hope he's
happy with the pain he's caused me.

The last few pages were blank. Instead of ducks
and fresh air, her mother had ended up in a nursing
home.

She picked up the phone and rang Albert. 'Hey,
it's me, Cassie.'

When he answered, his voice was sluggish.
Recently retired, Cassie guessed he was taking
advantage of a Tuesday lie-in. It was close to ten
a.m.

'Hey, little Cass, how's the family research
coming along?'

'Good, good,' she replied. 'I went through some
of those papers, but they were all ordinary,
everyday, household things. Hey, when I was in the
bedroom I found a journal that belonged to mum. I
don't know if you noticed.'

'Ah, to be honest, I saw you put something in the
box - brown book or something. Wasn't it a ledger
of some kind? Your father always loved keeping
those ledgers.'

'It wasn't a ledger, it was like a diary. I didn't
even know my Mum kept things like that. Listen,
when did Mum have her accident? I've been trying
to remember, but everything is blurred. I was so
young. Do you remember the month? I mean I know

the year because I turned seven and Mum had a little party - just the two of us. My birthday's in July. I kept that memory with me because I never had another birthday party again. And...'

'September, mid-September,' he said. 'I remember because I was headed out to Birmingham that day - had a rave to go to that night. Heard the news when I got back. Shocked me to my heart.'

'Okay, um, Albert, do you think I could go by the house where we used to live. I know I probably can't go inside. I just want to see it while I'm here. I leave in a few days. Who knows when I'll be back.'

'Yeah, sure, Cass. Meet me at Stratford Station; I'll take you by there. You owe me a tea date, remember?'

'Sure, sure...think I'll hit Soho or Piccadilly this evening; maybe have dinner in China Town. See you around one tomorrow?'

They hung up. Cassie looked at the last journal entry her mother made. The date was 19th September 1977.

The next day Albert drove her past the house where they used to live. The years had not been kind and the front yard was filled with tires and the remnants of discarded car parts. The paint on the red front door was peeling. Crooked blinds hung unhappily in dust streaked windows. It bore no resemblance to the tidy, smiling house of her childhood.

'Damn shame,' Albert said, 'used to be such a nice place. I haven't been down this way in a few years. Looks like one of them council derelicts now. House is crying out for care.'

'Wonder if there's anyone there?' Cassie was curious.

'You must be joking; you want to go inside that house of horrors?' Albert looked at her in disbelief.

'If I can, if they don't mind - whoever they may be.'

'Cassie, there's no telling who lives there - junkies, drug dealers, the IRA, who knows! No, it's not safe.'

'Albert, I'm going to knock and see. All I can do is ask, and all they can do is say no. Can you go back?'

'Crazy, just plain crazy. But hey, I have to look out for you; after all, you're George's kid.'

They pulled back up to the house. Together they approached the red door and knocked - and knocked, and knocked some more.

The door was yanked open. A large woman sporting curlers and dressed in a worn, orange robe, stood in front of them with a not too pleased expression on a face, wrinkled by years of hard living. A cigarette hung from one corner of spaghetti-thin lips.

'For Pete's sake, can I fuckin' help you?' she rasped.

Cassie gave her one of her sweetest, deep-dimpled smiles.

'I am so sorry to bother you, and I know this might sound like a strange request, but when I was little I used to live here. I was wondering, if at all possible, just to help me relive some of the best times of my life, if I could do a quick walk through, for old time's sake. You know, both my parents died and...'

Cassie thought for sure the woman was going to tell her to get lost, but the rheumy eyes softened. The woman said, 'I lost my daughter a few months ago. You got fifteen minutes. The man stays out.'

'Okay.' Cassie was in the house so quick that Albert's protest bounced off the front door as it was closed in his face.

They went into the small living room where a TV was loud and a large bird was squawking. It was filled with collections - porcelain elephants, porcelain dogs, porcelain cats, in fact, most animal species were represented in porcelain, and they were everywhere.

Cassie decided not to go upstairs. She entered the kitchen followed by a huge ginger tom-cat. The walls were oil-stained, and the stove was caked with years of crud. The smell of old food was strong. A grimy door led to the basement. Cassie hesitated. She knew it was foolish, but the basement seemed to pull her. She had always hated the basement with its steep, wooden steps leading into the dark unknown. She had ten minutes left. She flicked the light switch, hopefully, and was overjoyed to see a murky light illuminate the darkness. She began the descent. The cat remained in the kitchen.

The basement had not changed much in all those years. An old water heater groaned and moaned and gas and electric meters hummed. The floor was cold concrete, blanketed with layers of dust and the overpowering smell of mold. She could feel her allergies acting up and began a rapid session of sneezing.

Various piles of junk - broken furniture, piles of clothes, and boxes of who knew what were scattered everywhere. A rat ran across the floor, and she had to stifle her scream.

She stood at the bottom of the wooden stairs and closed her eyes. She remembered being in the kitchen. Her mother had gone down to the basement - she had been running around all morning getting this and that while Cassie sat eating a bowl of cornflakes, waiting. Suitcases appeared; her mother must have hidden them in the basement. Cassie was wearing her going out clothes. Someone knocked at the front door, followed by talking, loud voices. Her mother was back in the kitchen, upset. She was crying. The basement door was still open. Her mother stood in front of the open door. A man had followed her into the kitchen. Her mother was waving something in his face. The man was shouting, and then … she opened her eyes as a sense of agitation descended on her.

'I hate you, Dad,' she whispered into the murky light of the dank room, feeling overwhelmed as confusion entwined with shadowy memories.

A hand gently touched her shoulder but when she turned no one was there. Between two piles of junk something caught her eye in the dim light. She moved closer. Slipped into a crack, something white peeked out. It looked like paper, even though the corner that was sticking out was grimy with dust. On her hands and knees, she pulled it out, got up, and tucked it into the back pocket of her jeans.

A raspy voiced yelled from the upstairs, 'Time's up, chickie!' As she emerged from the basement, she heard again the same sigh she had heard in her father's flat. A gust of cold floated up the stairs behind her, and the hairs on her arms rose.

121

She thanked the woman who showed her the front door, closing it behind her without saying a word. Albert was waiting outside, looking distressed.

'You had one more minute, and then I was busting that damn door down,' he said. 'Foolish thing to do, Cassie, and foolish thing for me to let you do. Your father would never let me live this down. Well...any revelations?'

She shook her head. Two hours and three cups of tea later, she was on her way back to the tube station with the content of her back pocket still in its place.

It was probably nothing, she thought. She could only guess how many people had lived in that house over the years. She laughed at herself. Who was she? Nancy Drew or one of Charlie's Angels? She had kept her find to herself as she made polite talk with Albert.

As soon as she was back in her hotel room, she retrieved the thick, folded paper from her back pocket. It was an old, faded, Polaroid instamatic shot. She could make out a man and a woman. It was her mother.

Despite the blurred features, she recognized the long, black, wavy hair, but the man's face was almost obliterated by time and the photo's degeneration. He held something in one hand - a long, black, gentleman's umbrella with the handle carved into a peculiar but indistinct shape. Something about it looked vaguely familiar. The other arm was draped around the woman's shoulders. It could have been her father, but then she remembered her mother mentioning a photo in her journals. Why was it in the basement?

She recalled a story she once heard of a valuable coin which had been lost in a house for thirty years and was eventually found stuck in a radiator when the new owners were in the process of renovating.

No one had really done much to that basement in years. She wished she had had more time to scrounge around. But the photo, despite its condition, was still a major discovery, and something she felt she had been led to find. She debated whether or not she should tell Albert about it. The umbrella was on her mind ... where had she seen something like it before?

It was time to think about packing, but she felt the need to make her last visit to her father's gravesite. When she mentioned it to Albert, he offered to take her. The flower sellers were directly in front of Stratford tube station. Cassie picked up three bunches, one for her Dad and two for her great-grandparents.

Albert picked her up, and she put the flowers on the back seat of his car. Rain fell - light, casual, and unhurried; rain that planned to last all day.

As she got out of the car, a murder of crows rose from a tree in a cemetery devoid of mid-week visitors.

Pulling her raincoat's hood over her head, she walked ahead with her flowers in hand and thoughts whirling in her head like the earthy, damp mist she was walking though.

Albert went to get his umbrella from the booth of the car. He hurried to catch up to her and gallantly held it over her head. As he did so, regaining the position of his hand over the handle, she noticed it was fashioned into the head of a lion. She stopped walking. Albert almost fell against her.

'Oops, sorry. Missed my step!' she stammered.

'Steady, girl! I thought you saw a ghost for a moment.' Albert laughed as he helped her to regain her balance.

Arriving at her great-grandmother's grave, she quickly placed the flowers in the flower holders. Her mother used to bring her here to do just that when she was little. Cassie's mother had always said they had been the best grans a girl could ask for and were completely different from her own mother who had caused such tension in Etta's life.

She said a prayer, but her mind was flooded with images. She tried to put them in order. A spark lit a gas lamp and a flame began to grow.

They went to her father's grave. Cassie closed her eyes tight, seemingly deep in another prayer.

Behind her eyelids, a movie unfolded. Her mother was in the kitchen. She was arguing with a man. She was screaming at him, asking him why he wanted to ruin her life. She waved a photo in his face.

They were standing at the top of the basement stairs. The man moved to grab her mother's arm, but she stepped back.

She heard her mother's screams as she fell - the sound of her hitting the concrete floor. Cassie jumped up and pushed past the man. He did not come down but stood at the top of the stairs as her screams mingled with her mother's moans.

She heard the front door open and close as he left without coming to help her. The man was Albert.

124

Without looking up from the grave, she said, 'It was you that morning, wasn't it, Albert? That morning my mother fell. You were there. I always wondered why Dad would knock when he had a key.'

'Girl, Cassie, don't be daft, to my knowledge, I was speeding along the M25, don't be...' he started to say.

She turned to face him. She felt incredibly calm. 'All this time I thought my father pushed my mother. I thought he was mean because he was going mad. But it was you all along. You planted those thoughts in his head. You made him think my mother was cheating on him. You made him think she had cheated on him with you before they got married. No wonder he thought I wasn't his child. How did you find out she was leaving? Did she call you? The lies were coming from somewhere close to home, weren't they, Albert? You pretended to be in her corner. You used to bring me little toys! I know who you really are now! You used to drop by to have tea with her when Daddy wasn't there. You used to make her laugh. Is that why you stayed and waited for me after the funeral? You wanted to see how much I remembered. Why did you do it, Albert? Why did you want to destroy her marriage? You said you all wanted her, but I think you wanted her the most. You watched her fall! You didn't help us, Albert, you didn't help us! You knew she was hurt, possibly dead, and you walked out of that house. Everyone thought my Dad had something to do with her fall, even the people who adopted me. Why, *Cousin* Albert?'

Albert looked trapped, then angry. His eyes narrowed. When he spoke, his voice was full of ice. 'You talk nonsense, like your lunatic father,' he said, taking long, angry strides away from her.

He crossed over graves, stepping on some as he made his way back to the Peugeot.

She heard the car start up. He wasn't going to wait for her, so she stayed with her father.

Across the cemetery, a lone man in black stood, head down, a black fedora dripping rain, low on his head. Slowly, his head came up. She could not see his face. He turned and walked away - his figure blending into the raindrops as a sense of peace enveloped her.

Two months after she returned to the States, a parcel arrived in the mail. It was the oil painting of her parents.

PAPA

My father was a spiritual man;
well-worn spiritual shoes soled with Psalms and Revelations,
He spoke with the voice of Leviticus.
The Bible, his umbrella,
Protection from Satan's reign.
He went, door to door,
Late nights on London's granite streets.
He came home,
head bashed and bleeding,
Jesus in an ill-fitting suit;
Set upon by wolves and Romans who saw
Only that his skin, khaki brown,
Was different, desired to devour him.
'Go back to Asia,' words soldered to bats and fists.
All he could reply, before one tooth let fly,
'Lord, Lord, me Jamaican, man.'
The blows became a flood.

SPIRIT

The first time I saw a Spirit, I was five years old. Mami was asleep. You see, sometimes I couldn't sleep. Our apartment had one room of a nice size and two small bedrooms. It had a tiny kitchenette and a little bathroom. We had a few pieces of furniture and places to put the few bits of clothes we had.

My room was the room that had cradled me since I was a baby of four and which I called my own until I was fifteen years old. I loved my tiny space in this world, but sometimes I didn't always sleep right, even when I was really young.

Many nights I would take a walk. Mami would be fast asleep, cooing like a dove, her mass of kinky hair wrapped up in a bright blue silk scarf; her mocha skin damp because of the heat and because it was never cool in our apartment on the top floor.

She always talked in her sleep about things I didn't understand but which I later understood to be about my father. At nights she cried for him. She missed him every day we lived in the apartment.

I missed him too because I never got to know him and because I looked like him - a chocolate little him, with dark, dark eyes, like him, long skinny legs like him, and what Mami called 'a killer smile' like him. But while I didn't know him, I knew my mother. She was all I had. It was enough for me.

My father left us and so he really didn't matter as much as she did. If he ever came back, I would think about giving him another chance. But I doubted, even when I was four, he was ever really coming back. I had my mother, Uncle Pas's family, and my Spirits. It was enough for me.

Uncle Pas's house was directly behind the building housing our apartment. To get in or out of our home we used the door in the back of the house (never the front entrance which was made up of huge, wide, double, dark-cherry-red, mahogany doors) that led to the outside garden where a path split into two paths, one leading to Uncle Pas's house and one which went around the left side to the front of Robinson's Funeral Parlor (Caring Passionately for Your Deceased Loved Ones - as the sign in front read). It joined the wide concrete driveway leading from the front entrance to busy Tulane Road. Our apartment was the top floor of the funeral parlor.

It was shortly after we moved in. I woke up in the middle of the night and walked to the top of the stairs because a sweet, sweet voice was calling me. 'Le-ah! Leeee-aaaah!'

I had heard it in my dreams, and it pulled my steps from my bed, out of our apartment door, and to the top of the stairs. I looked down, and a lady, young, in glowing white, was floating at the bottom. As soon as I got there, she looked up at me with her see-through face and her see-through smile. Then she melted and became mist, drifting under the funeral parlor door to the other side.

She was my first Spirit. A lady in her twenties, who simply fell asleep, never woke up and lay on the other side of the door after being dressed by Pas, his wife and her own family. She would be ready to meet God the next day.

I never liked to ask their names - just who they were - but my mother told me she was the daughter of a policeman who, himself, had lain in the same room not too long before. He had been killed by a bullet in a Kingston shoot out.

Names made my Spirits too earthly - too connected to me. If they had no names, I could be sad for them and then go on with life without their names coming back to follow and haunt me.

Mami never went into the parlor, but she knew from Pas or saw from the window of our apartment, when family and friends came and went. Where we lived was a small but busy part of Kingston.

'It not 'ard to figga out who goin' back an' who comin' and stayin',' Mami said. She had grown up in the area.

My mother always knew who was who in our area, despite the fact that she spent most of her time inside reading books which Pas and Miss Matilda got for us, and listening to the transistor (except for market days and the few times she went out to church). She never spoke much to anyone but me and Uncle Pas but still she could say the names of people we would see passing by the funeral home.

Sometimes, I would watch them, the ones who lost loved ones, from Mami's bedroom window which looked out on to the street, coming in to help dress the bodies, coming in crying and leaving crying; or sometimes coming in and leaving looking neither happy nor sad, just relieved.

I would watch people and feel sorry for them. I liked to be sad with them; as if I could offer them some kind of comfort. I never knew the people they loved or sometimes didn't seem to love. Because I only left with Mami on market days or when she went so rarely to church, I had no real friends; I felt the Spirits were my friends.

But I was especially close to those Spirits who had no real family or only one or two people who knew them. They came in and stayed without any family to see them get dressed.

Uncle Pas was a strange but kind man. He sometimes gave proper service to those who had no name and who were brought in by the police or others. They would bring them in if the body was in good condition and especially if it was only a few hours new on the journey to meet its maker.

Every so often they found people in a ditch or in an empty, abandoned house, or on an empty lot, or in the gully in rainy season. They believed these people deserved some dignity, though a wooden cross might never mark their spot in the cemetery situated a few streets over. I felt there should be at least one other person, another friend who felt something soft for those who had unloved special days.

The room had air-conditioning and cold air blew into it. From the hallway you could feel the cold seep from under the door. On these occasions, when the ones going home were the lonely, the unloved, or the unnamed, Pas left the door to the parlor open; the cold air flowed out and stroked my usually hot skin as I stood in the hallway.

I would sing, "Swing Low, Sweet Chariot" or "I come to the Garden Alone".

These were hymns Mami taught me, and I sang while Uncle Pas and his wife, Miss Matilda, worked. Mami knew I did this. She never tried to stop me. She said it kept me in touch with my own 'humanness,' and it was part of living because all things came to an end one day.

Later, sometimes, a Spirit would visit with me at the top or the bottom of the stairs.

Uncle Pas, tall, too straight, too dark, with a face never visited by a smile, would sometimes sing with me, interrupting himself to boss the boys around if they were helping, or to boss Miss Matilda if she were the only one with him.

He was always making sure nothing was out of order. His eyes would flick across me, register my presence - he accepted me as the strange, quiet child of his renter, a distant cousin - a child who liked funerals - and then he, and, sometimes Miss Matilda, (but never the boys) would sing with me.

Uncle Pas had straight white hair and green eyes, and his color always reminded me of the dark, black, wood furniture that was scattered around the parlor. Mami said, laughing one time, he matched his décor.

He had long, long fingers and a forever look of concern and sadness. He wore stiffly ironed black suits with white shirts and a black tie. I never saw him in any other clothes my entire time living there or for as long as he was alive. Mami said if he didn't look so unhappy he would be kind of good looking.

His wife played the organ at the funerals. She was tall, dark, and thin just like him except she wore a pleasant smile most of the time and liked to curl her long, heavy hair so it fell like a waterfall around her shoulders; but when she worked, she made it into an enormous poof on the top of her head. I envied her her hair since mine was a massive halo that hated combs and had a temper all of its own.

Miss Matilda was twenty years younger than Uncle Pas and looked pretty no matter what time of day it was.

The boys were fourteen and fifteen years old, strong, sturdy, strapping male children and, when their Dad wasn't looking, they were rowdy, playful boys. They changed, though, when they were in Uncle Pas's company. They stood straighter, wore serious expressions and were all business. At times, in-between funerals and dressing 'bodies,' they played catch with me out in the back behind their house where there was plenty of room for us to be children.

I never went to school. Mami taught me in our apartment. She said the other children were too mean. I believed her and did not miss what I had never had, friends my own age. I considered the boys my only friends in a very transparent way; they never spoke to me except for those sometime times when we played catch.

This August night, Kingston raged with temperatures over one hundred degrees day and night. The air was so heavy it pressed against me like a dead weight hugging me too tight. It was hard to breathe.

Mami said a hurricane was being born, somewhere. Sure enough, the warnings came over the transistor radio in our room. A hurricane was growing up fast - changing from a baby to a toddler, a little pickney storm.

By the time it reached us it would be an adult, a big somebody, and everyone made to get ready for the strong winds. The marble sized drops of rain kept coming faster and faster, off and on, for days and days, and they got heavier and bigger.

I had turned eleven the day before on 26th August 1969. No big party was ever held on birthdays. On this birthday, no one was thinking about anything more than there was going to be a storm. People had things to worry about - like getting wood to board up windows and stocking up on canned food and big plastic bottles of water. They pushed along the street in front of us, loaded down with all kinds of hurricane supplies and protection.

Mami and I said quiet prayers to give thanks for being able to make it through another year with the hopes we would make it through the next few days of the coming storm.

All day I had been checking the thermometer on the wall between our bedrooms, listening to the radio, and trying to stay close to the standing floor fan. Ever since Mami taught me how to read the wall thermometer, I was fascinated with knowing how hot or cool it was at any given time of day or night. The day was so humid, and the two ceiling fans and the one electric floor fan in the apartment blew only hot air around.

On this hurricane-bearing day, they brought her in through the rain and the wind. Pas and his sons went to Parker Street to the family home and brought the little girl, who drowned early in the morning in the overflowing gully, too close to her house, back to the parlor, so they could get her ready for her special day.

Mami said, coming back, after going to the kitchen, with plates of food, 'Poor t'ing. She was playing, Pas tell me, and drop in the gully on accident. Dey fine her washed up almost two miles away. Some other pickney see when she fall in but couldn't get to her. De wahta was too, too fast. Nobady dare try to save her.'

Later on, a woman arrived, all in black, with a black umbrella; she was not crying as she walked up to the funeral parlor. There was something familiar about the way she moved, the shape of her face, but I did not know why this was so. I thought maybe I had seen her pass by because, after all, Tulane Street saw many people on foot as well as in donkey carts, cars, buses, and vans, going about their business, mingling with the goats, cats, and dogs which lived and moved along the street.

She came and stayed long enough to dress the little girl. She left, walking slowly by herself up Tulane. She held on to the umbrella with both hands, tilting it in the direction of the ripping wind as she tried to shelter from the hard drops of rain as best she could. Mami said the drowned girl was the only daughter of this woman and she, Mami, had gone to school with this woman - once, long ago. They had been best friends until something bad happened between them.

Mami never spoke to her again. She would not tell me anything more except: 'It was not too long after de friendship end, dat your father decide to leave.'

I felt sorry for my mother. She had lost my father and her best friend almost simultaneously; her parents died when she was little, and her wicked Aunt Joyce had caused her to suffer after their death.

Mami never spoke a lot about her Aunt Joyce but I knew this woman had made my mother and Uncle Pas very unhappy when she was raising them. I knew terrible things had happened in her house with the children in her care. My mother only hinted, but never spoke about it in any great detail. No wonder she didn't trust people. No wonder she always told me, 'Don't trus' anyone but God, me, and your own soul.'

'Not even Pas and Matilda and the boys?' I enquired.

'Not even them,' she would say, quietly.

My mother looked out of the window with her huge, brown eyes steadily planted on the back of the woman with the long, black hair rolling down as she walked so very slowly away.

The little girl was ready for her special day. She lay alone in the cold, cold room on the other side of the door. Mami called funerals *special days*. It was better than saying the actual word, *funeral*. It sounded like a happy occasion - a send-off party. I always wished I could tell the people who cried they should not cry. They should think of the occasion as being a celebration.

I had no idea what time it was, but it was late night or early morning when I woke up. Mami was asleep in her room, cooing like a dove as she always did.

The rain beat hard on the roof and swaying trees made crazy shadows on the walls of the apartment.

A streak of lightning split the sky and the following thunder made the windows shake.

On bare but slightly moist feet, I walked down the stairs leading from our apartment into the funeral parlor. The key was always left in the lock of the parlor door, even though the door was always locked.

I wondered why Uncle Pas bothered turning the key to lock the door if he was going to leave the key in the lock. He would lock the front entrance and back entrance when he left.

Pas did strange things sometimes; but we were grateful he had invited us to stay after father left. We never had any real reason to open this door after Pas left for the night or really at any other time.

When Mami needed to speak to Pas, she would knock at the door of the funeral parlor, and Pas would open it and talk to her in the hallway which connected the stairs, the back door, the front entrance, and the parlor door. He always had work to do, so he was always in the parlor until late into the evenings or late into the night.

That night, I turned the key and went in. They kept the bodies ready in coffins after they had been dressed. It was very dark, but I wasn't scared even though I had never actually been inside the room. I felt I knew my way around. The stillness made me feel as if I were in a walking dream, but I was awake as I wandered around the cool shadows and the quietness.

I was awake because the light touch on my arm was real. I could sense small fingers, smaller than my own, but not by too much. I heard a laugh - a light laugh - a happy giggle - a naughty but friendly giggle.

'You come to see *mi*, Leah?' a voice as light as warm breezes whispered. 'Mi was so hopin' you would a come!'

'Is who dis?' I whispered back to the darkness.

'Why is me! Israela!' the voice whispered again with the same little giggle.

'Oh,' I whispered, 'mi neva know your name. You died, you know.'

Israela sucked her teeth and laughed, 'Of course, mi know. Why else would mi be here? Silly girl! An' you supposed to be de old-a one. Not smart like mi tho'.'

I had no idea what she meant by this. I answered the voice in the dark, 'Israela is a pretty name.'

'Yes, so is Leah. You know dey picked out we names when dey was little girls like we - when dey used to play togetha - one day, down by de gully when it was shallow an' no rain was falling. Dey said when dey have dem girl chil'ren, one will be Leah an' one will be Israela.'

'Oh, mi neva know dat. Mami jus' now tell mi dat she was friends wit your Mami.'

'Oh, more than friends, Leah. So much more than friends,' Israela whispered.

'Oh,' I said, 'mi doan know much 'bout it at all. Mami neva said anyt'ing before today. Is like she holdin' somet'ing back. But Mami hol' a lot of t'ings back, you know.'

'Yes, mi know, same with mine. Doan talk, don't tell. Secret, secret, hush, hush. Somet'ings best leave not said.' Israela's voice was full of soft echoes.

I laughed. 'You sound like Mami!' I paused. 'Israela, can mi see you? Is 'ard to only talk to a voice. Spirits can light up, right?' I asked.

'Oh, Leah, you is a funny girl! You mek mi sound like a Christmas tree!' She sounded as if she were right next to me.

I stretched out my hand to feel for her, but all I felt was the empty darkness. Suddenly, a strange light illuminated the room, and I was looking into what I thought for sure was my own face - except my hair was longer and straighter. Instead of an old pink nightie, I was wearing a white, lacy, satiny, frock. I realized it wasn't me, but a face that looked just like mine, except a little bit younger.

Israela was not like the others - she was more solid - I could reach out and touch the fingertips she stretched out to touch my fingertips.

'Do you know who mi is now?' she asked, her eyes shiny in the glow that surrounded her.

I nodded my head, 'Of course, why you is de little drowned girl!'

She looked at me and suddenly her smile faded, and she looked very sad.

'An' you sistah,' she whispered, 'we never 'ad a chance to know each adda because dey neva tol' us.'

'Oh, you mus' be an evil spirit, come to tease me. Are you a witch spirit? You doan feel evil or look evil. Who is dey? An' why you t'ink we related? Mi 'ave no sistah. True, tho', we look too much alike. Maybe we cousins? Your Mami an' my Mami used to be really good friends. But mi doan know much more dan dat. So maybe dey was cousins? Mi see you Mami today. Seems like she was someone mi should already know.'

If a Spirit could sigh, Israela sighed.

'Oh, Leah, Leah, Leah! You still cyan't see. Did you know about their Aunty Joyce?'

'Mami said Aunty Joyce took in Aunty Joyce's sistah an' Aunty Joyce's brothah's chil'ren after dey get kill in a car accident in Mo bay. Mi always wondered what 'appened to the sistah's chil'. Mi know Pas was 'er brothah's son.'

Outside the wind was howling and the rain beat down even harder.

'Yes, Aunty Joyce was a wicked, wicked woman. She suck all de joy from Pas an' 'im soon forget how to laugh. She suck all de joy from you Mami, so she run away, an' she suck all de joy from my Mami so much so dat she grab on to t'ings that wasn't hers to grab on to.'

Israela's voice was sorrowful, but I was still unsure of what she meant by this although I now understood that her Mami and my Mami were more than best friends, they were cousins. Her Mami was Aunty Joyce's sister's child. The one no one ever talked about. I was confused; why would Mami not tell me this?

'All too late now, all too late. No time for us to play and dream. No time for us to hol' hands an' sing. No time for us now,' she said in a sing song voice. Then seriously, 'You mami neva tell you why you Papa leave? Why dey bruk up di friendship? My Mami an' your Mami? Ask her one day, Leah. But me going miss not knowing you. At least we had dis one chance. Is a pity de gully tek me away so soon. Maybe one day we would 'ave meet on the street an' you and mi would 'ave known who we is, why we look so much alike. We would a figure it out; we

140

could a mek dem tell we the 'hole story 'bout we. No matter 'ow 'urtful the telling would a been. Mi would 'ave liked to 'ave somebady like you as mi sistah. We jus' alike – you and mi – we 'ave nobody - father gone an' lef' us, jus' like he gone an' lef' you an' you Mami. Ask you Mami who mi is.'

I felt a light kiss on my cheek and then the room was dark again. I locked the parlor door and left the key in the lock. I wandered back up to my room, fumbling my way into my bed. My body was cold - a kiss still tingling on my cheek.

'Leah.' My mother was awake.

I was surprised. She usually slept so soundly she never was awake when I crept back up from my wanderings to the top of the stairs to meet some Spirit that wanted to tell me 'Hello'.

She called to me from her bedroom. 'You alright, baby?'

I did not answer, I wanted to think. Soon I heard Mami cooing like a dove, but the cooing changed to weeping, and in her sleep she was saying names - my father's name, Israela's mother's name, my name, and Israela's name. Then her weeping began to sound like a wounded puppy and she kept saying over and over again, 'Why? Why? Why?'

In that moment, I understood it all.

The next day, I woke up to Mami standing by my bed, dressed in black and holding one of my best dresses. She just laid it on my bed.

'Hurricane pass us by, the radio said,' she whispered in my ear as she kissed me.

Outside, the rain was still falling but not as angrily as it had done during the night.

That day I went to my first funeral. The boys dressed in pall-bearer suits sat in the back. The little white coffin looked so small. Miss Matilda played the organ, and my Mami Marva and I took a seat beside Mami Mervaline, the lady who looked so much like her.

We cried together. We were, after all, all we really had. It would have to be enough for us.

GRATITUDE

She looked up to the sky to blessing;
gift of water that washes away layers of dust from
fields from crops, from the ever present ever
looming haunt of Hunger.
Water feeds hunger; water keeps them here on this
land, in this place;
keeps them from becoming dust.
No water, no life.
But now the rains fell;
Deluge, it was truly a deluge!
The fields heave with new breath, quietly at first as
if awakening from a deeply, comatose state.
The land pulses; water flooding its veins.
And the rain, it fell, swirling muddy rivulets
forming.
And the rain, it fell, Quenching, quenching, water
hitting dirt.
And the smell of it, the rising, aromatic, earth scent
of rainwater blending with dirt. It made her giddy.
She felt the earth drink deeply, drunkenly as if to
forget being made brittle and unyielding.
Symbolism of loss and of hope, it fell and water
careened into dry riverbeds.
Children ran screaming and laughing; clutching
buckets, pans, tin cans,
so that they too could drink and become drunk, with
water the rain clouds had brewed stored, distilled,
now released.
She looked up to the sky and felt those giant
teardrops of gratitude roll down her cheeks.

VOICES
A Poetic Memoir

When I was a young girl, I was as formless as the universe before the big bang. I was filled and fired with passion, and I desired to change the world. I was a meteorite blazing a trail through space. I was big thoughts and dreams, had a big mouth but no grace. There was nothing you could tell me I didn't already know. I was an old spirit trapped in a young me and so my search for individuality was ruthless.

I was a wild Caribbean child, with flying braids, living my school uniform days. I tried to fit in with whatever was the in-thing because it seemed the in-thing to do. I was wound up tight like coiled springs in a time machine; like tension in tectonic plates bursting at the seams. I was metaphors and symbolisms and I had no clue except I wanted to change the world.

I wanted to be true to my dreams. I was home grown in Jamaican soil. My mother made sure of that. She returned to the island from the grayness of England, heavily pregnant with me because she wanted all her children to be born in sunshine.

When I was a young girl, my mind exploded with the brilliance of knowing for a fact I was invincible. I was nubile and fresh, untamed and untainted by the scars of rationality life tends to cut into our flesh.

Yet I was scared shitless of anything, of everything, of nothing. I imagine I was scared of myself. Under shady mango trees I caught lizards and cut off their tails just to see them (the tails) wiggle. My rationale was that they (the lizards) would grow another. I was curious and lost.

In high school I wondered how all the other girls seemed to be so together while my moods changed with the weather. I felt I could feel the earth sigh and wondered why no one else close to my life could feel it too.

But then they came, as posterity had planned... the woman voices. They would come to me late at night, and they taught me wrong from right.

They were voices which sung me stories of lamentations and celebrations; stories in which the women of my ancestry anticipated my birth story.

When I was but a young girl, my feet floated three inches above the ground at all times. Everything I experienced was profound and deep and scary and exciting and so, so, so brand new.

I will never again feel the first times of my actions. The first time I washed a dish, or made a friend, or cried over a dead pet fish, or did something brave or stupid, or made someone cry, or the first time I noticed boys, or had my first heartbreak when I thought I would die ... or got my period when I thought for sure I truly had died, or the first time I put on a training bra and demonstrated sheer bravery because the harness felt like slavery; or when I shattered my mother's dream of the perfect girl-child and watched her cry as her eyes asked me why, because I wasn't the Jamaican debutant she wished I would be; cultivated, as she wanted me to be, with piano lessons and a private taxi to school. I was always just a little bit street.

First times...

First times of emotions and thoughts and feelings made me tingly all over, pinpricks of life's energy raking over my body. When did feelings stop feeling so intense?

When did life stop being so immense? The voices in my head were choruses and choirs and songs of angels and the echoes in empty cathedrals ... whisperings at first, heard since the day of my birth.

When I was a young girl, I was the *Swan Lake* princess in a raggedy as hell yard dress trying to stand on tippy toes on freshly polished veranda tiles gleaming gold as the day grew old and a warm tangerine Jamaican sun laughed at my efforts, deciding it was time for me to go inside. But even though it hurt like hell and passers-by thought I was just a bit retarded, I practised and practised, no matter how hard it got.

My mother at the door saying, 'Chile, you know how long ah been calling you? Cho, come in and eat nuh'.'

I had it almost perfect. Because the voices told me I could dance and so I would dance; even though I know my mother was sure I was touched in the head. I listened to what those voices said, the way she had taught me.

I wasn't afraid of life, just some of the people in it. People who came and went in my young life. Good people, whose kind words are lost in my memory and people who hurt me. Isn't it funny how hurts remain like stains on the deepest parts inside of you, and no amount of meditation or medication can really undo. Misplaced words taint our youthful

146

days, linger, and seem to always stay ... a part of you...

When I was a girl-child, it was all a part of life. The Therapist and Prozac would come later. I was always surrounded by angels who enfolded me in soft fragrant wings of sweet protection and surrounded me with good karma, tender affirmations and affection.

These angels gave me hints on understanding life's lessons. Angels kept hands away from my private parts, and got me home safely when I was out way past a good girl's time, and angels later kept me from dying in places I would not have wanted to be found in ... even if I were dead.

Voices that chanted praise nightly in my 3D colored dreams. Great, grand relations; old people generations bent with this wisdom that was so awe-inspiring you were reverent. People who came in all shades and textures for the tapestry of my family is a rich work of West Indian exotic trails and cross continental resilience.

When I was a little girl, wild with impatience, my mother would tell me stories of the strong voiced men and women of my ancestry. But mainly she talked about the women, the women who had raised her; the women who took the brunt of living, took life's blows and came out swinging - my grandmas, Mima and Mari, who planted and harvested the land; who kept the power of the wind within their hands; who buried stillborn babies with no time to mourn; who made strong coffee way before dawn; who wept for nine nights when husbands were gone ... gone home. My grandmas and their mothers before; their tears nourished soils which became me. The women who whispered in my ear even as I back talked my mother, and she said that I must have been smelling my damn self, thinking I was grown. Right before she knocked me upside my head, not only was I hearing voices, I was now seeing stars of every color. Had I known then what I know now, maybe I would have paid a bit more attention ... at the very least learned how to cook.

The women who told me I could be a *Swan Lake* princess. They were un-named and faceless; they were impressions from the past, pressed on my future like a wax seal. I could not break it, no matter how hard I tried to be bad. You know, all of those crazy misinformed actions I committed when I was young and dumb; when I thought I knew everything when in reality all I did was get myself into one sad situation after the next (then have the nerve to be vexed with God).

In reality I had simply been ignoring the woman voices who had been singing symphonies in my head as they tried to turn my silliness around. Step away from the drama, they said, step away.

LALALALALALALALALALA. I put my fingers in my ears wishing them away, reluctantly remembering my childhood years. They were right. The fact is they were and still are right. I still don't know my rear end from my elbow.

Mama used to say a hard head makes for a soft behind ... and, you see, when I was a young girl, those dang women and their voices would not leave me alone; would not let me be complacent and accepting of my condition.

I danced because they said I could, I dreamed big world dreams because they said I would. I knew this even when I was just a little, little girl. I knew that all this fire springing up from the nether recesses of my soul was coming from the smoldering embers those interfering women had placed there; something I would have to learn to control.... my restless spirit, my constant searching for the who I was meant to be; this never putting up with *just* living.

My wanderlust came from those strong West Indian women, women who came out swinging. These were the women who went into the making of me. All this angst had to be harnessed, but positively.

When I jetted off to foreign lands and lived a life of foreign plans, I lost sight of home and somehow lost sight of me. I was like a square cube fitting into a round hole, like a cat in pajamas, itching and scratching and getting nowhere.

The voices were drowned by the voices of wants, needs, must haves, status, and show and, at times, I could not find myself anymore.

Later, when I was busy experimenting with a little bit of this and a little bit of that, late at nights the woman voices pounded on my already intoxicated head like a hailstorm, like fire alarms and hurricane warnings. It didn't matter that all I wanted to do was curl up in a fetal position and fail because it was easier than living up to bygone tales of strong women who never used the F-word, never had the option of thinking of the word fail. They would not shut UP!

'Girl, get yu trifling self in order and get yu self together. Yu cyan figet wheh yu come from, yu can't figet who you are. *Swan Lake* princess, a rising star. That is who yu are!'

You know what ... I did get off my cushion of self-pity and self-rejection. I got off my melancholy dilemmas, took a deep breath and started listening. At first it was hard to hear, but the voices were persistent and clear. I have never looked back since.

Maybe I won't ever really dance in *Swan Lake* and maybe we have to pay for the choices we make. But back then, back then when I was just a young, little girl ... I was raised by righteous women; I was raised by God-fearing women; I was raised by women who were divine; by women who took the blows of living full in their stomachs and came out swinging. The women who would not shut up and leave me alone.

The woman voices which always called me home when I had wandered just a bit too far into The Forest. Those women of grace forcing me out of beds I had no business getting into in the first place; the women, bold and thrilling, who went into the making of me. I am their prophesy fulfilling.

I am being all that I can be. The un-named ones, and those I call by name: my mother, Moraine, her mother, Mima, and my father's mother, Mari.

These great women, these wonderful women of strong Caribbean elegance. Despite the calloused hands and burning feet, these women, all honored here, inside of me. I claim this proud legacy handed down to me through eons of time. I am the vessel, and they are my content.

As I see myself grow, each day I realize that the voices have become mine.

'Train up a child in the way she should go, and when she is old she will not depart from it.' Proverbs 22 Verse 6.

WOMAN

Once a woman of magic walked...
Like Eve inhaling in the Garden of Eden
her body brushed against the heavens;
a Greek Goddess, Aphrodite; love made
her whole and broke her heart as she wept
like the Mother of Jesus crying for a crucified son.
She was paint on canvas; a Picasso rendition of
pure unaltered womanhood;
the Arawak maiden watching from the shore;
Madonna and the Mona Lisa of lost dreams;
the innocence of women.
Once she was a woman of magic
mystically gracing the streets of New Orleans;
a roaming spirit, soft, misty, cosmic, transcended;
the goddess of the Nile, an Egyptian princess
swathed in layers of gold and fragrance
while floating in the Ganges;
a baby, sacred, returning to its creation.
Iron Maiden, they whispered, as she saved children
and rescued men who were drowning
or died for men who were crowned.
She was once a woman of magic...
She bore children in hulls of rocking ships and
more screamed from her hips as she bent picking
cotton or macheting sugar cane.
Mulatto woman, crossing Sargasso seas.
She was broken and then built;
growing strange herbs,
sanctifying new medicine like women in white.
Mary Seacole holding the casualities of war;
Mother Teresa comforting the lepers of our time,
her love entwined with their suffering

as protesting suffragettes claimed the rights
to be first class citizens.
She was oh so much a woman of beautiful magic...
She wore Angela Davis afros, long blonded stresses,
swirling with a sense of purpose and bell-bottom
pants, boho skirts, peace signs, and black panthers,
an end to the war in Vietnam,
stalking injustice and marching to Washington.
She became Oprah, Hillary, Freya, Benazir,
becoming us.
We are women who have forgotten; some of us,
have forgotten, or maybe we were never told
that we are not bitches and hoes and nothing more
than the parts that are us - breasts, asses, hips,
sassy, us...
Our spirits unfulfilled at times...
them becoming us becoming them becoming the
magic.

THE SNAKE

The snake was mortally wounded, and Tuumba sat in the house with an angry mind - angry at her husband, Dibba, for raising the alarm which had sent the landlord, Mohammed, running from the front house and the watchman, Alhaji, racing from his post under the palm tree at the front of the front house.

She was shaking because no one had listened to her when she begged them to spare its life. It was dangerous, they said, it was for her own safety, they said, as they ran to get big sticks the size of small trees with which to beat it to death. This was followed by a cacophony of voices and the slapping of worn sandals moving quickly.

But Tuumba remained upset. The snake had not meant to cause trouble. She wished Dibba had let it go on its way - had allowed it to continue slithering through the grass in the front of their little house. She knew, eventually, it would have made its way to some other place and safety.

Her husband had not been so hopeful. He had seen it days earlier as he went out to prepare the little table on the patio for their breakfast coffee. He had called the landlord and watchman then, but it had been too fast for them. Tuumba, herself, had gone out to see if she could find it and possibly persuade it to leave, even as her husband yelled at her to put the broom down and come back in the house before coming out himself to force her inside. It was nowhere to be found.

She hoped, despite the dire warnings and dark predictions, it had left, and she would be spared having to bear witness to what surely would only be a brutal demise. She forgot about it; joked it had probably made its way to Tanje by now; teased her husband about his overwhelming fear of snakes; and felt enough at ease to consider the snake safely gone.

But Dibba had kept a wary eye on the grass since spotting the thick, black rope sliding from the steps of their house, raising its head and slithering into the grass even as he called out for help. It was his greatest fear - the snake.

It was said fear was sometimes mainly in the mind, but it could kill you even if the bite of the snake was non-venomous. The mind would scream you had been handed a death sentence even before the fangs sank into your flesh. Fear makes the danger more real than reality.

This was not a harmless snake, they had all said from the first occasion of its sighting. So, when it was spotted the second time, it signed its own death papers. This time it did not escape the blows that broke its head. She learned from Dibba, who came in briefly, it was not yet dead and had managed to find refuge in a deep hole in the garden. Its death would be a matter of time.

On the second sighting, before the fatal wound had been inflicted on its head, Tuumba had begged the men not to kill it. She had been especially angry with her husband whom she felt was directly responsible for all the commotion and the snake's unfavorable predicament.

'Why did you just not let him go?' she asked, giving him an angry eye.

'Honey, you do not understand. These snakes are poisonous; they are fast, they can get into the door before you realize what is happening. I cannot even bear to look at it.'

'Can't we call someone? The snake farm? They collect snakes. Don't kill it.'

'And how would we get it to them? We do not even have their number. They are hours away. No, this is best. You do not understand.'

She had walked off in a huff.

Alhaji explained, as she brushed by him on her way to open the door of the hot, little house which was their temporary home, 'It is for your safety, you must understand. This is a cobra, a very dangerous snake, not a pet snake. I have never seen a snake so big.'

She nodded, her hand on the screen door handle, and said, over her shoulder, that she did understand even though she did not believe it was really a cobra.

Tuumba had been raised in America, although her parents were from the islands, and in America she would have called someone to come and take the snake away; perhaps to a snake sanctuary. If not to a sanctuary then, (and this outcome resided at the very bottom of her list of humanitarian acts towards God's lesser creatures), at the very least, the decision to kill would have been something decided by experts on snakes and would have been out of her sight and her mind.

She tried her best to nod with understanding; she tried her best to understand that they were doing what they felt they had to do, but later, as she listened to more thudding of the wood planks, she tried to disassociate herself and not think about it.

No matter how hard she attempted to distract herself, the snake's dying spirit remained heavy on her mind; it was almost as if the wayward serpent were calling out to her for mercy. Its impending death went against her sense of fairness.

Muhammed came to the door to apologize for what he had to do, while Dibba got ready to leave on a short mission. She said she understood, but the landlord said, 'I can see on your face, you are not used to this - it is not your way. I am sorry.'

She tried to reassure him everything was all right, but he left, unconvinced. It seemed to matter to him how she viewed him.

He did not want her to think of him as a killer. She was surprised. This was Africa, and she was a woman. Perhaps the fact he considered her a toubab, a foreigner, had something to do with it. Perhaps he genuinely respected her strange outlook on life. Perhaps he pitied her.

She was aware the whole street observed (in a bemused manner) how Dibba treated his wife - differently. Before he left again, Dibba went to get his camera.

'You're taking pictures?' She was surprised.

He nodded. She gave him a look and went back to absent-mindedly watching a TV program. He returned a few minutes later to put the camera in the bedroom.

Since she had not been able to save the snake, she begged Dibba to have the men put it out of its suffering. Her words floated on the hot, breathless air behind him as the screen door swung shut once more, leaving only the voices on the TV speaking a language like the women who used to speak in tongues in her old family church, and the whirr of the struggling fan.

He returned once more.

'They are sorry they have upset you,' he said, as he prepared to leave again.

'Tell them I am not angry, and I am not upset,' she replied, but her face did not match her words.

He left, still unconvinced. She could tell *he* was a little upset with *her*. After all, this was *his* country, she thought, this was the way things were done. She was just not used to this way.

She sat and thought about the snake and the fatal mistake it had made by sticking around; by not going away when it had the chance. It had not followed the normal way of a snake, and now it had ended up dead.

She heard the voices of little children in the street. They were laughing. They were playing. They were unaware the snake, an alleged cobra, had been mere feet away from them.

She heard a woman call to another woman from the backyard of the compound next door. A man called out to a friend from the front yard of the compound on the other side. A rooster crowed loudly. She heard the sound of a cat crying as it was chased up a tree by the next door neighbor's dog.

There were many things about her husband's country she did not understand, but she understood these sounds. They were the sounds of those who believed they were safe.

Killing the snake may not have been her way in her country, but she was no longer in America and

158

her ways were not always going to be the same as the ways of her adopted home.

She got up. It was time to speak to Mohammed and Alhaji.

VILLAGE

I see a village
Where the lion walks
And the children play
Hand games with stones.
Where babies carried on strong backs
Are sages, newborn wisdom.
Where women, proud and tireless,
Balance baskets on their heads.
My village...imagined...
I see a village...
Where the mist that rises
From the coast
Descends like rich gray mesh, a tapestry
Of spirit voices,
Falling, dew-like, on masks and carvings.
A village, where warriors stalk,
Bodies lithe and swift, sculptured art.
And the children sing; like old men,
Whose footprints linger in
The sands of time.
A sacred musician
Creates magic,
Instills harmony, beats the drum
And the people come
To gather in praise
Of birth and dying.
Yellow mealie is in the pot
And the village fire is lit.
I see a village
Where the mist so gray
Is heavy with the souls of those
Whose fingers touch wistfully

The masks and carvings,
The women, the babies, the warriors
And old men.
I see a village.

GHOST BABY

'Vincent was too pretty to live,' my mother said about her younger brother who died mysteriously when he was five years old.

Her eyes would fill with tears and, despite the many years which had passed since Vincent died high up in the mountains in the village of Worsop, my mother continued to miss him.

I had heard about this little boy all my life but speaking about him brought my mother great heartache. I never asked her too many questions.

But I would not have to wait too long for a story, even a story about Vincent, because when my mother felt like talking about the past and about her life growing up in the village, she became lost in her memories and transported back to a time and place completely alien to the modern life I knew in the 1970s when I was a young teenage girl.

A born storyteller, the hours would slide away as she reminisced about the events and people who had gone into the making of the woman she had become - strong, resilient, poetic and loving.

My maternal grandparents were farmers - growing hills of yams and cassava, corn, coffee, and vegetables. They raised pigs, chickens, and goats. Edward and Agnes had already had my Mom (born 1913) and two sons, Silas and Ivan Waite born circa 1914 and 1915 when they moved from Mahogany Grove, Manchester to Worsop, Trelawny.

Vincent was my grandfather Edward's last child with my grandmother, Agnes (Mima), before he died. When Vincent was born, he was described as a 'doll baby'. Since both his parents were mixed with black, Indian, Spanish, and white, Vincent came out with light olive skin, jet black curly hair, pink lips, and liquid brown eyes. He was a thick, healthy baby boy.

My mother said, 'He was sweet like sugar cane and mango juice!'

My grandfather Edward died when Vincent was still a baby. Since my grandmother often went to the fields to work with Ivan or Silas, or both at her side, my mother would stay with Baby Vincent.

There were many in the village who loved the family and looked out for their well-being, but there were some who looked on with a jealous eye. Although my grandmother's Indian skin was darker than many people in the village, there were murmurings that the family was uppity because grandfather, baby Vincent, and my mother were so light in complexion.

It did not seem to matter that many other families were descendants of the Germans and the British who had once settled in this area and were varying shades of black, brown, and beige themselves; old colonial prejudices still lingered and the specters of caste and color hovered over the village, pervading an otherwise sociable community. The lighter you were, the more you were envied by a few who held on to old propaganda from Worsop's slavery days.

My grandmother and my mother felt that their faith would protect them, and my mother was deeply committed to her Catholic faith. The Virgin Mary smiled down from her portrait in my grandmother's bedroom; a large crucifix graced the walls of the tiny cluttered living room with the deep-burgundy, mahogany furniture handed down from my grandmother's side of the family. Sacred candles burned day and night to keep evil at bay.

At nights, the baby and my mother slept in my grandmother's room while the boys slept in the only other bedroom. Prayers were said, Bible verses were read, and the sacred candles flickered and shimmered as the family slept.

'I remember the first time I felt something was wrong,' my mother once said to me. 'I was having a strange dream about Vincent - he was calling out for me; but it was strange because he was still a baby and could not talk yet. But, as clear as a bell, in my dream I heard a little boy's voice calling me to come and get him because he was cold. I woke up, and mama was still asleep, but when I rose up to look in the cot, the baby was not there. My heart almost stop beating, and I scream. Mama jump up. All of a sudden, we hear the baby cry, and when we run into the living room, the door was open, and the baby was lying half in and half out like something was dragging him away. Mama grabbed him up so fast, and I slam the door. I look outside, but there was nobody there. We both start to pray. The boys come to find what was going on, and then they start to pray with us. But I knew that something was evil. It was watching us. To this day no one can explain to me how Vincent got out of that cot!'

My grandmother told my mother, 'Is Ole' Haig come to tek we baby to drink him blood. We have to get Vincent blessed soon. Lawd Jesus, but I feel bad things a come pon we.'

After that, my grandmother made sure there was always someone to watch Vincent. He was never

164

left alone. But still it would not be enough. Poor baby Vincent. He seemed to have been cursed from birth, haunted by a poltergeist because of some spell put on him by an old witch - someone unknown to the family and therefore much more dangerous.

Shortly after his third birthday, things started to happen to Vincent which caused my grandmother to go against her faith and see the local obeah man.

It all began when Vincent was playing outside and rocks fell from the hill under which their house stood. It was as if someone was actually throwing them or as if they were falling from the sky.

Big rocks and stones flew at the boy - a few hitting him in the head and other parts of his body, causing cuts and bruises on his delicate skin. My mother, who had been feeding chickens nearby, dropped the metal bowl she was holding and ran to pick him up, holding him tight as she raced into the house - all the while Vincent was rubbing his head and bawling.

Another time, he was running in the yard and almost fell down an old well because the boards they had used to cover it had become rotten and useless; one of his legs had gone straight through, and it took quite some time to stop the bleeding from the ragged gash in his little thigh. Once again, my mother was only a few feet away playing chase with him when he nearly fell in.

On another occasion, when Vincent had malaria, a strange wailing was heard going around and around the house, causing the dogs to howl and bark at three o'clock in the morning.

The obeah man agreed to come by and bless the boy. He said the boy was haunted and did not want Mima, my grandmother, to bring him to his house in case the evil spirit imposed himself on him. It is a bad thing when even an obeah man is scared of a spirit.

He came in the dead of night, sprinkling the house with oil and powders and burning black candles, chanting as he made his way through the small house, and finally sprinkling Vincent with the same oil, powders, and chants.

Instead of getting better, things got worse. Vincent would wake up in the middle of the night and sit up in his cot talking to something my mother and her mother could not see. When they asked him who he was talking to, he would tell them a black, black man who said he was his father.

My grandmother would say with great panic, 'Is not you father that is duppy!'

She would curse at the unseen spirit and tell it to go away and leave her son alone. All three of them would clamber into Mima's bed to spend another night praying.

An old lady, whom my mother had never seen before, was passing their house one day and called to her, 'Girl, come here. Do you see dat tall, black man with a top hat an' wearing a black coat sittin' in the tree in your yard? Be very careful of dat man; him is a John Crow - a bringer of death an' disease. Is dat you little brother over dere?'

My mother looked, but she could see no one in the tree, and she kept one eye on Vincent who was playing on the tiny verandah of the house. To her

166

shock, Vincent looked up at the tree at almost that same instance.

'And my heart drop when him smile bright - bright so and wave his hand like he was waving at somebody!'

The old woman called after her as she ran to get Vincent. 'Dat is not a real person dere, me chile - is a spirit who always watchin' you brothah wid an evil eye. Chile, dat little boy is not long fah dis worl'. Pray for 'im soul an' protect 'im as bes' you can, but him not goin' to live long.'

When my mother turned around to answer the woman and tell her that Vincent was in God's hands, and so nothing could hurt him, the woman had vanished. She was nowhere to be seen on that lonely stretch of road. When Mima and the boys came back from the fields, she described her to Mima, but Mima had no idea who she could have been. My mother never saw the woman again.

My grandmother tried to protect her son, but the old lady was right. When Vincent was only five, he became very ill; his brow was covered with sweat, his fever was so high that no amount of cold well-water could help to bring it down. He passed away and was buried by his father, not too far from the house.

My mother was devastated. He had been her heart - her favorite brother. In fact, she was more like his mother than his sister. She never got over his death.

My Mama always said, 'He was too pretty to live.'

BEACH WALK

It was past dusk and African skies had long since descended to blend with African seas. Stars and moon were scattered like jewels in the velvety fabric of night time as it graced Kololi Beach. A few people were still out, for the wind was more forceful than usual - whipping up stinging sands and softly moaning as night winds often do.

Some tourists were gathered, seated on the sand, outside a small bar and restaurant, listening to local drummers perform. The sound of drumming blended with the waves, rolling and frothing, hitting the shore and complementing the moaning wind. If it got much windier, the tourists would leave soon. People were out walking to get to places they needed to be.

The lanky woman who walked along the shore just out of the ocean water's reach was not the usual. Each step she made was sure and steady, even in the shifting sands of the beach. She was walking against the wind, bent forward, pressing on, holding her white shawl close around her shoulders.

The wind snatched her long skirt in all directions and whipped her long, bushy, dark, kinky hair into fantastic creations. With one motion, graceful and fluid, she removed the shawl from her shoulders and placed it, hijab-like, over her head, to protect her from the stinging sands. She squinted, long lashes acting as netting, but it was still difficult for her to open her eyes fully. They were gritty and dry.

The wind blew across fishing nets and empty boats, picking up the smell of fish, salt-water, and heat. Kololi would not cool off until the early hours of the morning.

The woman walked with a purpose, but there was nothing out along the beach that late in the day. She seemed unreal to people who glanced in her direction. Every now and then some boy or man whom she happened to pass would ask, 'Sistah, you okay?' But she kept walking and did not answer.

They concluded that she was rude and uninterested in their concern and obviously a tourist. Good Gambian girls were never out on the beach so late. They were home with their mothers in the safety of their compounds - as they were meant to be.

The African man was out later than he had planned. He needed to get home to Serrekunda by nine; his television was ready to be picked up from the shop. He had missed it, if for nothing else than his newly acquired DVD player was useless without it, and the hot nights in his little one bedroom abode, in the safety of his compound, were uninteresting.

Times like these he was grateful he had a friend like Assan, whose place was bigger and nicer with a real flush toilet and shower in the house. Assan had three fans in his living room and a rather nice TV. But then Assan had a sponsor ... a German man who was the real owner of the apartment. All this meant little to the African man. He was satisfied with his life and happy for Assan ... Allah was good.

The African man was returning from visiting his friends, eight guys living in an unfinished bar and restaurant. It was in a rather stalled stage of construction and needed a front wall and an entrance. It was open to the sea, and the boys slept with ocean breezes, composing reggae songs in their dreams. It was true. Sometimes a boy would start singing in his sleep.

Tonight, they had listened to music, done attaya, a ritual involving sugar sweetened Chinese green tea, and smoked numerous beefy spliffs before he realized that time was escaping, and he would miss the TV appointment.

He had many things to think about as he left. There was the problem with the Nigerians and the fact that he had turned them over to the police for trying to scam him out of money. Now they had threatened him ... without actually using any threatening words. But he knew, yes, he knew, that the strange phone calls on his mobile were threats seemingly covered up with strange questions from strange voices which he did not recognize.

He was worried. But he trusted in Allah. And he trusted in the Marabou and his devil and his magic. He guessed he would eventually come out of this all right. It was more of an annoyance when all he wanted to do was get on with his healing and his teaching.

The wind felt good against his skin, warm and enveloping, overzealous. His frame was slight, but he was a strong small man. The wind was like a woman trying to push herself up on him. He liked it. It felt sensual and earthy. But the stinging sands were worrisome, and his worn out T-shirt was not much protection.

He didn't have far to walk to get off the beach and make his way to the main road where he could flag down a taxi to Serrekunda.

He wished he had brought his motorcycle, but there was still a small problem with the paperwork and paying off the police was costly. He had chosen to leave it at home and take a bush taxi instead.

As he walked along the beach his thoughts were everywhere.

At first he thought the spirit coming towards him had no feet. It floated a few inches in the air, slightly hunched over, head down, head covered. His heart stopped on a beat, wavered for a second, and then continued in a rather doubtful manner. He decided he would not demonstrate fear in the presence of what could possibly be a devil, the bad sort.

He got closer. The spirit wore a long skirt which was flapping in the wind. It held on to a hijab of some sort and appeared to be human.

The African man's heart resumed its normal conscientious beating and his breathing slowed. He noted the complexion was not of a Gambian woman. Some crazy tourist, out late, but this was not normal - white women were not known to venture out too late alone on the beach.

She was sad. He could feel her sadness coming towards him on the fingertips of the fretful wind. This soul shadowed by the moon was not a happy spirit.

The woman's head was hung so low, she did not see him until she had almost bumped right into him.

She was startled like some exotic night bird and loosened her hold on the scarf, which was ungraciously grabbed by the wind and whisked dramatically out into the dark horizon above the shadowed and frothing waves.

He made an attempt to catch it as it zwipped by his face, narrowly missing his left eye. Allah, not yet three minutes with this creature, and I am almost injured. This could not be a good omen.

She glanced up, stepped back, and stopped. He stopped.

She looked frightened, caught, with the moon behind her, framing her, making her appear like something magical. He knew in that moment, he was in love with her.

'Good night,' he said, in his best English. His front teeth clacked regally as he over pronounced the "t" in 'night'.

She waited for about ten heartbeats before she replied, 'Good night.'

It was not very friendly.

She was beautiful, and she was sad. The African man wanted to be her savior. He wanted to save her soul and put her on the path to Mohammed, but he was too far ahead in his thoughts. After all, they had not yet really met - not an official greeting - only one made because she had no other choice.

But his thoughts were simple and to the point. No need to waste time, he reasoned. He made his mind up without hesitation, knowing with certainty that his thoughts were divinely inspired, direct from Allah. No need to waste time worrying over the small details. Those would eventually take care of themselves, Allah took care of everything.

The woman stood steadfast against the wind with a slight rock of her body; she was just looking at him.

He began to wonder yet again if she wasn't some trapped spirit ... perhaps some poor tourist who had drowned long ago on a day when the sea was so rough a strong wave could slap you in the eye and almost blind you; a day when the sea was so angry it would rough you up and swallow you. Only then would people see one hand, your hand, waving as if to say goodbye before you were swallowed whole by fat-bellied waves. But she appeared real.

He was scared to speak. And this was not the usual because he always had something to say.

She was some kind of mixture of races. In the shadowy moonlight, he couldn't tell which ones. But it didn't matter, she was beautiful.

A white lady, though ... is what she would be called, no matter her mixed-up heritage. Being with her would create jealousy in his community, especially with the police, especially if she ever rode on the back of his beloved motorbike. They would find a reason to take the bike away - no papers, wrong doing - no real reason. They would just take the bike for spite and jealousy; he knew this for a fact.

It had happened the year before, in the rainy season, with the young Peace Corps worker visiting from Senegal, the young lady with the light hair and blue-as-sky eyes who never stopped talking about how much she loved Africa. He was sure she did because it was a great place to practise doing good; and then she could go home to her nice big house in some American city and talk about what she had done in Africa. Everyone would look at her, admire her and say how brave she was.

But she was a nice girl and wanted to see Serrekunda in the night time but not in a tourist taxi ... out in the open ... with the people. So they rode from Senegambia into Serrekunda, and it was a beautiful night, warm winds, no rain, and people greeting them as they passed by.

It was all going well until the police car, loaded with five, big bellied, bored policemen, pulled up beside them and made them pull over and get off the bike.

His smile had stayed in place, his heart was calm, he was polite and humble, he respected their position, and still they took the bike. He would need to come to the police station in Serrekunda to negotiate getting it back. His papers were at home. No good, they said. He did not have papers and would have to produce them in order to bring his bike back, but still he must come by the police station and perhaps they could talk.

The young woman from the Peace Corps felt the whole thing was her fault. As they walked into town - not knowing whether or not they should feel embarrassed as the stares of the curious became stronger and stronger with every person they walked by - she offered to pay whatever the police asked to get his bike back.

He knew that was what the police were betting on. So he refused, and the bike stayed until he eventually got around to taking the papers and sorting it all out with the help of one of his police friends.

It helped to know people who knew people. This was The Gambia ... sometimes it was better just to take your time...

The African man decided he was worrying too much into the future. They had yet to exchange any real words. Yet, in his mind, he had already ridden around with the woman and her crazy hair on the back of his bike - her hands clutched around his chest like a baby clinging to its life giver.

'Cool man,' he told himself. 'Cool your mind.' He heard the sound of Beres Hammond and nodded his head in time ... music often popped into his head ... he was a musical man ... a cultural man ... he always had reggae music playing in his head. One day he would buy a CD player. Music kept him calm ... like this moment...

The woman was still standing. Then she spoke. 'Listen,' she told him, 'I don't want to buy anything, I don't need a taxi, and I don't need a friend.' She had a pretty voice, American.

He didn't mind her words although he should have been offended. She was rude.

'Cha!' he replied. 'How do you know I was going to offer you anything? I am out walking, like you, and we meet up. Do you see me with things to try and sell you? And taxi is way out on the main road, and I have a big hope I will find one as well. I am not so sure though you don't need a friend; you look like you are lost, my sistah.'

'I am not lost,' she said. 'How can you get lost walking along the beach?'

'It is a straight way either way,' he agreed.

'Well, if you will excuse me, I want to continue with my walk.' She began to stride away from him with feet sliding into the sand.

The wind blew harder, and the waves rolled in, loud and raucous. They had had to raise their voices just a bit above the natural conversations.

'Well, in all good conscience, can you tell me as to where you are walking to?' He smiled, less one tooth.

It was a handsome smile. He used a toothbrush and toothpaste unlike so many other Gambians who preferred chew sticks. Not him. He used both. He was lucky. People always said he had pretty teeth. So he smiled.

She did not smile back. In fact, she was getting more and more disturbed. 'That's not really any of your concern.'

He certainly did not care for the sound of her voice ... it was not pleasant.

'Bless, bless,' he responded in as gentle a voice as the whistling wind and fussy ocean would allow. 'Well, then I will walk a few steps behind you to make sure you get to where you won't tell me you are going, safe. Ok, ok, my sister, you don't even have to say a word to me or take notice that I am there.'

'You must be crazy.' She looked at him as if he had lost his mind and was running around a compound in circles and naked.

'Just walk, my sistah, walk.'

And she did. She heaved a weighty sigh of deep aggravation and walked around him and past him, squinting, more determined to get to where she was going. He had all night. The TV could wait. No hurry to go home; it was hot, and the fan was also in the repair shop.

The Marabou had told him he would find his woman in an unlikely place. By day, the beach was not so unlikely but, by night, it was a very unlikely place to meet your woman although here she was. She just didn't know it yet.

They walked along the beach; the man with the shoulder length dreadlocks, walking in his hip and dip style behind the woman with the long kinky hair and the slanted eyes. They walked for long minutes, long time with long silence. An occasional bat zig-zagged over their heads.

They walked past a group of young men sitting on the tourist-free beach loungers who were speaking Mandinka and Wolof and English, all mixed up in true Gambian style.

They were smoking weed and doing attaya. They were like his boys at Kololi Beach. The beach was their home. The men said, 'As-Salaam-Alaikum' and the man answered, 'Wa-Alaikum-Salaam.'

The woman said nothing, even though she was greeted. She kept walking.

The man walked a few feet behind her; the woman walked ahead. The moon slivered in and out of wispery clouds, and the stars were dazzling, so much so they did not seem real.

The man was thinking. The rainy season was in full swing. But the rain was not yet falling even though it could come with suddenness and, as he thought of this, he remembered he did not have his umbrella with him.

They walked from Senegambia Beach almost the whole way to Palm Beach Hotel. Really and truly, any further would be out of the way of the taxi he needed to Serrekunda, but he persisted in walking behind the strange woman with the slanted eyes, the African hair, and the American voice.

177

As they walked, the woman tried to control her wild hair. In less than a few minutes, she had managed to plait it in a fat braid; she knotted the end so that it would not come loose.

They walked past fishermen's boats at rest for the night until such time at the beginning of the morning when the fishermen would head out to open sea. Later, they would come back with butter fish, lobster, angel fish, and shrimp.

He hoped she would get tired soon or scared. Hopefully she would stop walking before they ran out of beach.

He walked because he was in love.

Everyone has a story; everyone has something they have come through to arrive at the place they eventually find themselves. He rather doubted anyone was predictable because the past makes you act in certain ways in certain times and, since no one knew everyone's past, no one could tell how a person would act. People no longer surprised him with their crazy actions. He had seen all different versions. He knew this woman was not a predictable woman.

She stopped. He stopped. She turned around, she sighed, she shook her head, she took a moment to look at him, and then she spoke.

'This is silly,' she said. 'You are not my squaw. Either go home or walk beside me if you insist on walking with me.'

He had no idea what a squaw was, but if she didn't want him walking like one, perhaps it was ok for him not to know. It did not sound like a good thing.

Humbly, he moved steps forward until he and she were the same. Humbleness was his best policy. He was beginning to understand why no other approach would suit her.

She was an independent woman. You could not expect a foreign woman to have the training of an African woman. They were Western, they were not Muslim, and they had too many freedoms and knew too many words. In the Western world, a woman spoke to a man as if she were the same ... even young women who had not earned true status as women.

No wonder the destruction of America and Europe was for sure. It had begun when they destroyed their family. He had read about it in books and saw it on the Internet and TV and in movies. Couples whose divorces were public knowledge, women who did work which should only be done by a man, and children who spoke to adults as if they were on an equal footing. These issues, and more, were as common as mangoes in season and a part of daily life for Westerners. Help her, Allah.

From this world came this woman, and her world was slowly creeping into his world.

He saw changes in the youth; they were not interested in anything traditional, only what they saw in videos and what they heard from Gambians who returned home with clear, soft skin and smart clothes. They were losing their sense of pride, always wanting someone to give them.

They wanted the newest mobile phones, the newest gadgets, and the latest American styles. No one worked on the farms except women, children, and old men.

So many young men, as soon as they dropped out of school, crowded around the tourist areas hoping to find a marriage ticket to Europe. And so many did ... it gave the others more encouragement. He was worried that The Gambia was losing her youths.

He understood her madness. It was a result of her pain. He could help her. He would be humble. He walked beside her.

After several minutes of silence, he ventured, 'Why are you walking so late, sistah?'

She did not answer. She stared straight ahead and concentrated on every step she made.

He sucked his teeth.

'Come on,' he urged. 'Have I done something to you? All I have done is express my concern for your safety. Perhaps you should look at me in a different light.'

She looked at him as if he had wings.

She shook her head.

'Where can I get a taxi from here back to Bijoli Beach?'

'You walked from Bijoli Beach to Senegambia? That is far.'

'Which doesn't answer my question.'

'We can go up through the path, and then there is a road that leads to the main road. Taxis go by there.'

'Ok, let's go!' She clapped her hands together.

'You are a bossy woman.' The words had escaped before he could stop them. He was really trying to be humble.

'Listen, I didn't ask for your company.' She tried to walk faster but the slipping sand impeded her progress, and she uttered a curse word in frustration.

The sandy path continued upward, and for some more minutes they concentrated on their steps. Walking in the sand in sandals and in the dark took careful planning.

'I am someone you can talk to,' the man told her, interrupting the silence between them.

'Right, you are. I just met you, some guy on the beach, in Africa, and I don't even know your name.'

'You never asked.'

'You have a point. I wasn't that interested.'

'So are you now?'

'Am I what?'

'Interested.'

She smiled. 'You don't stop, do you?'

'My name is Ibrahim Saidou Taft.'

'What kind of Gambian name is Taft?'

'It is my name.'

'Hmm…'

'And you?'

'Sarah Morgan.'

'Very English for an American.'

'Hey, what can I say?'

'But you look Chinese - your hair is like mine except much more of it.'

She had to laugh.

'My parents are from Jamaica. Both of them are mixed with Chinese.'

'Jamaica? Bob Marley, man, Luciano, Buju, Peter Tosh. Irie…no problem, man!' He paused. 'Chinese people live in Jamaica?'

'Please, lots of them do, from a long time ago. It's not all Rastafarians like people seem to think, you know. Don't Jamaican people come to the Gambia?'

'Yes, but I have never met one that looked like you; most look like us. Like Buju and Luciano...'

'Yes, yes, I gathered that they are the ambassadors of Jamaican culture.'

''Scuse me?' He did not understand.

'Listen, Jamaica has black people, Indians, white people, Jews, Germans, all kinds of people make up Jamaican people. No one is pure anything.'

'I am pure African,' Ibrahim stated with conviction.

'Yes, maybe in Africa, it's different.'

'You don't talk like a Jamaican.'

'I have lived in America since I was a kid.'

'America is a big country,' he observed.

'Yes, that it is.' The silence came down on them again.

'Why are you out walking so late?' he repeated, after a few moments.

'Listen, I really, really don't want to talk about anything to do with me right now. The less you know, the better.'

He laughed.

'What are you? Secret police?'

'Very funny,' she replied.

'Come on, sistah, you can talk to me.'

'What is the use of my talking to you? You won't understand.'

'I understand people will hurt you in life, but it's life. Did someone hurt you?'

182

She stopped walking and looked directly at him as the light of the moon washed over them both.

'I came on this trip because I had nowhere else to go, and I needed to get as far away as possible from my home. I got here earlier today, I took a long nap, and then I got up and decided to walk along the beach. So far, with all the men hollering at me, it has not been even close to any semblance of peacefulness, but I figured the later it got, the more people would leave me alone. Then I bumped into you, and now you want to ask me all kinds of questions about my life. And you are a perfect stranger to me. There, enough information?'

'Thank you.' He humbly bowed his head. 'Sorry to disturb your night. I am just trying to be a friend to you.'

'I told you earlier, I am not interested in friends at the moment. Don't you get it?'

'I get you, but I am here, in this time, and I can listen to you tell me why you are so sad and maybe Allah will give me the right words to give you some peace.'

Again she looked at him as if he had wings. But, surprisingly, she continued to talk.

'What does it matter to you, some man I just met on the beach? Don't pretend it matters to you. You're probably just wondering if I will pay your taxi fare home.'

'Well, if it is what you would like to do, please free up yourself, but the words did not come out of my mouth.'

'You think I'm rude, don't you?'

'Exceptionally!' he replied, quietly.

'Good! People normally take me for a pushover. I think that rude is one step away from gaining respect.'

'Sometimes it is a necessary action. But tonight it is not necessary.'

They walked for a few minutes in silence. The waves had become sleepy, and the further they got from the beach, the quieter it became.

They walked, avoiding sandy pitfalls still full of water from previous rain. It was dark, with light only coming from the heavens and the tiny fires of the occasional men they came upon who were doing attaya. The sounds of the night summoned meditation.

In the dark, people they happened upon spoke too loudly; their voices made even louder by the heaviness of night. They spoke loudly to show the night that they were not afraid.

'My life is a joke.' Her voice was so low he barely heard her. For a moment, he doubted his hearing.

''Scuse me?' he asked, respectfully.

'Don't worry about it. Nothing.' She shook her head, quickly.

Her voice was sad, and she looked straight ahead.

'I cannot imagine your sadness.' The words came from his heart.

'Where is your family?' he asked, hoping this would be a more pleasant subject. Family was always important. Family was always good.

'The last family I had died a few weeks ago. She was my twin sister. She killed herself.' She said it simply, but there was nothing simple about the way

184

her shoulders seemed to drop. He could sense the weight beneath the light tone she used.

He did not know what to say. Taking your life was a deadly sin, a sin Allah would not forgive. But he did not say the words.

He told her he was sorry for her loss; hopefully her sister was in a place where she could find peace. He knew in his heart her sister was doomed forever.

She said thank you, and then he got the feeling it was perhaps best to leave the subject alone for a little while.

But he wondered why this had happened. In a country where he believed people had everything, why would this sister take her own life? What was a twin?

He searched through Mandinka and Wolof and all of his English but could not get an understanding of the word. But he would have to wait for an answer; perhaps he would never know. For now, Sarah Morgan was the most important of concerns. She was here.

Since he was unfamiliar with how to deal with this situation, he was quiet and his mind drifted back to his own family. Both of his younger sisters were married and pregnant. They lived in Jamestown with his mother and father. Jamestown was a great distance from Serrekunda, where he now lived, and he had not been back to visit in two years, but they talked on his mobile, and his family would send letters by people they knew who were coming to his part of The Gambia.

His elder brother, Lamin, worked at one of the tourist lodges in Jamestown, and he, too, was married. His wife was a pretty Mandinka girl from the area. Unfortunately, the woman was not giving his brother any children. They had been married for three years, and his brother was now contemplating taking another wife.

Ibrahim remembered the day he and his cousin, Alagie, decided to leave Jamestown. There was nothing there for him. Despite the fact that Jamestown was famous for being the birthplace of Kunta Kinte and that the man who wrote about Kunta was a descendant of the great warrior, there was nothing there but ruins and struggling farms.

He left home with his parents' blessings and after many prayers of indecision. He had heard that Serrekunda had jobs and boasted a better life. He consulted with the local Marabou who saw great things in his future, and after scraping up enough money for taxi fares, he, along with Alagie, arrived in Serrekunda.

They were welcomed at the compound of Alagie's Aunt Loly and her husband, Ibo. Ibo drove a taxi van back and forth from Serrekunda to Kololi. Aunt Loly owned a cloth shop in Serrekunda's market. They were both well-known for being very religious and giving money and food to the poor. They were always in a good mood.

Loly was a tall, healthy woman - rolls of fat attested to her love of life and good food. She was an excellent cook. Ibo was thin and slight. He was a peaceful man, and always had a joke. Loly tried to feed everyone and anyone who was willing to be fed.

Alagie eventually married a Fula woman and moved to his wife's family's compound in Brikama. Later, he too would go into the taxi business - this

186

time running a small van between Brikama and Brusubi. Ibrahim was the favorite 'Uncle' of his three children.

Around this time, Ibrahim discovered he had a talent for healing and teaching. For a few years, he healed in the back room of Loly's shop and worked at a local school. The pay from both was unsteady, but with the help of people he healed, he opened a small healing shop of his own. It was located in Latrikunda where the rent was cheaper, and he could live in the shop as well as do business.

He had very little in the way of personal possessions. A few pairs of jeans, some old T-shirts, one good shirt, trousers so well worn and creased they were shiny from ironing, his robe for prayer, a new pair of shoes, one pair of sandals, and a prized pair of Nike's, three pairs of underwear, a towel and a large piece of mud cloth to cover himself with at nights. The back seat, taken from a long abandoned van, covered by an old spread served triple duty as his bed, consultation seat, and a place from where he performed his healing. He had his candles and his ointments.

Later, when he moved into his one bedroom unit in a compound of rented units, he moved with everything, well almost everything. The clothes and shoes were replaced, as they wore out, by newer clothes which became as old as the ones before. He moved with everything except for the van seat. A patient gave him a small sofa as payment, another gave him an old stereo system, still another contributed the sagging bed he slept in, a small table and some chairs.

He continued to work at Latrikunda's Basic School, teaching English to girls and boys aged ten through thirteen. The problem was that his English was in need of remedial help itself, but teachers were rare and English teachers were rarer still. In any case, he felt he spoke the English language very well, spelling words based on how they sounded with no one to correct him. At least the children were speaking English.

He had always had family of some sort. He was sure there was some relative whom Sarah must have forgotten. He could not imagine otherwise.

Death by one's own hands was a delicate matter. He was curious. Westerners could not survive a rough life - not like in Africa where hard living was a daily reality. African people did not kill themselves; their time was often short enough.

Most Gambians savored every minute of every day, even when they did nothing except sit in their compounds and watch the breeze ruffle the dirt that had already been scratched and pecked at by the scrawny chickens. It was just good to be alive.

The night air was cooling down, and the smell of impending rain was pungent. They had reached the main road, and their sandals were soaked from stepping in sandy potholes full of water. He needed to go to the left, and she needed a taxi which went in the opposite direction.

They hadn't talked much since she had told him about her sister. He cleared his throat; he did not want to leave her. 'You can get a taxi here that will take you back up to Bijoli way. But if you want, I can ride with you to make sure you get there ok.'

'I thought there was no crime here.'

'It is a crime if you are lost.'

He saw the corners of her mouth struggle to keep the faint smile from emerging.

'That's ok. I will be fine,' she said, and her voice was warmer.

They stood on the side of the road. It was past ten-thirty, he imagined, although he did not have a watch; he always knew the proper time without looking at one. She was gazing up at the sky, at the stars, and the first drops of rain began. They had been lucky. The rain had held off until they got to the main road.

'Rain,' she said, her face still facing up. Caught in the moonlight again, she was so pretty that it made his heart ache.

'Rain,' he repeated, looking at her, taking a photograph with his mind of her image, knowing he would remember every detail of her - her clothes, her hair, her strange color and eyes, the way she moved, the sound of her words. In a few minutes they would both be soaked.

He was right. The raindrops sped up, and the scattered drops soon became a deluge. They stood on the side of the road, getting very wet, when a taxi van going in her direction pulled up.

'Round Table!' The sliding door clanged open. A boy who looked about ten, but was probably more like fifteen, yelled from the safety of the van.

'Yes!' The man yelled back and grabbed her arm. He helped her in and jumped in just as the van took off. She gave him an annoyed look but then, as if she realized that she was new to The Gambia and really didn't know anything about taking taxis with strange local people and walking in the dark, the look became less hostile. She gave him a smile that was so small, it looked as if her face barely moved, but her eyes were softer now, less ready to fight or run away.

They found two separate seats, one behind the other, towards the back. The inside of the van was dark, full of the dusky outlines of other people, lit up only when they passed through Senegambia which was the only place along their journey that had street lights. The other passengers had boarded before the rain descended.

The van picked up three more soaking wet passengers, two women and a man on their way home from work in a nearby hotel. They squeezed on to the ends of seats, holding on precariously to the seat backs in front or to the side of them. It was extremely hot in the van, the air was moist, and the rain prevented them from lowering the window.

Ibrahim felt the steam rising from their wet clothes. The van soon smelled of wet hair; some rather nice men's cologne mixed in with some rather arresting but definitely quite inexpensive women's musk. Stirred into this was end-of-day sweat and old van odor which combined to create a unique, slightly overpowering, but not totally unpleasant, aroma. It was the natural smell of everyday living; it was their being in this part of African life - in a warm van, full of people, on a warm, rainy night in The Gambia.

Up front, the driver was blasting the latest compilation by Luciano and talking in Mandinka to the passenger beside him. In the seat in front of them, a young girl laid her head against the shoulder of a young man who was obviously her boyfriend and less likely her husband. Boyfriends were more likely to display public affection.

Ibrahim made out the girl's white T-shirt and the boy's oversized bright red football jersey. The rest of the women wore traditional clothes, as did a few of the men, as far as he could tell in the bad lighting. Two women were fanning themselves with straw fans, and grateful passengers were trying to discreetly lean in their direction.

Ibrahim paid close attention to each person in the van. He liked to watch people; it helped him in his work. Every so often, he would try to peek at the woman in the seat in front, Sarah Morgan, but mainly he rode in the van with only the back of her head directly in front of him.

Every so often the bus stopped for someone to get out or in as the boy collected fares with speedy efficiency. Ibrahim could tell he was a good boy. He was honest. You had to be honest to have your fingers in someone else's money and not be tempted to sneak a few dalasis into a trouser pocket. Pity, he probably did not go to school.

Like many boys, school soon became a place which kept you away from trying to find a job to help your family. Many boys made it to their second or even third year of high school and then gave it up. Even more so, the girls left in earlier grades, preferring to get a husband and a baby rather than learning things from books which would not help them to buy bread for breakfast from the corner shop.

Ibrahim and the woman, Sarah Morgan, got out of the van at Bijoli Beach hotel. They were followed by the stares of people who did not try hard to disguise their curiosity.

It was still raining. They stood with the rain washing down on them, and Ibrahim was convinced he would probably end up with some kind of fever or even malaria before the night was through. He had gotten wet earlier in the day on his way to Kololi and had never fully dried off. But it did not matter. He only had a few more minutes with her. She would be gone. Any promises she made, he was sure she would not keep, and he doubted she would make any promises.

They stood looking at each other without saying anything. She was waiting for him to say his goodbyes, so she could start walking down the walkway to the hotel. She was trying to be less rude. He could tell. Her huge mop of kinky hair was a cascade of wet waves.

He realized he was still not sure what she really looked like; her strange bright-as-star eyes and high cheekbones were evident, her yellow color, the blackness of her hair might not even be real shades in the light of day. He wanted to see her again, in the light of day.

In all their time together, she had smiled two times. She was a serious woman.

She had waited long enough for him to speak.

'Well, I have to go,' she said.

'I know,' he replied. He waited for her to make the first move.

'Will you be ok?'

He smiled at that. She was actually showing some concern.

'It's my country; no crime.'

192

'Yeah, I remember.'

'I will catch a taxi in a moment. Will I see you again?'

'Listen, Ibrahim...'

'You remembered my name.' He interrupted her, pleased by this simple yet meaningful occurrence.

'Yes, well, I have to go.'

'Will I see you again?'

'I am sure we'll bump into each other around the area.'

'Perhaps...'

'Listen, I didn't come to get caught up in anything, ok.' Her tone was reverting to the lady he had first met walking on the beach.

'I don't have a net.'

He could tell she wanted to smile.

'What I am offering comes naturally - to be your friend,' he said. 'I am not a bumster, a beach boy, looking for a white woman to marry him and take him out of The Gambia. I want nothing from you but your friendship. I have a job, I am a teacher, but it is summer, and there is no school. I have time. Surely you don't want to do one of those tourist things when I can be your own tour guide. Why pay a great deal of money when I can show you the real Gambian people; you can eat real Gambian food. I know a lady who is a good cook, the best in all of Serrekunda. Her name is Loly. She has been to America. She has a brother there. She speaks very good English.'

'Thanks, thanks for the offer. I have to go.'

She started to walk away, then stopped and turned around. 'I'll be on the beach around ten in the morning. Gotta go, ok?'

'Bijoli Beach or where?'

'Not sure. Good night. Thank you. You were very kind.'

The words floated back to him over her right shoulder as she made her way down the walkway towards the lighted entrance and dry haven offered by the canopy of the hotel. The security guard greeted her as she entered.

'You alright, ma'am?' the guard asked, loudly. She said something, he could not tell what, in return. He wished her 'Good night, ma'am.'

Ibrahim watched her till she was gone, with the rain still beating down on his head. He would have to take some herbs and drink plenty of tea to make sure he did not get sick.

He crossed over to the other side of the road and hoped a taxi would come along soon and pick him up. His dreads dripped with water. He was starting to feel cold, and this was a difficult spot to get transportation.

He was in luck. Standing on the embankment, he had to jump a good three feet away from the side of the road as the taxi pulled to a stop in front of him.

'Ibraham! Nanga def? How are you, man?' The driver shouted at him in Wolof. 'Are you crazy out in this rain? Get in!'

The taxi driver was a good friend of his. Ibrahim had performed numerous healings for the man's family, as well as curing the man of a bad back. He had suffered for many years until Ibrahim helped him. Not to mention, Ibrahim had been present to help deliver the taxi-driver's only child when his wife had suddenly gone into labor. The child had come one month too early and lived. The family had repaid him in many ways over the past two years since the birth, and yet again, Laurent was here to help him.

Laurent and his family and the now thriving two year old baby girl, Radiate, lived not too far from Ibrahim in Latrikunda. Laurent was on his way home. He apologized for his broken tape deck. They were soon engaged in a happy discussion about the new roads the young president planned to build in the near future which would link up many villages and help communities work more closely together.

In the next breath, they talked about the Buju Banton concert scheduled to take place in a week, if Buju really showed up. He had mysteriously cancelled on two other recent occasions.

Ibrahim's mind was half in and half out of the conversation. He was thinking about the woman and how long the beach walk would be when he tried to find her the next day.

For many days after their meeting, Ibrahim roamed the beach at different times trying to find her. He even visited other beaches that were popular. It was as if she were truly a ghost and from another world. It was as if that whole night had never taken place.

Then one evening, a group of boys came running up the beach towards him, breathless, excited, and loud. They had found the body of a woman - a toubab - lying on the beach where the woman and he had first met. The boys ran on, calling for the police.

Ibrahim felt his heart drop. He knew without a doubt who it was. He ran in the direction they had come, and soon he came upon a crowd gathered around her. Some were shaking their heads; some were praying; others spoke loudly of the trouble this would bring to their country.

Was it murder? Ibrahim knew differently. He had seen the sadness in her eyes, and he had thought he would be her prophet, her savior. Allah had sent her to him, but she had not been able to understand.

He turned and walked away along the same beach where they had first met, and prayed that Allah would forgive.

GRIOT

My Father spoke of spiritual things
Of African Queens and African Kings
My Father spoke of these.
My Father spoke of wonder;
Of Ruwenzori veiled in splendor;
Of Kalahari sands
And Baobab trees,
My Father spoke of these.
My Father spoke of bravery;
Of Bornu Princes before times of slavery;
Of Royal Kilwa and timeworn customs;
Of Kush and Mali, bygone phantoms.
My Father spoke Ogoni, Shona, Bantu, Swahili,
Wolof, Mandinka, Ibo, Twi,
Sang in Yoruba, prayed in Zulu;
Offered Izibongo to his God
On bended knees.
My Father spoke of these.
My Father spoke…
Who by foreign rivers toiled…
Stranger in a distant land.
My Father spoke…
Whose feet had never touched her soil.
My Father spoke…
Through years that laughed and worried,
My Father spoke, unhurried.
No crowns bejeweled my Father's head.
Yet, as I listened to each word he said
I thought My Father royal.

DREAD
A Story in Verse
(for Judi and her son Liam)

Verse 1

My friend Jerome looks like a lion. Dreadlocks stream down his back, cascading like the waterfalls of Zion. Each lock chosen, transposed, and transplanted by his ancestors. Each lock tended daily by invincible hands of fore-fathers whose own locks had grown so long, they reached into eternity and infinity.

His locks were moistened by ancient tears, linseed oil, and beeswax. Twisted into shape by wisdom so old, it had never been written only told, only whispered in dreams, echoed in the winds of time by Griots heralding Jerome's birth on earth.

Jerome has not always had locks. Once, he was a conformist who wanted nothing more than to move ladders reaching the sky and helping him to soar. He talked the accepted talk and walked a conditioned walk. Jerome's hair, upon a time, was weekly cut and shorn, was worn with textured confidence, perfectly neat, a public testament to his sense of identity. It was acceptable and guaranteed him a place in the corporate world - a world where he would not be seen as a threat, a rebel, and yet, it never really was what he truly wanted to express. He was groomed for future success as a lawyer, a doctor, or a CEO of a Fortune 500 enterprise.

Railing against convention was not appropriate in his world. Jerome put aside his artistic side; buried his unfinished paintings, his lyrics, his poetic pen. Coming from a line of successful men, Jerome

198

told his sprit to be quiet. He would be a strong contender in the battlefield of business. Jerome looked the part, even as a teenager. A bona fide member of the status quo, he would not draw unnecessary attention, as his father never failed to mention. He would not be associated or mingle with those kinds of people. His head in books, he regarded his looks as the foundation for a bright and conventional life.

Jerome's father, proud and secure, was happy that his son's future and life would be without unwelcomed strife. He fitted in with the best of education at the best of schools and had a healthy regard for societal rules. A proud sire and well-pleased with life, Jerome's father had settled into old age with relative ease. He knew all was well with his lone offspring. He realized he never had to worry about anything, that he could peacefully enjoy his remaining years without the anguish and fears of so many of his friends, whose sons, and sometimes daughters, had met vicious ends - prison, mysterious deaths at the hands of justice, black-on-black crimes, drugs, and other plagues coming without warning, taking young lives and scattering their promises on infertile soil. Jerome's father instilled in him the values of his own upbringing. He was, himself, set in his ways and as solid as a granite rock. And all was well, except Jerome was changed by an incident, an unforeseen occurrence. It happened while he was at college seeking wisdom and learning knowledge.

On the way to a Thanksgiving celebration, Jerome and his college love, Miriam, were driving though the South through the grand state of Mississippi with one of his closest friends. Leo was a man who could recite mathematical enigmas as if they were poetry flowing from his mouth, and from his lips, the enigmas of physics rolled with ease and formulations played games. Leo was a master of philosophy and rhetoric, and Jerome admired his intellect as well as his friendship. But on this fateful night with blaring sirens and flashing lights, these fine attributes could not save Leo from the slash of a police baton to his head and two long months in hospital until he was declared brain dead.

Jerome never forgot the sight of his friend being pulled from the car for saying 'No' to a cop. An experience which haunted his sleep state. He would wake up sweaty in the midst of the night. The scene played over and over again in his dreams. He could hear the sound of a scream ... and the fear would rise from the depths of his being. A sense of helplessness would descend because there was nothing he could do to save his friend. Nothing was ever going to be the same. Nothing was ever going to be right. Jerome's faith in the status quo crumbled. His belief in conforming stumbled. He was lost. But he plugged on through for the sake of his father who had always been the foundation for his ambitions even as a sense of losing self-enveloped him.

Verse 2

Jerome's father, proud and secure, had always felt he could not have asked for more than a son as well put together as his son. But his concern grew when

200

Jerome's visits home became far between and few. The voice on the other end of the phone line sounded strange and distant, and Jerome's father sensed some deep, dark intent was growing in the air surrounding him. He almost died from the shock of what he called 'losing respectability' when Jerome emerged from college with hair surging with unruliness, ungodliness, and rude-boy-ness. His heart felt like lead. 'No son of mine would look like this,' he said, 'like a ganja-smoking, red, gold, and green toting Bob Marley quoting dread! No son of mine will disgrace my name with bush-fire flaming from his head!'

Pops, after all, was old school in the highest sense of the word. Following all the rules, he stepped in the footsteps of the proper way and watched his words and what to say. He had survived in a world where it wasn't always the smartest course of action to say what was really on your mind or draw attention of any kind that went against the mores, norms, and all the hidden do's and don'ts and ingrained institutionalized methods society had to keep him in his place because of race. It was life.

His was not the battle. His was not a stand against what he felt he could not change. He had raised a family, bought and paid for his home, and retired with a well-endowed pension plan. All this was accomplished by the might of his hand. Sacrificing parts of himself was sometimes the only way to be a man when true colors weren't always an option. Having grown up in the South in a time of Jim Crow Laws, segregation, KKK, and black degradation, over time he learned to respect his position and abide by the should not's and should's.

After all, next to God, there was the job and surviving as well as you could.

Verse 3

Jerome's twists coiled themselves around each loving ancient moment bestowed on them by rituals echoing across the span of time; distant fingers lavished them with love and memories ingrained in his DNA came from a land where tall trees swayed hypnotically to songs roared by lions and trumpeted by elephants.

Four hundred years past, these songs transposed to the banks of rivers in Mississippi, Alabama, Texas, and so on, dripping with the lows of despair and the highs of hope and aspiration even in a nation where people of color were not conditioned to hope or to aspire despite being sung in a land where every success achieved was gained by the blood, sweat, and tears of martyrs who refused to watch their dreams die; refused to accept answers without asking why and why not; refused to lie down in beds made for them by others who wanted to keep them in their place ... simply because of race.

Jerome's locks became for him a symbol; an outward show of rebellion; his own method of saying he could no longer be silent because to him they meant more than words. And so they grew. Small and young at first, nubbies true. Then sprouting like tendrils from magical vines, they created artistic formations composed of magical rhymes and exotic incantations; causing women to take a second look and think them spiritual, erotic, rhythmical. Men would say, 'Cool, my brother!' or

202

give a manly nod of the head when no words were needed to be said.

Jerome's father tried to encourage him to wear a hat while attempting in vain to persuade him to visit the local barber shop again and again without success. Jerome was adamant in his stand.

When father and son faced the public throng, his father would continue to moan that dreads were wrong. They were just not mainstream. They looked unclean, uncouth, unwashed, and rough, and yes, he had had enough of Jerome's infantile and irresponsible demeanor; could he not get a hairstyle a little bit cleaner? Why could he not understand next to God was the job? Who was going to hire him looking as if he should be selling shells on a beach in the Caribbean or promoting reggae dances? Jerome replied, 'I'll sort it out, Dad. Let me take my own chances.'

Verse 4

Still, Jerome's locks grew esoteric in their beauty. Centuries of grooming had produced a black man's glory. 'But all that was long ago,' Pops mumbled, disgruntled and dismayed. 'I have heard it all before, and it makes great sense in poems by activists, but no sense in a world where snow lies deep on DC streets and empty bellies long to eat.

'Idealism is for those with time and money to burn. There are life lessons to learn, son, more profound than raising fists and growing hair in some misguided protest. I feel your unrest, but there are times when the only way to fight is to make it in this world. Success is the best revenge. It pays to have plans because taking revolutionary stands does not provide a pension plan or keep you off the streets!'

Jerome stayed strong in his resolve, and he tended to his dreadlocked garden with abundant patience and reverential care. The dreads began to flow in diverse directions everywhere upon his head. Some pointed to the North and South and others to the East and West until they settled into a waterfall heavy down his back. And his father came again. 'How much longer will you see me in pain? How much longer before you are the son I named?' Jerome hugged his father and assured him one day he would not even notice the locks upon his head and would only see him as the son he was instead.

Jerome's father was a high deacon in his church. One Sunday, Sister Pratt got off her high perch and, with the utmost of conciliatory concern, inquired if he required counseling now Jerome was selling weed or so it seemed from the state of his hair. Jerome needed to be redeemed. He needed to find Jesus as he had obviously lost Him somewhere along his way. 'Those things upon his head,' Jerome's father informed her, 'those dreads are merely youthful exuberance. A passing phase. They represent a young man's desire to exert himself against establishment's door and nothing more.'

Sister Pratt looked at him askew, and off she went to gossip more about the poor, poor, poor high deacon and his son who she knew for sure was up to no good.

Verse 5
Jerome's hair had started to metamorphosize into distinct personalities of their own - some

symmetrical, some obtuse, some spiraled, some fat and round, some reddened, some brown, some jet-black reaching down the center of his back - a lion's mane.

But the controversy went on just the same. CV in hand, Jerome went out to seek his fortune from the 'man.' The first man was black, spiffed, smarted, and confident.

'Our company has policies it has to uphold and doesn't look too favorably on fashion that blares ethnicity and the like. Bad for business. Conformity brings success, my friend. Now listen, just a word of advice. Shave your head and come back with a new look instead. Perhaps then we can talk.'

'But,' Jerome countered, 'you've yet to see my qualifications. You've left my resumé unread.'

'As I said, come back when you've shaved your head.' The man stood up. Jerome stood up too. They shook hands and exchanged pleased-to-meet-yous. Jerome was shown the door, nothing more.

The second man had ice-blue eyes and lips which barely parted in a smile. Corporate executive suit and tie, he politely asked the proper questions and waited the required time to listen to answers while all the time his eyes were glued to Jerome's head.

'Well, we sure would like to have you on our team. But our company is quite mainstream. What you lack is experience. Perhaps you could consider somewhere else, perchance? Perhaps even freelance? Your qualifications are all on par, and some minor personal adjustments will definitely get you far. Right now, you're just not right for us. In a few more years come back, and we'll discuss the possibility of a possibility.'

Three, six, nine times more he heard the same; twelve, fifteen, twenty-five times he barely made it past saying his first name. Each time he'd leave, he shook his lion's mane. Thunder roared and dead black men cried out in pain. Dark clouds fell low on turbulent seas. In the holds of ships, the wails and moans, the chafing of chains, the scalding smell of death and nightmares seeped into future years. The men and women with lost names kept Jerome pressing on just the same.

His locks continued to grow like the waterfalls of Zion. Longer and longer, stretching backwards and forwards to new knowledge. Money was tight, but he held fast to his resolve and grew his locks with love acquired and fed by dreams of Mali, Songhai, and voices singing from deep below frigid Atlantic seas. Voices which once sang songs with tall grasses and limber trees swaying in bygone breezes.

He poured out his desires on canvas - swirling images of dreadlocked men, women, and children - dreadlocked lawyers, doctors, and congressmen. A dreadlocked president.

Jerome's father looked at this son of his. He saw the strength it took to hold fast to his choices. Saw him as if surrounded by the fires of manhood rites. He learned to understand that young men must fight new battles differently and yet completely the same as his. These were battles fought with different weapons; these were battles for self and survival.

One day, he reached out and touched his son's mane; he ran his fingers through twists and curves, stroked the locks as he would stroke a lion, gingerly, and then boldly. His father reached back four hundred years, and the tears he had hidden from so long flowed. Softly he began to hum an ancient song which had always been in his heart. And the hum became a roar.

Tatiana stretched, unhurried, arching her back, and twisting her spine as she gently eased herself out of bed. A feeling of contentment suffused her, and she felt, at first, as if the day was going to be terrific.

A deep morning sleep had summoned a dream about her mother. Whenever she dreamt about mom, she awoke buoyant and happy to be alive.

She was so sure her day was going to be absolutely wonderful that it took a few seconds for her to realize her mother was no longer with her.

The deliciousness of eggs and sizzling bacon drifted away, carried off on layers of reality; the wetness on her forehead swiftly evaporated even as she touched the spot where her dream Mom had kissed her good morning.

Sleep-ruffled hair, mocha brown skin slightly damp with night sweat, blurred vision, the picture of the truly just awakened, she stared at herself in the dressing table mirror with both hands on her cheeks trying to give herself a quick facelift. The effect was only temporary and it sent her spirits plunging just like her cheeks.

'Damn!' she said out loud. 'Good God Almighty, not forty yet and could I be any more pathetic!' She tried to resurrect her enthusiasm for life, the hint of which had stirred her awake, but it was no use. The quick mantras she repeated beneath her breath lacked sincere conviction.

'I am all powerful. I am beautiful. I am successful. I am blessed. I am diva incarnate.' The words strung themselves together until they sounded like one, but she felt no positive connection with the universe. Her main concern was injecting some coffee into her system, quickly.

Tatiana grabbed her love handles, turning this way and that in front of the mirror. Shaking her head, she frowned at the extra ten pounds which stubbornly clung to her middle section. She rubbed her fingers over her dimpled thighs then threw her hands up in the air as if defeated.

'I am definitely going back to the gym!' she declared to her reflection. 'This is ridiculous!'

Grabbing a clean towel from the linen closet in the hallway, she made her way into the tub-less bathroom. There was a pretty, flower-and-leaf etched glass shower stall, her commode, and sink.

The room was cluttered with various hair, face, and skin products. Half painted in mint green, the little bathroom felt as unfinished as she did in the mornings. She had started the project the summer before but never completed it, although she seriously meant to.

The steamy water helped to wash away some of her moodiness but, even as she toweled herself dry, she felt herself sinking again. She popped two Xanax's instead of one - a bad habit, but one she indulged in when her days started off particularly rough.

She searched the cupboards for instant coffee, finally succumbing to the hope that she had put the jar in the refrigerator in a state of absent mindedness.

As she surveyed the contents of a somewhat chaotic refrigerator, she quickly ascertained there was no coffee, in any form, lurking behind the moldy bread, juice, still water, week old grapes and aging assortment of condiments.

She was now dressed, smartly, neatly, black skirt, ruffled purple top, dreads neat and controlled, heels, pearl necklace, pearl earrings, and a matching pearl bracelet and ring.

Standing in front of the open 'fridge door, she looked around her open plan, and modern (if woefully), minuscule apartment. She made a face, and, nodding to herself, decided everything needed sprucing up. 'Including me,' she thought.

Sighing heavily, she grabbed her purse and car keys as she headed out the door. Her determination to have a wonderful day was slowly fading.

It was six-fifteen a.m. as she drove across the Woodrow Wilson Bridge on her way from Temple Hills, Maryland, to her school in Fairfax County, Virginia.

It would be another exciting and inspirational day, teaching ninth graders the virtues of punctuation and differences between sentence fragments. Oh, and let's not forget the uplifting task of getting them to write more than three sentences to fulfil the requirements of a proper paragraph.

She sighed again. Lucky for her, grading papers was a breeze. Their work production was so low, she whipped right through their papers. A true Zorro, the educator, slashing across typos and grammatical sins with her trusty purple pen - red being politically incorrect these days.

Tatiana took her exit off the 495, the Beltway, and headed in the general direction of the school.

The DJ was doing the morning show, and his co-hosts were upbeat as they batted around funny lines like ping-pong balls. Their effervescence crept up the back of her neck like an entourage of cockroaches irritating her. They sounded so damned peppy; she wanted to reach into the radio and slap them into *her* reality. She decided to give them a few more seconds as she negotiated lanes in an effort to find one moving at a reasonable speed.

'What's up, DC! Another beautiful late summer day right here in the nation's capital! Tuesday, the eleventh of September. Aunt May, whatcha got to say about the day?'

'Well, I am feeling blessed to be here today, son, even though for the life of me I could not find my favorite wig!'

'Now, Aunt May, how you lose a wig?'

'That explains it!' another voice chimed in. 'I was wondering if you were trying to give new meaning to the phrase "bad hair day".' This was greeted by rounds of laughter and Aunt May protesting it was as easy to lose a wig as to lose false teeth. More laughter.

Tatiana found the whole thing plain silly and switched to a jazz station with music on the air and less nonsense. At about six forty-five, Micky, her brother, called her on her cell.

'Hey, Baby Sis,' he said, 'heading into work?'

'Naw, on my way to Tahiti!' she teased. 'I wish! Pulling into the teachers' parking lot as we speak. Oh, joy! How about you? Today's the day, Big Brother! Are you excited about your new position? First day on the job as CEO! Go, Micky! How does it feel to have all that power in your hands? Not to mention the extra cash. Personally, *I* couldn't sleep an everlasting wink! What with all the planning and scheming to help you spend all that green! Brother getting paid! Chi-ching! Tell a sister how you really feel!'

'Feeling good, feeling damn good! Got my new Armani suit on, fresh haircut, walking in like I own the joint.' He laughed.

He had the most joyful laugh of any man she knew. She could picture that yacht-sized grin on his handsome face, the way his brown eyes crinkled at the sides, those long lashes swooping down, and his perfectly orthodontised teeth, gleaming white. Hearing his voice lifted her mood a little, but he nevertheless picked up a hint of something in her voice.

'What's wrong, Tats?' he asked.

'Nothing,' she replied.

'Come on,' he coaxed, 'I know you better than that. You sound down.'

'A whole lot of nothing, I guess.' She wished, as she often did, he was not always so perceptive. Sometimes she wanted to be moody. Was this such a terrible personality trait?

'You been to the doctor?'

She sensed the deep concern in his voice. 'Don't worry,' she said, 'I am not going to go there, the dark place - doodoo doodoo!' She hummed the tune from the TV show *The Twilight Zone*. 'Don't stress, okay. It's not that serious. Really, I am okay, Big Brother, A.OK. Groovy!'

'Huh.' Micky seemed unconvinced. 'Now why is it that something's really missing in all that fluff... Aw, that's right, not quite picking up the happiness. Tatiana, you were always one of the worst liars I have ever known. Don't go working for

212

the CIA. Your voice gives you away every single time. Remember, that's why Mama always knew who stole those damn cookies when we were little. All you had to do was open your mouth, and one little trembly word would sneak out, and your little butt was toast!'

She giggled like she was five again. He was right.

'Are you taking your meds?' he asked. 'Tatty, listen to me. Tell me whenever you don't feel so good. I'm just a phone call away. New York's only four hours from Maryland, but I can drive like a demon when I have to. So, let's say more like three hours.'

'OK, Micky. Don't sound so dramatic.' She rolled her eyes, affectionately, as she looked in the mirror to check she had no lipstick on her teeth.

'Seriously, Tats!' His voice was deep. 'You and me, we're all we got, Sis. I can't let anything happen to you. I promised Dad, after Mom died, I would watch you like a hawk. I don't get why you don't just move in with Loretta and me. Brianna loves her Aunty, and she wants to know, all the time, when she's gonna see you. You never visit. Always one excuse after the other. She's starting to think you're just a voice at the end of a phone line. You're like candy to her, girl. Take a break for a while.'

'I know you love me, Micky, and I love you to the moon. But New York? All the smog and craziness and those crazy public schools! On the other hand, think about the perks I have right here in our nation's capital - well, just across the Beltway, in any case. My awesome luxury apartment (big enough for me and at least one small cat), my host of supportive, loving friends (seen at least on every Fourth of July), and the close proximity of Popeye's chicken, within walking distance, no less. Naw, give this all up? You've got to be kidding! I'll take my chances here, thank you very much! Seriously, don't worry. I will call you. Don't I always call you?'

'You didn't then.' Micky's voice had grown solemn. 'The hospital called me, remember? You almost didn't make it. Don't hurt me again, Tats. I can't go through losing you, too, like we lost Mom and then Dad, like we lost my son. You call if you need me, do you hear?'

'Spoken like a true son of Thomas G. Tate!' Tatty said, laughing.

'At least come visit on Columbus Day. It's a little over a month from now. You have plenty of time to get yourself mentally prepared for the trip, for New York, for *us* even!'

She heard him sigh heavily. He was always worrying about her, always being the big brother. She felt she was merely the bratty, baby sister.

He was Micah G. Tate. He had been the rock after their mother passed and her saving grace after their father's rapid decline and eventual death. She had never been one to face emotional turmoil head on. She lacked Micky's conviction that life had to go on no matter what took tragedy took place.

She was more like her Dad, extremely sensitive, and as brittle as candy glass. He didn't make it that much longer after their Mom died; he shattered and splintered, and then one night he passed away, peacefully, in his sleep. If she ever went, that's how she'd want to go, not enduring the agony her Mom went through as she battled stomach cancer. They had taken with them the sunshine of their birthplace, Jamaica.

Her parents had been grounded people, strong, West Indian folks, with a deep belief in God and hard work. They had always been sunny and optimistic, constantly expressing their wish to one day move back to Jamaica when they retired.

Only a short time into their much anticipated golden years, sickness and death had stolen their dreams and crushed her own spirit. Micky had been a tower block of strength, but even he could not save her as she plummeted into a whirlpool of depression.

'Micky, I'll make plans. I promise to make it there this time. I would love to hang out with Brianna, with Loretta, with you, silly. We girls can go shopping - Garment District - hey now! Micky, seriously though, I'll be fine, I will, I promise. You go take on those big financial coups that you're so good at. I've got to go educate the youthful minds of America's future! Your future employees, honey. Be afraid; be very afraid! Call you tomorrow. You have the best day New York can offer, and remember, I got you.'

'I got you too, Baby Sis,' Micky replied, 'right here!' She knew he had placed his hand on his heart. It was their thing, their symbol, a gesture they used with the people who really meant something, down deep, personal, and special.

They hung up. Tatiana got her bag of graded papers and other miscellaneous teacher items from the back of her little RAV4. She headed into the school building, greeting other teachers as she went. Theirs was an early school, and she did not have much time before the students started to arrive for class at seven ten.

The early morning was already warm, and it swiftly turned into a bright-sky, blue-tinted, bird-song, kind of day. As the sun rose higher and began its day-time journey across the sky, the air got more humid. The windows were open in her classroom, blinds up, and the fan circulated moist air.

The students worked slowly through the daily oral language warm up. Tatiana's first two classes went well. As she read with them through the last pages of the first quarter's first short story, she walked over and glanced outside. Her classroom overlooked the front of the building and she saw a shimmer of heat hovering over the parked cars.

The kids filled out literature logs, discussing imagery and figurative language with varying degrees of enthusiasm. Themes of loss, redemption, and hope resonated with some; others passed notes to one another, zoning out to places she could only imagine they went to when their eyes glazed over.

They jumped like startled rabbits when she asked what they thought about the last paragraph she had read. It was now eleven forty-five a.m.

Lunch had come and gone, and she was teaching her third class of the day. One of the school counselors knocked apologetically at the classroom door.

Tatiana stopped midway in her correction of the morning's warm-up when she saw Mrs. Hayworth peering anxiously through the porthole sized window in the classroom door. Tatiana gave her an inviting smile and motioned for her to enter. The class stopped writing and looked up, curious, a pause in their quest for the correct identity of clauses and phrases.

Mrs. Hayworth, a middle aged blonde, cleanly put together, came close and spoke to her with all the minty-breathed calm she could summon up - considering she was usually in some degree of agitation about student issues. 'Ms. Tate, there is something going on right now in New York, and we are awaiting word from the district as to whether or not the school might close a little early today.'

'Something in New York?' Tatiana looked at her with surprise, raising one eyebrow. 'Why would it affect us? We're all the way in Virginia!'

'Just a precaution, just a precaution,' Mrs. Hayworth answered with a tinge of panic in her voice. 'Should be an announcement shortly. Mr. Orlando wanted us counselors to do some personal visits to classrooms … see that everyone is okay. Orderly exit, and all the usual procedures. You are aware of school policies regarding emergencies, yes? I know this is your first year, and I just wanted to make sure you understand. We never want to alarm the children.'

Still puzzled, Tatty replied, 'Alarm them about what? Do we know or will this information be on the announcements as well?'

'We can't make detailed announcements in emergencies, Ms. Tate. It might…'

Tatiana cut in, 'I know, upset the children.'

'I'm sure you agree.' Mrs. Hayworth gave her a tight smile.

'Well, keep me posted,' Tatiana said, her curiosity growing. She was still not overly concerned.

'Hey, Teach,' Pierre piped up. He had been eavesdropping from his desk in the front row. 'Maybe it's like the time we had the bomb threat and stood outside the elementary school across the street for two hours before they even *said* it was a bomb threat. We all just thought it was a really, *really* long fire drill.'

Mrs. Hayworth gave him an odd look and nodded quickly at Tatiana before she made a quick exit.

Tatiana shook her shoulders. New York was miles away. Why was Dale High, in Springfield, Virginia, concerned about some isolated incident in New York? She went on with the rest of that block's lesson and thought nothing more of it.

When Principal Glenn's voice came over the PA system, Tatiana paused again. It was noon.

'Staff and students, school will be closing for the day. All students will proceed in an orderly fashion to the bus area or student parking lot. Teachers will follow. There is currently a national emergency. At this time we have only limited information. We advise that you proceed directly home. School buses are waiting. Parents have been notified and should also be waiting in designated parking areas. Walkers, please proceed directly to your homes. Please check the school advisory TV channels or call the school hotline for information on school openings over the next few days. Safe journeys home.'

Her students started talking all at once as they gathered books, papers, and crammed them into book bags, switching on cell phones as they made their way out of the classroom. Tatiana walked with them and made sure they were heading in the right direction before returning to get her own belongings, locking up, and finding other teachers who were getting ready to leave.

Cell phone signals were jamming; everyone was saying something was wrong with the lines.

'What the hell is going on?' she asked Graham, the math teacher, who had his briefcase under his arm and car keys jangling in his hands.

'Terrorists! God damned terrorists!' He walked off, mumbling under his breath.

Everyone was scattering like mice escaping a pest exterminator. Since she still had no clue what was really going on, Tatty found her way to the parking lot.

She rang her friend, Lex, a Gambian immigrant who worked nearby. After two or three attempts, the call went through. 'What the hell is going on?' she said.

'America is going to hell, that's what. America's last days. Is all over, Tatty, all over! We doomed!'

Then she lost the connection.

'What the hell is happening?' she exclaimed out loud.

She took her cell phone out of her purse and realized there was a message. She always kept it on silent during class time. The missed call and voicemail message were from Micky.

For some reason, she was finding it difficult to breathe, as though ice was forming on her heart. Something felt very wrong.

She had spoken to Micky that morning. Why was he calling again? Her fingers were like icicles, like dead meat, as she punched in the code for her voicemail.

The car key was in the ignition, but she wasn't going anywhere until she heard his voice telling her everything was fine, everything was good, and all she had to do was take her meds.

She was convinced that was why he had called again - to make sure she was all right. The message was left at nine oh-five a.m.

Her heart beating painfully, she listened.

'Sis, don't panic. Something happened, there's a lot of smoke and dust, and it smells like fumes. Loretta came to meet me for breakfast. She wanted to see my new office, and she's here with me. But something is very wrong, like an earthquake or worse. People are going crazy! The elevators don't work. We're going to take the stairs, but it's hard to breathe. We'll call you back, so stay close. We got you...' Micky's voice was replaced by static before the line disconnected.

She sat there listening to the message at least ten times before it occurred to her to turn the radio on. Then she heard what was really happening. She put her hand over her mouth. She could not stifle the scream that came tearing out of her, involuntarily, shattering the blue of the sky, piercing through the sunny day.

'At eight forty-five a.m. EDT, the first of two airliners crashed into the World Trade Center, opening a horrifying and apparently coordinated terrorist attack on the United States, which saw the collapse of the two one hundred and ten storey towers into surrounding Manhattan streets and a later attack on the Pentagon.'

She called Micky's cell, but the call went straight to voicemail. Her heart froze. She tried his number again and again and again. It went to voicemail each time. She put the RAV4 in reverse and with screeching tires pulled out of the empty parking lot. She had to get home, she had to get home, and then she could think, then she could figure out this mess.

On the way back, she listened to the radio, to announcers recounting what they knew of the attacks. They said the towers collapsed. How could they? They were huge, magnificent, and as stable as American patriotism. None of this seemed real.

Traffic slowed to a crawl when she got to the Woodrow Wilson Bridge. There was silence, no horns, only the hum of engines, the sounds of arrested movement, and radios from cars and trucks which had their windows wound down.

Everyone was looking to their left. Instinctively, she did the same. She saw the smoke, heavy, real, black-grey, deathly, streaming across the harbor like a phantom. The Pentagon! It had not registered when she first heard the newscast. The announcer kept repeating himself and, in addition, he informed listeners that a plane had also plunged into a vacant field. They hoped there would be survivors; both towers had collapsed; crews of firefighters and paramedics were not responding; everything was in a state of chaos.

In the midst of her growing anguish, Tatiana felt the anger, the rising anger. It was as painful as her fear and uncertainty. She wanted to get home.

Maybe Micky had lost his cell phone when he escaped with Loretta, sweet little Loretta - just like her to want to defy corporate protocol and have breakfast with him on his first day on his new job. Maybe there was a message on her home phone because he could never remember her cell number. Why should he when it was programmed into his cell phone? It changed so frequently, he could never keep it memorized. He and Loretta were fine. They had gone to get Brianna. All was good. She had to get home.

Still stuck in the eerie traffic jam on the bridge, she rang his number again. Now, it wasn't even going to voicemail. It buzzed incoherently with the hopeless sound of nothingness. She tried Loretta's cell, and the same thing happened.

Traffic inched along, painfully and uncertainly. The air was heavy, pressing down on the creeping cars and trucks. The waters below moved sluggishly as the seagulls and other water birds stood like silent sentinels on buoys. The sounds of radios became more unnerving as she drove.

Then her phone rang, and she jumped. It was still firmly and desperately grasped in her hand even as she drove, even as she held the steering wheel in her own death grip.

Her hands shaking, she pressed the answer button. The number was withheld. Her heart stilled for just a heartbeat as she said with great faith and conviction, 'Micky! Where are you?'

'Aunty Tatty!' a little voice whispered, a voice sounding wet with tears. 'Aunty Tatty! I need you!'

It was Brianna. 'Baby, where are you? Are you alright?' Her words were as shaky as she felt. The traffic continued to inch along. She suddenly realized she really had not given much thought to Brianna's whereabouts.

'Do you know where my Mom and Dad are?' Brianna sounded much younger than her eleven years. And she sounded so alone.

'Baby, I'm not sure but, believe me, they're fine. Everything is just so confused right now. People are trying to get home on foot. It may take them a while to get home. Where are you?'

'At one of my friend's house. The school tried to reach all our parents, but they couldn't reach Mom or Daddy, and we had to leave, so since Leah's Mom came to get her, and she's Mom's best friend, she's my emergency contact, so they let me go with her. Can you come get me?'

Panic streaked through Tatiana. Micky would be home, she knew he would. Loretta, too. The radio had said the highway was blocked; cars were not moving in or out of New York City. Traffic was blocked in places that were nowhere close to New York. Life had come to a standstill across the USA.

'Listen, Baby. Your parents are going to come get you soon. You know something really bad just happened, right? But don't worry, I know they're on their way. Traffic's just really messed up, no subway, it might take them a while to get to you.'

'Aunty, our teacher said there was a big fire. But it's more than that, I know it. Ms. Williams won't let us watch the TV or listen to the radio. Melissa and me just been sitting in the baby's new room, waiting. Ms. Williams been trying to reach you. She had me come down so we could try again, and it went through this time. Can you come get me?'

'Alright. Well, listen, traffic is bad everywhere, so it would take me hours, honey. But, you're safe. Just listen to Ms. Williams. As soon as they can, your parents are gonna come get you. I'm gonna keep calling them because the phone lines are all tied up and it's hard to get through. We have to keep my line clear for a little while. I'm gonna call you back as soon as I figure out what's going on. Hang tight, sweetness? And please get me Leah's number. I promise I'll call you right back.'

There was whispering in the background before Brianna returned to the phone and gave her aunt the number where she could be reached. It was a landline. Then Ms. Williams came on the line and in a low whisper said they were not going anywhere - in fact, couldn't go anywhere if they had wanted to.

She said it was more difficult to get through on cell phones, so best to call the landline, though that was a matter of chance as well, and neither could she get on the internet. The communication highway was at a standstill. Everyone had questions; everyone was calling to find out where loved ones were.

Brianna came back on the line.

'Okay, Aunt Tatty. Ms. Williams says I have to go because she needs to keep the lines free.' A pause. 'Aunty,' Brianna said, 'I'm scared.'

'It's gonna be fine. I promise you. Just hang tight, little girl. I love you.' Tatty pushed the voice of doubt out of her head and her heart.

'I love you too, Aunty.'

It took Tatiana more than three hours to make it over the bridge and through the chaotic streets before pulling into her parking space at her apartment complex.

As soon as she got into her apartment, she turned on the TV. The images of planes hitting the towers, the rapid disintegration of those very towers, people jumping in futile efforts to save themselves, and the sudden realization Micky would have been on the seventieth floor, made her realize what she had given Brianna was, in essence, false hope.

The TV pictures looped themselves into what seemed like eternity. She had made a promise she could not keep, and her world had suddenly come crashing down like a heroin addict on a really bad high.

In her present condition, she could not go to New York, even if the roads were clear. Maybe she could make it there in order to give Micky and Loretta a piece of her mind for scaring everyone.

She went into the bedroom and then into the kitchen. She stared out of her living room window. For a while there was a rush of people coming home. She could tell by their urgent walks that everyone was on high alert.

As it got later, the coming and going slowed. Most people were home now, released early from various places of employment, hang outs (good and questionable), and school. People still came, a few still went, but most stayed put.

She held an assortment of pills in one hand and reached into the cabinet for the bottle of vodka with which she desperately needed to wash them down.

It was now almost five p.m. and there had been no word from her brother and his wife. She had written down the number of Leah's mom, but when she tried it she could not get through. She called again and again, hoping they had received some word.

Next, she tried calling the Red Cross, but it had taken an hour just to get the automated answering service. After she had pressed the numbers to get through to the right department, she was promptly disconnected. She tried eight more times, but there was no getting through.

She had the pills and vodka at the ready. She stood in front of the window, thinking unclearly. After a couple of her pills and two shot glasses of neat vodka, she felt warmer and calmer.

It was her usual habit - pills and vodka. It was the way she dealt with most things that knocked her to the ground with a sledgehammer. Then, she could sleep, thinking about her Dad ... thinking how lucky he had been to pass away so quietly. She walked out onto her tiny balcony. Sad memories crept up from her heart and, for a moment, she went back to another time, seeped in uncertainty. For a few minutes, she was consumed by her own self-pity.

She had slept her way through a divorce which had removed her very essence, stolen the light from her eyes, and sent her spiraling into a soul crushing depression lasting three years and controlling every sinew in her body and every aspect of her attempts at a normal life. The counseling never penetrated the fog in which she was surrounded, and the prescription pills only became another crutch.

The combination of pills, like the ones she held in her hand, and a bottle of vodka, like the one she clutched in the other hand, had caused her to end up unconscious in Prince George's County Hospital.

It was luck, and possibly divine intervention, because she completely forgot Lucy, her best friend, her only friend at the time, was stopping by to visit, and she had a key. If she had remembered, she would have put the top lock on, so Lucy would not have been able to get into the front door of the house. But, knowing Lucy, it wouldn't have stopped her because the RAV4 was parked in the driveway of the house she once lived in with Dante.

'Girl,' Lucy told her, as Tatiana lay in the hospital bed a day later, 'I know if your car is there, you're there. And I know if you aren't coming to the door or answering my calls, you're in trouble. I know you too well. You and Dante have been at each other's throats lately. I know this isn't the time, but don't you think it's time to let go? Tatiana, you can't keep trying to beg and plead your way out of a divorce from Dante Winters.'

Lucy had closed her eyes and instead of being grateful, she told her to leave. Their best friend relationship cooled after that. Lucy said she could not sit back and watch her destroy herself without saying a word.

'When you're ready to get it together, give me a call.' Lucy's voicemail hurt her, but she had shrugged it off.

Micky had brought her home from the hospital and had stayed with her for a few days while she recovered. She tried to get on with her mission to get Dante back. More fights, more futile attempts. She realized Lucy was right, but her pride held her back from trying to resurrect their friendship.

On this day, there was no Lucy to come and see how she was holding up. The days following Tuesday, 11th September, warped into long, tear-filled days. She spoke to Brianna every night on the phone. She did not want to see her. She knew it was cruel, but she wanted them to find her brother. At least so they could have a proper funeral.

She felt a void was taking her over. She had no feelings, not even for Brianna. She wondered what she could possibly do. She was terrified that, as much as she loved her niece, somehow the universe was playing a cruel joke on her, and she would lose her too. So she shut down.

She had never considered that anything would ever happen to her brother and Loretta; she had never had a reason to worry about who would take care of their affairs because they were the strong ones, the ones who were guaranteed to be around. Loretta complained about her relatives, but she always assumed there would be someone Loretta had pre-selected to be Brianna's guardian. At least then she could still see her.

In her own grief, Tatty found herself unwilling to go to New York to comfort Brianna. She was not that strong. More days, more pills, a few bottles of vodka, slurred phone calls to the child, and an indefinite leave of absence from work.

Micky and Loretta were reported as missing. They were not presumed dead because rescue searches were still in place. Everyone felt there had to be more people who had survived, cocooned in some section of the enormous, mind boggling piles of debris, fuselage, and building parts.

Ms. Williams had contacted social services, but things remained chaotic with public services in New York. They had promised to send someone out to see her as soon as they could.

No one from Loretta's side had come to Brianna's rescue. In fact, there were only one or two calls asking about life insurance policies. She remembered Loretta saying her family was somewhat unpredictable.

Her marrying Micky had been the best thing to have ever happened to her because it put distance between her family's creative ways of destroying themselves and her efforts to create a normal life. But she had never once indicated that they were all complete write-offs. They could not *all* be bad. Tatiana had never given them much thought but, since 9/11, she found herself praying there had to be at least one good, responsible, preferably sane aunt hidden somewhere in the fabric of Loretta's family who would rally up and provide Brianna with a home.

In every conversation they had, Brianna asked her when she was coming to get her, and Tatiana would give her some sagging excuse which bore no weight.

At first, Brianna asked a litany of questions about her parents. When it was obvious there were no more survivors, she asked heartbreaking questions about having a funeral for her parents. But then in subsequent conversations, she completely changed and asked where Tatiana thought they could be and was she sure all the hospitals in New York had been checked since they might be in one of them. Their conversations were often like roller coasters, and Tatiana felt emotionally strained.

Ms. Williams grew terser with each phone call from Tatiana. She told her she was waiting for word from social services and, if nothing else, she would be more than willing to foster Brianna, maybe even adopt her. Brianna stopped asking questions after three weeks. Instead, whenever Tatty called, she answered her aunt in monosyllables.

'Yes, Aunty. No, Aunty. Sure, Aunty. Okay, Aunty. Bye Aunty.' Tatty could almost decode what she was actually saying, 'Hey, you are really more messed up than I ever guessed. Don't you realize I just lost not one but both my parents? We haven't even had a proper funeral for them. Nobody who is supposed to be family has made any claim on me. What is wrong with you? You're my Aunty, and I'm just a little girl!'

Tatiana's father used to say, 'God has a twisted sense of the ironic!'

She had always wanted a daughter but not like this. Dante was right. She would make a horrible mother. In her mind, she still saw the look of disgust in his eyes the night he left.

'Baby, you're running around in circles. How are you planning on having a healthy baby, when everything you do is unhealthy? What? You're drinking and drugging your way to pregnancy? Shit! If it isn't happening, then you're the cause. I checked out just fine. You think I want a druggie for a wife? How do think that looks for one of DC's most up and coming black lawyers to have a glassy

230

eyed, can't-keep-her-balance wife on his arm? I will *never* forgive you for what happened when I won that award. You were drunk, Tatiana, standing up and clapping and swaying and shouting like a curbside wino, then throwing up over the dinner table. Get some help, Tatiana. You're always using this "I can't have a baby" song as a damn excuse. You're not fit to be a wife, much less a mother, to anyone.'

Tatiana rubbed her weary eyes as she stood on the balcony staring out at the cars coming in and going out of the apartment complex. She wished she could press an erase button and delete all those old, washed-up memories, especially when they kept clouding her thinking. She needed to be able to think - as an adult - not the complete failure the voices in her gut kept telling her she was.

She worried about how she was going to tell Brianna her parents were never coming home without back-tracking and making it sound like there was still such a possibility. How could she bury the people she loved the most when their bodies had never been found?

She was consumed with thoughts of what might have been her brother's last moments. She called and spoke to Ms. Williams who informed her that she had already spoken to Brianna about her parents.

'You were taking your time, and she needed to know the truth. The sooner she starts to grieve, the better it will be for her. She's been living with this for weeks. You know what she wanted to do yesterday? Go and get welcome home balloons! That's when I knew I had to put a stop to this. The child needs to mourn her parents because they are not coming back. And that's all it is at this point. She's really distressed right now. Leah's with her. I'll call you back when I think she can handle talking.' There was a pause, followed by, 'So, are you?'

'Am I what?' Tatiana asked her.

'Coming to get the child?' Ms. Williams's tone was dry.

'I'm working on a plan.' Tatiana's voice was tremulous.

'Sure, you are,' Ms. Williams replied. 'I'll call you later, Tatiana.'

She hung up before Tatiana could say anything more.

The weeks passed, heavy, hot, and dank. She wished to have someone, her mom, come and tell her in a dream that everything was going to be okay. They were all silent - her parents, Micky, Loretta, Dion.

Tatiana received a phone call from her brother and his wife's family attorney. He wanted to talk about the Will. In it, Tatiana had been named Brianna's guardian and the beneficiary of Micky and Loretta's assets. She was absolutely shocked. She was in no condition to be a mother. Heck, she barely got by with making those daily phone calls to Brianna to make sure she was in good hands.

'You've got to be kidding me!' she said to his attorney. 'Was he crazy when he did this?'

She sounded almost flippant. It came out wrong. She wasn't flippant, just flipped out. She was running out of her prescription pills and could not think of one more excuse to get more.

Her vodka got lonely without company. She felt the involuntary quiver of her limbs and the creepy-crawly feeling across her scalp. She needed something to calm her down.

On the other end of the phone line, the attorney was silent. She could tell he was not amused. He went on to review the life insurance policies, the properties they owned, bank accounts, mutual funds, and trust funds for Brianna, with her named as executor. He needed her to come to New York in order to go over everything in detail.

He mentioned her brother and his wife had a list of private schools they wanted Brianna to go to in the event of a move to Prince George's County, Maryland. They had apparently made up the Will when they first moved to Manhattan, right after Dion had been shot on his way home from middle school only a block from his front door when they lived in DC.

She told Mr. Lowry, the lawyer, she would get back to him with a date.

For an instant, she was really pissed at her brother. How dare he put her in this predicament, knowing full well she was a hot mess, whether it was a good day or a bad one.

'Micky, did you and Loretta lose your minds? What am I supposed to do with a kid?'

One night, she woke herself up, crying so hard she felt her neighbors must have heard her wailing. She had dreamt that Micky was holding her as he had done every night of that week when he came to see if he could rescue her. It was a sorrowful time. The air she breathed burned her chest.

As Tatiana recuperated after her overdose, Micky stayed for eight days before he had to go back to New York to his wife, his daughter, and the hole left by the death of his son a year earlier. She had assured him she was perfectly well, but every night the madness of losing Dante ate at her from the inside out.

He stayed as long as he could, dragging out those last few seconds because he did not want to leave her. He held her as she wept; he loved her so much although he was going through his own pain and loss. In her dream, he was holding her in the same way he had held her as she cried over Dante. In her dream, he changed into Brianna who, in turn, evaporated into a nebulous mist which floated away as she tried to hold on to her.

Tatiana paced the floor of her tiny apartment every night for five nights straight after the phone call from the attorney, and another three nights after her dream about Micky.

She was tormented by the decision she had to make. If she did not take her niece in, where would she go? Into foster care? Micky's daughter in foster care? He would never forgive her and neither would Loretta, not to mention the spirits of her Mom and Dad.

Micky and she had always said they had each other's back, but she was obviously hesitating about living up to their motto, especially now when it was truly crunch time.

She felt disgusted with herself but terrified at taking on the responsibility of being liable for someone else. She had her own demons to tame first; self-improvement could not take place using Brianna as a guinea pig.

Brianna could not be the crash dummy in her ever imminent downward spiral. Maybe she *would* be better off in foster care? And how could she give up her life-line, her prescription pills, and her beloved vodka? Didn't Dante tell her it was the only time he ever really saw her able to function in a somewhat normal state?

She stopped in her tracks on the afternoon of day nine as these thoughts scurried and burrowed their way through her sleep deprived brain.

Then it suddenly hit her. Fuck whatever Dante had said. Dante had moved on, had a new wife, had a child, and had a life. She wanted a life.

She realized she had not had a drink or taken any pills in eight whole days. She had been so consumed with trying to make the right decision for Brianna, for someone else, she had not even thought about it. True, the same went for eating much of anything and taking a shower every day (those thoughts having eluded her until she could no longer stand the smell of her own funk), but she had not been interested in getting high, in escaping. She was actually facing a decision head on.

Something clicked, some new revelation dawned on her. She had *truly* wanted to make the right decision and not make a decision by default.

She thought the situation through with a clear head, trying, albeit in her own muddled way, to come up with a well-constructed plan based on one of the most important decisions of her life. She could do this; she could still have a life. She could at least give it the best damn effort, even beyond what she 'felt' she could manage.

She had only one flesh and blood relative left to shower with love. All the goodness she knew was inside her might now have the opportunity to come pouring out.

She remembered what Micky had said after Dion died, shortly after he was gunned down because some young gangster-wanna-be had thought he was some other young gangster-wanna-be who had disrespected him on the playground.

'Tats, I can't handle this, girl, it's too deep, too cutting. I lost my boy. I lost my son. A part of me, Tats, and goddamn it, I can't fix it! I can't fix it!' He had bawled like a baby, cradled in her arms, in that big house she had once shared with Dante. 'There is no deeper pain than this, Tats. You, my girl, Tats, but I know, even you can't take away any of this load. Losing someone you love more than life itself is like losing life.'

She had lost them all, except for Brianna. She knew if she let Brianna go, it would end up 'cutting too deep.' She loved this child.

She stopped pacing and dialed Ms. Williams's phone number. Brianna answered. Tatiana was not surprised. It was as it was meant to be. 'Brianna, baby,' she said. 'I'll be there to get you in the morning. My little girl, I got you right here, okay? I got you right here.'

She put her hand over her heart.

At the other end of the line, she heard Brianna sigh deeply through her weeping, and say, 'Finally.'

236

THE DREAM

I awoke to find myself standing in the garden, barefoot, dressed only in my nightdress. I touched my cheek with one hand. It was wet. I touched the other, and it was wet. I realized there were tears streaming down my face. I had no idea what was going on.

I heard the screen door behind me as it swung - pushed by a gentle night breeze. Somewhere in the distance one dog howled and then another and then yet another.

I shivered as my body temperature dropped in the coolness of the night; my toes absorbed the cold squishiness of the rain-soaked ground. I raised my face to the cloudy skies hanging over me as I stared up at a depressed moon struggling to make an appearance, just as slow moving summer raindrops began their descent.

'Girl, what you doin' dere?' my grandmother's voice was a high soprano of panic as she leant out of her open window. 'Get your backside back in de house. Standin' out dere in de dead of night wid not'ing but a shift on. People goin' to t'ink you're mad!'

It was as if her voice brought me back from my sleepwalk. Without a word or a backward glance at the shadows which hid grandmother's pride and joy - breadfruit, mango, cherry, papaya trees, and her clusters of vegetable and flower beds - I ran to the back door and inside the dark kitchen, racing up the noisy wooden stairs on my way to my bedroom.

I met up with grandmother at my open bedroom door. I could tell from the look on her face that she was heavily concerned about me.

These night time expeditions of mine usually consisted of wandering around the house, waking her when I knocked something over or when my steps were 'like a cow plodding through the living room.'

It was the first time they had taken me out into the open. I could see the worry in her eyes. She stood there, her frail curved body covered by an old, much-patched, green nightgown. 'De dream again, chile?' she asked, taking my face in her wrinkled, arthritic hands as she held her face close to mine.

The smell of Colgate from her nightly brushing still lingered. Grandmother was mightily proud of the fact that she still had all her teeth which she claimed was due to her ritual of brushing twice a day. She had survived for over sixty years without losing one of them.

She was 'always taking care of the small t'ings' as she called them. Unlike many others of her generation, she relied on the Good God Above, to a certain extent, but she was often more practical when it came to leaving things to a 'wing and a prayer.'

'God 'elps those who 'elps themselves,' she said, whenever I moaned about someone being luckier than I was at whatever venture I had failed in. ''Stead of tryin' to figure out luck, t'ink more on what you can do to do bettah when nex' you mek your own chance 'appen. You mek you own luck.'

This night, she looked deep into my eyes, as if searching my soul.

'Dere is somethin' deep in you, child, somethin' only you can see. Mi can't tell you what, but mi can tell you jus' this much,' she said.

I was fully crying, sobbing, my shoulders rising up and sinking down.

'Mi don't know! Mi don't know!' I blubbered, as snot mixed with tears. 'Why can't you 'elp mi to stop, Granny?' I asked, looking into her eyes for answers.

'Because de ghost you 'ave inside you is only for you to know,' she replied.

'You not makin' sense, Granny. Mi is only a child. You should be protectin' mi.'

'Me can only try, but de real reason for dese dreams, dis late night ambling, is somet'ing so deep in you dat only you can fix it. You are thirteen years old now; you are not a child. You are grown. Your Mama had you when she was two years younger dan you, but she wasn't strong enough to face her own ghosts. She tek off an' lef' me wid you. No amount of searchin' brought her to light. No amount of askin' made her reappear. You 'ave more of mi character in you.'

I had heard all this before. There was nothing for me to say. My grandmother felt the need to remind me every chance she had that her daughter had run off. I think in some way it helped to keep her daughter, my mother, real.

Usually her remembrances of my mother would be followed by the story of the mysterious dead and bleeding goats which were found at the corner of our street on the morning of my mother's disappearance. They were a sign the whole neighborhood took to mean 'somet'ing dark' was invading the rather upbeat, if struggling, community we lived in.

'Tomorrow me will tek you to Brother so dat he can do a readin' on you,' she announced.

She helped me out of my wet clothes. I felt like a baby as I put on a dry nightdress and got back into my bed. She sat there on its edge, stroking my wet hair as she sang in low, dulcet tones, an old lullaby which she had sung to me all my life and probably sang to my mother. Sleep caressed my eyes with gentle fingers as I drifted off on the misty notes of her song.

My grandmother was a member of St. Anne's Roman Catholic Church. She attended church when she could, when her bones were not aching, and when she said she felt a calling in her spirit. Apart from that, she was all too content to say her own form of mass in our little house which was a few streets from the church.

Our house had a crucifix in every room and the Virgin Mary's altar, Our Lady of Compassionate Protection, was in the living room with its shining tiled floors and mahogany furniture. Old black and white pictures with their unsmiling occupants were placed on crocheted doilies around the Pledge-scented room which was kept gleaming and dust free by three of us: Granny, Esther (a girl who came every week to clean for us), and me.

I never knew who my Daddy was. No one ever spoke about him. There were no stories except one that said he was a drifter, a passing through man. It was as if he were dry dust carried away on a Kingston breeze sometime after I was born.

240

I would look at the pictures of my mother, few as they were, and see her large, almond eyes, her mass of straight Indian hair, her light skin, and realize I looked nothing like her or my grandmother. I had merely inherited my mother's long legs and her too soon grown-up appearance.

My grandmother said that when people called me 'black as a coal pot' they were just jealous of my perfectly even color and the way light reflected off my face as if I were surrounded by an angel's halo. I never really believed her. I knew she wanted me to feel better about myself.

I was picked on almost daily because of my blue-black skin, my kinky hair that had to be tamed by hot irons and Vaseline on an almost daily basis, my high cheekbones, my thick nose, and full lips, all of which were regarded as ugly and Negroid.

The few friends my grandmother had would make no bones or worry about sparing my feelings when they spoke about the chip falling many miles away from the block.

I thought my father must have been the devil himself because the devil was black in every picture I had ever seen. Even Esther was brown, with a fine nose and pretty, kissy lips, as the boys on the street would say.

The next morning, grandmother made us sweet tea and golden corn meal porridge with honey and evaporated milk.

I was dressed in one of my better yard dresses and wore a pair of pink sandals we had bought the week before at Coronation Market.

Grandmother wore her favorite blue, flowery smock and her long, straight hair hung down her back to her waist. She would only cut her hair when it reached below her bottom. She wore it in a ponytail despite the talk that this long 'horse hair' was not proper for an elderly lady. She did not care. It was her hair, she said.

We were on our way to see Brother, the obeah man and healer, who lived not too far from grandmother's church on Percy Street.

The day was hot. It was early June and school had been out for some time. Children played in the coolness of the trees as we walked by. We passed little girls playing jacks in the dirt or dolly house or sweeping verandahs and front yards. Boys, tinkering with this and that, created toys out of discarded bits and bobs.

Grandmother shaded us from the morning sun with a big, black umbrella and occasionally nodded in the general direction of this or that person who had greeted us with a cheery 'Mawnin', Ma Reynolds.' We took our time walking because grandmother's hips were acting up. She was sixty-seven years old and had had my mother when she was in her early forties.

Eleven years later, my mother had me. I knew that having a child at eleven was very young - even though I saw young girls of an early age who were married and with babies - I had yet to meet one as young as my mother must have been.

I knew there were many questions about my birth, but grandmother never brought them up. When I asked her anything, she would brush my questions to one side.

I remember my grandfather. He was a short man, shorter than grandmother, very light in complexion with red freckles all over his face, and red hair. I remember his laugh. He loved to laugh, especially after a few Guinness stouts or rum and water. He played dominoes every Sunday evening with three of his best friends while grandmother went to Mass. I remember that he left to find work with three best friends. They were on their way to Panama, and the boat they were on got caught up in a storm and sank. None of them survived.

I missed my grandfather even though I do not remember him ever being very nice to me. But he was my grandmother's world, and he made her talk and laugh. I was five when he died. My grandmother became quiet then. She took to being by herself, and we only had one or two people stop by to check on us even though we lived on a street full of people.

I knew people called my grandmother strange. Her hair, her choice of colors for her clothes, her overgrown front yard, and her hodge-podge gardens in the back yard created whispers behind her back and questioning smiles to her face.

I heard from the children that the grown-ups on our street said she was not 'all there' because of the way she would sometimes walk past people whom she knew and pretend she did not see them. Her eyes would be focused straight ahead on something in her head, they said.

They still talked about the daughter who had left after having a child when she herself was a child, and me, the child she had, who looked so different from all the rest. They had as many questions to ask as I did, and, like me, were scared to ask. The people who knew us or about us talked and gossiped and gave us funny glances whenever we were out and about.

We arrived at Brother's house. It was a nice house - painted in a pretty, mustard yellow, with a yellow fence - and there were two big, black and brown dogs called Garnarshing and Timoline. Grandmother said he named them from a Jamaican story about a giant with seven heads and a poor 'yassie' skin boy who had to kill the giant and bring the seven tongues back to a king in order to get a pot of gold.

The front garden was full of brightly colored flowers, Birds-of-Paradise, Hibiscus and Bougainvillea, and various kinds of Crotons and Lilies. It smelled of wet dirt because he kept his flowers watered, even in very hot times. When water rationing was in place, Brother managed to find ways to water his plants.

With all the trees and bushes, it was shady and cool. Brother had the best garden for miles. The dogs barked and ran back and forth behind the gate. I was not afraid.

This was not my first trip to Brother. Over the years, we had been to see him for one reason or the other. Our visits began when grandfather was lost in the ocean and when my dreams first started.

'Is who dat?' The voice appeared before the woman did. She was Brother's wife, a tiny, tiny woman. Her hair was wrapped in a red, green, and gold scarf, and she wore a long dress in the same cloth. She had many beads around her neck and huge, dangly earrings. She was dark but not as dark as me. She was standing at the front door, and I knew she could see us quite well.

'Tess,' my grandmother called, 'is me an' me grand-dawtah, Regina. How you doin' dis mornin'? Look like you gettin' ready to go somewhere.'

'Hey, Ma Reynolds,' Tess said. She walked down the short path that led from the house to the gate. 'Hush, dawgs, go lie down somewhere, nuh.'

The dogs wandered off and lay down under the large almond tree which was in the center of the front yard.

'How you doin' dis mornin'? Brother was jus' sayin' dat he had a feelin' 'bout you. An' 'ere you are! Yes, mi on mi way to town center. But come on in. It appears Brother is expectin' you.'

We made our way into the house, and she invited us to take a seat on the settee with its plastic covering. Mary, their helper, was dusting when we entered and stopped to get us some cool water and two hand fans while we waited for Brother.

We wished Tess a safe journey to the town center where she was planning to look for cloth. She made dresses, shirts, skirts, trousers, and things for the house. She was always busy sewing and her reputation was high around the area. People called her Tess, the Seamstress, as if that were her good and proper name.

'Walk good, Tess,' grandmother said to her.

'Stay well, Ma Reynolds,' she answered, as she got her handbag from the top of a mahogany bureau and walked out the door.

Her dogs stirred and ran to the gate with her.

We waited a few moments. Then Mary came to tell us that Brother was in the back garden, and we should go out there.

The back garden was as beautiful as the front except, amidst the shady trees, there were plots of herbs, all kinds and varieties, separated by different colored little fences. That was how Brother kept track of what was what.

There were also more flowers and bushes. He had a big yard - just like we had - but his was organized whereas ours was a jumbled collection of plants, bushes, and trees. Grandmother had not got a clue about many of them.

When we came into the back yard, Brother was pruning plants that were in a plot surrounded by a little blue fence. Brother was a beautiful man. Everyone said it. He was not tall or big, but he was just right. He had wavy hair and big green eyes, a smooth cocoa brown complexion, perfect teeth, and he was strong and well-muscled.

Even though I was only a child, I could see why women forgot themselves whenever he was around. I would often hear them on our street talking about going to see him for this or that and, when they did, they dressed up for the visit.

'Welcome, welcome!' He looked up from his plants and smiled at us.

'Sweet, sweet, Brother!' grandmother said. 'So good to see you, as always!'

'Tek a seat, my Sister!' he replied, getting up and making his way out of the patch of plants.

My grandmother and I took a seat on a garden bench, and he joined us.

'You were 'eavy on mi mind today, Ma Reynolds,' Brother said.

'Mi was led to come here again, Brother, for your advice,' my grandmother responded.

'Yes, me can see de worry on your face. Is it, you, Gina, who is causin' so much concern to put a hand on you poor grandma? It been years now.'

I bent my head in shame and nodded as I whispered, 'Yes, sah.'

'It's the walking dream dis child be having, still. Not'ing you give us so far has worked. Now, she walkin' out de house an' dere is no tellin' where she is goin' to end up. Mi very scared for her safety an' well-bein'.'

'As you should be, Ma,' Brother said.

I was sitting in-between them on the bench under the shade of a Bombay Mango tree. Little flies buzzed; butterflies wearing different coats of color flitted from bush to flower.

A black cat strolled into the yard followed by two smoky kittens. She lay for a few minutes in the sun before deciding it was too hot and moved to a more shadowed area. Humming birds came and went. We were silent for a minute or so.

A slight breeze rustled through the greenery, and the sun cast sprinkly patterns on the ground as it made its way through the leaves of so many trees.

'Dere is somet'in' you know - dat only you alone know. Somet'in' dat you keep searchin' for, an' only you alone know where to find it. Somet'in' deep inside you. Mi going to lay hands on you right 'ere before God an' all His goodness. De time for you to know dis is now, an' dat is why you dream walkin'. De older you gettin', de more you 'ave de

247

need to figure it out. Once you fine de answer, it will bring you peace.'

Brother stood up and then, standing over me, he put his hands on my head and prayed long and quietly. My grandmother said 'Amen' in all the right places. I kept quiet waiting for the peace to descend on me and for me to be all right. I wanted to remember what I was dreaming about because then I could figure out where I was walking to and what I was trying to find.

When he finished, Brother went to his garden and came back with a bunch of different types of herbs. 'Boil a tea for de child before she go to bed tonight. It should help, but dere are no guarantees.'

My grandmother took the herbs, and we left Brother who returned to his garden. Mary led us out past the dogs and to the gate where we wished her well and began the long walk back to the house.

I was anxious about the night - afraid and yet wanting it to hurry up and come.

The rest of the day passed. We cleaned, and we dusted. We tried to make sense of our own gardens. We cooked, and we ate. We listened to the transistor radio, and then we began to make preparations for bed.

The weak light bulbs around the house were turned off one by one, and grandmother came to my room just as I settled into bed. She gave me a warm cup of dark, green tea - the product of Brother's herbs.

'Me let it cool down first, so you could drink it up fast,' she said. 'Me will come back aftah me brush me teet'.' She left the room.

The tea was warm, but I drank it down quickly and put the empty cup on my little bedside table. Grandmother came in and kissed my cheek.

'Sleep well, child,' she whispered from the door. She turned off the light as she left, and soon the whole house was in darkness. I could feel my body getting sleepy. I closed my eyes, and soon I was in another place and in another time.

There was music playing, a swaying-to kind of music, a 1950s jazzy style of rhythm. I was in a place where there were people drinking, dancing, and laughing. It was me, but yet again it was not me; I knew I was the correct age that I was when I was not in a dream.

When I reached up and touched my hair, it was long, silky, and hung down my back in a ponytail. I was wearing a party dress and, when I pressed my lips together, they felt sticky. I realized I was wearing lipstick.

A man's arms were around my waist, and he was saying things into my ear - warm things, and my body was pressed up to him tight, tight. When I looked up, I saw he was dark as night with big, wide eyes and a wide mouth. I saw that he looked like the me I knew I was.

We were walking down the street, this man and I, both smelling of alcohol. We laughed and danced in the street. The moon made the road shiny, and more stars than there were numbers filled the sky.

His name was Samuel, and he kept telling me over and over again that he loved me. He kissed me long and hard, and I felt a warmth I had never known before flood my soul. I was young, but I loved this man.

We were almost at grandmother's street. Samuel would leave me here, and I would walk the rest of the way by myself and crawl back through the back downstairs window before anyone realized I was gone.

There was a group of men standing at the corner - four of them. One of the men was my grandfather, but the other men were in shadows. I heard the anger in my grandfather's voice.

'Mi did tell you long, long time, to stay away from mi child. You put baby in her once an' you not goin' to do it again. Not no black tar man like you! Mi did tell both of you time an' time again! You bring disgrace pon dis family. People callin' mi daughter tramp an' whore. No daughter of mine will bear dem names. Mi rathah you dead! No more!'

I saw the shadows gather around us and close us in. I saw the moonlight glint off the machetes; I felt the numbness take over my side and then my neck; I felt myself falling to the ground; I heard Samuel's scream begin and end as blood filled his throat in a matter of seconds. But no one came to help us.

It was early, early morning time, a long ways from sunrise. It all happened so fast only the howling neighborhood dogs knew that something was not right. But they howled every night, so no one paid them any attention.

I awoke, and I was standing at the corner of grandmother's street. There was an open piece of land where there was once an old cemetery, no longer in use, scattered graves with broken down and weathered tombstones. It was overgrown with macca thorns and prickly bushes, and not even the goats bothered with it. People would often throw a dead dog or other dead animals to rot there. It always had the smell of rotting flesh. The neighborhood had long since become impartial to the odor that sometimes drifted on gentle breezes and shy winds.

I was dressed in my nightshift, and the moon was shining down on me, full and sad. I looked down the street towards our house, covered in the distance by the dark, and realized that grandmother was standing halfway between our house and where I stood.

I looked out across the darkened cemetery. They were in there somewhere - my mother and my father. I turned and walked towards my grandmother.

JUDY

It was 1924 when I arrived in New York City at the age of twenty-two. I was a timid, little Jamaican woman entering a new phase of my existence, but I had always had a fearless nature. As I searched the sea of faces along the harbor for Aunt Delores, my mind was ablaze with the possibilities lying ahead.

I had traveled with only one suitcase, a small one, but in it were all the possessions dear to me. It held a framed picture of my parents and my brother Charles when he was young, around seven, a handsome boy with an anxious expression, and me, a little girl of five with large white ribbons at the base of two short plaits on either side of my head, and a faraway gaze in my eyes. My parents exuded youth and were so full of life. They never possessed a stern atom in their nature and were known for their laughter and good spirits.

Perhaps it was the Lord's plan for them to die as they did - together. They could not have survived without each other. An old bus crammed with passengers tipped over a gully on its way back to Kingston. Mother and father were returning from a visit to relatives in St. Elizabeth. It had been a horrendous accident caused by a slippery, winding, country road, faulty mechanics, and the reckless speed of the driver.

In my suitcase, I had a nice suit, a deep blue and carefully folded between scented paper. My Aunt Toni (short for Antonia) had given the suit to me as a going away present, and I had kept the paper which had come in its stylish Harrod's box. She had bought it on one of her trips to England in her younger days.

'It seems I have gained a little weight, Judy, and it's a shame for such a beautiful outfit to languish in the armoire.' I had hugged her. It was a beautiful suit. 'I never had a chance or really an occasion to wear it. I know at this point,' (she patted her belly), 'I never will.'

Aunt Toni always had good taste and had even lived for some years in England with other relatives of our family. They were distant relatives to me. I had never met them since they had little to do with us. We were the product of a family who had come over to the newly emancipated Jamaica, some forty years after slavery ended, to start businesses. The family they left behind in England was particular about the family members with whom they remained in frequent correspondence. By the time I was born, most of our English relatives had become nothing more than vague names.

Aunt Toni was very light, but her husband was very dark. After she married him, she never went back to England because she could not take him with her - not because England would not allow him in the country but because she would be unable to have a proper relationship with her English family. They would never have accepted my Uncle's dark skin.

'I saw no need to go where there would be no family support, and where the focus would be on the color of my husband's skin rather than on who he is as a person and the man I love,' she explained, when I asked her why Uncle Frederick had never been to England. 'Why let family bias intrude on us when

253

my husband and I have a great life together? Judy, family is of the utmost importance, and I have always wanted to please them, but my loving Frederick is more important. He is my everything.'

My mother found herself in the same situation when she married my dark-skinned father a few years later. My brother came out very light brown, but I was dark like my father.

Mother's parents died when she was young and were buried in a Kingston cemetery. Grandfather died before my mother and Aunt Toni married, and Aunt Toni said, 'It's probably a good thing as I never had to fight with him over my choice of a husband.'

I often wondered if my mother, Charlotte, the sweet, gentle person she had been, had felt the same way. Their mother, Marcia, passed away when I was ten yemars old, but she lived a solitary life after her husband, Angus, died. When both her older daughters went against her wishes and married men she considered 'common', she stopped speaking to them.

I met her once. For some unknown reason, shortly before she died, she sent for me. I spent a day with her, and she showed me around their rather majestic family home in the hills overlooking Kingston.

She took me to grandfather's tomb and showed me pictures of various family members, all of whom were unknown to me and lived, or were living, in England.

'These are your family on the right side of the fence,' she informed me as we flipped through many, many, family albums. 'They come from a long line of highly respected English men and women. Your great-great-great Aunt Margaret was married to a Duke, so you have royal blood flowing through your veins. It's a pity about your complexion. Still, if your parents send you to the proper schools and you mingle in high society, there is hope you will become a success of sorts. You might even attract a good husband. The world is sadly changing. People of all levels of society seem to be intermingling more and more. There is some hope for you, my dear.'

We had delicate cucumber and watercress sandwiches for lunch, which left me as hungry as I had been before I ate them, accompanied by strong British tea, which I drank with a stolid expression. It was not to the taste of a ten year old who preferred hot cocoa tea.

I was returned home, courtesy of Oswald, her unsmiling, ancient (in my young eyes), white-haired, male servant, and deposited on my parents' doorstep.

A few days later, she sent for my brother Charles who had a similar experience, except he was told he would have a relatively easier time becoming part of high society than I ever would because he was not as dark as I was.

My mother told me not to mind her words, but whereas Charles bounced along happy in a future that was guaranteed because he was the correct shade of brown, I started to experience anxious thoughts about my position in the world around me. After my visit to my grandmother's, I began to pay attention to the make-up of my society and who were in the top layers and who were in the lower ones. Color dictated where a person fitted in and what a person could do.

The memory of this tiny, light-skinned woman, my grandmother, with her salt and pepper black hair, deep wrinkles around her mouth and corners of her eyes, and dry smile stayed with me for the rest of my life. She never sent for either of us again, and mother said she was surprised she had sent for us in the first place.

'My mother is a peculiar woman and an opinionated woman. She has seen you now in person and formed her own opinions. That's it. In her strange way, she has shown you a little bit of love. Darling, it will have to be enough for you because, knowing my mother, it will be all you get.'

My mother sighed, and we both agreed that I would have to love her from a distance. Grandmother Marcia died when I was a few months shy of my eleventh birthday.

The one room I was not allowed to enter on my visit to her house was the room which belonged, only a few short months before I was sent for, to my Aunt Delores.

Aunt Delores was a few years older than I was. After both her older sisters married against their mother's wishes, I had only seen her when she made quick, secretive meetings to see Aunt Toni and my mother. She was forbidden by Grandmother Marcia to have anything to do with her 'irresponsible' sisters, but she missed them. Whenever she could come to lower Kingston, she would stop by one or the other of her sisters' houses for an hour or so before going on to whatever errand she had to take care of for her mother.

Her driver was a young man, Morris, who was tall, handsome and the color of cool coffee with a hint of cream. He was very protective of her, and she told us he kept her visits a secret from grandmother. My mother would give her youngest sister and Morris knowing looks which Aunt Delores would ignore. Then one day, I was told that Aunt Delores had left, and I was not to ask questions.

I remember how in love my mother and father had been. He called her Charlie, and she called him Bertie (short for Robert). He brought her flowers every Friday, and she made his favorite meal of stewed salt beef with red beans and rice on Sundays. She told me once her parents would have called it 'slave food'.

It was a common sight to see my parents strolling along, hand in hand, whether by the harbor, through the parks, or downtown amongst Kingston's shop-lined streets.

When my parents were killed in 1917, I was fifteen. My relatives in England wrote to Aunt Toni: 'It's perfectly alright for Charles to come to England and go to school. Your Uncle Maynard states he seems to be a bright and well-mannered young man of obvious good breeding with a complexion that could easily be from one of the more olive-skinned European countries. We will say he has Italian blood.'

Charles would live with our mother's cousin, Edward Ivy, who owned, along with his wife, an enormous house in Enfield, Potter's Bar. The pictures Charles received and shared with me caused a little tinge of jealousy to stir in my chest, but I was happy for my brother.

He was a good boy and worked hard at everything he did. They were right. He was intellectual and when other boys had been outside playing 'boy games', he was constantly engaged in some advanced reading activity. Edward and Miranda Ivy had two daughters who had married and moved out to the Cambridgeshire countryside.

This house, they wrote in one of their letters to Charles, *seems to echo with a great deal of empty space now the girls have left. It would be wonderful to hear the sound of youthful conversation once more. We are absolutely positive you will be ever so happy living with us.*

My brother would be an ideal fit for them because he would be the son they never had - although more exotic looking than their real son could have been. I was not extended an invitation. I was not exotic. I was obviously black, and no one would be even remotely convinced that I had an iota of Italian blood in me.

In my suitcase was a pearl necklace and earring set which had belonged to my mother, and a silver pocket watch of my father's. I was keeping the watch for Charles who said he was too afraid to take it with him as he had the habit of losing any form of jewelry he was given. The watch was engraved with Papa's initials - RSB III (Robert Stanley Brownstone, III). It had been a gift from his father who had been one of the first, dark-skinned barristers in Kingston.

My father chose not to go into law. It would have meant leaving the island to go abroad to study. He worked for many years with a printing firm in central Kingston.

Shortly before their deaths, many of my father's friends had gone off to help England to fight in the war. Although the British West Indian Regiment was comprised of many brave men, my father was always of the opinion that the Caribbean militia went unrecognized.

He had a deep-seated fear of traveling. His brother, Samuel, did not, and readily signed up to fight for the honor of England.

'He never came back,' father said. 'I firmly belief his loss hastened the deaths of Mam and Pop. Many never came back, but Samuel was ours. When I thought about it later on, I never saw how any of them were shown appreciation. They died for a country where they were still seen as less than human. Perhaps I'm a coward, but I've got a young family to take care of.'

After my paternal grandparents passed away, my father decided he was going to move back to the country. He had inherited the family home with its acres of land in St. Elizabeth, a few miles from Savanna-La-Mar, and planned to extend the house and learn how to be a gentleman farmer. It was an area where he had been born and spent his younger years before moving to Kingston with his new wife, my mother.

'It's time to leave this rat race and go back to a simpler life,' he told her. 'It will be good for Charles and Judy to know the other side of their roots.'

The accident put an end to his dream and, after their death, Charles and I lived with Aunt Toni. She had a large house with a wrap-around verandah close to downtown Kingston, and the house staff was complete with two cooks, two servants, a gardener, and her own personal driver.

Her husband was a successful man who owned a construction company. He was one of the few black men to own a lucrative business in Kingston. But, in his dealings, he had won the respect of many people because he employed such credible and reliable skilled laborers. There was never a shortage of projects for him to undertake.

Aunt Toni's house was chockfull of intricate, Victorian furniture and paintings of the English countryside. She adored nature - her gardens were landscaped and luscious with intriguing and colorful tropical plants, bushes and fruit trees.

Aunt Toni wanted to send me to one of the finest boarding school for young ladies, The Hampton School in Malvern, St. Elizabeth, and she was willing to pay for it. She had no children and told me that Charles should not be the only one of her sister's children to be presented with such a golden opportunity.

'This way you keep your inheritance intact and untouched. Your parents stipulated I was to keep the money in a trust for you and Charles until such time as you both turned thirty. I imagine they wanted to make sure you were mature enough to handle the responsibility, and they wanted you to either go on to higher education or obtain employment. Right now, you have nothing to worry about. Frederick and I have discussed it, and we would like to take care of you as if you were our own.'

'But, Auntie, I have to earn my keep. I'm not interested in more schooling,' I insisted. 'There's no better teacher than real life. Papa would've had it no other way; he never raised either of us to be a burden to anyone.'

Eventually, Aunt Toni agreed and decided to do what she could to help me find employment, even though I was still quite young at only sixteen.

I went to work in a Mr. Jonas's barrister's office in Kingston. They needed a secretary, and Aunt Toni was a close friend of Mr. Jonas's wife.

I was not quite the right color, said Mr. Jonas, as gently as he could, and only secretaries with the lightest complexions were needed in the main office. The result would have been the same if I had wanted employment in any other establishment.

A dark-skinned teller or bank employee in general, for example, was unheard of in Jamaica during this time as were hotel clerks, receptionists and any other position which required the importance of "the first impression".

My desk was far in the back. The firm already had an executive legal secretary and an assistant legal secretary. I was, in effect, a secretary to a secretary.

In addition, and as part of my secretarial duties, I was required to clean the office and the toilets, and make sure there was always a fresh pot of coffee brewing, hot water for tea, and imported biscuits ready for the staff and clients.

Mr. Jonas - a Jamaican white who had traced his heritage back to significant land and slave owners - preferred to choose the fine gin, whiskey, and rum himself as these were reserved for his 'special' clients.

The two other lawyers in the firm were white and had come over from England, years before I started to work at the office.

The firm's specialty was Estate and Property Law. What I learned during the time I worked there helped Charles and me figure out what to with our land in St. Elizabeth.

Our decision was to sell all of the land, which we did, albeit with a great sense of loss because we knew how much it had meant to our parents. Charles said he doubted he would return to the island, and I wanted to leave one day as well. The money was for our future.

At the office, I grew used to being ordered about, to being looked through as if I were invisible, and to being talked down to in conversations. Sarah Watson, the executive legal secretary, was a light-skinned girl and Mrs. Jonas's youngest niece. She never failed to bring up this difference in our social status to my attention as she, too, placed herself in a superior position above me. She ordered me to run the office and, sometimes, personal errands. But I was happy for the salary which allowed me to save while still giving Aunt Toni and Uncle Frederick some money for my room and board (despite their protests).

I had been brought up to be frugal. Even though I would have money available to me from my trust once I was older, I wanted to save as much as I could from my current earnings. I was always planning for the future and was careful with my spending. Every now and again, I allowed myself a frivolous treat such as perfume, a new dress, or a pretty bracelet.

I had been working for a few years when I received a letter from Aunt Delores asking me if I would like to come to America where she had moved to after her sudden disappearance. Aunt Toni had known her sister's whereabouts but never mentioned it. I had asked once or twice, but she had only given me vague responses and then changed the topic. It was obvious to me, Aunt Delores was a sore subject. When I received her letter, I was elated. I had wanted to travel and here was an opportunity to live in America. Aunt Toni was far from happy.

'This is not what your parents would have wanted!' she protested. 'DeeDee is not well known for her sense of responsibility. She left our mother like a thief in the night without even thinking how her leaving would affect an aging woman's health. She was all our mother had left after father died and we married men she made no bones about disapproving. That was bad enough, but we were here, if she needed us.

'She may have stopped speaking to us because of our choices, but we were still here for our mother. DeeDee should have waited before leaving the way she did. She was little more than a child at fifteen but as stubborn as a mule at times. I have no idea how she thought mother was going to react to her leaving! You cannot go to America. I forbid it.'

We argued back and forth for weeks until Aunt Toni and Aunt Delores engaged in written communication, including urgent letters and a few wired telegrams. I was relentless while also being respectful.

'Auntie, you're going to have to trust me.' I knew Aunt Toni was looking out for my best interests, but I wanted to convince her I was no longer a child. 'I will always do the right thing. Father, mother, Frederick, and you have instilled this into my character. What is there for me to do here in Jamaica? I want to, at the very least, see a little of the world. You have been to England, and you have a fulfilling life. Give me your blessings to go and do the same! I promise you, I will return if I truly believe I will not succeed in my life. But I want to give it a chance!'

Although I could tell she was far from pleased with my wanting to leave, Aunt Toni did agree that perhaps America would provide me with more opportunities to advance myself than Jamaica.

The lawyers gave me a beautiful cashmere cardigan as a parting gift. I had been a loyal and dedicated employee for almost six years. The cardigan was like the suit, folded in-between fragrant tissue paper, although it had not come from as fine a store as Harrod's. It was very good quality and extremely soft to the touch.

Sarah Watson pressed a tiny bottle of French perfume in my hand on my very last day.

'Judy, we will truly miss you,' Mr. Jonas told me personally. 'You have been a bright star in this establishment, and I can only hope you will take your brilliant shine to places where it will be as appreciated as it was here. We have learned to really value you over the years, Judy.'

'Hear, hear!' rang out, as a round of cheers went up from the staff and glasses were raised in my honor. I felt a somewhat awkward pride in this acknowledgement since it came as such a surprise.

My suitcase contained my Bible, much read and much underlined, and the hymnal from Mount Sinai Church in which the Pastor had written a message of good wishes for me.

'Now, remember to keep the word of the Lord close at all times. And when there are times of sorrow, open this book, and God will lead you to a song. He will bring happiness back into your heart.'

Pastor Dalton called me up to the pulpit to receive the book as the whole church prayed for my safe going and coming. One day, everyone hoped, they would see me again.

It made my heart glad to see how much I would be missed. After all, I had run the Sunday school for all those years, and the children's choir was my personal triumph.

'We goin' miss you, Miss Judy,' they chorused, before bursting into a sweet rendition of ''Til we meet again'.

They were as perfectly pitched as angels and, for many years, they had been my children. An ache rose in my throat as I kissed each and every one of them and accepted their gifts of flowers, candy, and childish hand scrawled messages. These gifts were also in my suitcase. I swore I would never eat the candy.

I longed for a child of my own - a little girl to teach how to sing and how to praise the Lord. But first, I had to find a husband. I hoped New York would be the place where true love finally found me, and I would be as happy as my parents had been with each other before they went to glory.

I had a few new skirts and blouses, two pairs of sturdy shoes, a copy of *The Pilgrim's Progress* - which had been my mother's when she was a little girl and was inscribed *To Charlotte from Nana, June 1871* - a few petticoats and other items of lingerie. The suitcase was quite light.

Having survived my segregated quarters aboard *The Cabana*, a steamship which had stopped in Cuba before its final destination of New York Harbor, I was grateful the trip had been a short one. It had been nothing like the horror stories I had read in my brother's first letter home about his journey to England. Regardless of how he was perceived in our family, to the rest of the world he was still a Negro.

As our ship approached the promised-land, I stared eagerly at the Statue of Liberty on Ellis Island. My feelings of elation were so overwhelming, tears slipped from my eyes. I was leaving behind the land of my birth - a land of class distinction, color consciousness, sweaty heat and hurricanes.

I felt as if Lady Liberty's torch represented everything that would become right and honorable with my world. I would be more than the color of my skin.

Making my way off the ship and through the formalities of immigration, I was happy to see Aunt

Delores waving in my direction through the milling crowds of the newly arrived and the soon to depart. She was the spitting image of my mother.

It was a hot summer's day in New York City. I was happy to start a new adventure although the humid air caused me to perspire and feel as though I was back in Jamaica.

'Judy! Well, don't you look a treat! Can't believe the last time I saw you, you were just a little, bitty girl - how long has it been? Over twelve years now? You're all grown up!' Aunt Delores hustled me along, talking a mile a minute, hands gesturing, and laughter pouring out of her trim, elegant, well-dressed frame as frequently as the horns tooted and people shouted on the busy streets of New York City.

We sat in the back of different tramcars as we made our way from the harbor, and sometimes we had to walk when the cars were full. Eventually, we made it to Harlem.

Aunt Delores was close to me in age. It felt strange calling her Auntie. After a while, she said, 'You really should call me DeeDee! Everyone either says DeeDee or Ms. DeeDee or Ms. Ivy - depending on where they fall on the friendship or acquaintance scale. The really low end means I'm Ms. Ivy; the really high end means I'm just plain DeeDee because you're special in my world; and you, little niece, my little all grown up Judy, are very special in my world. Don't you agree it's a much better name? "Auntie" makes me sound like a spinster. Why I'm only five years older but, when you call me Auntie, it might as well be twenty.'

DeeDee told me, as we got closer to her apartment, how she had declined an offer to rent an apartment in one of the buildings Phillip A. Payton, a visionary businessman in real estate, had promised to fill with Negro tenants since nobody else wanted to move into them.

Over-enthusiastic real estate agents had swamped the area with buildings they had hoped would be filled by everyone except black folks. Turned out, no one could stop the influx of Negros moving into Harlem, so those 'other' people moved on out. In the end, the developers had no choice but to encourage black people to rent the apartments or risk them remaining empty and generating no money.

Aunt Delores informed me with great pride how she had put the sales representative in his place. 'I said to that beady-eyed agent when he came knocking on our door trying to promote his property, I said, "I do declare, it would be too many people of questionable character in my personal space. It seems you are trying to grab everybody and anybody to occupy your tenement buildings. I am very particular about my surroundings." I ignored the look he gave to my then accommodations. He had no idea where I had been in my life or where I wanted to be. As he walked away, I believe I clearly heard him call me a snobby something or other, but my ears could have been playing tricks on me!'

She laughed. 'Later on, Alberta told me someone she knew mentioned that the renovations had been completed on a house in central Harlem, and there was a possibility of three apartments ready to rent out. It sounded like a much more attractive idea than his by far. The good Lord above knew I had grown tired of a landlord you had to beg and chase to get any repairs done, and the apartment was so small, if you turned around in it, you would bump into your own self. Positively claustrophobic for what they were trying to charge me for rent! Scandalous!'

She continued talking without missing a beat as she put a coin into the tin cup of a rustic old man who looked as if he had not taken a bath in over a year.

'I feel living in a house, even if it's an apartment in a house, gives me a feeling of having a proper home. And we met with the landlord, a Mr. O'Leary, who had bought the house for rental purposes. He assured us he had the highest respect for Negros and would never allow our house to fall into disrepair. Alberta told me later he couldn't take his eyes off me. I never noticed, I was far too busy admiring my soon-to-be home.'

DeeDee rented the top floor apartment in a row house made up of three floors and said she felt sure she could tolerate her neighbors. The middle floor had already been rented to a couple. Alberta rented the bottom floor apartment.

'They may be crazy, but these are some of the most industrious people I've ever met, even if they all have their peculiarities. And the best part is they're salt of the earth people from the West Indies and the South. There are so many things I miss about Jamaica. It's good to be around good people from my island in the sun.' She sighed.

'Why don't you go back for a visit?' I asked her as we entered the apartment.

She pointed to a place for me to put my suitcase, tossed her hat onto a green chaise longue, then made her way into the tiny kitchen where she put a kettle on the stove.

'My parents are dead now; Charlotte is dead now. I really don't have much of a reason. Even though I know Toni's forgiven me for running off like I did, sometimes I think she's never forgiven me for hurting mother. I was, after all, the baby, and the worst part is that I could not afford to come home for mother's funeral.'

Before the tears could get in her way, she went on to describe the people who lived on the street.

DeeDee's street was composed of a colorful and eclectic collection of West Indian Negroes and American Negroes. We were the same in many ways and yet oceans and timelines apart.

Our one bedroom apartment was surprisingly big. The house, like all the others on our street, had once been a single family home belonging to a well-off Jewish family.

The ornate fixtures, large windows and high ceilings were still beautiful even though many of the other houses in our neighborhood had fallen into disrepair after the original owners made a gradual exodus over the years. Many of the houses had been divided into single rooms which were, in turn, rented out to more than three tenants a room.

The neighborhoods in Central Harlem had become over-run with black Southerners seeking a better life in the North, and West Indians who challenged anyone to call them 'Monkey Chasers'. All they were trying to do was achieve the American Dream of working and raising their families, without having to eke out a living and survive hand to mouth. Our street was better maintained than most, and many of the landlords were black.

Loud mouthed Priscilla had come over from Kingston a few years before I arrived, toting two boys with her. The boys were surprisingly well-behaved and soft-spoken, considering the loudness of their mother.

'Oonu bettah get you all back side back in de 'ouse before dem street light come on!' she yelled on a daily basis out of her top floor window which was directly across from our house.

The boys would break off from playing with the other boys in the street or rapidly remove themselves from stoops.

'Coming, Mama!' they shouted back as loud as they could as they made their way home.

Priscilla was one of the few Jamaicans I had ever known who had taken their children with them when they left the island. Most Jamaicans parents, when they decided to leave the island, left their children in the care of relatives in the hopes they could send for them at later dates. Priscilla's husband had died while they were making plans to emigrate as a family.

'You t'ink Ah even consider leavin' my babies wid my fathah an' his wife?' Priscilla told me when I became more comfortable with her.

She was a pretty brown woman with a deep dimple in her chin, large sad brown eyes, and a passion for satin head scarves and hoop earrings. 'No way on God's eart' - aftah me mothah pass, dat man married dat witch an' instead of bein' beat by jus' 'im, we chil'ren 'ad to deal wid her. Trus' me when Ah say, she nevah satisfy wid any switch we pick from bush or tree. She like to get de switch herself - a nice, green, young branch dat would slice into you skin an' leave welts an' marks dat took weeks to go away.' Her eyes became distant as she relived those harsh days.

'What about Calvin's side?' I wanted to know. 'Couldn't they help until you got settled and then send for the boys?'

'Calvin's parents were just too old to take de boys,' she explained. 'Dey is good hardworking people - still alive to dis day - live out dere in Ocho Rios. But no way me coulda leave my chil'ren behin' like dat - no way me coulda leave dem to de mercy of who-knows-what. T'ings hard fe true, but me keep my promise to Calvin when he dying. Me was able to get all of us 'ere. Bad minded people did kill my 'usband cause dem jealous 'cause we leavin' Kingston slum.'

Priscilla cleaned toilets all day in Grand Central Station. She walked the boys to a nearby cousin's house at four o'clock every morning. The cousin's wife would take care of them along with her own three children before she, in turn, walked them to a Catholic day school.

She picked them up again at eight o'clock, after a twelve hour shift. If the days were long enough, they would have an hour to play after dinner before she called for them.

She was determined that her boys would not grow up to be porters, chauffeurs, or servants in any form. They would be more than she was and more than any member of her family had ever been.

Everyone on the street looked out for Priscilla's boys.

The house they lived in was smaller than ours which was reflected in their apartment size. Priscilla would take in lodgers, but she had only one bedroom and would end up sleeping in the tiny living room with the boys.

Midway down our street in another smaller house lived Rina, her husband, Joe, and Joe's teenage brother, Troy. They were from Trinidad and their one and only child, Darkus, had been born in America. Rina was a tiny, dark, Indian woman with a high voice and long hair which she wore in a ponytail hanging down her back.

Joe was a dark man, over six feet tall, and broad like a boxer. He had a deep, heavy, booming voice and worked as a launderer in a local Chinese cleaners. Their constant fights often took to the streets, and Joe's clothes sometimes fluttered down from their second floor apartment, accompanied by the loud bass of Joe and high soprano of Rina engaged in a torrent of angry words.

Troy would go off on long walks whenever they were fighting. More often than not, he was too busy working at one odd job or the other, and he was rarely at the house.

Rina took in washing, ironing, sewing and watching children, to make ends meet, and cooking up a storm when we had street parties. She made the best West Indian pies and cakes for sale.

Tottie Harris ran the numbers on the sly and had a top floor apartment in the largest row of houses on the street. Her apartment was positively grand despite the constant flow of 'friends'. She was the only person on our street with a car, and she usually had a driver. Well, the driver was whoever was in debt to her. It was a way of paying back her money. She was a blossoming numbers queen.

'I don't expect her to be around forever,' DeeDee remarked. 'Business is good at Tottie's place. Soon she's going to be looking for someplace bigger and better than our little street.'

On paydays, there was often an increased flow in the river of people who came and left her house.

Tottie dressed in expensive clothes, fur shrugs, and costly coats; she smoked a cigarette from a long holder, and her conversations were always seasoned with French words. Her 'bienvenues', 'bon amies', 'bonjours', and 'au revoirs' would ring through her section of our street until the early mornings. Her hair was straightened, coiffed, and styled, and she claimed to be personally acquainted with one of the top beauticians in Manhattan, although I had personally seen her in Naomi's Hair Salon a few blocks from our street.

'Don't let her smooth, pretty voice fool you! She can turn ice-cold and deadly if you wrong her,' DeeDee warned me. 'She moved to Harlem from New Orleans, and nobody knows her real age; she could be thirty, she could be sixty; woman has old eyes just like she can read your mind, but her skin looks soft like caramel with not a wrinkle in sight. Men still go ga-ga over those curves of hers.'

Tottie carried herself like a queen and, in our neighborhood, she gained a great deal of respect. Tottie would always help you; you just had to make sure you always paid her back or there would be hell in the form of two strong Negroes appearing at your door with a bat.

The saddest man on our street was Trevor, a Bajan who loved his rum. He was an ordinary looking, brown-skinned man - the kind you would pass by without a second glance. He was short, skinny, with a dour expression and a scratchy personality. He was 'temporarily' sharing an apartment with two other West Indian men with whom he had nothing in common except drink and long hours working.

Trevor's great-grandfather had owned Trevor's great-grandmother and had long since returned to England when slavery ended. Trevor boasted he was related to aristocracy. People called him 'The Duke' behind his back and to his face. He was a dishwasher at the Hotel McAlpin, the largest, tallest classiest hotel I had ever seen, and he lived in the middle apartment in the house next to ours.

He liked to talk about his wife back in Barbados who was, he said, from a well-to-do Creole family who were influential people back on the island.

'My wife is a goddess,' he was heard to say. 'She is the best woman I know - clean, well-bred, and well brought up. You all know I don't deal in coal. Only the best complected women for me. I going send for her soon. You will see when she come; she will put all you Harlem women to shame.'

'But Trevor, how is a white woman going to live in Harlem? I don't think any of us Harlem women have much to worry about when it comes to her moving into the neighborhood!'

He never did send for her, and she never did come. She became a myth on the street. People said things like: 'So you're paying me back when Trevor wife come, is that what you're saying?' or 'So I guess I only have to wait until Trevor's wife comes for you to do/fix/get/give back/receive etc.?'

Whenever Trevor extolled his wife's beauty and fine attributes, someone was compelled to remark something along the lines of, 'Hmmm - woman need man. If you here, and she there, I wonder who else admiring all that beauty and refinement out there in the sunshine with that gloriously, sweet, white sandy beach and sky full of night stars. Romantic setting, Trevor, and where are you in that painting? Right here in Harlem.'

Upset, Trevor repeated the same response almost every time, and often you could see those nearby mouthing his words along with him as he indignantly and loudly retorted, 'My wife is a virtuous woman. Somet'in' you people don't understan'!'

He was a melancholy alcoholic and talked about his beautiful wife and beloved Barbados non-stop when he was drunk and to anyone else he met as he made his way to or from the local drinking establishment which in our neck of Harlem was called "Aunt Bessie's". Strangely, he never mentioned his wife's name. When pressed, he replied he did not want anyone to know her name in case they had an envious or bad-minded mind.

The only poor Jew I had ever met was Old Mr. Levine but his house was not sectioned into apartments. He lived alone at one end of the street.

'Now, Mr. Levine,' DeeDee said, 'from what we know of him, seems like he's been here since they built the street. Old Martha - you know, the lady we met down at the diner? - well, she said when she was younger, she was actually a maid for him when the wife was alive.'

'You don't say,' I replied.

'She says he's from Hungary and used to be some kind of art dealer back in his day. They were a peculiar couple; never spoke to each other; never had any children; and never seemed like they had any real joy in their lives. She said he was a tight-fisted man and the wife never left the house much and suffered from a bad case of the blues and was addicted to morphine. She had a nasty fall in that house, and the morphine was the only thing to help her with her back pains.' She paused.

'What happened to her?' I asked.

'No one knows for sure. She disappeared.' Her voice took on a mysterious tone. 'When he moved to Harlem, it was nothing like it is today, and both he and his wife were getting on in age. I guess they figured it was a good place to retire. He never has any visitors, and every few days you'll see him shuffling down to the grocery store, then shuffling back home with his brown bag of groceries.' DeeDee shook her head sadly. 'Growing old is a bitch, no matter what color you are!'

Occasionally, workmen would show up to hammer and unclog, as was appropriate. They would be at Mr. Levine's house for a brief time, and the house would relapse into its customary lifelessness.

'Good day, Mr. Levine,' was always met with a low grunt; 'Nice weather we're having, Mr. Levine!' was greeted by an upward glance at the heavens which reverted to the ground as he proceeded on his way to or from his house; 'Need help with your bags, Mr. Levine?' was ignored.

A small-framed and frail man, he walked with a severe stoop and had a partially bald head with a smattering of stark, white hair, so soft it ruffled in the slightest breeze. Rumors traversed the street. It was said there were thousands of dollars stashed away, under or in his mattress, as well as boxes of gold coins hidden in his basement, and the jewelry once owned by his wife was hidden in sugar and flour containers in his kitchen cabinets; it was also said he had either buried his wife in their small back yard or her corpse was seated in her favorite chair in his dark-windowed living room which overlooked the street.

The wife, rumor had it, stopped making public appearances many years before I arrived, and no one knew for sure when she had disappeared or what had happened to her. Some nights, he played somber songs loudly on his gramophone. Two rooms on the floor above the living room had two windows facing the street - one was always open, no matter how cold the weather, and the other was always unlit.

The despondent notes of grand symphonies mingled with the sounds of the street below, swirled around the laughter and conversations of our neighbors as they sat out on their front stoops, which clashed with the sounds of peppy jazz spilling out of the top floor apartment in a house, not too far from his, which had a blazing red door.

'Death music, nothing but the melodies of the dead,' was how people referred to Mr. Levine's musical taste. If the depressing, eerie notes floating out of his open window were examples of classical music, we all preferred to plug our ears.

Aunt Toni had loved to play classical music on the piano, but it was always something upbeat and happy. In Harlem, jazz or gospel ruled. Life was hard enough and music was required to lift the soul, not dampen it.

If we did not see Mr. Levine for a few days, or hear his music, we started to wonder if he had died and whether or not we should call the police. They never came into our neighborhood at any great speed when summoned. We figured we would have ample time to stroll out of his house before getting accused of killing the old man, even when it probably would have been apparent he had died of natural causes. Someone always said to give his absence another day. Sure enough, shortly thereafter, either the dolorous music would waft out his bedroom window or we would see him shuffling up or down the street on his way to or from the grocery store.

The house with the red door was two doors down from Mr. Levine's house. It was sectioned into three apartments - top, middle, and bottom. The top floor was rented by three brothers who were Negroes originally from Georgia.

'Those are three of the handsomest men I have ever seen!' I mentioned to DeeDee, as I struggled to control my admiration after meeting them all at the same time.

Instruments in hand, dressed in baggy, wide-legged zoot suits and rakishly tilted fedoras, they were on their way to "Aunt Bessie's" when they passed our house as we were sitting outside, daintily fanning ourselves.

'Well, listen to you! Just a short time ago, I couldn't pry your hands from the Holy Bible. My, my! Well, thank the Lord! One religious fanatic in my life is enough.'

I knew Aunt DeeDee was referring to her best friend, and staunch Christian, Alberta.

'I'm glad to see you've got some fire. The Lord never said there was anything wrong in looking at a fine man when you see one. It's more hypocritical to pretend he didn't get your juices flowing. Don't look so scandalized. You know I'm right.'

The brothers played the trombone, the clarinet and the saxophone, and they practised every day or every other day. And they were loud. The synchronized and syncopated layered blend of horns was such a part of life on our street, you found yourself opening up all the windows to hear them better, and wiggling just a little because the rhythm was so sweet you had to move just a little as you dusted, sewed, cooked, or read a book. They were more entertaining to us than listening to the radio.

All three worked at "Aunt Bessie's" which, in addition to being a bar and speakeasy at nights, was a restaurant in the day time and located in central Harlem. They served real soul food - Southern cooking - real people's food.

'Caleb Johnson plays the trombone and cooks; Carter and Clarence Johnson play sax and clarinet and wait tables. Whoowheeee! Those boys were born to jive, honey.' DeeDee slapped her knees as she rocked with laughter.

On the weekends, the Brothers Johnson performed for an energetic and enthusiastic audience who loved to jitter-bug, boogie-woogie, and jive on the dance floor. Before the dancing started, food was served until midnight, at which time the tables were rearranged to produce an area where patrons could gyrate and kick up their heels until the morning sun lightened up the sky.

DeeDee took me to "Aunt Bessie's" a few weeks after my arrival in New York, despite the cluck-clucking of her friend, Alberta, the devout Christian.

'In my home town in Mississippi, if the Lord didn't burn down a den of iniquity like "Bessie's", you had best believe the Klan would. In which case, it would be safe to say, the Klan was doing God's work!'

'Bite your tongue, Alberta Williams. I'm sure the Lord can find better help than the Klan. If not, you may want to reconsider who you call Lord of Lord and Host of Hosts.'

DeeDee flounced past her, sat on the dresser stool, and began plucking her eye-brows, looking cross-eyed into the mirror and contorting her mouth in concentration. Alberta said she was on her way to prayer service and would pray for us and especially for me.

'I thought you would be a good influence on DeeDee, but I see I'm too late. She's already corrupted you.' She gave me an accusing look.

I tried to restrain the smile by pulling down the corners of my mouth. I looked dutifully repentant. I liked Alberta.

'Have fun at Bible studies, Berta!' DeeDee murmured, now fully engaged in putting on makeup. 'We'll miss you! Toodleloo!'

'I won't put any money on that lie!' Alberta left the room, as she often did, morally offended. She would be back the next day, so neither of us was unduly concerned.

DeeDee loaned me one of her red, shimmery, betassled, party dresses for the night, and I donned Mama's pearls. I wore the cashmere cardigan, which I had been given as a parting gift, casually over my shoulders although I would have preferred the little mink stole DeeDee wore. She had already encouraged me to cut my hair into a bob which she had helped to smooth and hot comb for the night's outing.

We were escorted by DeeDee's male friend, Richard, and his friend, Earl, both of whom were porters. We danced the night away, and the Black Bottom dance quickly became a favorite of mine.

I knew that if my Aunt Toni ever saw DeeDee or me doing this dance, she would never have recovered from the affront to her sensitive sensitivities because Aunt Toni had never been to a dance in her life which did not involve waltzing and other such sedate dancing.

Women and men kicking up their heels, skirts twirling high, and lower body regions gyrating in joyous abandon would have appeared lewd and too close to devil worship. But it was all for laughs. We Charlestoned, Shimmied, Rumbaed, and Black Bottomed our way from late night to a sunrise morning.

282

I led such a sheltered life in Jamaica and had never attended any dances. I realized, out of necessity, that I had chosen to spend my time at church instead. DeeDee never went to church even though Alberta was constantly berating her about her heathen ways. Theirs was truly an odd friendship, yet they were fast friends. I liked to think of them as the show girl and the deaconess.

It amazed me how quickly I wanted to follow DeeDee's lifestyle although, until my arrival in New York, my life would have had more in common with Alberta. I reasoned that perhaps the demure girl and woman I used to be was merely due to the fact I knew nothing else.

In a matter of months after arriving in Harlem, I began to see changes in myself and in my personality; I discovered I liked a bit of a drink, men, and flashy clothes. I longed to make friends with Tottie, but she merely nodded at me while giving DeeDee inquiring looks.

I eventually put two and two together. DeeDee must have told Tottie I was still too green for her world. I didn't know whether to feel upset at being treated like a child or appreciative of the fact I had someone who was truly concerned about my well-being.

DeeDee was a strange one, highly strung and verbose; she could be a dancing cyclone at the clubs and speakeasies then lapse into quietness because she was praying for her sins or reading Zora Neale Hurston. I had never heard of Zora Neale. The Brontë sisters, yes, Shelley, yes, Thomas Hardy, yes, maybe even Claude McKay. I wondered why she didn't go to church with Alberta and get her repenting over and done with between the hours of eleven in the morning and two o'clock in the afternoon.

I don't think anyone back in Jamaica really knew the authentic DeeDee. DeeDee had been left out of her parents' Will. Aunt Toni would send her money sporadically, but there was tension between the sisters. If she sent nothing, DeeDee would never write to ask for a pound, no matter how badly off she was.

Before I arrived in Harlem, I had envisioned a woman who was as proper and demure as my other aunts. This was not the DeeDee I came to know and adore. Nonetheless, her quiet times annoyed me. I had discovered I was a bit of a chatterbox.

DeeDee's arch enemy was Sonia Hutchison. Sonia lived on the second floor of our house and had once had a husband. He had worked for Tottie but, when he stole money from her, he left town before Tottie's folks came looking for him. He was lucky. Sonia kept Tottie's people from finding him and doing him serious harm.

Sonia went to work at Tottie's apartment for a couple of months in order to pay back her husband's debt. She cleaned and waited on Tottie all night long every night for no pay before heading out to her real job as a cook in a local diner. She did it all, so he could come back one day without having a leg or arm broken or worse in retaliation for stealing from Tottie. Her husband never returned.

'The woman is a she devil! A thief and a liar!' Sonia had slept with DeeDee's man a couple of years before I came. They had never been real friends. They had tolerated each other. 'She's a bitter woman. Her man was a stupid man and what he did shamed her. But at least we were cordial to each other and, after he was gone, I tried to help her. Then the no good, lying, cheating dog of a man of mine had a big fight with me. Coming in when he wanted, going out when he wanted, and me staying here waiting on him. I had enough and that's when he told me he'd been getting busy with Sonia. Maybe if he would've been as busy trying to find and keep a job, he wouldn't have had all that free time on his hands. Sitting up here in my house, eating my food, lying around on my furniture. Do me wrong once, shame on you, do me wrong twice, shame on me, and you can bet there won't be a third chance or trust me somebody will get cut. The woman should have a red "H" for hussy etched into her forehead!'

DeeDee huffed into our apartment after we encountered Sonia in the stairwell one day, and there was an exchange of dagger-looks as they tried to pass without touching each other.

'What happened after he told you?' I inquired innocently.

'You don't see him here is what happened!' DeeDee exploded. I was a little taken aback by her reaction. 'I hit him over the head with a wine bottle; he tried to kill me; Tottie heard me screaming; next thing I know, two men the size of buildings bust down the door and pull him off me. I haven't seen him since.'

'Oh,' I said, realizing he wasn't a topic she liked to discuss. She did not mention his name. 'Tottie asked me if I wanted her to take care of the situation as in take care of Sonia,' she continued, 'but the witch is not worth my time of day or a black mark on my conscience. I have enough to ask God to forgive me for - hating her. Now, neither of us has a real man, so nobody won!'

'Little Judy,' DeeDee remarked one evening as we watched the street go by, 'life is not for the fearsome, only for the fearless. This America is not what you think. You are a black woman and slavery is alive and well and living in every state of America. It doesn't even need to wear a disguise. It doesn't even need those white hoods and gowns they like to wear so no one knows who they really are. It's ten million times worse than Jamaica. I used to think all the "better than you", "better bred than you" and "better shade of brown or beige than you" was bad, and I remember truly admiring my sisters for bucking tradition and marrying for love. I saw it as being so brave. But here you can lose your life on the turn of a dime just for saying the wrong thing, for walking on the wrong street in the wrong neighborhood, for being black.

'Here, the night riders still ride, even here in the North where we think we are so much more educated; where black folks think they found a way to escape all the hate,' she continued, her voice grey and heavy. 'Huh. I still can't get a job in one of those fine ass offices or Macy's or Lord & Taylor's. I can't say what I really feel unless I'm saying it around my own kind. I work as a maid in a high rise fancy apartment building for people who think they really do own me. I put up with shit on a daily basis. Sugar coated shit, straight in your face shit, it doesn't matter. Shit is shit, but it pays my bills, and

286

when I get home after the "yes ma'am-ing" and "no sir-ing", I put my feet up, swallow down some good wine and smoke my tobacco like a queen in my own little palace. That's why I hold my tongue and clean those toilets and mop those floors as if my life depended on their lemony smell and gleaming shine. It's why I don't knock the bitch out when she calls my name or when her husband makes his remarks about my high ass and big breasts, as if I were an animal, and then tries to fondle said breasts and ass in the hallway when she's not looking. I know I'd be lynched for sure for laying a hand on either of them but, God knows, I had to hold myself back from acting out how I really felt on many a trying day! Even if this isn't the South.'

I was horrified she would say these things. I had seen a man in Kingston beaten to a pulp by a group of white businessmen because a customer in one of their stores claimed he was 'fresh' with her.

She sighed and took a sip of her favorite wine. 'I don't need a man, Judy. I need to hold on to my self-respect. I'll leave Harlem, perhaps go back to Jamaica. More Europeans are coming to New York. Most of them are as poor as church mice, but they make more money than us blacks - may not be much more, but it's more. It's a slap in the face when this is our country!'

'This isn't your country, DeeDee... We're like those poor Europeans - immigrants,' I reminded her.

'We're not quite like them, Judy. No matter what you think, a poor white immigrant has rights far surpassing a rich Negro, hands down.'

'DeeDee, I could ask Aunt Toni to let me have my money now instead of when I turn thirty. It's

287

enough. We could even buy our own house somewhere in Harlem if we want to stay in the city or maybe somewhere else!' I volunteered.

'I'm already in the doghouse where Aunt Toni is concerned. You loaning me money would not go across well and I would never ask you to do such a thing, no matter how bad things get. If you need it for you, then you ask her. But I will never touch a cent of the money your poor mother and father left for you.' She ended the conversation by lighting up a cigarette and blowing a twirling flume of smoke out the window.

In our little pocket of Harlem, I knew I was more protected than DeeDee had been when she first came to America, on her own, at fifteen.

She came out of defiance to parents whom she felt were stifling her. She had stowed away on a ship to America with three other young girls and a young boy. Although they had all made it off the ship, she never knew what became of her traveling companions after they parted a few days later.

DeeDee slept on the streets until she was taken in by Bethel Baptist church where she met Alberta and her family. She moved in with them until she could fend for herself. Her past explained why Alberta was her best friend.

'She's a crazy, Bible hugging, Jesus-Forever-on-the-Cross Christian, but she loves me,' she told me, 'and I love her, regardless of all her habits and opinions and even when I come this close to hitting her over the head with her own Bible.'

Evenings would often find us observing the antics of the street. We shared the bedroom. I was glad our personalities were so much alike because the arrangement worked.

I quickly went from being a solitary human being to staying up late into the night, gossiping and giggling with DeeDee about events and people as they became a part of my story. She had never been married. In fact, she called men evil, and Harlem men were just plain devils. She was lucky. Most of the other renters lived in buildings which were not well taken care of, even though the rents were more or less paid on time.

Mr. O'Leary, who owned our building, was Irish. When he came round, I could tell he had a little 'sweet spot' for DeeDee. He was a big man with enormous hands, closely cropped red-hair, heavy freckles, a crooked smile, and large, thick lashed green eyes which softened the instant DeeDee came into view. He had a pleasant disposition and was always respectful.

When circumstances got tight, we would throw rent parties. Even though he specifically told his tenants 'no parties,' he would turn a blind eye to ours.

I wondered why DeeDee didn't take him up on his inviting looks and attempts at softening his gruff voice. He seemed a nice man. I fully understood the color issue. Blacks and whites weren't supposed to mix, but they did, although it was usually in secret. There were many Northerners with Southern frames of mind, who mentally wore white hoods and white gowns.

I saw life differently as I grew more accustomed to the American way. I knew DeeDee wanted a baby just as much as I did. I was surprised how I sounded like a blatant heathen when I mentioned this to her.

DeeDee laughed. 'How the good has been corrupted! Listen to my fresh-from-the island little niece!'

'Not so fresh,' I reminded her. 'I have been Harlemized for quite some time!'

'He's married, and I'm not desperate,' she responded, as she flipped too casually through pages of a volume of Langston Hughes's poetry. 'I get what I want now without giving him anything he wants. We've been doing the same dance since I moved in here. If he gets tired of it, I'll leave.'

She said this with confidence, but she knew I knew that moving house was not an easy accomplishment for Negros in New York. Color blind landlords were a myth; slightly color myopic landlords were a legend. We had a legend in Mr. O'Leary, but for how long, only the Lord knew for sure. Was a cute little red-haired baby such a bad thing? Neither of us had family or church to answer to if we really were to consider our options.

The rent party was the fifteenth one since my arrival. We had them at least three to four times a year when money was scarce. I worked sporadically, but DeeDee always made sure I never needed anything, despite my insistence I was not her responsibility.

I found part-time employment at a fruit and vegetable stand not too far from where we lived. I walked there and back.

'I'm an adult woman, and I need to find work. I just never imagined it would be so difficult. I can work as a maid like you, DeeDee. I don't know why you think I shouldn't be doing what you do!'

'Because I promised your Aunt Toni we would find you something in an office. You're young and more qualified than me. Mr. Jonas gave you a top-shelf commendation letter. You deserve better.'

She refused to listen to my opinions on the topic and swore she would send me back to Jamaica if I tried to find work behind her back without clearing it with her first. I promised her I would do exactly as she asked while, at the same time, my mind was scheming with ways to do just the opposite.

The previous parties had been huge successes. We had no trouble getting folks to come and drink bootleg liquor and feast on pulled pork, fried chicken, chitlins, greens, salads, and a variety of sweet cakes and pies. We charged an entrance fee and a fee for each plate of food and for every drink.

This party was no different. Neighbors cooked and brought dishes; bootleg alcohol poured from moonshine bottles as well as imported ones; everybody felt good; the music cascaded out of open windows as a soft summer night tried to slip in and cool the smoky heat.

Rent parties were a way of helping each other out. We had attended many on our street for others as well as the parties we had hosted since I arrived. At least twice a month, a party would be in full swing, and appreciative landlords, realizing it was for their benefit, would make sure we never got raided by the police who would, on occasion, drop by for food, liquor, and a little kick back from the proceeds.

Tottie always provided security. At times the combination of alcohol and a sensually charged atmosphere created altercations.

'Just in case, honey-child,' she cautioned in her voice of raspy silk, 'you never know when some fool is going to need the laying on of hands, if you catch my meaning.

Tottie also provided the alcohol.

'Damn those "dry" crusaders,' the rest of us said.

'Bless them!' Tottie would gush. 'Their dry asses making me rich.'

'You smilin' from ear to ear like a fat cat 'cause you rakin' in the change fist over glove, Tottie,' said Rina's husband, Joe. 'It costing me too much to be a bona fide alcoholic, which is my God-given right.'

Trevor, melancholy as always, nodded in agreement.

I think in my circle of acquaintances only Tottie, Tottie's "employees", and Alberta (as well as any other member of Bethel Baptist who did not sneak their own moonshine) were happy about Prohibition.

We had people come from blocks away. The music of Duke Ellington, Billie Holiday, Louis Armstrong, Hines, and Jelly Roll Morton blasted as loud as the scratchy gramophone would allow. Women and men, draped down and dressed as if they were going to the Cotton Club, crammed into our apartment and spilled over into the hallway.

Sonia yelled up a few times. After one of our guests threatened to come down and drag her up the stairs so she could join in the festivities, she left us alone. We never understood why she made a fuss. When she had her parties, we refrained from going, but we threw in what we could and someone put our money in the hat on our behalf.

'Just 'ornery, plain 'onery, old dusty-butt!' Dee would shake her head and Sonia would be forgotten.

On rent party night, our little street had a small assortment of old jalopies parked where they could be stationed without threat of damage, depending on the state of the car. Usually drivers stuffed as many passengers as they could into their cars because not everyone could afford the luxury of a motor vehicle.

At the party, there was even a little reefer and opium floating around. DeeDee never touched anything and neither did I, but I will admit we turned a blind eye to Tottie and the help in the form of the narcotics she provided.

I met Red Johnson the night of the rent party, and I fell in love in a matter of hours. No one knew for sure where Red lived. He was often present at these functions, and we had seen each other at "Aunt Bessie's" but had never spoken. He always had a bedazzled, hotsy-totsy girl on his arm and was one of the most popular men in the borough.

Even with DeeDee's coaching, I was a little on the shy side and no match for the flashy flapper girls who were drawn to Red and who seemed to be his preference.

Their smooth American accents intimidated me; I continued to speak a peculiar, clipped version of the Queen's English, ripe with a Jamaican intonation - at times I spoke a bit of patois, especially if I was speaking to another West Indian.

'Where have you been hiding, little gem?' Red stood in front of me in our small and crowded living room. He had gold caps on his teeth, his wavy, ebony hair was slicked back and lustrous with pomade.

My awkwardness bubbled to the surface. I longed for the ease with which I saw other single women flirt with the men in our apartment - some single, some not.

Red laughed. 'Baby, you're smoking-hot cute. Don't be afraid; I ain't gonna bite you. Just saying hello. Been seeing you over at "Aunt Bessie's". Wondered who you were. Someone said you were related to DeeDee. You know, DeeDee and I know each other real well.'

I raised an eyebrow in surprise. She never mentioned knowing Red Johnson.

'Oh, really?' I replied, in as cool a fashion as I could muster.

'Yessiree!'

Damn, I thought to myself, he has the most gorgeous smile of any man on this earth.

'DeeDee was sweet on one of my boys,' said Red. 'Gerald, Geri. He had to leave town unexpectedly a year ago. But that was some time after they had a major falling out. Turns out he had a habit of double crossing his friends. I introduced them when he was new in town - fresh up from Alabama - a real Bama till I took him under my wings and showed him how to be a man in the city. Fool thought he was too smart for his own good. Anyway, that's an old story. I heard he bought a farm somewhere out in Oklahoma.'

I acted as if I knew nothing. 'DeeDee keeps a great deal to herself.'

'Sometimes, it's the best way,' he responded, with dancing brown eyes which I found way too piercing, even in the fuzzy light of our apartment.

I looked away and took a sip of the rum punch I was holding.

'You *are* a fine looking woman,' he said. His eyes held mine. 'Very fine; the Bees Knees, girl, the Bees Knees.' He took a long sip of his rum punch.

He was not too much taller than I was, but he made me feel like a young girl. I found his proximity disconcerting and hurriedly made an excuse to go mingle. I could feel him watching me wherever I went in the room.

The party was coming to a close. As usual, thanks to our landlord and a street good at keeping lips tight, we had no trouble from any law officers - not even our friendly neighborhood "patrol" officers who only showed up if the smell of cash became overpowering. DeeDee had already put aside their cut, but we were both relieved when no one came.

In time, people started leaving in twos and threes, until only the stragglers were left, nibbling on the last of the food and guzzling the remains of any liquor. I went outside to sit on the stoop since our apartment had become extremely sticky and stuffy. I was tired of smelling my own sweat as well as the sweat of our partiers. The early summer morning air felt good against my skin.

'Night, night, Judy!'

'Great party, Judy!'

'Hope you and Ms. DeeDee made out well, Judy!'

I nodded, 'Glad you folks could make it. You know, times are hard, and po'folks need to stick together.' There was laughter as there always was when I put on the vernacular of a black American.

A voice from a few steps up said, 'Feel like taking an early morning saunter with me? Just a few minutes strolling under the stars 'cause I only want to say how much of a pleasure it has been to finally meet you.'

I turned my head. Red was standing at the top of the stoop.

'Naw,' I replied, 'what would people think?'

'That you're taking an early morning stroll with one of the finest Negros this side of the Mason-Dixon line!'

I laughed. He bounded down the steps and held out his hand to help me up.

'Come on, live on the wild side for a moment.'

I was thankful for the bright moon lighting up the street. Only one, flickering, spasmodic street light was working. The city had yet to send anyone around to fix the ones which had been deceased for as long as anyone could remember. This was central Harlem. We were grateful we had lights, even when they weren't working. They symbolized a form of recognition for us. There were streets in Harlem with no lights - working or not.

I took the hand he offered, thinking what harm could there be, and we began to walk. As we walked, I found myself telling him about the people on our street. I made him laugh with tales of Rina and Joe, Priscilla's boys and other neighborhood children, and Trevor's mythical wife.

I told him about Jamaica, my life there, and my parents. I felt a real connection with Red especially when he insisted we walk hand in hand. I sighed.

The night could not have been more perfect. We reached Mr. Levine's house, and I told Red what people said about the elderly man having piles of money hidden throughout his old house.

'You don't say.' He looked at the silent, dark house with interest. 'Has anyone seen this money?'

'Course not. You think that old Jewish man is going to trust any of us Negros in his house? He never speaks to us. We figure he's too old to move, has no one and nowhere to go to, and has no other choice but to stay put. Death will be the only way he'll be rid of us. Anyway, I don't think those stories are true; you know how street gossip can be. Mr. Levine is probably poorer than all of us put together, except he owns that house of his.'

'Yes, death...' Red clapped his hands together and stopped our walk in mid-stride. 'It's getting late or is it getting early? In any case, I best be heading home. I'll walk you back. See you again?'

I smiled, 'Of course, if you want to. You know where I live.'

We walked back to my stoop, making small talk. He waited until I opened the door and was about to step inside when he hurried off saying he better watch out for police, although we both knew the police were rare in our neck of Harlem.

I floated up to the apartment. I was blushing when I entered. He had kissed me passionately on the lips before striding off with his hands in his trouser pockets. It was my first kiss. My stomach ached, and I was convinced I was in love.

'Young lady!' DeeDee was sitting on the chaise longue, counting coins and bills. The apartment was a mess and smelled of stale tobacco, alcohol, and food. She caught my eye.

'Leave it till the morning. I was told you were out walking with Red. You be careful of him. He isn't all he seems. Be careful of storm buzzards, Judy, they're never up to good. But you're an adult. You'll have to decide for yourself. I know I had to.' She went back to counting the money. 'Think we did mighty fine tonight. Looks like we got enough for two months.'

'I *am* no longer a child, sweet DeeDee, as you've told me since I came here. Just believe, you don't have to fret over me. Glad we don't have to worry about rent for a couple of months. I still don't understand why the Rothsteins don't pay you when they go on holidays, especially when they are away for weeks at a time. You still have an apartment to take care of while they're gone. You're expected to show up there every day, whether they're away or not.' I walked over and kissed her cheek.

She continued to count her money but looked at me sideways.

'They claim the place doesn't get very dirty with no one there, so they cut my wages. Judy, you just watch out for yourself where Red is concerned. Some of us had to learn the hard way.'

'See you in the morning!' I felt a little lightheaded as I went into the bedroom, quickly tidied up, put on my nightdress, put DeeDee's warning words out of my mind, and snuggled under the warm, clean sheets of our bed with a hand on my lips as if trying to touch Red's kiss.

I had hoped he would come by on some pretense the following day. There was no sign of him. I did not think it was ladylike on my part to go looking for him. I also had no clue where he could possibly be, and I certainly did not want to draw anyone's attention to my infatuation. No matter how nonchalantly I tried to bring up the subject of Red, DeeDee kept repeating I needed to watch myself. I did not tell her Red had told me about Gerald, but I was interested in what she knew about Red. She was as tightlipped as a clam.

A week before our rent party, I had finally gotten a job as a nanny and was due to start in two weeks' time as the current nanny was going to have a baby.

I told DeeDee about the position a couple of days after the party. She was miles from being happy about it but, after arguing with me got her nowhere, she acquiesced and, with great reluctance, gave me her blessing. More than anything, I was looking forward to the weekend.

DeeDee grabbed me by the shoulders when she got home from work. 'Time to kick up our heels, Judy. Seems like a lifetime since we heard the Brothers Johnson and let our hair down a bit. We done well at the rent party. We deserve a night out to have a good time!'

I had hoped she would say exactly that, and I hoped I would bump into Red. I prayed he would be with his 'boys' and not with one of his usual made up, too-hot-to-trot, female companions.

Alberta popped up to say she was off to a lecture about Marcus Garvey who had been deported to Jamaica in 1925 because of fraud charges. He had recently toured a variety of countries speaking about repatriation and injustice, and a co-lecturer was traveling with him. She thought we might be interested because we were Jamaicans, and also because DeeDee and she had gone to see Garvey speak before his deportation.

I had heard about Marcus Garvey when I was living in Jamaica. His views were regarded as radical and almost blasphemous. He offended the Jamaicans in my circle who declared they were Jamaicans, not Africans. To my knowledge, except for the lower classes of Jamaican society, he was not very popular.

'I'll come with you next time,' I told Alberta.

What I could not tell her was I wanted to stay in and start planning which one of DeeDee's dresses would be the best to borrow for the weekend. I had to coordinate shoes and jewelry and find out who on the street would do my hair. My list grew longer the more I contemplated our night out.

DeeDee thought going to see a representative of Marcus Garvey was a brilliant idea. She had been impressed by him and had wanted to see him again. 'Work got in the way. Seemed like the minute that woman and her husband heard about Marcus Garvey, they needed me to stay later and later, especially on the weekends. I would be bone tired by the time I got home,' she told us in a voice tinged with exasperation. 'I knew it would be only a matter of time before the authorities put a stop to his black repatriation talk by any means they could. The press said he was pompous and a laughing stock. Jamaicans have disowned him. He went to England because it's the only place someone might not shoot him in the head.'

300

'I would've thought America might've done the opposite,' Alberta said. 'You know, since they brought us here, they've been trying to think of a way to get us to up and leave and take our black selves back to Africa. Garvey might be solving their problem if they give him half a chance.'

'Yes, I can see Rina, Trevor, and Priscilla going back to Africa.' DeeDee made us laugh as she walked across the room imitating Trevor's drunken teetering gait and then wagged her finger in our faces as Priscilla would do with her sons. 'Imagine the chaos. On second thoughts, maybe Sonia could join them, and I would be spared the sight of her forever. She might find her Zulu warrior and leave other women's men alone. I think I better go and listen to this man's thoughts on this whole repatriation mumbo jumbo I've been hearing so much about.'

It had been three full days since the party. Still no sign of Red.

I was awakened the next morning to loud voices coming from the street. DeeDee had left early for work, despite coming in late from the Marcus Garvey lecture. We had not had a chance to talk about her outing with Alberta and what she thought about Garvey and his ideas. There were handouts and pamphlets on the dresser. I would read them as soon as I figured out what the commotion was outside.

I leaned out of the window and Trevor, Rina, and Rina's husband, Joe, were in the street below, talking loudly. It was nine o'clock. I knew Trevor was on nights that month. He should have been asleep, not waking me up at this ungodly hour in the morning when everyone knew I liked to sleep in until at least ten! I was no longer working at the fruit and vegetable stand as I had been replaced by the owner's teenage son.

'What's going on?' I yelled down to them.

'Is Mr. Levine!' Rina yelled back up to me.

'What 'bout him?' I asked.

'No one see 'im since the day of de rent party. No music, no lights, no'ting. You see 'im at all?' Rina shouted

'Not in some days. I don't really pay much attention to his schedule. I'm sure he's fine.' I tried to reassure them.

Even though he avoided us, the street was always concerned about him. He was probably all right, but I realized I could not recall when I last heard his tearful music drifting out into the evening as it settled into darkness. It must have been a few days. Yes, I remembered, the night of the rent party. I had heard it faintly behind the strains of Louis Armstrong's trumpet before it was drowned out by Satchmo's "Potato Head Blues" and a bunch of drunks cheering along to the rhythm.

'What y'all thinking of doing?' My question fell on upturned faces which wore expressions of uncertainty. The police were not our friends. Mr. Levine was not really our friend. But he was a neighbor, and it would be the neighborly thing to do to find out if he needed any help. We all knew he was old and had no one. Whether he liked it or not, we were his unofficial family.

'I was talking to Priscilla yesterday about it,' Rina shouted up. 'She say we should check on 'im today while she at work. If he sick, she will see if he will accept 'elp from her. You know, he smile at 'er when he see 'er wid de boys. He never smile at de res' of us. So maybe he will accept 'elp from her, if he need it.'

'Listen, why don't you go knock while I get dressed. I'll be down soon.' I ran around and found something to put on and eased on a pair of slippers. I hoped Red would not pick this time to show up. I needed powder and lipstick. It was not the time to meet the man you had decided was the man of your dreams.

I had barely dragged on some clothes when I heard yelling outside the window. I hurried to it and leaned over. It was Trevor, and he was not looking well.

'Somet'ing's not right. The curtains are pulled shut tight, de back screen door close but de inside door open. We goin' inside. Rina and Joe waiting for me.'

My intuition told me this was not a good idea but, before I could say anything, he ran off in the direction of Mr. Levine's house.

'Oh, Lord,' I thought, 'I hope he didn't die in his sleep.' But why would the back door be open? I might not have known him well, but Mr. Levine was not the kind to leave doors open, whether he was there or not, and I had never known him to have visitors.

I was running down the steps of the stoop when Rina, Trevor, and Joe came running back. Rina was out of breath. The three of them dripping sweat.

'Lord Jesus!' Rina was saying over and over again.

I wondered who was watching the baby, until Sonia poked her head out of her window. I could hear the little girl crying from inside her apartment. 'Well, what you fine out?' she asked, telling the baby to hush-hush. 'Rina, your child is going to drive me insane. Hurry up with your detective work and come and get this baby. Whew! She needs changing!'

'Lord Jesus! Lord Jesus! He dead! He dead!'

It took me a few seconds before I understood Mr. Levine was, indeed, dead in his bed. I ran back to his house with Trevor and Joe while Rina went to call the police.

I had never been into the house. It was dark, old-man musty, full of ornate wood furniture and fussy, heavy drapes. An old piano was covered with dust, as was everything else.

A grandfather clock had stopped at some point in time; its hands were on four o'clock. It was now after ten in the morning, and it made no ticking sound. The house was worryingly quiet.

Mr. Levine and his late wife had preferred the darkest most disturbing hue of any color ever created by nature or man.

The hair rose on my arms and a shudder rippled down my spine. Any curiosity I had ever had about being inside Mr. Levine's house was more than satisfied at this point. I had to verify he was well and truly dead, and then we could all leave the creepy house as quick as I could move my slippered feet.

There was a smell in the house. I recognized it as the smell of death. I felt as if I were trespassing and, trying to avoid the creepy-crawly feeling running up and down my spine, I followed Trevor and Joe

304

There, on his bed with a pillow on his face, was Mr. Levine. He was obviously dead.

'Why does he have a pillow on his face?' I whispered, but it sounded so loud in the quiet, still room, the men jumped as if they had been touched by a spook.

They shook their heads, nervously.

'Let's get the hell out of here,' Trevor murmured, clearly frightened.

We turned to make our way, as quickly as possible, down the stairs. I had seen dead bodies before at funerals. Mr. Levine's posture looked peaceful, but the pillow obscured his face and none of us dared to move it. The police would be there soon enough.

There was a bedroom next to Mr. Levine's room. Why he did this, he could not later explain, but Trevor swung the creaky door wide open, and then let out a less than manly scream as he took a step or two back from the entrance to the room.

Sitting in a rocking chair was the skeleton of a woman dressed in dust-drenched black, with sparse, soft white hair clinging to her scalp. She was covered in spider webs. Her hollow eyes and skeletal mouth were embedded with eerie, wispy, grey-white spider threads. On her skeletal nose was a pair of grimy, wire-rimmed reading glasses. A dusty book was lying to one side of the chair as if it had fallen off her lap ... its pages yellowed with time. The chair was by the window, but she was facing the door as if someone had spun her around.

Lying sprawled on the floor with blood pooled around his head was Red. There was dried and congealed blood on the back of his head. From the blood on the sharp angular corner of the marble topped dressing table and the disheveled rug, he appeared to have tripped, fallen against it, hit his head, and then attempted to crawl to the door.

He was lying face down, a couple of feet from the room door. My unbelieving eyes scanned the room in a matter of seconds. The shock of seeing Red dead caused my knees to give way. Luckily, Joe caught me before I fell.

Trevor stood frozen. 'Holy Mother of God!' he uttered in disbelief and made the sign of the Cross.

I looked up at him as Joe raised me to my feet. His eyes flicked back and forth from the skeleton in the rocking chair to Red lying dead. We looked at each other, stunned. No words came out of our mouths until Joe broke our horrified trance.

'We gotta get outta 'ere!' he commanded Trevor, as he dragged me down the stairs. 'Three scared Negros and two dead Jews won't sit too well with de law! Not to mention the dead Negro lying where he ain't supposed to be! It don't matter who died when!'

Rina had called the police from a house a block away because no one on our street had a telephone except Tottie, and it was too early in the day for anyone in Tottie's house to be awake. No one answered the door when she knocked, so she took off to the next street where there was a phone box. She did not give her name when she called the police. We knew theirs would be a delayed sense of urgency. This was Harlem, after all. For once we were truly grateful we were low on the priority list for the police.

Joe and Rina holed up in their apartment, Trevor went to work, and I sat by the window looking out at the quiet street. Everyone had heard the story, and folks decided it was best to stay low.

Hours later, a police car took its time to ease along our street before stopping in front of Mr. Levine's house. I knew questions would be asked.

We had conferred, as a neighborhood. Our stories were solid and memorized before the inevitable questions materialized.

As I sat waiting for the knock on the door downstairs, I touched my lips, but the kiss had long since faded.

DANCERS

Seems like all we ever did was dance on the corner,
long, long, time ago.
Sweet bodies swaying in perfect time;
Steady beating of a rhythmic heartfelt drug-like
drum
(You later said it was the beating of our hearts);
We were young, and we could dance.
It was all about the music
flowing in our veins and making our hips swivel,
gyrate, curve, merge and blend as we sculpted
patterns with our bodies.
We were music.
The only place that we could go was the corner.
Didn't have to worry, and grown folks wouldn't
know.
Late night corners in hidden parts of our
neighborhood,
The music was all around in the night, and in the
way people whispered and touched;
in the way our hips would sway.
Man, oh, man...could we dance?
We had it then, boy, you and me.
Had all the right reasons, had all the right moves.
Cool smooth like chocolate ice cream.
We could dance outside convention;
we could dance like it was God's intention.
Dance circles 'round any care
Man, oh, man, we had it then.
And I wonder, wherever you are, boy, does the
music still move you?
Get you on your feet and make your body itch all
over with the rhythm and the beat.

Do you dance till the sweat flows down, makes you wringing wet?
Do you dance?
Do you dance when your body's pressed up tight against your woman?
Do you dance late at night in secret places hidden from sight?
Do you dance?
Do your hips still swivel, gyrate, and sculpt patterns into the night?
Do you dance out sorrow?
Do you dance for today and not care about tomorrow?
Do you dance to preserve your freedom?
Or has the music become so low, you no longer hear?
Has your mind grown so old you no longer dare ... to dance?
Like all we ever did back then
when we danced for life.

LIFE

I have worried with the wind.
She has taken my pride as if it were a leash
Strangling me, as she dragged me around the world.
She has gnashed and torn me into little pieces;
with her vengeance she destroyed the pathway to my
home.
I have cried with a hard rain that beat
Upon my dreams as I lay in a barren place.
The rain, my tears, washed the shredded
remnants of my soul into the soil.
I have taken root,
I have grown and blossomed.
I have laughed as the sun
Kissed me and made me whole.

Getting old was the most difficult thing Ezekiel Hodges had ever done. He could feel old age taking over his body, wedging into the marrow of his bones, creeping into his back, roughing his voice, corroding his eyesight and hearing.

He fought the thought of aging for many years, but one day he woke up to bones that creaked loudly as he struggled out of bed, feeling stiff and rigid. Thinking he was getting sick, he promptly took himself to see Dr. Andrews in town and ended up sitting in the waiting room sans appointment but in crisis.

Ezekiel was not used to feeling aches and pains in his sixty-five year old body. After a brief examination, Dr. Andrews said it was normal, quite natural, and laughingly told Ezekiel his body was catching up to its chronological number.

Ezekiel saw no humor in the matter. In his eyes, he was still youthful and virile. Since that day, some six years earlier, Ezekiel felt the aging process taking over like vines slowly creeping up the side of a building. He had always prided himself on being strong and considered himself a man whose prime had never left him. He had slid effortlessly through the decades doing his business as man about town and the perpetual lady's trophy.

He was handsome, fit, muscular and toned, straight as a ramrod, and a catch. He survived two wives not because of death but due to divorce after they got tired of the competition from younger women in town. Their loss, he always maintained. His grown children called him by his first name since he felt father, dad, papa, pops, and the like really did not suit him. His grandchildren called him 'Mister'.

Ezekiel dressed in whatever was the latest wear, wore whatever was the latest haircut, and used whatever was the latest street expression.

His friends were at least thirty years younger. After his last wife packed her bags and headed out the door, he only had eyes for young shapely calves and bellies free of any kind of jiggle. Yet, he deeply resented the term 'sugar daddy'. He would say that, in general, he was more like honey than sugar with his entourage of young girls.

Behind his back, the people of the town of Vineberg, just outside Brownstown on the island of Jamaica, wondered how Ezekiel would get his come-uppance. It was, they said, not a matter of when, as that was a given, it was simply a matter of how much and how soon.

Ezekiel was so busy being young that people thought he must look in the mirror and see himself as he had been forty years before and not as he was in the present.

One day, a new couple moved to Vineberg. The wife was a vision in the most fashionable of fashion and the most elegant of coiffures. She was close to twenty-five, a newly-wed, with perfect creamy olive skin, huge sparkling green eyes, and a laugh which made men turn their heads as if they had heard a siren.

Her husband was not much older - a strapping man with a Herculean build, a deep brown complexion, and a booming voice. He was involved

312

in a liquor business which he ran down by Kingston harbor, so word had it; although there was talk that he was involved in other more shady enterprises but nobody knew the definites.

He was often on the road, leaving his honey-complected beauty alone, and he was gone for long periods of time. Some said he was away at sea on pirate ships which was why he was so secretive about his business. Others said he was off dealing in the prostitution trade in Kingston. Some said he was security for rich white men who dibbled and dabbled in illegal gambling and the selling of stolen goods. Some said he was a hired assassin, a merchant murderer, who got rid of people for a high price.

Nobody knew for sure what he did. What they did know was that his pockets were deep and full, and he kept his wife well. They had no children.

Many drones would find a reason to buzz by the young wife of this intriguing couple's home which was on the outskirts of Vineberg. Her name was Charla. It was a nice, comfy cottage which they had bought from the heirs of an old woman upon her death. Charla had revived the dying flower beds around the cottage and, while her husband was away, she spent many hours tending to the flowers, accompanied by a little white dog of undetermined breeding called Tutu.

Her flower beds were a beautiful symphony of colors. Fragrant Heliconia, Lilies, Lavender, Ixora, Petrea, and night blooming Cereus surrounded the cottage, filling the air with their essence. Three large Eucalyptus trees graced her property, and a garden plot full of Black Mint added to the medley of sweet aromas.

Her husband had hired a young girl, Ella Mac, to help her with the less delicate aspects of housekeeping such as washing dishes, sweeping, making beds, and tending to their vegetable patch, so that Charla could concentrate on her flower gardens and her sewing. This indulgence was highly admired by some in Vineberg while others, especially other women, regarded it as frivolous.

When she was free, Charla dressed in her best and went shopping in the tiny town or visited a friend or two for tea. Her dresses were imported from England or made of cloth from France. They were bright and colorful and, to some, just plain uppity.

She had the airs and graces of a Jamaican debutant. Being a quadroon (possessing only a quarter of black blood), with fine looks and long jet-black hair, when she walked, she walked with the air of a gentle woman. The women of the town glanced at her sideways, while the men looked at her and sighed because even old hearts could thrill with desire tinged with jealousy and a longing for younger, more agile, days.

The moment Ezekiel's eyes alighted on Charla DesMoines, he felt a rumble in his chest. He bumped into her as she was coming out of Ruskin's Haberdashery on Lime Street.

'Oh, pardon me!' she twittered, as she, enveloped in a sweet jasmine scent, maneuvered her way around his bulk. For a few seconds, they did an awkward dance until they both found room to go around each another. Ruskin's entrance was crowded with merchandise.

'No, pardon *me*,' he said.

She carried a neatly tied brown paper package of cloth, which she had just bought, to make a new tablecloth with matching napkins and curtain, she told him as she floated out the store door, although he had not asked. Charla loved to sew.

That was the first time she had gone into town on her own. Since then, Ezekiel had seen her alone on numerous occasions but only rarely was she accompanied by her husband. She was always with her little dog and often with a white parasol, which added to her demure demeanor.

Most women did not pay attention to these finer details, thought Ezekiel, ignoring the fact that many women still slaved in the nearby cane fields, with or without husbands, or toiled till the late hours in other crop fields, or sweated as maids for the more well-to-do, or ran here and there after a slew of babies which they had to feed, tend to, and keep from death's threshold in infancy or early childhood - all the while trying to keep ramshackle houses in some semblance of order.

It was ninety years since the 1835 abolition of slavery in Jamaica but, for many, very little had changed.

At first, Ezekiel had deep respect for Charla's institution of marriage, but, as time went by, he noticed, as did everyone else, that her husband's absences were quite long - weeks at a time.

She was young and vibrant, wasp-waisted, and delicate - just the way he liked women - and she surely must have lonely nights, Ezekiel thought. There was only so much sewing and gardening one could do before the soul would yearn for more passionate pursuits.

Ezekiel was amongst the few blacks in town who had money. His was inherited from his grandfather, Samuel Hodges, a cane plantation owner with a penchant for the black female house servants who worked for him.

His father's wife, long deceased, had never had any children, and Mr. Samuel Hodges had never remarried. Ezekiel was a product of one of those liaisons. There were no other children born despite the fact that Hodges remained, until his death, a sprightly old man. Ezekiel was born when the old British gent was well into his eighties.

With no other heirs and no living relatives whom he cared to own, Ezekiel had been left Mr. Hodges' entire estate - well, what there was left of it after debts were collected and parcels of land sold to cover those debts. Still, he had a good ten acres and workers to call his own.

Vineberg had steadily become darker and darker in complexion. The old gentility was dying out and many were mixing as they openly intermarried with those who, less than a century before, had been slaves. Some families simply died out.

As time passed, the families which owned and worked the land were black. True, the amount of land they owned wasn't much at first. It mainly consisted of small parcels for personal cultivation and a place to build homes made of wood and mud-clay bricks. Yet, with each purchase, a sense of pride enveloped the town. Vineberg was, after all, mainly a few odd shops, shacks, land, more shacks and abandoned plantations, but it was fast becoming a predominantly black town, albeit an impoverished one.

On one particular occasion, Ezekiel paid Charla a visit. She was out tending to her prized flowers. Bulbs of yellow, red, purple, and orange brilliance flourished in the rich soil of her garden and waved in the subtle breezes of a Jamaican fall day. It was late in the afternoon.

'Afternoon, ma'am!' he greeted her, tipping his hat. He had worn his best dungarees and plaid shirt and was riding one of his prized mules, George V.

He had seen her straighten up the minute he clip-clopped up the road. Now, shielding her eyes as she looked up at him, even though she wore an enormous straw hat, she smiled and replied, 'Why, hello there. Ezekiel, is it? What brings you 'round my way?'

He smiled in return. 'Jus' thought me would come by to see how you an' your husband are settlin' in. Ah 'aven't seen you in town for a while.'

'Why, Mr. Ezekiel, are you keeping an eye on me?' Charla batted lashes the length of cane fields.

Tutu yapped at him. He decided in that moment that he did not care too much for this little ball of moving fluff.

They talked for a short time until Ella Mac emerged from the cottage. 'Miss Charla, me finish up de house, an' you dinner is ready an' waiting - so me t'ink me'll be off home now.' She gave Ezekiel a querying look.

'Well, Ella, I will see you in the morning then. You hurry on home to those little ones of yours. My husband should be home by the end of the month so you can get your pay.'

Whenever Ezekiel heard Charla speak, he was enthralled by her command of the English language. She spoke like a proper English woman. It was a delight to listen to a voice which lacked the coarseness of most Jamaican women who were bereft of refinement. He felt his manhood tremble with admiration.

Ella Mac nodded to them both. Having come out with everything she needed for her walk home, she wished them both a fine evening while leaving behind her lingering questions about Ezekiel's presence.

'I should be going in now,' Charla informed him.

'Well, Ah guess Ah will jus' have to let you,' Ezekiel responded in his best English.

Charla's high, angelic laugh made his skin tingle.

'Ah, Miss Charla!' he called after her, as she turned and bent to gather her gardening tools. 'Would you like to 'ave dinner with me some evening? Ah know how lonely it mus' get wit' your husban' away. Don't seem to me like the women in our lickle town have been at all courteous when it comes to takin' pretty ladies under them wings. But believe me when Ah say dat my offer is merely one of concern, an' Ah sincerely hope you don't t'ink it a breach of social manners.'

Charla straightened and removed her straw hat to give her hair a chance to breathe. She looked at him.

'What I do I tend to think is my business and mine alone, but I am sure tongues will wag if they were ever to hear talk of a married woman eating alone with a man who is not her husband, father,

318

brother, and so on. But that is for me to decide. Perhaps you should come again in a few days and extend the invitation one more time. In the meantime, I will give it some thought and give you a more defined answer at that time.'

Her words were like music to his ears. The voice of an intellectual woman who could read. He was not even perturbed that she had dismissed his presence. Gardening implements in hand, Charla sashayed to the veranda of the cottage where she deposited them and primly went inside.

Ezekiel watched her every movement and stood for a few minutes, long after she had closed the door. There was something about this woman which drew him like a bug to an oil lamp.

He got on George V and rode slowly down the dusty road.

The next time Ezekiel came to Charla's home, it was again late in the evening. In all honesty, he had real business to tend to, and her home just happened to be on the way there and back. He decided to stop on his way to Moses Hampton's farm where he planned to discuss the purchase of five of Hampton's prized cows. He wanted to add some new blood to his own herd.

Charla was not in her garden. He hitched his mule to the tree outside her gate and boldly went up to her front door. He gave it a hearty rap-a-tap and, before the last tap, it opened. He stood face to face with Ella Mac who was, once again, on her way home. The look she gave him spoke the unspoken, and her smile never made it past a slight curve in her bony, high-cheeked face.

'Oh.' She acknowledged his presence with cold surprise.

The temperature of a slow to cool country evening got a little cooler. Ella Mac was dressed in her strict, blue, gingham dress, starched severely. Her hair was held hostage in a bun so tight it made her eyes appear more slanted than they were naturally.

With her dark face shiny from her day of domestic duties, and her little traveling bag clutched grimly in her right hand, she stared at him without one iota of a proper greeting.

'Why, good afternoon, Miss Mac.' Ezekiel managed a tone of nonchalance, despite her icy stare. 'Is your mistress available to see a passer-by? Ah was on me way over to the Hamptons - t'ought Ah would see how Miss Charla is doin'.'

'Hu-huh.' Ella Mac looked at him with eyes slanted in disbelief. Her mouth had settled into a straight line.

At that moment, Charla came into view. 'Why, Ezekiel!' she chirped. 'What brings you this way again?'

'Hampton cattle. T'ought Ah would see how you is holdin' up since Ah heard in town you husban' still away.' He gave her one of his brightest smiles - the one where the dimples in his broad handsome face deepened and the twinkle appeared in his large brown eyes.

Decades of practising his debonair air in the mirror had led to a polished expression of gentility. He remained standing at the door since no one had invited him in.

He heard Ella hiss her teeth and ignored her. He wished she would hurry up and get on her way to that sad effigy of a man who hugged a bottle of rum tighter than he ever would his bony wife or his nappy headed daughter and son.

Ella wished Charla a good night and threw some parting words of farewell in Ezekiel's general direction as she brushed past him.

Charla wished her safe journeys, and then turned her attention to the man on her veranda. 'I imagine you're also here for an answer,' she said, smoothing her apron. She had been adding the finishing touches to her sweet potato pone and had just placed it in the wood stove to bake.

'Well, 'ave you? Given it much more t'ought, you know?' he asked.

'Mr. Ezekiel, I believe I see no harm in it,' she replied, 'but then it's what others will say and how they say it that will bring the harm. With all respect, I respectfully decline, although you are right, it gets lonely with no one but Ella and one or two others to talk to. The people of this town seem a bit slow to extend true warmth in my general direction. But my husband has a vile temper, and he's not always the most reasonable of men. I apologize if I gave the impression of a more positive outcome to your quest. I truly hope you didn't go out of your way to come by tonight and, if so, I apologize once again. Good night, Mr. Ezekiel, and good luck with those cattle.'

With that, he was left standing on the veranda, staring at a closed door. Deflated, he remounted George V and decided he was too disappointed to discuss cattle.

He turned around and went home to the comfort of a large bottle of whisky and the remains of the roasted goat from the previous night's dinner. Later, he went for a walk and took out his disappointment on the oldest daughter of a local widow who only required a few shillings to keep her mouth quiet. He decided that Charla DesMoines was an uppity bitch, and he had no use for her anyway. There were too many who were willing to come to his bed. He was not a man to beg.

The news of an affair between Miss Charla and Ezekiel snaked through the town, with little bits added as it made its way.

Ella Mac mentioned Ezekiel's visits to her mother, who mentioned it to her neighbor, Miss Lizbeth, who mentioned it to her daughter who lived in the town with her husband and children who, in turn, mentioned it to the owner of the haberdashery, while her husband mentioned it to some folks who came into his smithy shop.

Sizzling and smoking like gunpowder leading to a keg of dynamite, the whole town crackled with talk of Ezekiel and the dainty and lonely Charla.

Reginald DesMoines returned from his long trip, pumped and primed, with money to burn and the yearning to make up for his long absence. Charla loved to sew and adored beautiful cloth. He wanted to surprise her. He had just bought a car. The first one ever owned by an actual resident of Vineberg. It was being serviced in Brownstown, and he would ride there the next day to get it. He was excited.

He rode into town on a borrowed horse and tied it up at the horse troughs. It was a short walk to the haberdashery store. As he reached the entrance, he overheard a parcel of four women talking as they stood at the counter waiting for Sara, the owner, to bring back some merchandise she had stored in the back.

'Shame, me hear de husband's still not back an' de little hussy probably get tire of waitin' dis time. Me was wonderin' 'ow long she goin' to keep up de pretense of bein' de innocent wife,' one of them whispered loudly.`

'Hope, for her sake, he none the wiser,' said another.

'Ezekiel always 'ave an eye for dem young ones. Guess she jus' couldn't say no to de old goat's magic!' cackled yet another, laughing. 'Ah guess it get too quiet out dere at Miss Mae's old cottage. Not'ing but de creickets and owls at night. Scary for such a lady such as she.'

'You would t'ink she 'ad more class dough - her wit' her airs an' fancy clothes. Never gives us de time of day; always looking down her nose at de likes of us. Ella Mac says dey been seeing each other since de 'usband lef'. He been goin' by de house on de basis of one phoney reason or another. An' she a married woman! I guess when de cat ain't aroun', de rats go to town!'

'Well, you know how dey say some women jus' couldn't swat fly. Dem's de ones you hav' to watch out for - dose quiet ones who don't wanna mix - sometimes dey ain't got not'ing to say for a reason. Dey got secrets.'

At that moment, Sara came into view and caught sight of Reginald standing at the store door. She coughed loudly and the women, turning with smiles, caught sight of him, too.

Like four rabbits caught by a fox, their eyes widened. They hurriedly zipped lips and turned back to the counter as Sara came behind it, holding out a large box of assorted buttons over which the women began to make a loud fuss.

They turned their backs to Reginald, although it was way too late for them to act as if they did not see him. Secretly, each one of them hoped he had overheard their talk.

The town was often boring, and a little more drama would surely add to the entertainment, especially if it was at the expense of the uppity young miss and that condescending old man who was forever lamenting far too publicly what he saw as the rapidly diminishing air of class in the town.

Ezekiel often sounded as if he wished they would reinstitute slavery because he feared Vineberg was losing her colonial roots. He was an irritation to many of the townspeople who were even now struggling to figure out what it meant to be Jamaican.

Reginald stood still as the wheels turned rapidly in his head. He could feel rage rushing up from some lower primitive part of his body. He had never been a man to control his temper. Never been a man to put up with being the butt of a whole town's joke - especially not a run-down patch in the woods town such as Vineberg. He was Kingston born and bred, not a country bumpkin like these backward negras.

Without a word, he turned. Heavily, but slowly, he walked away from the store. He had cleaned and loaded the shotgun for a hunting trip he had planned for the next day. He was going to shoot a wild hog for Charla so she could have some real meat for a change. He would have to find out more about this Ezekiel and his wife.

The gun was strapped to his horse, ready and waiting to make someone talk.

CRY
and MAMA (An Essay)

I stood at my mother's grave-site and watched my brothers and sisters cry. I couldn't cry. I watched them, wondering why my well of tears was not bubbling to the surface and remembering I had not cried on that day when walking home from school, my Pastor, after passing me in his car, had reversed, pulled up, and said he was sorry for my loss. I remembered climbing, brain-numbed, into his car.

Mama died on a Monday morning while I was at school. No one had come to get me. I had gone through the day, blissfully ignorant. Sitting in Pastor Cameron's car, I received the news as if I had been told that Mama was still shopping at the market. I wasn't fazed when he told me they had already taken her to the morgue, stripped the bed sheets, and blessed her room.

'Your mother must have left plenty money,' my boyfriend said, mystified and upset by my pleasantness.

I wanted to walk the dogs that evening, although it was an unusual practice in Jamaica because it was viewed as pretentious and foreign. I had spent the first ten years of my life in England. At sixteen, I clung to certain British ways, regardless of the funny looks.

My mother loved dogs; she made special food for them, mixed with table scraps. I took them for an upbeat jaunt around the neighborhood. My best friend, Lisa, and my boyfriend, Huntley, trailed behind me.

326

'You know,' I said, making conversation with the night, 'we were reading from *The Merchant of Venice,* and it was so funny. Michael was trying to read as if he was from Shakespeare's day and...'

Huntley grabbed my shoulder; he spun me around. 'What is wrong with you? Your mother just died, and you're talking about stupid school and playing with dogs!'

'Leave her,' Lisa said. 'Let her go on. Give her time.'

'But she hasn't shed one teardrop!' Huntley shouted. 'I never knew she had no feelings!'

He turned and, shaking his head, refused to continue our walk. He strode back to my house. I stood looking at the ground. Then, I merrily clapped my hands together. I began walking again. Lisa walked wordlessly beside me as the dogs yapped on ahead.

I stood at the grave-site of my mother thinking how she had changed from a plump, healthy, independent woman with long, strong hair and glowing, olive skin. My beautiful mother was naturally happy. The world rose with her smiles. The cancer had taken all of this away as it ravaged her essence, stripped her of her joy, stifled her spirit, dulled her skin, and withered her to a shadow with pain-stricken eyes and deep-valleyed cheeks.

But, in her coffin, she seemed to have aged backwards. She looked angelic and peaceful. Death held her in a gentle embrace. Some days before she died, I heard her humming "Nearer My God to Thee" as it played on the record player. It was her favorite hymn. I found solace in the fact that she suffered no longer. But I could not cry.

I went back to school the day after the funeral, just as I had gone back to school the day after she passed; school was my sane haven. My foreign siblings, who had taken over the planning of the funeral, eventually left with their plethora of Mama-mementos, tossing remarks about my emotionless state before their departure.

I was alone in the emptiness of a motherless house while my living arrangements were decided. No mother shouted my name to wake me up, to tell me off, to tell me dinner was ready, or to ask me how my day at school had been. There were no more off-key Mama-renditions of Jim Reeves and Elvis. The house had lost its voice. None of us ate much. My remaining brother hid in his own grief; the dogs moped. We were silent and lost. No tears came, only wide-awake nights, a rueing of every wrong I could no longer right, and a sense of dying inside.

'You are wicked,' my neighbor, Mrs. Johnson, said, 'not to mourn your own mother. I haven't seen any eye-water drop from your eye. Shameful!'

I wanted to explain, but the nebulous explanations could not get past the constricting lump in my throat. I was adrift in a tragic black and white movie, struck color-blind and deaf. I found myself reading lips.

Months passed. I was living with Sheila, my guardian. She was patient and understanding. I was guardedly jovial. I participated in the school play, the Glee Club, the French class trips, and studied for the upcoming 'O' level exams. I bypassed the concern of others with a ready smile. I was sent to speak to the principal and told him I was just fine.

One morning, rain sprinkled against the bus window as I made the two-and-a-half hour journey from Sheila's house by the sea to my high school in Spanish Town.

The fresh day was tinged with diamond-like greyness. The skies swirled with black clouds and the bus was crowded with the usual eclectic assortment of morning travelers. Heavy-hearted raindrops beat rhythmically against the bus windows as we passed lush fields being passionately kissed by the downpour. Emerald green mountains loomed in the distance.

I thought about my mother and our last trip to where she had grown up, met, and married my long-since deceased father whose voice was now lost to me. We had gone to those Trelawny mountains on a day such as this. I remembered how she had been so alive that day. I longed to never forget the sound of her. I wanted to hold on to her voice.

The rain beat harder against the bus windows and played music on the roof. I heard Mama calling my name, and I began to cry.

MAMA
An Essay

My Mama, Maureen Angelica Palmer, née Waverly, was born in 1913 in a place which no longer exists called Mahogany Grove, situated somewhere in the parish of Manchester on the South side of Jamaica.

Her mother was Agnes McLean, a lone woman from India who, in the late 1800s, eventually found her way around the world to Jamaica in a time when Indian women were not very independent or lone travelers.

Towards the end of the 1800s and beginning of the 1900s, many Indians sought ways to escape their condition of extreme poverty and abuse and had, before, during, and for a time after my grandma's youthful days, been offered the limited opportunity to work as indentured servants on plantations in Panama and other parts of Central America and the Caribbean.

They were little better than the African slaves who, newly freed, had proven difficult to control by the British who had occupied the island since 1655, when the Spanish were unceremoniously ejected as conquerors and rulers of Jamaica.

The indentured servants were, indeed, slaves themselves, based on their ill-treatment, their deplorable living conditions and the cruelty which was imposed on them in terms of labor.

No one knows if Mima (her pet name) came by herself or with her parents or siblings but, somehow, she ended up in Panama. Nothing is known of her time there; Mama never spoke of it.

What is known is that, probably, during a mass conversion to Christianity when the newly converted gave up their heathen ways and names, my grandma denounced her possibly Hindu roots and adopted the name Agnes McLean. Apparently, it was common practice for entire members of congregations to take on the pastor's or priest's name. Her true name has never been recovered.

My grandma became a Catholic, which was the predominant religious denomination in Panama and still is, to my knowledge.

My grandmama was dark-skinned and, from what my Mama told me, a very pretty woman, which explains how she might have attracted the attention of my grandfather, Edward Waverly.

Grand-daddy's family had immigrated to Jamaica from Cuba, and his father was British (hence the name Waverly, which we have been able to trace to a Cuban family from Santiago, Cuba). His mother was a Cuban creole. They were high yellow, as we say today - or red-boned - light, bright, damn near white kind of folks.

It is a mystery how the two met but meet they did, to the utter and horrified dismay and distress of my great-grandparents who could not believe their son would marry this black 'coolie' woman. Oh, the disgrace!!

My Mama said that if the Waverlys were walking down any street in Mahogany Grove, and her siblings and she were walking on the same street, the Waverlys would cross the street so they would not have to speak to them or pass on the same side. My grandpa was disowned and disinherited, and his marriage was never acknowledged.

The Waverlys were prejudiced and color conscious - products of an age when black skin was synonymous with every negative human characteristic.

In the early to mid-twenties, when Mama was still quite young, her parents moved to Worsop, Trelawny, high up in the mountains, and acquired a few acres of land. The rest of the story, the jigsaw, is based on bedtime and dinner time stories which Mama told me.

My grandparents were deeply committed to their Catholic faith (hence the picture of the Madonna which used to hang over my Mama's bed. The picture was subsequently secreted away by one of my older sisters, when Mama was dying, and now graces her bedroom wall - much to my distress).

Edward and Agnes had my Mama (born 1913) and sons, Silas and Ivan, who, in turn, were followed by the ill-fated Vincent. When Vincent was only five, he became very ill and passed away. His demise was attributed to obeah. My Mama was devastated. He had been her heart and her favorite brother and, in fact, she was more like his mother than his sister. She never got over his death. Even when she had me (the last of her fourteen children), she would cry whenever she talked about him.

She always said, 'He was too pretty to live.'

My Mama's youngest brother was Rudolph (Ruddy) Robinson (named, perhaps, after Rudolph Valentino), the product of my maternal grandmother's remarriage.

When she was a young girl, Mama went to the little, broken-down, school house in Worsop. She told me stories about dancing the Charleston in secret with her friends on the red dirt, silver-misted and, at times, rain drenched roads of Worsop, as she made her way home from school.

Where she got to know these dances is a mystery, unless she learned them on infrequent trips to movie houses in rural big cities such as Christiana or Brownstown. She stopped going to school when she was around fourteen so she could be a full time help in the fields, and with the boys.

She was full of stories about country life, ghosts (duppies), strange happenings, crazy weather and unusual people. The tales she told were addictive, when I was young, but when I turned thirteen - with hormones and attitude raging - I didn't have time for them. Funny, right? There were probably volumes of short stories right at my fingertips.

She was alive when everything major was happening in the 1900s - world wars, revolutions, the gramophone, television, telephones, wireless radio, the Blimp, the Zeppelin, glamorous movie stars, the Titanic, Marcus Garvey, great writers, influential religious leaders, the Suffragettes, and so on and so forth. My Mama was a walking history book, and nothing is more boring to a teenager than 'all that old stuff.'

When she was around thirteen years old, my Mama really got to know my father. Worsop isn't big although it was once a thriving, vibrant, farming mountain village during its heyday. He was, by her account, the prefect at her school, and they did not get along at first.

In fact, Mama caught the attention of other male admirers in the village and, by the time she was sixteen, she really wasn't paying my Daddy much attention.

He was her senior by five years. Daddy would have been getting ready to leave school, while she was still in lower classes. Somehow, my charming, handsome Daddy won Mama's heart.

My Daddy was half German (his Mom) and half black (his Daddy) but that is a whole other story in itself.

The Palmers owned many acres of land in Worsop, and these acres had been bequeathed to Daddy's Daddy's father, back to sometime in the late 1800s. It would only be logical to assume our family name came from the Palmers, who had owned our fore-fathers as slaves. The English Palmers either amalgamated with the local population or went back to England, or both.

My Mama and my Daddy had their first child out of wedlock when she was twenty (I found this out by matching birthdates and their marriage certificate). This was my eldest brother, Victor, born 6th October 1933. My parents married on 25th April 1934, and she proceeded to have a baby every year or every two years, depending on how low the mists hung over Worsop.

Papa was often gone to market in Brownstown for days or weeks, so I guess they had a great deal of making up to do when he returned to the farm. I have sets of siblings who might as well be twins because they were born only nine months apart.

Somewhere along the line, my father discovered the Seventh Day Adventist Church and became one of its most ardent advocators. They gave up pork and other unacceptable food (according to Leviticus 11 and the tenets of Ellen G White, the Adventist prophetess) and began a strict observance of the rules of the church, much to the amusement of my Daddy's relatives, parents, and siblings who all lived in that section of Worsop.

My Daddy's share of the property was directly across the road from his sister, Zara Belle, my Aunt Zar, whose name eventually metamorphosed into Anzar. Her husband, Harold, who, no questions asked, also had the last name Palmer but came from another part of the island and was not (hopefully) related to my aunt except (hopefully) as a very, very, very distant cousin.

Anzar and my Mama were extremely close. She was also close with my Daddy's youngest sister, Darkus, who was deaf and mute. My father's younger sisters, Patsy and Inez, lived along the road leading from our property. My Daddy was the only male child who survived for his parents.

The land was lush and green with rolling fields. On our property, we had a hill with an amazing view and a bubbling, happy, little stream which provided fresh water.

My Mama helped her mother in her fields while her own children and my Daddy took care of their homestead and the livestock. From Mama, I learned to love dogs. I knew the names and the stories of her favorite dogs back then, Rover and Dover.

Once, when her four oldest children were still babies and toddlers, Mama went to the fields to meet up with her mother and found her unconscious. She had had a stroke. Mama was with her then, managed to say her goodbyes when my grandma was cognizant, and held her when she took her last breath in their old family home. There were no doctors close at hand - just local healers who came to help as best they could.

Ivan moved to the UK, Silas to America, and Ruddy to Kingston. My Mama never recovered from her mother's death. Every time I had a rude mouth on me, days when Mama said I was 'smelling myself', she would remind me that one day I was going to miss her and the worst part would be I would not have been the good daughter she had been.

She always talked about her mother with such love and reverence I truly wished - even at my worst - I could have known Mima. The name 'Mima', I have since found out, is the Spanish pet name for mothers/grandmothers. It is a term of affection. So, I imagine Edward, with his Cuban background, called her Mima, and the name is now entrenched in the history of our family.

I never knew whether Mama got along with my Daddy's mother, the German woman, Mari. I do know she always said I was just like her - contentious - but she would also tell me I was like my Daddy - a dreamer. She would say both things with love. So, Mari couldn't have been all bad.

In the early 1950s, with more and more Jamaicans moving to the Motherland (the UK, not Africa), Mama made a scouting trip to find out what it was like. She went by ship. She liked it, came back and, since farm life was becoming rough and not as profitable, my parents agreed to move to the UK.

By 1952, Mama had birthed thirteen children - eight boys and five girls. One or two were in college, some working, one or two involved in petty crime, a couple had already left for the UK, while others had moved to Kingston.

Aaron and Clara were still quite young. Aaron, unbeknownst to my mom, was autistic. She knew *something* was wrong with him - he was a difficult and needy child who would often sit and rock back and forth and cry unceasingly. He was also exceptionally bright, especially when it came to mathematics and art, and had an outstanding command of the English language, which was demonstrated in his writing skills.

My Mama and Daddy took him with them when they left the island in the mid-1950s for the UK, and left Clara with relatives until they could get settled and send for her. I do not think Clara ever got over being left behind.

My parents suffered through the crises and humiliations of trying to find accommodation in a London where immigrants were not accepted with open arms. The treatment of West Indians after masses of them emigrated to the UK is a favorite subject for a lot of West Indian writers.

When WWII was in full force, many West Indians fought in the war, but they were never expected to settle in the UK. When they did, and as others came in search of work, many of the English public were not happy with the influx of 'coloreds'.

Mama told me about the indignities of signs that said upfront 'coloreds need not apply' for rooms available to let; the shock of having doors slammed in their faces when there were no signs, just incredulous or angry faces to greet them; and the insincere politeness emanating from property owners as they were told vacancy signs in living room windows should have been removed because the room, flat, cellar had been let out thirty seconds before they arrived to inquire.

At first my Mama loved England, but then the greyness, the rainy, gloomy long wintered damp weather, the endless hours of work while still trying to take care of Aaron, the chill surrounding British people as if to protect them against people of color, and British life in general, got to her. She began to hate the place.

My Daddy, on the other hand, despite being beaten up on a constant basis by white street gangs who thought he was Pakistani or some hybrid of sorts, was proud to be British. He loved England with a passion. The rain never bothered him. He was deeply religious, and quickly became a high standing deacon in a predominantly white Seventh Day Adventist Church.

In spite of his poor education, my Daddy was an avid reader. Years later, I would find classics such as *How Green Was My Valley* and *Far From the Madding Crowd*, various books of poetry by renowned English writers as well as a first edition of *The Philosophy and Opinions of Marcus Garvey* in the old house in Worsop.

He wrote poetry about being a black man. Like many Jamaicans, he struggled with the dichotomy of belonging to two worlds - being black and British. He was a highly intelligent man, and I am sure he wrote more than poetry, but if he did, it has been long lost. I am positive his mind echoed with all of the wrongs he started to see in a society he had always been brought up to believe was so incredibly right and the essence of civility.

When she became pregnant with me at forty-nine in 1960, Mama said she wanted me to be born in Jamaica. They went back and had me on April 27th, 1961.

I was the only child born in Ulster Spring Hospital. All my other siblings had been brought into this world by the village midwife, Kubba. I often wish I could say I had been as well. How amazing she must have been to have assisted in the births of many, many children throughout the village for many decades. She carried on a tradition passed down to her from her ancestors and fore-mothers.

My parents returned to the UK when I was an early toddler. Once they got settled again and bought a house in Stratford, East London, they sent for any remaining children.

There is so much to this story and to life in the UK. Mama worked in a peanut oil factory where she consistently got her hands burnt. Later, as a seamstress in a garment factory, she accidentally sewed across a few fingers and had to make an emergency visit to the hospital. She eventually developed a better understanding of industrial sewing machines.

When I was four, my Daddy died of anthrax which he contracted in the factory where he worked. The factory made unregulated feed-meal for cattle from animal by-products.

He didn't wear his protective gloves on the Monday and was dead by the Wednesday. He died in my brother Aaron's arms as they rode in a brother-in-law's car on the way to hospital.

I remember Mama falling out flat on the floor when we arrived at the hospital when she was told he was dead. She had to be heavily sedated and cried for years to come.

In the commotion, a kindly nurse took pity on me because everyone had forgotten I was there.

On his death certificate his death is listed as a bacterial infection of the blood. They did not want to cause public alarm but, in private, our family doctor, Dr. Levy, told Mama and my older siblings it was anthrax. It was 1965, and they had been married for thirty-one years.

Mama never had much of an education. Sitting in a dark, dreary, and dusty barrister's office, she really did not understand just how many violations the factory had committed over the years.

One of my brothers, who was with her, was not very helpful, and the lack of proper advice Mama received cost her dearly in terms of compensation. She was in a position to be wealthy but, unaware of how the legal system operated, she did not know she could have asked for substantially more. She accepted a very low settlement. The factory was shut down, and we received a small stipend for each child under twenty-one. Mama received a widow's pension.

She wore black for the funeral - a black pill box hat, covered by a long black veil; a black crêpe dress, black stockings, and black shoes. She walked beside my sister, Rachel, at the head of the procession. The rest of her children followed in rows of two, followed by more relatives and friends. I walked, somewhere in the mix, flanked by two tall boy cousins. The procession made its way to East Ham Cemetery, following the creeping hearse.

Close to two hundred people attended my Daddy's funeral which included church people, friends and family. The day was rainy, the trees were green and lush, and except for the fact that we were in a cemetery, it was just another typical, London morning. The mist rising from the saturated, muddy ground had fingers which caressed my little legs as if it felt sorry for me - for us.

I refused to toss the handful of sand on to the coffin - as was customary for good luck. I wanted to go home where I was sure my Daddy was waiting for me, warm, solid, and safe.

His funeral marked the unravelling of my family. The seeds of bickering had been dormant while Daddy was around, but they gathered strength and sprouted into arguments and disagreements about property and money.

My Daddy did not have a Will. His children resented the fact that Mama was his sole benefactor. One of the oddities about my siblings is whenever we speak about Mama, we never say *our* mother, we always say *my* Mama. It is as if the births of my siblings happened at different times; my Mama was a *different* mother to each and every one of us.

Daddy's passing took another big chunk out of Mama's heart. The next chunk taken out of her heart took place a few years after my Daddy's passing.

Clara, the red, shiny apple and true beauty of all us girl-children, had a baby at sixteen and broke my Mama's heart. Mama beat her with a high heeled shoe the day she announced she was pregnant and thereby increased the intensity of their already tumultuous relationship. Clara left shortly after the beating. The silence between them grew thick for many years..

One day, I went into Mama's bedroom. She was sitting at her dressing table crying and holding a picture of my Daddy. She never looked at me; she just kept looking at the picture.

I knew she was crying for him and for the fact she had wanted Clara to be all the things she had not been able to be. She had wanted her to go to school and become someone of importance. I was never able to take Clara's place. I loved my sister dearly, but she blamed me from the day of my birth for taking Mama away from her. We never bonded.

My Mama always admired nurses. Four of her daughters were nurses by then. It was a profession she had always coveted. After one short, icy visit to see baby Mona, Clara and Mama never spoke again until Mama was dying of cancer in Jamaica, and Clara came to see her.

Clara's baby was the turning point in Mama's life. Mama knew for sure she had had enough of the UK. Her longing for her old life had never left her, and she had always hoped to go back to Jamaica.

With Daddy's passing, there was nothing to keep her in the UK and, with the exception of me, her children were long since grown and busy with their own families. Continuously plagued with severe bouts of bronchitis, Mama's local GP agreed leaving the damp, polluted air of London was probably a good idea. Mama began to plan for her departure.

In the years following my father's death, my Uncle Ivan was allegedly murdered by his wife - she had

342

moved her boyfriend into their house while he was suffering from a mysterious illness which had kept him bedridden for months.

Once, after he had been admitted yet again to hospital, his colostomy bag mysteriously unattached itself, resulting in a serious condition. He died the same night.

His wife, my Aunt D, had just visited his room, and the unattached colostomy bag was discovered some time after her visit. Family gossip was, of course, rampant. Mama was strangely quiet about the whole thing, although one day I heard her discussing with another relative how D killed Uncle Ivan. They stopped talking when I made my presence known.

The year we moved back to Jamaica, Aunt D, who was on the island visiting family, came by our house to see Mama and brought some items from the UK. They had been sent by one of my sisters. I was nine.

As I came in from a day out with our landlord's daughter (who was also nine) and her nanny, a young girl of around eighteen, I recognized D as she sat at the Formica kitchen table with Mama whilst they sipped on cool drinks. Mama discovered then that not only had I overheard her conversation years earlier, I had also remembered it.

After cordial greetings were exchanged, I told D she was wrong to have poisoned my Uncle and what did she have to say for herself. I will never forget the look on Mama's face, and I will never forget the sore bottom because it plagued me for about week. I, once again, had interfered in the world of a

Jamaican adult. The name 'mouth-a-massy' subsequently became Mama's nickname for me.

After my Daddy's death in the UK, I went to Colgrave Primary School around the corner from our house, and Clara would take me there and back when she lived at home.

After she left, I went, after school, to a Jamaican babysitter, who lived a few streets away. When one of her sons began using me as a football and cut my fingernails down to the quick, I became a latch-key child. Mama said there was something 'not right with that boy!'

I found out years later that Mrs. Colton, the babysistter, and Mama remained friends although I never went back there for babysitting. Not even after I locked myself out of the house numerous times because our front door locked automatically once it closed.

There were occasions when I tried to sneak back outside and forgot the key. Mama would come home from work and find me either sitting in the cold on the front steps or at a neighbor's house. Eventually, I just started going to the neighbors after school.

At first, we were one of only a handful of black families in the neighborhood, so we always had endearing things happen to us, which included our door splattered with dog faeces or names such as 'Gollywogs go back to Africa' hurled at us.

I remember, as a little girl of seven or eight, running for dear life from a group of white children who would wait for my friend Sandra (another black child of Jamaican parentage who had a constant runny nose and cough) and me at the corner to chase us.

344

I told my Mama I wanted to be white and almost burned the house down trying to straighten one of my doll's hair on the heater. My savior came in the form of a little red-haired girl with freckles whose name I have sadly forgotten. She took it upon herself to walk home with me. She could fight like a wild cat - a proper East End cockney girl - and dared anyone to lay a hand on me.

My sense of loyalty to my old friend Sandra quickly evaporated in lieu of self-preservation. I left Sandra to fend for herself, and I walked home from school in peace with my own life-size white doll.

On one day of the week, a neighborhood Irish boy around thirteen or fourteen years of age, who was one of the nicest boys in our neighborhood, took me and another black child in the neighborhood to our swimming lessons. I believe his name began with a K – so, in my memory I call him Kevin.

He was the son of a friend of my mother's. Once, I fell and hit my nose on the edge of the pavement because I would not listen when he told me to stop running. The road was icy. He was mortified when he brought me home with a bloody nose. But my Mama knew that I often did not listen to good advice. She gave Kevin his tip and, after they both made sure a doctor's visit was unnecessary, Kevin went on his way.

I don't know whatever became of him, but I have happy memories about how protective he was of his two little 'colored' charges.

My Uncle Ruddy, who had become a full blown alcoholic, died of cirrhosis of the liver. He was thirty-six years old. He had been my favorite Uncle.

Despite the fact that he and my Aunt Etta had passed out from drinking by eleven a.m. on most of my visits, I enjoyed my weekends at his house which was teeming with his five energetic sons who took surprisingly good care of me and were exceptionally protective of their 'sister-cousin'.

After his death, Mama adopted a stolid and impassive attitude. Her smile became less joyful. We attended funerals as if they had become an everyday part of life.

Shortly before I was nine, Mama sold our house, and packed up. The next thing I knew, we were leaving all my nieces and nephews (who were the same age as me), brothers and sisters, cousins and other relatives behind, and boarding a cargo ship called "The Plantain" with twelve other passengers. We were bound for Jamaica. It was the best thing Mama did for herself, and the worst.

Jamaica was stunning. Our life there was intriguing and full of color and vibrancy. Mama bought a house in Washington Gardens, Kingston, and I went to Duhaney Park Primary until constant gang warfare in the area resulted in Mama selling that house (where we even had a helper and a maid's quarters in the back).

The final straw had been a massive shoot-out between the police and gangsters on Washington Blvd. The rat-a-tat-tat of gunshots was loud, even though our housing scheme was some distance from the boulevard.

The next day after school, unbeknown to my mother, the girls and boys I walked home from school with decided to take a route which included going by where the shooting had taken place. There was dried blood everywhere. As children, we were fascinated yet appalled by the violence.

We moved to the outskirts of Spanish Town to a new housing estate called Horizon Park, just off Old Harbor Road.

In our extensive backyard, Mama grew peppers, corn, yams, mangoes, vegetables, cherries, and papayas. She raised, much to my chagrin, chickens, and part of my chores was to pick up chicken feed after school on a regular basis. I found it so embarrassing because my group of friends were mostly from families who were more sophisticated than I felt we were. They were off to other countries on holidays, lived in nicer homes, and many had telephones.

On the other hand, I could tell you the most wonderful stories about our life there on the island, about our trips to the country where so many things from Mama's early life had been kept safe, such as paintings, books, clothes; I could tell you about our visits to our relatives - my aunties and all the people Mama had grown up with, such as the enigmatic Ms. Rayma and her room with its walls papered with newspapers dating back some thirty odd years; I could tell you about visits to the graves of my grandparents.

I remember picnics and trips to beaches; packed lunches of stewed chicken and rice and peas, bammy and fried fish, escovitch fish, curried goat, curried chicken, callaloo, and johnny cakes; Mama's famous Cornmeal Pone, grater cakes, sorrel, and ginger beer; the markets, the Denbigh Agriculture Show in May Pen, and festivals; rainstorms when our roof leaked like a sieve, and little pans and pots were all over the house to catch the water; kooky, lively neighbors with blasting reggae music, entertaining arguments, or general busybodiness.

I could tell you how news about any of my misdeeds which were witnessed in public would reach home way before I did at the end of a school day (a mystery, when phones were not common in our neighborhood at the time) because back then we were raised by a village mentality that kept us on the straight and narrow; I could tell you about my first school, which was outside under a large tree, and which was cancelled whenever it rained; then Duhaney Park Primary, Spanish Town Primary, and my incredible years at St Jago High School - days made more special because my mother was still alive and I was trying to understand these 'new t'ings.'

I could also tell you about trips to Kingston, Port Royal, Mandeville, Ocho Rios, Dunn's River Falls, Port Antonio, and Falmouth; my Mama telling me stories by moonlight, our many assorted cats, dogs, and chickens – oh, those darn chickens and roosters; our church, the Seventh Day Adventist Church on Brunswick Avenue; learning to plant flowers, our Christmases, chatting on the veranda (yes, in Jamaica we call patios verandas); our celebrations, our nights sleeping in the same bed because I was afraid of the dark and could not sleep in my own room; our tears, our arguments, our closeness, and our separateness.

Everything is all jumbled together for me in a brightly lit slideshow of my times with my Mama.

348

When I turned fifteen, Mama's last remaining brother, Uncle Silas, who was living in Buffalo, NY, USA had a stroke and died at the bottom of the staircase in his house. He died alone. He was later found there by my Aunt Helen (who was an American black woman with a wide-mile smile and a soul stirring laugh).

When the telegram came, Mama almost had a stroke herself and was bedridden for days afterwards. She never spoke about Silas after that. It was as if saying his name would cause her already broken heart to shatter into a million pieces.

Mama played mediator between her autistic son, Aaron, and myself. We had grown not to like each other, and our fights and arguments were often epic.

Another brother of mine, who had a significant criminal history, came from the UK and proceeded to smuggle marijuana in huge quantities and later became part of the Jamaican mafia. He would use my dead father's name to import cars and vans into Jamaica. The vehicles would have drugs stashed in a variety of places and for years he managed to fool immigration as he went back and forth between the island and the UK. Then they got wise. He stayed put in Jamaica after that, leaving his wife and children. He could not risk trying to go back to the UK. His constant stream of loose women was scandalous. Mama was mortified, but I also think she was a little afraid of him. He treated her like the hired help.

Life went on. To supplement our income, we rented out half of the house. First, Mama rented to a single mother who according to Mama, was a nymphomaniac (moaning sounds emanated loudly and regularly from her side of the house when her boyfriend came to see her and stayed the night).

Then Mama rented to two brothers with a love for motorcycles and pretty young girls. The main girlfriend of the older brother eventually became pregnant and moved in with them. She was a half-Chinese girl and very pretty with crazy long kinky hair. She told my best friend Lisa (who lived up the street) and me all about sex and how great it was. She showed us the latest sexy dance moves (her pregnant belly keeping in time to her dance steps), and she talked to us about grown up business. She was funny, and I liked her. Mama thought she was scandalous and eventually forbade me spending too much time around her.

Mama continued to take in sewing and washing, grow her vegetables, scotch bonnet peppers, papayas, and sell freshly killed chickens – oh, those darn chickens.

Various brothers and sisters visited at various times. Mama would use what resources we had to plan elaborate dinners and then spend hours cooking for them, washing their clothes, and taking care of their needs while they did the 'tourist' thing in their own country. I was very resentful of the way they treated her because when they left we went back to making ends meet.

With the exception of my eldest sister, Vivica, and one other sister, Rosa, no real help was ever forthcoming.

I understood that two of my other sisters, including Clara, were struggling to raise their own families, but Clara was still not speaking to Mama.

Of the boys, my brothers, only my brother in Canada sent anything for my mother.

What did come were angry letters arguing about property my father had left to Mama. I saw Mama shed many a tear, especially when her own children threatened her with legal action over property in Worsop.

Mama made sure I had all the best she could give me. I learned to play the piano and took voice lessons. She even sent me to Haiti with my French class despite the fact I seriously doubted she slept one wink during the eight days I was away.

She adored hearing the crazy stories I loved to write and which were often influenced by the crazy stories she liked to tell me. Her biggest worry was I would get pregnant. She was wary of boys.

On one occasion, I returned home and Mama was in the back yard. She could make anything grow, and the yard was lush and green. I had had Glee Club right after school. It was early evening, around six.

When I came into the back yard, she called me to her. She looked lovingly into my face as she smoothed my eyebrows and remarked how much I reminded her of my Daddy and how I was a dreamer just like him. It was a very special moment, and I can still see her in my mind's eye with the settling day silhouetted around her, her soft, tearful eyes, her stained apron, the touch of her calloused hands, and the love and gentleness in her voice.

I went to the Manning Cup Soccer playoffs at the Stadium in Kingston on a school night. I went with some other friends, but I did not tell Mama because I knew she would never have let me go. When I got home, around eleven p.m., she was not at the house. She had gone to the police station in Spanish Town to report me missing or dead.

Needless to say, all hell broke loose when she did come home via taxi. She wanted to find a boarding school for me, but she knew full well she could not afford it. After the talking to I received, death seemed a pretty good option.

Then there was the time I went to a party and did not make my midnight party curfew. The party was just getting started then. I got home at one-thirty in the morning, and Mama let me sleep on the verandah in a verandah chair in the company of our dogs.

It was cold, dark and, being terrified of the dark, I kept banging on the front door. She would not let me in. Finally, I resigned myself to being eaten by duppies, and I curled up in the chair awaiting the inevitable.

She let me in the house at around five (taking pity on my crying and caterwauling) but refused to speak to me for a week. No more outings for me. I was grounded for life. I had to be home right after my extracurricular activities at school.

Mama was in the process of extending the kitchen and adding a new bedroom and bathroom to the house. The work was slow because she was on a tight budget. The extensions were almost finished, and I was nearly sixteen when she got a searing pain in her back. She wanted to make a bigger house so her children and their children could have a place to stay when they visited Jamaica.

I realized she had not been feeling well for months, but she had not wanted to spend money going to the doctor. She needed that money for the house. The majority of our funds went into this project.

Even in pain, she refused, at first, to go to the doctor. When she finally went, it was too late. The cancer was in her stomach and spreading fast.

That April, she became extremely ill. My Mama displayed amazing strength during her illness. She rarely complained, and she was loving and forgiving of those who took advantage of her home and her possessions while she was not able to defend herself.

So many objects mysteriously disappeared from our house while I was at school - the most significant of which was her beautiful wedding band with the star shaped diamonds. It had become too loose for her finger and stayed in a glass bowl on her dressing table with her other jewelry. The bowl and its contents disappeared one day.

There were trips to the Spanish Town hospital where, on one occasion, I arrived to find my mother in a gurney in a hallway because the rooms were full; a failed trip to the US Embassy to try to get her to the US to my eldest sister so that she could receive treatment (the visa was refused, and I never understood why my siblings would consider this an option); and one brief stay in a picturesque nursing home in an upper class section of Kingston, which Mama cut short.

My sisters, Rosa and Clara from the UK, and Vivica from the US, came at various intervals to see Mama. Vivica would later return for Mama's funeral as would three of my brothers and my sister Mayvis, who put aside her own long standing feud with our mother and appeared genuinely devastated by her death. My quiet but very sweet sister, Pru, in the UK was financially unable to attend but sent her blessings.

My mother left the nursing home and turned up at her front gate after making a four hour long trip by public transportation on her own from the nursing home to our house. She said she wanted to spend her last days in her own bed. I urged her to go back to the UK since she was a British Citizen, but she refused. She never spoke about doing so. Perhaps she realized it was just too late for her, no matter what country.

There was a night when I heard a ghost. I was studying in the little alcove which used to be our old kitchen. We used the old space as a dining room. It was late when I heard one of the chairs in the living room drag itself across the tile floor. I called out. No one answered.

It happened again and, in fear, I called out to my Mama. She told me to come to bed, and it would be all right. I hurriedly turned on the lights in the living room and, sure enough, the chair had moved a couple of feet. I was positive. I ran through the living room, flicking off the light before running and jumping into bed with her. She laughed, and only then did I feel safe.

When she became too sick, I began to sleep in the new bedroom she had built for me, which was directly behind the one in which she slept.

Then one night, Mama called out and begged me to come to her room and sleep in her bed with her. I was tired and said no. She eventually stopped

354

calling for me as she moaned herself to sleep. It was a week before she passed away.

To this day, I can still hear her calling for me. The guilt has never left, and I often dream I am cuddled up beside her as she wanted but, of course, it can only ever be a dream.

On 7th November 1977, I was walking home from school when a young lady who was walking up the road came up to me and said she was sorry to hear of my loss. I was puzzled and replied my Mama was very sick but still very much alive.

Then the pastor of our church almost passed me in his car, reversed, and said the same thing. That's when I froze in my tracks. I vaguely remember climbing numbly into his car, and nothing he said made any sense.

My Mama died on a Monday morning, while I was at school. No one had come to get me. I had gone through the whole day blissfully ignorant about what was taking place in our home at Tropicana Drive.

The weekend before she died, I kept putting off going into the room where she lay in a semi-coma and telling her I loved her. I was busy. There was homework, a French lesson the previous Sunday, getting my uniforms ready for school, household things, killing a scorpion the Saturday night - important stuff. I peeked in but did not go into the room. I was going to tell her the coming Monday when I got home from school.

I did not get a chance to tell her goodbye or to hold her while she took her last breath. She left me, and for years my life felt as unfinished as it did on the day of her passing. Life is funny.

I have forgiven myself for being the child I was then and not always being the best daughter I feel I could have been, but my mother's legacy is in my soul.

I hear myself repeating things she used to say and doing things the way she used to do them. I have her weird sense of humor and I have her kindness, love of children, animals, and learning.

I have her tenacity, determination, and sheer grit, no matter what life throws my way. I see many of the same qualities in my siblings who have mainly done well in their lives. I only wish they had been kinder to her.

When I look in the mirror, I see Mama looking back at me. And I am comforted.

LOVE SONG

This is a love song for the mothers
who bore this earth rich mosaics of sons and
daughters;
who sang their lullabies to still the fears and cries;
who gave strength and honor through their pain;
who never stopped giving despite poverty's disdain.
This is their love song.
Mothers tempered like strong steel.
Mothers knowing how they often feel
the weight of all creation resting on their shoulders.
Mothers with aching backs and burning feet.
Mothers calling out your name and
even in your sleep, you can feel them
loving you.
Mothers with calloused hands.
Mothers' eyes, they understand.
Reaching back to listen to ethereal voices
whispering rites of motherhood.
Mothers digging deep into their innermost
soul remembrances left them by
before-mothers - old voices
who still speak and never will
be silenced.
With their touch, they healed a million wounds.
Mother instinct always in-tuned
Always knowing.
Mothers who comforted us, fed us, and chastised us;
with words of faith, baptized us.
They watched us grow.
Gave us legacies of hope and pride;
and mourned our passing when we died.
Mothers who kept the fires burning

although their souls were often yearning
for just one moment of rest.
Mothers who have labored long.
For them, we sing this love song.
To you, our debt eternal.

ACKNOWLEDGEMENTS

Many of the stories contained in this collection are based, albeit fictionally, on my family history, stories my mother told me, and events I experienced and witnessed as I grew up in England, Jamaica and America.

I am forever grateful to my mother for teaching me to love and to be creative, to my siblings for teaching me to be persistent, and to my wonderful life-long friends, Alfredia DeVita, Jackie Hightower, Vielka Phillips, Pennie Partee, Jeri Brittain, and niece Grace Kennedy, for always encouraging me.

I am also grateful to my husband, Lamin Jabang, for his support, and to my beloved dogs, Mischa and Myiah, who have been faithfully at my writing side (despite hating the laptop) for so many years.

I would also like to thank my publisher, Lindsay Fairgrieve, at AudioArcadia.com, for her help with editing and choosing the name for this collection.

Shona Jabang

#0040 - 250116 - C0 - 210/148/0 - PB - DID1337294